AT THE DOG SHOW

An absolutely gripping cozy mystery filled with twists and turns

PETER BOLAND

The Charity Shop Detective Agency Mysteries
Book 3

JOFFE BOOKS

Joffe Books, London
www.joffebooks.com

First published in Great Britain in 2023

This book is a work of fiction. Names, characters, businesses, organizations, places and events are either the product of the author's imagination or are used fictitiously. Any resemblance to actual persons, living or dead, events or locales is entirely coincidental. The spelling used is British English except where fidelity to the author's rendering of accent or dialect supersedes this.

Cover art by Nick Castle

ISBN: 978-1-83526-293-1

PROLOGUE

People think that there is safety in numbers. That somehow being around others makes you less likely to come to harm, while being alone is when the really bad stuff happens. We're all conditioned to believe that, because, well, it's just common sense, and it's a well-worn phrase — safety in numbers. It doesn't help that umpteen crime dramas reinforce this myth, usually in the opening scene: a solitary figure stumbling along gritty, wet pavements in the dead of night. You just know that something nasty is about to befall them. Because they're alone. No one around. No witnesses to see any dastardly deed and crucially no one to come to their aid. So it stands to reason that it's a lot safer when more of us human beings are clustered together, acting like a collective police force to keep an on eye on things, preferably in the middle of the day when it's easier to see everything. Which is why it's even more of a shock when bad things happen in broad daylight — that's another well-worn phrase used to shocking effect: "The crime took place in broad daylight." We don't expect bad things to go down when it's time for elevenses, or when the kids are coming out of school and piling into the local newsagent, because traditionally we feel a lot safer when the sun is up and there are people going about their day. But it's just a perception. Fake reassurance.

There is danger in numbers. There is danger in the daytime.

For a start, our guard is down, and let me tell you, crowds are the worst place to be. Things happen in crowds that no one notices. People make the best camouflage, there's no better cover for a crime. Just ask a pickpocket. All those bodies and faces pushing past you. Too much stimulation and information for your brain to process so it just ends up becoming a blur, one big mush of homogenised humanity, and that means distraction. Today, there's an even bigger distraction, because this crowd has dogs in it. Lots of them. Big ones, tiny ones, noisy ones, quiet ones, fluffy ones, hairy ones, shy ones, boisterous ones — all sniffing and barking and getting under feet. This is going to be so easy. One casual brush past someone and you could have their valuables without them even knowing.

But today I'm not going to be taking a phone, a watch or a wallet. Oh no. I'm taking something far more valuable. I'm taking a life.

CHAPTER 1

An unmistakable tang hung in the air. Several to be precise. The strongest of these being grass. Slowly compressed, its crushed essence was released into the atmosphere by hundreds of busy feet, clad in sensible footwear. That was the trouble with holding events on grass. The stuff was unpredictable — would it be wet and slick, muddy, or dry and dusty? As it was the month of March, the organisers had sensibly erected a marquee and had escaped with it being damp, bordering on soggy underfoot. The majority of visitors, Fiona included, had quite rightly selected something from their shoe rack with a sturdy grip and at least a degree of water resistance. However, most people had begun shedding a layer of clothing to cope with the humidity of all those bodies, which included dogs, hundreds of them. Their hot, sweaty breath and freshly washed coats incubating their collective odour beneath the stifling canvass.

Fiona was at the annual Christchurch Dog Show. But it wasn't just the smell and humidity that threatened to overload her senses. Noise was having a pretty good go at it too. Beneath the marquee's sagging curves rose a collective canine cacophony of snuffling noses, swishing tails and panting tongues mixed with chuntering, yapping, crying, barking and the never-ending array of odd noises that dogs utter. Fiona hadn't registered any howls yet but give it time. Add to this their chattering owners and the racket was deafening, but in a good way. A happy way. She couldn't say the same about the public address system. It should've been called the public assault system. What was it about this technology? It never seemed to improve, making everyone sound as if they were in the 1940s. Fiona's tinnitus had been behaving itself recently, but she was sure she'd have a good dose of it after the poor-quality PA acoustics currently hacksawing through her skull.

Fiona scooped up Simon Le Bon, her diminutive terrier cross, into her arms, so called because his hair bore more than a passing resemblance to the New Romantic singer. His normally pretty brown eyes became indignant as he was denied his God-given right to sniff the behinds of every fellow dog he passed.

A whoop went up from the crowd ahead of her, swelling around the main arena. Fiona's steps increased, as she threaded her way through the masses, careful not to tread on any paws or resting tails, not that there were many of those, they were all wagging with uncontrollable abandon. She'd left Daisy and Partial Sue to look after their charity stall. Normally they all volunteered at the Dogs Need Nice Homes charity shop on Southbourne Grove but today Christchurch Dog Club had kindly bequeathed a free stall for all the local dog charities — a big opportunity for them to raise money for their particular doggy good causes. However, it wasn't as big an opportunity for them as it was for the other charities, as Malorie Granger — chairwoman, chief organiser and not their biggest fan — had taken it upon herself to strategically position their stall near the smaller rear entrance of the marquee, where footfall dropped significantly. The reason being that this entrance led outside to not much — a line of Portaloos, some noisy generators and a couple of plastic chairs where some of the caterers would nip out for a cheeky cigarette. Every time there was a breeze, the ladies would get a waft of cloying chemical agents and nicotine. Not the best combination when you're trying to flog charity lanyards, mouse mats, water bottles and other branded paraphernalia for homeless dogs.

Just in case the ladies hadn't got the message that Malorie really didn't like them, their fellow charities had delightful spots, nudging shoulders with the trade stands adjacent to the arena, where there was more of a buzz, not to mention a good view of the action. The only action the ladies could witness from their stand were people's backs and dogs' wagging behinds. This had led them to design a system whereby one of them could briefly duck out of fundraising duties to watch a category of their choice while the other two looked after the stand. First up, it was Fiona's turn, and she was desperate to see the Best Biscuit Catcher category, the start of which she'd missed, judging by the cheers from the densely packed crowd that had gathered. Fiona seized the opportunity to claim a gap left by an inconsolable chihuahua that had to be escorted out by its owner as it had taken to snarling its dislike to everyone around it.

Fiona slotted herself at the roped-off edge and placed Simon Le Bon by her feet, who pulled on his lead, desperate to join the fun. Although judging by the faces of the people and the dogs taking part, this wasn't fun. This was very serious indeed. The rules were simple: entrants had to form two parallel lines — one consisting of dogs, the other consisting of their owners facing them with a gap in between. The dogs had to sit still while their owners took it in turns to toss them a biscuit. At the moment, the gap between dog and owner appeared to be about three metres. If a dog failed to catch the flying biscuit or moved off their mark, they were instantly disqualified. A tense, sudden-death knockout. But it was as much about obedience as it was about catching prowess, although, human throwing skills were also put to the test. This was borne out when a cocker spaniel, tongue lolling to one side and bursting at the seams with energy and eagerness to please its owner, had a biscuit lobbed in his general direction that was so far off course that it was caught by the next dog in line.

Malorie Granger, judge and compère of the show, clad in her trademark quilted green body warmer and flannel shirt, wasted no time in giving them their marching orders in the severest possible tone. "Disqualified!" she blurted into a microphone headset clamped around her mass of wiry red hair. The bearded owner of the cocker spaniel glared in her direction as he was ejected from the competition in an undignified fashion. His dog, completely oblivious to his owner's biscuit-throwing blunder, bounded towards him and licked his fingers, whether that was out of affection or to snaffle biscuit residue, Fiona couldn't tell. The pair made the walk of shame off to the side, the man having angry words with himself.

Malorie continued to bellow orders at the remaining contestants. "Next round. All competitors move back one metre." The human contestants jumped at her order, and took a large reverse step, while their doggie counterparts stayed put. It was all too much for one quivering wreck of a French bulldog who couldn't bear to be parted any longer and made straight for its owner.

Malorie's response was swift and merciless. "You're out!" She then produced a large, wind-up tape measure and proceeded to adjust the distance between each remaining dog and its owner, aided by Kenneth, a small man with a scrunched-up face who held the other end. He appeared to subscribe to Malorie's school of thought that though this was classed as a fun dog show, the fun had to be strictly monitored and could not under any circumstances escalate into light-heartedness or, God forbid, any form of jollity.

"Pull the tape tighter," Kenneth demanded. "It can't sag, or it won't be accurate."

Malorie didn't like being told what to do and took her displeasure out on several contestants, shunting them back to the correct distance. When she was satisfied by their positioning, the competition resumed for several rounds until just two dogs remained: Lord Bob the Boxer and Frances the Border collie. The distance was now a staggering eight metres — a new record for the show, Malorie announced. Excitement fizzed through the crowd as everyone considered the prospect that they might be witnessing history in the making, admittedly history of a very specialised and localised nature, but history, none the less.

Malorie soon quelled their exuberance. "Silence! I will have silence! Our contestants need to concentrate."

The crowd obeyed. Frances' owner went first, favouring an underarm throw. The biscuit rose into the air, and the collie locked onto its trajectory, tracking it with its keen eyes. But the throw was long, forcing the dog to leap and snatch the biscuit out of the air.

The crowd groaned with disappointment and commiseration, as did Fiona. At least Malorie took a more forgiving tone. "Oh, bad luck. An amazing catch but sadly against the rules. Let's have a big hand for Frances and her owner Suzanne." A hearty round of applause followed the pair as they exited the arena to stand with the other knocked-out contestants.

Malorie commanded the crowd to be quiet again. Silence swiftly followed. "Lord Bob and his owner Ewan have the chance to enter dog show folklore and set a new record. If successful, people will remember where they were when this happened." Malorie's spiel had become a little melodramatic, it wasn't as if this was going to make the evening news. "Good luck. We're all behind you."

Ewan coolly nodded his acknowledgement and turned to face his dog. Lord Bob had hardly moved a muscle such was the level of his unwavering obedience. Looking at Ewan it didn't surprise Fiona. With neatly parted hair, shoulders as wide as a bridge and dressed in a smartly pressed white polo shirt tucked into his equally smartly pressed chinos, he was clearly ex-army. Lord Bob had probably been drilled every morning like a sharp shooter to catch biscuits with killer accuracy.

Ewan prepared himself. Poised and focused, he slowed his breathing. Changed his stance to stand sideways on. He leaned in and raised his right arm, holding the biscuit between his thumb and forefinger. His hand metronomed back and forth like a darts player sizing up the shot. Not a sound could be heard, apart from Lord Bob's snuffling, his body still as a statue but his eyes burning with alertness.

Suddenly the biscuit was released. More of a flick than a throw. It sailed high into the air. Time almost stopped, and the doggie snack appeared to defy gravity, hanging at the zenith of its arc. Fiona's eyes switched to Lord Bob. He remained still, eyes fixed on the moving target, but his sinews shifted beneath his slick brown fur, readying himself. With laser-perfect aim, the biscuit dived towards the dog's saggy muzzle. The aim was true. Now it was up to Lord Bob. A millisecond later his jaws opened. A flash of a thick, pink tongue, and the biscuit landed square in his mouth. Then his jaws clacked shut with the ruthless efficiency of a Venus flytrap.

A roar erupted from the crowd. Lord Bob, who'd waited so patiently on his spot, sprang forward, sprinting towards his owner. Ewan threw his arms open, and Lord Bob leapt into them. He smothered his owner's face with sloppy licks, as if it were covered in beef stock.

"A new world record!" Malorie's enthusiasm had got the better of her. "I mean, a new show record! Ladies and gentlemen, give Lord Bob and Ewan Fitch a big round of applause!"

Lord Bob hopped out of Ewan's arms and the pair did a lap of honour to a gleeful crowd who clapped and cheered them. When their circuit was over and the crowd had quieted, Malorie beckoned them over for a quick interview. "I have to say that was truly magnificent. How did that feel?"

Before Ewan had a chance to answer, someone shouted out, "Cheat! He's a rotten cheat!"

CHAPTER 2

The multitude of onlookers gasped in shock. The giant, simultaneous intake of air almost created a vacuum that threatened to collapse the marquee. Hundreds of heads snapped in the direction of the accusation, desperate to discover who had levelled it.

The bearded man who'd been knocked out in an earlier round when his biscuit went awry, stepped out from the group of other contestants, pointing his finger at Ewan Fitch. "He cheated. He knows he cheated. Go on, ask him."

All heads swung in the direction of Ewan, eager for his reaction. Poker-faced and unflappable, he didn't offer one. Malorie regained her composure and marched over to his accuser. "This is neither the time nor the place to throw around false accusations."

"But it's okay to throw around a chopped-up sausage, is it? Go on, ask him. He's got a leather pouch on his belt. When Frances and Suzanne were having their go, he swapped his biscuit for a bit of sausage. The category is Best Biscuit Catcher. Not best sausage catcher."

"Did anyone else witness this?" Malorie asked.

A couple of arms rose from the gathered group of contestants, plus a few in the crowd.

Malorie turned to Ewan, who'd joined her next to his accuser. "Well, is this true?"

Ewan Fitch made no attempt at contrition, shrugging his big shoulders. "I didn't think it would matter. It's just a bit of sausage. It's no big deal."

A murmur went through the crowd. Debates quickly broke out, discussing whether substituting a sausage for a biscuit could ever be justified, especially under competition conditions.

The man with the beard had already made up his mind. "He should be disqualified."

"Now just hold on a second," Malorie replied.

Fiona had never seen her flustered before. She could be blunt, bolshie and bad-tempered, but she was always sure of herself. Not at the moment. Malorie paced up and down, appearing to have deliberations in her head, unsure about what she should do. Eventually she stopped and barked into her microphone. "Can all committee members of the Christchurch Dog Club assemble at the main arena. We have a code red."

Fiona didn't know whether to be scared or impressed that they had devised a coded alert for emergency situations. Was it a catch-all alert to summon committee members, or was it part of a multi-coloured system specifically designed to inform them of the nature of the emergency? If that were the case, then red was normally the highest level of alert, reserved for the most volatile of circumstances, surely not disagreements over the choice of flying dog treats. Maybe a mauve alert or a teal alert would've been more appropriate. Perhaps she was underestimating the severity of the situation. Two dog owners were having a disagreement, and she knew from experience that those never ended well.

Turning off her microphone, Malorie pulled Ewan Fitch and the bearded man aside, close to where Fiona stood. Kenneth, the bitter-faced chap, who'd held the measuring tape just minutes ago, appeared by her side. Backup from the other committee members came swiftly, in the form of another man and a woman, which was just as well, as Ewan and his accuser were having a stand-up argument. Like a couple of fighters, they were sent to stand in opposite corners of the arena with their dogs, who didn't know what all the fuss was about.

The committee gathered in a scrum. Standing nearby, Fiona overheard them debating what they should do. "Well, he should clearly be disqualified," Kenneth snapped, then his face softened, which was not easy for someone with a perma-scowl. "Or maybe we should just let it go."

"You're not getting all Zen on me, are you, Kenneth?" Malorie asked.

Before he had a chance to answer, the man next to him, who had hair like Shredded Wheat scraped across his head, posed an important question. "Is a slice of sausage really that different from a biscuit?" He'd managed to acquire one of Lord Bob's offending meat snacks and was comparing its heft with the standard-issue dog show biscuit. "They feel the same to me."

"Not to a dog, David," Malorie replied. "A sausage is far more delectable, thereby giving the dog more incentive." The other committee members nodded in agreement. "Think about it. If someone offered you a plate of biscuits or a plate of sausages for breakfast, which would you choose?"

"True, but would a dog know the difference at that distance?" David asked.

Malorie huffed. "Dogs can smell the difference between a sausage, a biscuit and an old sock from a mile away."

"That's a definite advantage, I suppose," David conceded.

"What do you think, Delia?" Malorie asked.

Delia, the fourth member of the committee reminded Fiona of Jilly Cooper with her thick white bob of hair. "We're damned if we do, damned if we don't," she said. "If we disqualify him people will be disappointed. He's just smashed the record. But if we allow the result to stand, people will think we're letting someone get away with cheating."

"Why don't you run the last leg again?" Fiona blurted, thinking out loud. "Just between Ewan and Suzanne. All the other contestants had been knocked out, so it really only concerns these two."

The gathered committee stared at Fiona, surprised at the interruption and oblivious that anyone was listening. From what Fiona could tell, everyone around her had been earwigging their conversation, eager to hear how this would play out.

"That's not a bad idea," Delia said.

Malorie glanced at her other committee members for their reaction. No one else appeared to have a better solution. "Well, what do we think? Shall we run the final leg again, ensuring both use official dog show issue biscuits?"

"That would be fair," Kenneth said.

There were nods from the other two. Malorie beckoned Ewan and Suzanne to join them. Suzanne appeared blank-faced as she trotted over, wondering why she had been caught up in the controversy.

"In the sense of fair play," Malorie explained to them, "we're going to run your leg again. Make sure you both have biscuits. Does that sound acceptable?"

Before Ewan could agree or disagree, Suzanne smiled and said, "Oh, gosh. Don't worry. You don't need to do that. Lord Bob won, as far as I'm concerned. It's only a bit of fun, isn't it."

Her last words were probably the smartest Fiona had heard since the debacle had begun — it was just a bit of fun. Everyone had appeared to have forgotten this. Or was she being naive? The second you added a competitive element into anything, no matter how silly or insignificant the activity, from flicking playing cards into a cup to Pictionary, it ceased being fun and became extremely serious. In Fiona's experience, competition brought out the worst in people.

Malorie and the other committee members were flummoxed by Suzanne's sensible indifference. "Really?" Malorie asked.

Suzanne chuckled. "Oh, sure. It's not a problem. I mean there's not much difference between catching a biscuit and a sausage."

"That's what I said," David blurted.

Malorie ignored him, double checking with Suzanne. "You're happy for the win to go to Ewan?"

Suzanne snorted. "Of course."

"Thanks," Ewan said, quietly embarrassed and almost certainly regretting his sausage substitution.

Switching her microphone back on, Malorie proceeded to the centre of the arena. "The dog club committee has come to a decision. Helped in part by second place winner Suzanne, who I must say, has been incredibly magnanimous, and has let the win stand. Ewan and Lord Bob are this year's victors."

The controversial decision divided the crowd. Some clapped generously, others shook their heads, and she heard one woman say, "But he didn't even catch a biscuit. How can he be Best Biscuit Catcher if he didn't catch a biscuit?" However, the majority of people weren't really that bothered and examined their programs to see what category was up next. Fiona knew it was Sweetest Eyes and wondered whether that would create a similar controversy.

"What a sham!" Over in the far corner of the arena, the angry bearded man took his bouncing cocker spaniel and stormed out of the arena, chest puffing. Fiona followed him through the crowds with her eyes. It wasn't difficult as he left a trail of disgruntled people he'd shouldered out of the way, forcing a path towards the main entrance. With his berating lips still going nineteen to the dozen, he disappeared out of the marquee's main entrance accompanied by his cocker spaniel. She hoped he wasn't about to do something stupid.

CHAPTER 3

Fiona didn't stay for the trophy presentation and bustled to the rear of the tent, where the crowds thinned out enough for Simon Le Bon to be set back down on the grass without getting under too many feet. She needed to return to the stall, as she knew Daisy would be desperate to catch the start of the Sweetest Eyes category, which would begin shortly. The pair of them could perform a kind of charity stall tag team switch over, like a couple of wrestlers, but without the theatricals and the garish singlets.

She noticed Partial Sue, another member of their charity trio, walking in her direction, step for step alongside a young couple, collection tin in one hand, phone in the other, pushing its screen into their personal space. From Fiona's limited perspective and the uncomfortable expressions on their faces, it appeared her colleague had opted for the hard sell when it came to raising money, not the softly-softly approach they had all agreed upon before the show. The couple stopped briefly while the woman folded up what looked like a five-pound note and slotted it into the top of the collection tin. Once the donation was made, the couple increased their pace, as if they couldn't wait to get away.

When she caught sight of Fiona, Partial Sue grinned widely, her slight frame not nearly enough to contain all that gleeful energy. "I am partial to this fundraising lark." She'd earned her nickname from her penchant for putting the word partial before anything that took her fancy. "I think I'm getting the hang of it."

Fiona frowned. "You weren't pressurising those people into parting with their money, I hope."

"Gosh, no. Not pressurising them." Her smile dropped. "Well, maybe a bit. Just a smidge of guilt-tripping. But it's positive guilt-tripping."

Fiona couldn't see how there could be such a thing.

Partial Sue explained. "I pulled up pictures from the Dogs Need Nice Homes shelter in Ferndown. All the oldest dogs that don't have much chance of being rehomed." She turned her phone around to reveal the saddest, most forlorn dog Fiona had ever seen. A portly, grey-muzzled beagle cross named Bovril, who'd been denied affection for so long that his eyes were devoid of all hope. Sad and bewildered at why no one wanted him, he stared up at the camera from a harsh concrete enclosure with just a dented water bowl for company. "That lovely couple were thinking about getting a puppy, until I showed them this. They changed their minds and want to adopt Bovril. They're heading over there now to meet him."

Fiona went from suppressing a tear and being heartbroken at the sorry sight of Bovril, to elated for the little fellow. He didn't know it yet, but all being well, he'd soon be off to a loving new home, having walks and cuddles, and being spoilt rotten, no doubt. It reminded Fiona of why she loved volunteering for this charity. "Oh, Sue, that's great news."

Partial Sue looked pleased with herself. "Raising cash while rehoming dogs. It's not a bad system."

"It's a bloody brilliant system."

They joined Daisy, the third member of their charity trio, managing the stand. Although managing wasn't really the word. Sanitising it would be more accurate. With her sweet round face and playful curls spiralling out of control, Daisy had a gentle nature but took a harsh approach to germs, which sounded like the tag line for an organic surface cleaner. In the short time Fiona had been gone, the charity's merchandise, already pristine and fresh out the box this morning and arranged in neat regimental rows, had received several deep and unnecessary cleans, judging by the stack of spent wet wipes piling up. Daisy currently rubbed a water bottle so hard that the Dogs Need Nice Homes logo was in danger of coming off, either that or a genie would emerge from its flip-top lid any second.

"Daisy, you don't need to clean that stuff," Fiona said. "It's brand new."

"I know," Daisy replied. "But I don't mind. I find it relaxing."

Partial Sue put her phone back in her pocket. "You can come round my house. I've got lots of relaxing you can do. You can relax in the kitchen, the lounge, the hall, the loft and especially the cupboard under the stairs, it's a right old mess." Partial to not throwing anything away, her house was a delightful clutter of books and dusty tat, which included a great deal of horse brasses, giving it the feel of a country pub, crossed with a library and a junk shop. Many thought she was eccentric, but Fiona knew that her hoarding was a coping mechanism. After losing her partner Kate, Partial Sue couldn't bear to lose anything else in her life.

Daisy moved onto giving the hessian tote bags a once over. Something about that made Fiona wince, as a disinfectant wipe was dragged over the fuzzy material. A textural equivalent of fingers down a blackboard.

"I've sold a ton of merchandise." Daisy smiled. "A portable dog bowl, a fleece, three lanyards, three pens and two car air fresheners."

From her vantage point, Fiona could see Daisy's bag behind the stand. In amongst the backup cleaning products poking out of the top, Fiona spied the exact items she had just listed. "I hope you haven't been spending your own money, Daisy."

Daisy ceased cleaning. "No. Well, yes. Business was a bit slow, so I thought I'd move things along a bit."

"But it's your own money," Partial Sue pointed out.

"I don't mind. It's all for a good cause."

Partial Sue changed the subject. "Hey, what happened in the Best Biscuit Catcher category? We could hear someone shouting 'Cheat' and Malorie talking about running it again."

"Oh, yes. Bit of drama. I'll tell you all about it. Oh, wait. Hold on." Fiona glanced at her watch. "It's gone half eleven. Daisy, you're going to miss the start of Sweetest Eyes."

Terror swept over Daisy's face. "Oh my gosh. I completely forgot."

Partial Sue, never averse to a bit of mild fearmongering, nodded in the direction of the main arena. "You need to get a move on. Look at that crowd. It's getting packed over there."

Normally, Partial Sue preferred to exaggerate for pessimistic effect, but Fiona had to agree. One side of the marquee swarmed with people, thickening by the second and it wasn't to gather around the main arena. The crowd had encircled someone or something. Curiosity, like gravity, pulled in more and more people from all across the show, intrigued to discover what all the fuss was about.

"That can't be just for Sweetest Eyes," Partial Sue remarked. "Hey, you don't think it's that celebrity dog, do you?" Rumour had gone around before the show, that an ex-Crufts winner might show up. Fiona had dismissed it as a bit of gossip or unfounded PR to attract more people, but witnessing the massing crowd, it appeared that it might be true.

Daisy put her wet wipes away. "I need to get over there, otherwise I won't see a thing." She came around the front of the stall and headed over to the stream of curious bodies moving towards the ever-increasing throng. A lad with a Staffordshire bull terrier and a spider's web neck tattoo, hurried against the flow of people. Not looking where he was going, he collided with Daisy. The impact sent her stumbling backwards into the path of a petite woman with a coffee in her hands. She screeched as the lid flew off her drink, spilling it all down her smart front.

Without losing pace, the lad muttered a worried, "I'm sorry. I'm really sorry," before scarpering away through the small entrance by the Portaloos.

Fiona, joined by Partial Sue, rushed over. "Daisy, are you okay?"

She seemed only a little dazed. "Yes, I think so."

"Oh my God!" The petite woman was blonde and yappy, exactly like the Maltese dog by her feet. "Why don't you look where you're going?" A spreading patch of coffee, roughly the shape of Africa, covered her long, grey sweater dress, but the short jean jacket she wore over it appeared to have escaped unsullied.

"I'm terribly sorry," Daisy apologised.

Annoyed that Daisy had apologised for something that clearly wasn't her fault, Fiona said, "That young lad with the neck tattoo and the Staffie knocked into her. There was nothing Daisy could do."

Daisy produced a small, emergency wet wipe from inside her coat. "I can sponge off some of it."

She was about to embark on the fruitless task when the woman batted her hand away. "That's not going to do anything. You'll have to pay for a replacement. It's from Zara."

Partial Sue, always vigilant when it came to saving money, was having none of it. "Don't be daft. It's a coffee stain. It'll wash out."

"This is pure wool," the woman protested.

Daisy, from her vast encyclopaedic knowledge of cleaning, supplied the solution — literally. "Mix half a teaspoon of baking soda in a cup of tepid water, dip a cloth into it, rub the stain gently then wash on thirty degrees. It'll be right as rain."

The woman continued arguing for a replacement dress, refusing all reasonable alternative settlements. Clearly, she was an opportunist, using the situation to score a new frock. Curiously, Fiona observed that the woman appeared to be shrinking before their eyes, not unlike the Wicked Witch of the West. Glancing down at her feet, Fiona noticed her huge, spiked heels, which added at least another six inches to her diminutive stature, were slowly sinking into the soft grass. The woman was digging her heels in before their eyes.

They came to an agreement. They'd foot the bill for the woman's dress to be dry-cleaned, but nothing more. Details were about to be exchanged, when a scream came from the centre of the massing crowd, followed by gasps of shock and outbursts of disbelief. Over the PA, Malorie appealed for calm, which had the opposite effect, like a politician announcing there's no shortage of petrol will guarantee that everyone will immediately queue up to fill their tanks. People swarmed to the already over-subscribed spectacle, although some fled, abandoning the marquee, horrified expressions on their faces, and phones held against their ears with shaking hands. The ladies caught a fragment of conversation from a trendy man in a Gatsby hat as he passed by, rapidly speaking to someone on the other end. "I think someone's just died at the dog show."

They abandoned the coffee-stained woman and the stall, and headed towards the centre of the commotion. More people were coming away now, clearly upset by what had happened. Threading their way through the throng, in the middle of it all, they found the traumatic sight of Julie Sheers, the show's vet, in her green scrubs, kneeling beside an unconscious, sixty-something woman, lying flat on her back, an obedient standard poodle beside her. Julie drove her two clasped hands onto the woman's chest again and again, attempting CPR. Every thrust of her arms was accompanied by an abrupt, breathy count, "One, two, three, four . . ."

The cycle repeated itself, over and over, the frequency of Julie's pummelling increasing as the situation became more desperate. Until there came a point when it was clear the CPR was having no effect. Malorie appeared through the crowd, concern gnawing at her face. "Ambulance is on its way."

Julie's solemn gaze rose to meet Malorie's. She slowly shook her head. The woman had passed away.

CHAPTER 4

Mondays were normally the chattiest of days at Dogs Need Nice Homes. To be fair, there weren't any days that were unchatty. But Monday had the edge on other days when it came to spoken word count. At the start of every week, although the ladies had only been parted for one day, they would arrive bursting with banter, desperate to know what the others had done with their Sunday. Okay, there would be a bit of grumbling about the donations left outside unattended despite the very clear and unequivocal warning sign in the window. But once the splitting bags and ruptured boxes had been dragged in, tea would be sloshed into cups, cake cut into generous wedges, and they'd sit around for a good old natter.

Not today.

Words were in short supply, as there wasn't much they wanted to say. They knew the conversation would inevitably lead back to the tragic events of yesterday.

Sombreness filled the shop. Only the vast clock set into the dark-wood panelling, a relic of when it used to be a jeweller's, interrupted the silence with its deep, dependable ticking. Any words the ladies spoke were hushed and to the point. They quietly busied themselves with tasks that could usually wait. Daisy defaulted to cleaning while Partial Sue dived into the weekend donations, sorting them in the storeroom.

It didn't seem the right occasion for cake, so no one had bothered bringing any in. The morning ritual of gathering around the communal table for hot refreshment and a slice of something sweet had been postponed.

As amateur sleuths, all three ladies were quite accustomed to dealing with death, but it was always after the fact. The fatality had occurred long before they'd become involved. Yes, they were never happy that someone had lost their life, which was what drove them to catch killers, but it was less emotional and more intellectual, akin to puzzle solving, pitting your wits against the criminal. A game of chess with an unknown opponent, already several moves ahead of you.

This was different. They weren't used to seeing death up close. To witnessing its cold hand at work, taking a life before their very eyes. And although they didn't know the woman personally and she had died of natural causes, it was disturbing, leaving a clammy residue clinging to them, thick and heavy, reminding them that what separated life and death was tissue thin.

They'd discovered the poor lady's name after she had passed away. It had swept through the show and was on the lips of every horrified by-stander who'd witnessed her passing: Sylvia Steadman with her ex-Crufts-winning dog Charlie. So the rumours had been true: a famous dog and its owner had turned up at the show. From what they could tell, the moment she'd entered the marquee, Charlie had been recognised by several sharp-eyed dog owners. Immediately surrounding Sylvia, they'd requested selfies with her show-winning dog, and she'd been happy to oblige. Others soon became curious as to why this woman's dog was attracting so much attention. More people swarmed around them creating the big crowd they'd witnessed next to the arena. Many different versions arose about what had happened next. The most common and consistent was that she'd started coughing. The coughing intensified, becoming deeper, harsher and hacking, although a few said it sounded more like she was choking. She'd certainly begun to have trouble breathing at some point. Sylvia collapsed on the ground gasping for air, then lost consciousness. Her heart had presumably stopped, which was when Julie Sheers the vet turned up and valiantly tried to save her. Julie's unofficial verdict, although she wasn't a doctor of humans, was that Sylvia had suffered a fatal heart attack. A likely verdict as all the tell-tale signs were there.

Malorie and the other organisers quite rightly brought the dog show to an abrupt end and sent everyone home out of respect.

Fiona thought about Sylvia waking up that morning, not knowing what was ahead. She wouldn't have had the slightest inkling that death was waiting, its shadow slowly creeping up on her. As far as she was concerned it had been just another day in her life, like any other, starting with the first glimpse of morning light and a warm welcome from her dog, in that way that only dogs provide: a fidgeting mass of fur and joyful enthusiasm, accompanied by a snuffling wet nose, a licking of fingers and a manically wagging tail. She'd probably gone about her daily routine; got dressed, made the tea, sat down and had breakfast, possibly followed by a brisk morning walk with Charlie, chatting away to him and having little conversations with herself in her head, making micro-decisions about the day ahead, reminding herself of things she needed to do and where she needed to be, which, of course, included the dog show. What time should she get there? Where should she park? Should she go before or after lunch? Among those little debates, Fiona was one hundred percent certain that none of them included having a heart attack on the damp grass under a marquee erected beside Christchurch Quay, witnessed by an astonished crowd. Then losing her life.

Fiona sat at the till with the laptop in front of her, overwhelmed by a sad curiosity about Sylvia Steadman. She hadn't had the stomach to look her up last night. It felt morbid and disrespectful somehow. It still did if she were honest, but she felt compelled to find out more about her. A Google image search filled the screen with shots of Charlie winning Crufts. Sylvia posed beside a sizable trophy, not unlike the FA cup, dressed in a tweed trouser suit, her mousy hair cut into a smart page boy style for the occasion, while Charlie sat next to her, his tightly curled coat thick and glossy. In other shots she trotted around the packed arena with him, an artificial acre of emerald lawn beneath their feet and paws. Fiona didn't know whether this was before or after they'd won, but Sylvia gazed down at Charlie, adoringly, a slightly smug superiority in her expression. And why not? Completely justified if she'd just scooped Best in Show at the world's most prestigious dog event.

Daisy and Partial Sue silently gravitated towards the till, curious to find out what Fiona was doing, or had they realised that her inquiring mind would've got the better of her, provoking her to want to know more about the dead woman.

"When did she win Crufts?" Partial Sue asked.

"Four years ago, according to this," Fiona replied.

"She started doing those adverts after winning," Daisy remarked. "The posh ones on the telly."

Fiona and Partial Sue both stared at her, neither having any recollection.

Daisy put on a plummy voice. "Only the best for your best friend."

"What was it for?" asked Partial Sue.

"Dog food. You must remember it. Her and Charlie were always in exotic places, being all hoity-toity. Then every ad ended with a posh fellow saying, 'Only the best for your best friend.' But I can't remember which dog food it was." Daisy highlighted the major pitfall of creative advertising. The ad got remembered while the brand got forgotten.

"Oh, I remember them, but what was the name of it?" The pain on Partial Sue's face as she strained to recall the celebrity-endorsed dog food became too much for Fiona to bear. She put a search into YouTube with the terms 'dog food' and 'Crufts winner'. A column of thumbnail images appeared down the right-hand side of the screen, various dog food commercials past and present. Fiona scrolled down them.

"That's the one!" Daisy thrust out a pointed finger. The still image showed a kaftaned Sylvia reclining on a sun lounger with Charlie stretched out on the one next to her. The title beside it read: *Good Companion dog food beach advert.*

"Good Companion!" They spoke at once, confounded at how they'd forgotten now it was so obvious.

Fiona clicked on it and pressed play. The commercial opened on a Caribbean beach, water of the clearest blue lapping at pure white powdery sand. The camera panned over to Sylvia and Charlie both on sun loungers. She sucked on a straw poking out of an extravagant cocktail then addressed the camera. "When your dog is a Crufts winner like Charlie here, you want, no, demand, only the best for them." The script was suitably trite, but Sylvia wasn't a bad actor, and her haughty delivery dovetailed perfectly with the brand's luxury credentials. She sat up and snapped her fingers. Right on cue a waiter delivered a gleaming terrine to the end of Charlie's sun lounger. "For me, nothing but Good Companion will do." The waiter snatched off the lid, revealing a plate piled high with gravy-drenched meaty chunks and the tin they came from. "Nutritiously balanced and full of vitamins and minerals, it's not dog food, it's canine cuisine — as any sophisticated dog with a discerning taste like Charlie will tell you." Completely at odds with Sylvia's description of her dog, Charlie leapt up, gorging on the food with wild abandon.

After demolishing it in seconds, his long damp tongue rasped over the plate. Sylvia glared at him. "Now, now, Charlie, remember one's manners. It's rude to lick one's plate." The ad cut to an end screen with the tin of dog food being held in white-gloved hands, accompanied by an upper-class voiceover: "Good Companion. Only the best for your best friend." The ad cut back to Sylvia on the sun lounger with Charlie. She smiled and raised her cocktail glass to the camera. "Toodle-oo." The image froze on her.

Additional thumbnails of Good Companion ads were listed down the right-hand side, featuring Sylvia and Charlie. They watched a few more. The concept continued throughout and was fairly obvious to grasp: The pair of them living the jet-set highlife in different James Bond-esque locations: ski lodges, health spas and penthouses. Each one ended with Charlie devouring his food, sucking it down in a wild feeding frenzy, to contrast with the classy environment and the product.

"Nice work if you can get it," Partial Sue commented. Sylvia had appeared to get a lot of it, judging by the number of ads she and Charlie had appeared in.

"I think I would've been good at coming up with advertising slogans," said Daisy. "Catchy ones like that."

"Really?" This surprised Fiona, especially as Daisy often forgot what day of the week it was.

"Oh, yes. I thought of one for the Devon tourist board the other day."

"Go on. Let's hear it," Partial Sue said.

Daisy deepened her voice, like a radio announcer. "Devon. It's like Cornwall but closer."

"Well, it's definitely true," said Fiona. "And it would certainly get remembered."

"And it has a money and time-saving benefit in it," Partial Sue added.

Daisy smiled, pleased that her creative tagline had been well received.

The ladies went silent, their gaze held by the haunting image of Sylvia paused on screen, toasting them from the past. A woman who would have had no idea what a terrible end the future had in store for her.

"What happened to her dog, Charlie?" Partial Sue asked.

"He's with Kerry Pritchard, the dog fosterer, poor thing," Fiona replied. "Waiting for a new home."

The bell above the door chimed. The Wicker Man, so called because he sold old-school second-hand wicker furniture in the shop next door, popped his head in. "Greetings on this fine morn. You three look like you need a spot of merriment in your life. And I've got just the thing."

CHAPTER 5

Fiona had to admit, they were all in dire need of cheering up. "What do you have in mind?"

The Wicker Man stepped in and closed the door behind him, an impish grin on his rosy-cheeked face. "I plan to dabble in the fine art of stand-up."

Partial Sue grimaced. A grimace of confusion rather than disgust. "Stand-up? You want to do stand-up? But you're not . . ." She caught herself before rounding off her sentence with what Fiona presumed would be the word funny.

His faced dropped. "I'm not what?"

As a full-time cravat wearer with a penchant for peddling outdated phrases and archaic wordplay, the Wicker Man was certainly entertaining, in an eccentric, Terry Thomas, born-in-the-wrong-era kind of way, but he wasn't necessarily funny.

Partial Sue hesitated, her eyes searching for an inoffensive ending to her outburst. "Er, I mean, you don't have any experience."

He strode across the shop, enthusiasm radiating off him. "That's where you're wrong. See, I have more than a modicum of stage experience. Treading the boards in many an am-dram production. My timing is impeccable, and I've been told my King Lear is outstanding — the envy of the menfolk."

Partial Sue produced a micro snort for some childish reason.

He ignored her and continued. "Only difference is in all those instances the words were quilled by some other bard. This time, it shall be I supplying the verbals. Homegrown, as it were. There's a talent show on at the Regent Centre in Christchurch. I've added my name to its illustrious list of performers."

"So what style of stand-up will it be?" asked Fiona.

The Wicker Man's eyes lit up. "I'm glad you asked. I plan on doing sharp, observational comedy. I thought I'd call myself the Wicker Man and perch on a wicker stool, like Dave Allen, but without the whiskey and the missing digit."

Daisy was all smiles. "Well, I think it's a wonderful idea, and we'll all come along to support you. I love a good laugh. I love watching videos of people slipping on ice and falling into hedgerows. That's my favourite comedy."

"Thank you, Daisy. But it won't be slapstick. It'll be everyday stuff we all notice but with a mirthful spin."

"Let's hear some then," said Partial Sue.

The Wicker Man froze on his feet. "What?"

"Let's hear your material. I've heard stand-up comedians try out their material in front of small audiences first. See if it works."

"We're a small audience," Daisy said.

He gave a twitchy smile. "Oh, are you sure? Aren't you a tad busy?"

"No," Fiona replied. "Like you said, we could do with cheering up."

His confidence departed and he lost the playful twinkle in his eye. "Well, it's not perfected yet by any means."

"Doesn't matter," Partial Sue replied. "Wouldn't you rather test out the raw material first before you do it for real?"

There wasn't any logical reason why he shouldn't. "Er, yes. That would make perfect sense. But I'm not warmed up yet."

"Take your time," Fiona said.

He took a moment to gather himself, stepping away and turning his back to them. He cleared his throat then began shaking his arms and legs while uttering gobbledygook to ready his vocal chords, "Zoo, zoo, zoo, zoo. I want to go to the zoo, zoo, zoo, zoo. How about you, you, you, you. Me, me, me, me, me. Yes, yes, yes, yes. I like the zoo, zoo, zoo, zoo. Ping pong, ping pong, ping pong ball."

Fiona wondered what they had let themselves in for. Without warning, the Wicker Man spun around to face them. All bright-eyed and smiley, he cavorted back and forth, not able to keep still, as if he had ants in his pants. "Have you ever noticed when you go to a restaurant and ask for the dessert menu, there'll be all these amazing sweets like apple crumble, sticky toffee pudding, lemon sorbet and chocolate mousse, then right at the bottom they put cheese. Anyone else find that strange? Cheese. Not one type of cheese either, there'll be lots of them. Several types. I mean, who are these people who are eating lumps of cheese at the end of a great big meal? They must be like, 'You know, that meal didn't fill me up, what I could do with now is a big plate of cheese.' And why is it cheese? Why not bread, peas or slices of potato? Who decided on cheese. What's that all about?"

He paused, presumably leaving a spacious gap for all the hilarity to ensue. None came forth.

"I quite like cheese at the end of a meal sometimes," Daisy said.

"Me too," Partial Sue added. "I am partial to a spot of cheese, especially if I've had a fairly sweet main course, like sundried tomato pasta. And some people don't have a sweet tooth, so it gives them an alternative, otherwise they'd just be sitting there with nothing to do while everyone else tucks into pudding."

The Wicker Man became agitated. "No, no. You're missing the point. You're not supposed to take it literally. It's observational. I'm pointing out how it's weird that a dessert menu has cheese on it." He went back to his stand-up persona, held out his arms as if pleading. "What's that all about?" As if somehow adding that phrase at the end transformed it into humour.

Fiona smiled sympathetically. She so wanted it to be funny, but it just wasn't. Anything that had to be explained, that needed verbal footnotes wasn't working. She tried to salvage the situation. "Maybe we just need warming up first as an audience. Don't comedians have a warm-up act beforehand. Let's hear something else."

The Wicker Man stared at his feet and mumbled something.

"Pardon?" asked Fiona.

He looked up, sheepishly. "I don't have anything else."

Fiona felt a collective wave of guilt pass over them. Perhaps they should have forced their laughter and spared him the humiliation. But then, surely it was better that he found out here and now, in a safe environment that this particular skit wouldn't elicit any laughter, not even the merest giggle or even the hint of a chortle, rather than discover this awkward fact in a packed regional theatre in front of people who'd paid good money.

Sparing him any further humiliation, the doorbell chimed and in walked the familiar figures of DI Fincher and DS Thomas. Never comfortable around the law, the Wicker Man made a swift exit.

DI Fincher was her usual immaculate self, wearing a slim black Crombie-style wool coat, while DS Thomas, impervious to any cold weather had thrown on a battered hoodie, missing its drawstrings, and shiny tracksuit bottoms, the kind of clothes that people keep only for doing odd jobs in the garden. He took up his usual position at the door, as if he were guarding it, folding his meaty arms and not saying anything.

"Hello, ladies." DI Fincher's tone was friendly but formal, definitely not here for a social call. "Mind if we have a word with you?"

"Not at all. Would you like a seat?" An unashamed police fangirl, Partial Sue always became a little star-struck in the presence of the two officers. She led DI Fincher over to the small round table, joined by Daisy and Fiona. DS Thomas stayed put. "Can I make you tea, coffee? I'm afraid we don't have any cake, but I am totally prepared to go and get you some."

Both officers declined.

"I'd rather get straight to the point." DI Fincher spoke plainly. "You had a charity stall at the Christchurch Dog Show yesterday, I believe."

"That's correct," Fiona replied. "Is this about Sylvia Steadman, the woman who had a heart attack?"

"That's correct. Although, we believe she was murdered."

The detective's last words gave Fiona shivers like a sharp icicle had been dropped down her back.

CHAPTER 6

"Murdered?" All three ladies posed the shocking question at once.

DI Fincher gave an imperceptible nod, her expression unchanged, unemotional.

Fiona felt that cold hand of death again, its frigid fingers picking their way over every joint in her spine. "How do you know it's murder?" She'd seen Sylvia collapsed on the ground, being frantically given CPR for a heart attack. Dying of natural causes was nasty enough but now murder. And if that were the case, how in the world had the killer made it look like a heart attack?

"Do you have any suspects?" Partial Sue asked.

"Why would anyone kill Sylvia Steadman?" Daisy joined in.

"And why do it at a dog show of all places?" Partial Sue added.

Their questions came thick and fast, a verbal bombardment. The police detective patiently listened to each one in turn. Eventually she held both hands up, appealing for silence. "You know the drill by now."

They did know the drill, all too well. DI Fincher had disclosed too much about a case once before and wasn't about to repeat the same mistake. "I can't reveal details of an ongoing case. However, I will say this. Even at this early stage of the investigation, the dog show is proving to be a headache for us. There's no CCTV inside or out, or anywhere nearby, and apart from organisers, competitors and stall holders like yourselves, we have no idea who attended. Entrance fee was two pounds, all cash, paid on the door. By the time we discovered it was a murder and not a heart attack, everyone had packed up and gone home. Hundreds of suspects and witnesses have slipped through our fingers."

DS Thomas added, "We'll appeal for witnesses to come forward and we'll get the details of people who paid for items using credit cards but it's likely to be a tiny fraction of everyone who attended."

Fiona repeated her initial question, "But how do you know it was murder? I'm no medical expert but it looked like she'd had a heart attack. I saw Julie Sheers performing CPR. What makes you think it was malicious?"

DI Fincher hesitated, face full of consternation. She sidestepped the question but did drop a few crumbs. "I can't tell you exactly how at this point, or how she died, and before you ask, no I cannot let you see the autopsy report, but I will say this, we're working on the theory that it was someone in the marquee because that's where it was busiest. Crowds are dangerous places. Very easy for the murderer to get close to the victim then melt away into the masses."

"Eye witnesses have told us a lot of people had their phones out, taking pictures of her dog Charlie," DS Thomas said. "We're hoping to track them down."

"Killer's hardly going to hang around for a selfie with a prize-winning dog," Partial Sue replied cynically.

Without so much as a raised eyebrow, he replied, "No, but it may help us identify others in the crowd."

"Talking of people not hanging around," said Fiona. "We did see a young guy with a neck tattoo and a Staffordshire bull terrier."

Daisy nodded eagerly. "Oh, yes. He couldn't wait to leave. Bumped right into me, sent me flying, he did, right into someone else, knocking coffee all over them."

DI Fincher brightened. "When was this?" Realising she'd let her normally cool exterior slip momentarily, she returned to her usual calm-and-collected state of affairs.

"I'd just come back from watching Best Biscuit Catcher," Fiona replied. "Maybe eleven twenty-five-ish."

"I'd like to take a statement from all three of you, if I may."

"We'd be more than happy." By the look on Partial Sue's face, she couldn't wait to be caught up in police procedure. An important cog in an even more important wheel, she leapt to her feet and made a beeline for the storeroom, calling out from inside, "Now you'll need somewhere private. It's a bit cramped but this should do." For the next minute or two, the scrape and scuff of cardboard came from the little room as she shouldered boxes out of the way, some of them full of unsold merchandise from the show. She reappeared red-faced. "Shall I go first seeing as I'm already here?"

"Why not?" DI Fincher headed into the makeshift interview room followed by DS Thomas.

"Should I make a sign?" Partial Sue asked. "Something like: *No entry. Police interview in progress.*"

"That won't be necessary," DI Fincher replied.

After they had all given statements and signed them (Partial Sue's had taken the longest — more than Daisy's and Fiona's put together, presumably because she enjoyed the process so much she wanted to string it out by drowning them in minutiae), DI Fincher promised to keep in touch. Both officers handed them their contact details, even though the ladies already had them saved in their phones. As DI Fincher left, she reminded them to not hesitate to call her if they thought of anything else.

"You can count on it, Officers." Partial Sue stopped short of saluting as they walked out of the shop.

Fiona collapsed into a chair at the round table. "Can you believe it? That poor woman murdered right in front of us. Well, not in front of us. But you know what I mean."

Daisy hung her head. "Dreadful, just dreadful. Who would do such a thing?"

Partial Sue headed back to the storeroom. "I think we could all do with a cup of tea. Hey, you don't think DI Fincher thinks we did it, do you?"

Fiona's head bobbed up, astonished. "Whatever makes you say that?"

Partial Sue filled the kettle, switched it on, then came back out. "Well, Sylvia Steadman was declared dead at eleven thirty-seven by Julie Sheers. Ambulance didn't get there for another half hour, then say another half hour to get to the hospital morgue. Now this is all pure conjecture, I have no idea what happened next but let's assume someone had to fill in all the paperwork. That's maybe another hour, putting the time at roughly one thirty. The coroner's probably just coming back from lunch, needs to get settled. Probably doesn't get around to having a proper shifty at the paperwork until two thirty and the body until about three. Probable cause of death is a heart attack, nothing out of the ordinary but the coroner notices something off, obviously we don't know what that is yet. Reports his or her suspicions to the police at three thirty. Say, they turn up around half an hour later, takes them at least another hour to listen to the findings and process it all as a suspected murder. It's now five o'clock, at least. DI Fincher told us they headed over to the dog show and found everyone gone. Place is empty. Let's say that's six o'clock. Place is a crime scene. Now they have to seal it off and wait around for Forensics to do their thing. It's a big space. Gonna take hours before they can get in and have a proper look. Probably not much to see, apart from grass, an empty marquee and the odd abandoned trestle table. Now it's late evening. First port of call is breaking the horrible news to her next of kin then maybe telling the organisers that a murder's taken place at their show, which is easily going to take them up to midnight at least. They probably call it a night and decide to start questioning people first thing next morning — that would be us, probably." Right on cue the kettle huffed, puffed and bubbled, then clicked itself off.

A frown slowly formed on Fiona's face as the information filtered into her brain. "You know, I hadn't considered that. Is that why you were being so accommodating?"

"Well, I'm always accommodating when it comes to helping the police. But, yes, more so this time. I wanted to show we had nothing to hide. I mean, I could be paranoid and they're simply in the process of collecting statements."

"But still, why come to us first?" Fiona replied. "I mean, all the other traders and charity stalls were a lot nearer to where the murder happened."

Partial Sue sighed. "It could be that our old nemesis Malorie has done the dirty on us and made out that we had something to do with it. Just to get back at us." As well as being Chairperson of Christchurch Dog Club, Malorie managed Southbourne Community Centre. The ladies' paths had crossed several times, and where those paths crossed, they had become potholed with mistrust and puddled with the deep muddy waters of dislike, and were best avoided.

The ladies grew silent. Three minds chewing over some rather unpleasant and grisly thoughts. Partial Sue went back to making the tea. She returned and placed a tray in the middle of the table, dominated by a big brown teapot, chipped here and there, together with three mugs.

While they sat waiting for the tea to brew, Daisy broke the silence. "You know, it could be rather flattering."

Snatched away from their thoughts, the other two ladies turned their inquisitive heads in her direction.

Partial Sue's eyebrows knitted together. "In what way is it flattering?"

Daisy took her time answering. "What if DI Fincher's asking us for help?"

Partial Sue baulked at this suggestion. "Asking for help? How do you work that out?"

"Well, she said she couldn't talk about the case," Daisy replied. "She always says that. Tight-lipped with details and the like. But then she started talking about it, in a roundabout way, outlining its difficulties. No CCTV, very few witnesses. Why would she do that? I'll tell you why, because she knows we solve crimes, and we were there, at the murder scene. We have the home advantage, as it were."

"She'd be stupid not to use us," Partial Sue conceded. "But she didn't request our help at any point."

"She can't. Not officially," Fiona said. "It wouldn't be professional. So she gives us a gentle nudge. Gives us a heads-up, early doors. Gets us started on the case."

"Throws us a bone about the dog show murder." Daisy was quite oblivious to her canine pun.

"And she knows we can't resist solving a murder," Partial Sue added.

Fiona smiled. "Well, we better not disappoint her then."

CHAPTER 7

They had a suspect, a very promising one: the neck-tattooed lad. Anyone running away from the scene of a crime had to be. Only drawback, they had no idea who he was. But before they could proceed, homework had to be done. First things first. The phones came out as did the laptop for a deep online dive into Sylvia Steadman's background. Nothing would hold them back, apart from the laptop, which had to be restarted as it needed an update. The spinney wheel of doom, or caterpillar chasing its tail as Daisy more playfully called it, didn't seem in any particular hurry to get on with whatever it needed to do, delaying Fiona from making a start. Of course, she could've used her phone, but the wait gave her an excuse to make a fresh pot of tea.

Being a very minor celebrity, content on Sylvia Steadman was fairly plentiful. She hadn't been at risk of being asked on *Strictly* or anything like that, but within canine circles she had appeared in enthusiast magazines, and there were her TV ads from a few years ago. It also helped that she'd been active on social media. At just under ten thousand followers, Sylvia wasn't in the giddy heights of someone you'd class as a social influencer. She had more of a niche following of those who liked her harmless and inoffensive posts. Not what you'd call viral material, more of an online log of her life, going about her daily business with pictures to boot: her and Charlie in the park; her and Charlie in a forest; her and a wet Charlie by a river; her and Charlie at Christmas — both wearing festive jumpers. Posts were rarely shared by her followers and would normally earn around ten or twenty likes and a few pleasant comments. Although Sylvia never once replied to any of them, leading the ladies to deduce that Sylvia Steadman liked having followers as long as they stayed in cyberspace, and didn't come any closer. The classic doggie person who preferred the company of her pet to other people. Fiona read several interviews in online articles that confirmed as much. They also discovered she was an only child who'd lost both her parents several years ago. Sylvia Steadman was a loner, but not one you needed to feel sorry for. From what they'd gleaned, she'd preferred it that way.

"Oh, look at this." Daisy flipped her phone around to reveal several posts of what appeared to be an office leaving do, complete with party poppers and champagne and a table full of nibbles. A colourful banner Sellotaped to the wall behind read: *Happy Retirement!* Sylvia appeared to be putting on a brave face for the camera; attempting to smile, but she couldn't camouflage the melancholy in her eyes.

"She looks sad to be leaving," Daisy commented.

"Unless she's fed up and couldn't wait to get the hell out of there." Partial Sue justified her deduction by reading out the comment above one post. "*Last day at work. Bye-bye Bristol City Council. Going to miss it. Hello new challenges!* Notice how she says, 'Going to miss it', as in the place, not going to miss you, as in her colleagues."

"Definitely not a people person, then," Fiona said.

Daisy jumped onto LinkedIn, the site where professional people showed off about how important they were. "Her profile's still up. Says she was Chief Administrator for Bristol City Council."

"That's a hefty role if ever there was one," Fiona commented.

"Hey, here's a post from two weeks ago, February twenty-seventh." Partial Sue flipped her phone around, showing a social media post dominated by an image of Sylvia in a smart empty kitchen dangling a pair of keys in front of the camera. In the background, Charlie has his nose pressed up against the French windows, yearning to get at the vast garden beyond. The comment above it read: *I'm in! Just moving into my fab new house and starting my new life in gorgeous Christchurch. Now to unpack about a million boxes! Wish me luck!*

A fresh pang of sadness stabbed Fiona in the heart, seeing Sylvia's happy face and the copious number of smiley emojis she'd posted after her comment. Just two weeks ago she'd moved to the area. A fresh start to her retirement, all that free time ahead of her and the pristine possibilities that came with it. New places to go, new things to do and discover. Every day a little adventure. Fiona wished she could climb into the photo and somehow warn her not to go to the dog show. Would that have prevented her murder, or would the killer have just found another way to end her life? This prompted the most important question that needed answering, the one they needed to know before they could move forward. How had she met her end? Had her death been a random, unprovoked assault? Had she had a disagreement with someone at the show, perhaps an argument with the neck-tattooed lad — had their two dogs got into a fight, and that had led to her having a heart attack? Charlie didn't appear to have been in a fight with another dog. Physically he was fine. Maybe Sylvia's demise had been planned and premeditated by someone with a grudge? That was what they needed to find out. Without details from the coroner, moving forward would be a stumbling, clumsy affair. Neither DI Fincher, DS Thomas, nor any other police officers were going to divulge that information to members of the public, but perhaps it might come from someone else who wore a uniform.

The doorbell rang. The ladies had been so engrossed in what they were doing that it gave them a start. In walked a face familiar to Fiona, distinctive by her oversized glasses and the big mournful eyes behind them. She removed a large pompom hat, revealing dyed hair the colour of faded mustard, contrasting with dark roots that really needed doing. Fiona recognised that sad face all too well, but it took several awkward seconds to recall her name. "Molly?"

Molly forced a nervous smile. "Hello."

Fiona introduced her to Partial Sue and Daisy. They'd never met before, but knew of her sorry tale. Molly's parents weren't quite who she thought they were. Without her knowledge, they'd become involved in some rather nasty and obsessive behaviour that had led to someone losing their life and others nearly losing theirs. They were now serving a very long time behind bars for murder, leaving Molly alone in the world, and her daughter Dina wondering why her grandparents didn't take her out for ice cream anymore. Subsequently, Molly appeared to be in a perpetual traumatised state of shock at the secret lives that her hitherto gentle parents had lived. She had to be handled delicately.

Molly took another timid step closer to the table. "I've just dropped my daughter off at school. She's in reception now."

"Oh, how wonderful." Daisy smiled with as much warmth as she could muster. "How is she enjoying it?"

"Oh, yes. Dina loves it. It's me that's not coping so well. My mornings are a little empty without her. Giving me too much time to think. My mind won't stop dwelling on my — you know I can't even say their names."

Partial Sue gestured to an empty chair. "Please sit down, would you like a cup of tea? Although it might be a little on the strong side."

"Oh, I don't mind that." Molly took a seat. "The stronger the better in my opinion. If it's not the colour of HP Sauce then it's not worth drinking, I always say."

"Ah, a woman after my own heart." Partial Sue chuckled.

"How have you been?" Fiona asked.

"I'm okay. Some days are better than others. Having murderers for parents, it's not something you get used to. I still refuse to see them or talk to them, despite their requests. It's worse than if they'd passed away. At least I could mourn them. Instead, I just feel shocked and disgusted . . ." Her voice trailed off and her head slumped forward.

"I'm so sorry, Molly. I shouldn't have asked."

Molly sniffed back a tear and prodded her glasses back up her long straight nose. "It's okay."

"If there's anything we can do to help, just name it," Daisy said. The others nodded enthusiastically.

Two pleading eyes regarded the three ladies. "Well, there is actually. I know this is probably a long shot, but I'm looking for volunteer work. I desperately need something to do when Dina's at school, to stop all those unhelpful thoughts buzzing around in my brain. But it needs to be flexible, you know for nipping to school assemblies and if Dina's off sick. I wondered if you might have any positions."

Truth be told they were already at full capacity. Realistically, it only took three of them to run the charity shop, and even then, they could've easily managed it with just two. But they liked each other's company so much and since they were volunteers, and no wage bills were involved, head office turned a blind eye. Could Fiona justify having four staff at once? It would certainly give them more freedom if they wanted to head out together, investigating. One of them usually had to stay behind or they would have to close up the shop if they all wanted to go. So far it had gone unnoticed, but it was only a matter of time before some busybody sent an angry email to their head office exaggerating that their Southbourne branch was always closed. Having a fourth member of staff to hold down the fort would be very handy indeed.

"It'd only be part-time," Molly said. "I have to leave at two thirty to pick Dina up from school."

"Of course, Molly, we'd love to have you on board." Fiona couldn't really refuse after what she'd been through, and she could square it away with head office later.

"Welcome to the team!" Daisy beamed.

"It'll be lovely to have you," Partial Sue added.

Molly was overcome, all breathy giggles of joy. "Oh, you don't know how much this means. You can count on me. I'm a hard worker and a fast learner."

"There's not much to learn. If I can do it, anyone can." Daisy grinned.

"Would you like to start tomorrow?" Fiona asked.

"Oh, that would be wonderful! I can't wait. I am so grateful." Molly was on the verge of tears again, happy ones this time.

Fiona had never seen her so elated, "Well, I think this deserves a toast." They raised their mugs over the centre of the table, clunking them together. After chatting some more, Molly left with a big smile on her face and a clutch of forms to fill in, to make her volunteering position official.

"Well, that was rather lovely. What a treat having someone new and interesting starting in the shop." Daisy's face suddenly became guilt-ridden. "Sorry, that sounds like I'm bored of you two. I'm not. Honestly. I love working with you."

Partial Sue reassured her. "Don't worry, Dais. We know what you mean. It'll be nice to have a fresh, young face around here, that's for sure."

"I think so too," Fiona replied. "Now back to more pressing matters. First things first. We need to know how Sylvia Steadman died. Police won't let us get within sniffing distance of that autopsy report. Next best thing would be talking to the person who declared her dead."

"You mean Julie Sheers, the on-site vet," Partial Sue said. "But isn't she just going to say Sylvia had a heart attack?"

"Probably, but you never know."

CHAPTER 8

While Fiona and Partial Sue took the short walk to visit Julie Sheers, Daisy stayed to look after the shop and delve into the comments on Sylvia's social media posts — a gargantuan task of sifting through each one to discover if there were trolls among them. Anyone who felt the need to post nasty comments on a regular basis might also be a possible suspect. They also thought it best to leave Simon Le Bon at the shop, to spare him any unnecessary trauma, as last time he visited Julie it was to have a gloved finger up his behind.

As Fiona crossed the bustling high street of Southbourne Grove with Partial Sue, they noticed the designer-clad shape of Sophie Haverford emerging from the Cats Alliance, the charity shop opposite. A spontaneous and simultaneous groan emanated from the pair of them. Sophie had that effect on people. An encounter with Sophie Haverford was not unlike watching the end scenes of *Titanic* — distressing with a great big sinking feeling, knowing throughout that it would not end well.

Because their charity shops were directly across the road from each other, Sophie had decided that they were in competition and used every opportunity to prove to Fiona how much better her shop was than theirs. The Cats Alliance had the slick, clean interior of a Mayfair boutique, whereas Dogs Need Nice Homes had the slapdash aesthetic of Steptoe and Son. Sophie was an out-and-out snob who looked down her neat, rhinoplastied nose at them, not just belittling their shop but everything they wore and everything they did. Sophie had better dress sense, better clients, better stock, better everything. The only thing she lacked was a troop of flying monkeys to do her bidding, but as someone who always got what she wanted, that was probably just a matter of time.

Too late to turn back now. They stepped onto the other side of the pavement, right into her path. "Hello, Sophie," they said reluctantly.

Dressed head to foot in black with a sleek bob to match and blood red lipstick, she looked like a vampire and smiled like one too. "I am so glad I bumped into you." A complete lie. Sophie made it sound like a chance encounter. She never left anything to chance and had probably been monitoring the street to catch them the second they stepped outside. Her expression immediately changed to one of deep concern. "I heard about that dreadful business. A murder at the local dog show. Terrible." News travelled fast along Southbourne Grove, although being an ex-PR maven (her words), Sophie knew everything that went on. Uncharacteristically sympathetic, she was up to something, or wanted something, or more likely she was laying the groundwork for a set piece that would result in a cheap insult.

"Yes," Fiona agreed. "Just awful."

"And I'd heard her dog was an ex-Crufts winner."

Fiona and Partial Sue nodded.

Sophie frowned, although her Botoxed forehead didn't join in. "I do hope they catch her killer."

"So do we," Partial Sue added. The ladies edged sideways, hoping to slip away, unscathed.

She held them back verbally. "Tell me, are you investigating the murder yourselves?"

Fiona nodded. "Yes, we are."

"Any suspects?"

Fiona thought it best not to mention the lad with the neck tattoo. Not until they knew more. "No, not yet. We've only just begun."

"I mean, there must be so many."

"Yes, the dog show was a very busy place, could've been anyone."

Sophie smirked. "And dog owners all look the same, don't they?"

And there it was, the insult she'd been itching to unleash. "What do you mean by that?" Partial Sue asked.

"You know, dog people are all very similar. Bit scruffy. All muddy wellies, grubby gilets and split ends, wearing strange little pouches on their waists filled with treats that smell like last night's discarded kebab meat. And those funny little rolls of poo bags for picking up unmentionables, that sometimes get left on park benches and hung in trees, like little presents. What do they call those poo bags?"

"Poo bags," Fiona answered.

Sophie gave an artificial giggle. "Gosh, really? If ever there was a product in dire need of rebranding it's them. But coming back to the murder, it doesn't really surprise me. Dogs are aggressive by nature, always fighting and barking at each other. I suppose the same goes for their owners. You'd never get that among cat people."

Fiona had had enough. "You do know that cats fight too. Hence the phrase cat fight, which is what this is turning into. I'm sorry Sophie. We need to go. Lots to do."

"Well, don't let me stop your amateur sleuthing. Off you go. Ta-ta."

Fiona and Partial Sue hurried away before Sophie changed her mind and thought of more nasty things to say. When they were out of earshot, Partial Sue huffed, "What is that woman's problem?"

"I'm not sure. I suppose some people can only be happy if they're making other people miserable."

"Never a truer word spoken."

Five minutes later they stood outside the smart, white, clean and clinical veterinary practice of Julie Sheers. Partial Sue lingered on the pavement gazing up at the signage, reading it out loud: "*Julie Sheers Vets.*" She repeated the name quicker, eyebrows dancing on her forehead in confusion. "Julie-Sheers-Vets."

Fiona was impatient to get inside and get started. "What's the matter?"

"Forget poo bags. I think her practice could do with rebranding. Julie Sheers Vets sounds like someone who clips vets, as if they're sheep."

Now she had mentioned it, Fiona couldn't get the image out of her head of nice, middle-class vets penned in on a bleak Welsh hill farm, then herded one by one towards a rugged farmer, mechanical shears in hand, who would roughly trim their hair, then release them into the wild where they'd skip away, leaping now and again with relief that their brief ordeal was over.

Fiona smiled. "Come on, but don't mention any of that to Julie."

"Wouldn't dream of it."

Inside, Julie's practice was a sparse and pristine affair. White walls everywhere and a grey vinyl floor with pungent disinfectant rising from its surface. A reception desk sat along the far wall, complete with computer screen and phone. To the right, an opaque glass door led to Julie's treatment room. On the other side, stood a tall rack of pet products, ranging from extendable dog leads and shampoos to fresh-breath chews and worming tablets. Down the middle of the space, two rows of plastic chairs were arranged back-to-back. Almost every seat was occupied with concerned pet owners, their beloved animals atop their laps or by their sides, mostly dogs and a couple of cats in carry boxes, and a guinea pig in a cage. None of them sounded at all well, judging by their worried cries and whimpers. Fiona felt sad for all the poor creatures, and their owners.

They took a seat beside a teenage girl whose Yorkshire terrier reminded Fiona of a microscopic Chewbacca, although that was where the parallel with the ferocious Wookiee ended. The dog quivered with fear at being back in that place where they prodded and poked you and stuck you with pointy things for no apparent reason. Fiona smiled sympathetically at the girl who attempted to comfort her dog by massaging its ears. Fiona had heard that this calmed them down and released endorphins, although not enough in this case, judging by the way the dog continued to tremble. She'd definitely made the right decision leaving Simon Le Bon behind.

Dressed in her green scrubs, Julie emerged through the opaque glass door, her curly black hair pinned back in several places. She showed out an older lady carrying a cat in a carry box, which they couldn't see but they could hear well enough, as it hissed and yowled. "Make sure you bring her back if the infection persists."

The woman thanked her and left in a hurry, trying to spare her feline any further distress.

Julie caught sight of Fiona. "Oh, hi, Fiona. Simon not with you today? Hope he's okay."

"Oh yes, he's fine. I can see you're busy."

"I'm always busy," Julie replied, smiling.

"We were wondering if we could have a quick word with you about what happened at the dog show?" Partial Sue asked.

Julie's face became serious. "Oh, er, yes. I suppose. Just let me see to my next patient."

Julie ushered the young girl into the treatment room. The Yorkshire terrier, sensing an opportunity to make a break for it, hopped off her lap onto the floor, straining on its lead, heading in the opposite direction, its claws not gaining any purchase on the slip-slidey floor. He was unceremoniously picked up by his owner and taken to the treatment room.

Fiona and Partial Sue waited while mournful cries came from the poor creature, behind the opaque door.

"Is Julie a good vet?" asked Partial Sue, seeing as they were being presented with all signs to the contrary.

"She's an excellent vet. It's just that animals are very good at picking up on the fear of other animals."

After a while, the Yorkshire terrier reappeared, looking far happier than when it went in, especially as they were now heading in the right direction — towards the exit.

Julie showed the ladies into the treatment room and closed the door. "That was an easy one. Just had to remove a tick from his belly. Horrible things. Told her to avoid the long grass near the river when it's mild and stay on the gravel path."

Fiona gave what she hoped was a warm, unthreatening smile. "Sorry for taking up your time but we were wondering if you'd mind telling us what happened at the dog show."

Julie looked uncomfortable. "I'm not sure I'm supposed to. I gave a statement to the police this morning, just before I opened."

Fiona and Partial Sue exchanged glances. They'd wrongly assumed that they were the first port of call for the police, leading to Partial Sue's theory that they were the number one suspects. Clearly, they weren't, and maybe Daisy's theory was the correct one: they were being given a gentle nudge into investigating. With that in mind, Fiona decided to lay it all out on the table. "We're doing our own investigation. Was it DI Fincher and DS Thomas you spoke to? They've spoken to us too."

Julie nodded. "Are you working with them?"

"Not exactly," Partial Sue replied. "But if we make any breakthroughs, DI Fincher will be the first to know." She reached into her coat and pulled out the police officer's business card to back up what she'd said.

Relaxing her shoulders, this appeared to reassure Julie. "What would you like to know?"

"Start at the beginning," Fiona said. "What led up to the point where you were giving Sylvia Steadman CPR."

"Well, as the on-site vet, I get a free stand to promote my practice in return for offering emergency veterinary care to any of the dogs at the show. To be honest I don't really need to, I'm on the club's list of approved vets. Never been busier. But I do it as a bit of goodwill. So I was advising this woman about urinary diets for schnauzers — they're particularly prone to infection — when this brash-looking guy interrupts us."

"Did he have a neck tattoo?" Fiona asked. "And a Staffordshire bull terrier?"

"Yes, that's right. His face looked desperate, you know, a bit intense. He tells me someone's having trouble breathing. She's on the ground grabbing her chest."

"He alerted you?" Partial Sue appeared confused. This didn't fit with the narrative they'd concocted in their heads of the culprit escaping out the back, not when he'd made a quick diversion to tell Julie about Sylvia's heart attack.

Julie continued, "Yes, so he points to this great big crowd by the main arena, but before I can ask him anything else, he's off, running away with his dog. So I force my way through the crowd, and find Sylvia on the ground. I recognised her straight away. Like everyone else I'd heard that her and Charlie were entering the show. I tell everyone to move back. Check they've called an ambulance. Then I'm at her side, asking if she can hear me, I get no response and that's when I notice she's stopped breathing. So, I start giving her CPR. I must have done this for several minutes. And then, well, you know the rest." Julie's gaze drifted down to the floor.

Fiona tried to comfort her. "That was very courageous what you did."

Without looking up, Julie said, "Thank you. But it wasn't really. Veterinary CPR is not that different to human CPR except we lay the animal on its side, administer the compressions to the ribs instead of the breastbone, but the technique is the same." Her voice became quiet. "I'm used to pets passing away in front of me, but not people."

"You did everything you could," Partial Sue said, sympathetically.

Fiona felt numb, apart from the disinfectant cloying at the back of her throat. "I know this is difficult and the whole situation must have been traumatic for you, but did you notice anything about Sylvia that made you think it wasn't a heart attack that killed her, maybe it was caused by some-thing else?"

Julie glanced left and right, as if someone could be listening. "After Sylvia had passed away, Malorie, the chairperson of Christchurch Dog Club appeared, to let me know the ambulance was on its way. I indicated that it was too late. Sylvia had passed. Malorie disappeared quickly then reappeared with a dog blanket from one of the stalls. We draped it over Sylvia's body to give her a bit of dignity. That's when I noticed a spot of blood on Sylvia's fleece."

"Whereabouts?" asked Fiona.

"Just above the elbow, on the outside of her arm, her triceps. Without removing the blanket, I rolled up the sleeve. There was a puncture wound on the skin. I told the paramedics when they came to pick up her body."

"A puncture wound? What would've caused that?" Fiona knew the answer before she'd finished her own question. An injection. Had Sylvia Steadman died of a lethal injection?

CHAPTER 9

"You think Sylvia had been injected?" Partial Sue asked. "Is that what killed her?"

Julie took a deep, calming breath. "I wouldn't like to say for sure. However, some diabetes sufferers have been known to inject themselves through their clothing."

"Was Sylvia Steadman diabetic?" Fiona asked.

"I have no idea. But if she wasn't, it could mean someone injected her at the show. But I have no proof. You'd need a look at the coroner's report for that, traces of a toxin in her blood. A very fast-acting toxin, I'd say. Almost instantaneous."

The chances of three amateur sleuths getting within a mile of that report were as likely as David Beckham having a bad hair day. They'd have to assume she'd been injected with something that had a rapid effect.

"Would it work, injecting through material?" asked Partial Sue.

Julie nodded. "Yes. Diabetes sufferers sometimes do it when they're in a hurry. It's not ideal, but it's fine as long as their clothes are clean to avoid infection. A good quality needle, even a fine one, is strong enough to make it through several layers of clothes, apart from a really thick coat like a parka. A needle would've had no trouble passing through a soft material like Sylvia's fleece. However, injecting in the triceps would be an odd choice if she was diabetic. Most people prefer the tummy or the thigh as it's easier."

"But if someone did inject her, surely she would have felt it?" Partial Sue asked.

"Like I said, not if a fine enough needle was used, and it was someone who knew what they were doing," Julie explained.

"Crowds are dangerous places," Fiona said. The other two women regarded her. "It's what DI Fincher said. The show was busy, packed, and Sylvia was surrounded by people, distracted by all the attention. If someone wanted to inject her, that's the easiest place to do it. Killer could have brushed past her, stuck her with the needle. Even if she'd noticed, by the time she'd turned around, the killer could've melted into the crowd."

"And the next second she's fighting for her life." Julie glanced at her watch. "Sorry, I better get on."

Partial Sue and Fiona thanked Julie for her time and left her to attend to her next patient. As they were leaving, a small man with a vast Newfoundland, who appeared to be taking his owner for a walk rather than the other way around, was dragged into the vets, as if he were water skiing behind the mountainous dog. They side-stepped the mismatched pair and regrouped outside on the pavement, processing what they had learned.

Fiona blew out through her teeth. "Quite a lot to take in. So, we have our neck-tattooed lad who's gone from being our number one suspect to the person who tried to help save Sylvia's life by alerting Julie. What do you make of that?"

Partial Sue harrumphed cynically. "He's still top of the suspect table as far as I'm concerned. Just because he told Julie doesn't mean he didn't kill Sylvia. Or he might have done it then suddenly grew a conscience, like a hit and run driver calling nine nine nine anonymously. Or maybe he wanted to set up an alibi, so he grabs the show's vet, knowing it was too late for her to save Sylvia. If he does get caught, he can use it as an excuse."

"But what motivation would he have? He barely looked twenty. I doubt he even knew who Sylvia was."

Partial Sue scoffed. "Who knows? But he's a Staffie owner. Doesn't need motivation. You know what they're like."

Fiona didn't like the sound of this. "If you don't mind me saying, that's a bit prejudiced. You're saying he must be guilty because of his age and the dog he owns."

"Staffies are aggressive, aren't they?"

"It's a reputation they've earned because they're usually owned by macho men who want to show off or have mistreated them. They're supposed to be very friendly dogs by nature, if they're looked after properly."

"Okay, sorry. Point taken."

"I wish we could see that coroner's report so we can be sure what killed her."

"We need to know if Sylvia was diabetic or not, otherwise we'll be barking up the wrong tree, excuse the pun."

"Let's assume she's not until we hear otherwise," Fiona replied. "For now, we go with death by lethal injection."

Uttering those last few words sent a shiver across her back. They sounded outrageous and incompatible, more suited to a high-security prison in a foreign land than the familiar and genteel streets of Southbourne.

CHAPTER 10

Back at the shop, they found Daisy with her nose deep in her phone, so engrossed in social media she barely noticed her colleagues had returned. They joined her at the round table and filled her in about the puncture wound, the probable cause of death and the lad with the neck tattoo.

Daisy gasped. She'd been doing a lot of it since they got back. "I can't believe it. A lethal injection at a dog show. Who would have the nerve to do such a thing?"

"There's a chance that Sylvia might be diabetic and had simply injected herself earlier," Fiona explained. "On your journey through her social media posts, have you seen any mention of her being diabetic?"

"Not a sausage," Daisy replied, "but I've hardly made a dent in it. There's a lot to get through."

"Anyone had it in for Sylvia?" asked Partial Sue.

"Not so far. Everyone's very nice, unless she's deleted the nasty comments. I can't imagine who would have done this."

"Someone with a swift hand," Fiona remarked. "Steady enough to squeeze several CCs of an unknown poisonous substance into her bloodstream." They didn't know what name the poison went by, but it didn't really matter whether it was arsenic or window cleaner, only the effect mattered.

"What about Julie Sheers?" Partial Sue asked. "She could've done it."

Both women looked at her, shocked. "Whatever makes you say that?" Fiona asked.

"Well, she gives injections every day, to dogs. I bet she's good at it."

"Why would Julie Sheers want to kill Sylvia?" asked Daisy. "She tried to save her life by giving her C3PO."

"You mean CPR," Fiona replied. "She was surrounded by people watching. How's she going to inject her without being seen?"

Partial Sue was sticking to her theory. "She could have done it before then."

"But she said she was talking to the owner of a miniature schnauzer when the tattooed lad came up to her. She was nowhere near Sylvia."

"We've only got her word for that," Partial Sue replied. "What if she's lying? What if the two of them are in cahoots, giving each other alibis?"

"But why would she want to kill Sylvia?" Daisy asked again.

Partial Sue began scrolling through her phone. "I've been having a nose into the Kennel Club rules. There's a lot of them, pages and pages and they're very strict indeed. It's interesting what you can learn." Being a retired accountant, she knew what it was like to operate in a highly regulated area and had developed an almost sadistic obsession with red tape.

"But this was a fun dog show," Fiona pointed out. "Not a serious event."

"I know, but all dog shows require on-site vets for the obvious reason. At a fun dog show, anyone can be the on-site vet as long as they're qualified. However, for the bigger championship dog shows, right up to Crufts, all vets must be chosen from a pre-approved list of, well, vetted vets, you might say."

Fiona became interested. "Is Julie on the list of approved vets?"

"Yep. Got accepted onto the list the same year as Sylvia won Crufts. Bit of a coincidence, don't you think. Maybe the pair of them were at one of the shows that year and had a falling out. I've emailed the Kennel Club to ask if Julie was the on-site vet at any events Sylvia entered including Crufts."

"We could just ask Julie," Daisy suggested.

Fiona mused on this. "No, let's keep it under our hats until we know for sure. Then we can confront her with the facts."

"I did notice one other thing among some of Sylvia's social media posts," Daisy spoke quietly, unsure of herself. "Nothing nasty against Sylvia. But I read a few bitchy comments among her followers, aimed at other show dogs, criticising them for this and that. Silly things, really. But it got me thinking. What if the murderer were a competitor at the show? Someone who had their sights set on winning. Then heard this rumour that Sylvia had entered Charlie, so they killed her because they were worried she'd steal victory from them."

Now this was a theory that made sense to Fiona, one she'd bandied about in her own mind. "Winning is a powerful motivator if ever there was one. Imagine you'd been preparing to enter your dog for months, thinking you've got a good chance of taking first place, then some ex-Crufts winner turns up. That's not going to go down well."

Partial Sue was on her phone again, delving into the Kennel Club rules. "I'd been thinking that too, but I couldn't square it with the fact that it's just a fun dog show, nothing serious. You can't use a win at a fun dog show to count towards anything, certainly not qualification into Crufts. It's literally just a bit of fun."

"I don't know whether that matters," Fiona replied. "Speaking as a dog owner, I'm extremely proud and protective of Simon Le Bon. I would never dream of entering him for a show, he's too scruffy for that." The other two ladies gave impromptu ahs. Simon Le Bon popped his head up from his basket, his furry ears burning, knowing they were talking about him. "But if I did, well, I'm sure I'd be taking it seriously and eyeing up the competition."

"Okay, sure." Partial Sue went back to her phone screen. "There's bound to be a bit of friendly rivalry but is that enough to kill someone? I mean look at these categories: Waggiest Tail, Sweetest Eyes, Golden Oldie, Handsomest Boy, Prettiest Girl, Floppiest Ears, Dog Most Like Its Owner, Best Biscuit Catcher — hardly the stuff of cut-throat competitiveness."

"I don't think that matters," Fiona said. "Friendly football matches are never friendly. No one wants to lose, and someone who thought they were on track to win wouldn't take kindly to some jumped-up out-of-towner swooping in to snatch victory."

Daisy did a quick search on her phone. "It's not just about friendly rivalry, either. There's money at stake. Winner of each category gets fifty pounds. Each category winner is then eligible for Best in Show — top prize two hundred pounds. Most of the prize money being put up by local doggie businesses, judging by all the sponsorship plastered everywhere."

"Who won Best in Show last year?" Partial Sue asked.

"Someone called Pippa Stroll with her dog Barbie, also winner of last year's Dog Most Like Its Owner category," Daisy replied. "She'd be the most likely suspect, I guess."

"Maybe going for the double." Fiona said. "Her nose would certainly be put out of joint if she thought Sylvia and Charlie were going to stop her."

Partial Sue didn't seem to share their enthusiasm. "Okay, I admit this is probably the most plausible theory we've got so far — the competitive rival. But we don't even know if Sylvia had entered Charlie into the show. It was just a rumour."

Partial Sue was right. They needed to embark on some fact checking before they got carried away and went off at an investigative tangent. First port of call was obtaining a list of this year's entrants. Fiona went on the Christchurch Dog Club website. The one and only contact number was for the club secretary Kenneth Prendiville. "Hmm, I wonder if that's the same Kenneth who held the end of the measuring tape in the Best Biscuit Catcher category. Had a perma scowl."

Daisy found profile pictures of all the committee members on the club's website, including the one of Kenneth Prendiville who had attempted a smile, but it came off as if he'd sat on a cactus.

"That's him," Fiona said. "Let's hope he's in a sharing mood." Fiona tried the number. It went straight to voicemail. She tried it again, same result. "No answer. I know what we'll do. We'll go straight to the source of power at the dog club — Malorie Granger."

Both Partial Sue and Daisy shrank ever so slightly. "Is that wise?" asked Daisy. "Maybe we should hang on, wait until this Kenneth answers. He'll probably give us the information, whereas Malorie won't, seeing how she doesn't like us very much."

"I imagine," Fiona replied, "like all things Malorie is involved in, she rules that dog club with an iron fist. I bet he'd need her stamp of approval before he was allowed to give us that list. We'd be better off going straight to the horse's mouth as it were. Plus, we know where she is. We could go up to the community centre after work. Catch her there."

Daisy swallowed hard, as did Partial Sue. A confrontation with Malorie was not unlike a trip to the dentist — something you only did when absolutely necessary, which often resulted in a lot of pain and humiliation.

Daisy became downcast, accepting her fate. "What should we do between now and then?"

"Keep looking for any trolls in Sylvia's comments," Fiona replied. "Sue, you and I need to do something that we've been neglecting all day."

"What's that?"

She smiled. "Some charity shop work."

CHAPTER 11

Daisy served the last customer of the day. A woman who bought a slightly dented but still serviceable fireguard and a second-hand, well-thumbed copy of *Chocolat*. Fiona could tell Daisy's nerves were getting to her at the thought of visiting Malorie. Words tumbled out of her mouth, cascading in the customer's direction. "Oh, I love Joanne Harris, and *Chocolat*, such an adorable book, a book to devour, you might say. Have you read it? Of course not, otherwise, why would you be buying it. And you must have an open fire, if you're buying a fireguard. You could sit by the fire reading *Chocolat*, how lovely. Hey, I've just realised, you've got *Chocolat* and a fireguard. A Chocolat Fireguard. Isn't that funny."

The woman raised an eyebrow, completed her purchase and made for the door. After she'd gone, Fiona turned the shop's sign around to *Closed*. "Daisy, you don't have to come with us to see Malorie if you don't want to."

"What makes you say that? I'm fine." Daisy defaulted to her go-to comforter, squirting far too much Cif (although she still called it Jif) on the counter than was really necessary, then rubbing it as if she were using attrition alone to wear a hole in the top.

Confronting Malorie would be easier with three of them, although it might look as if they were ganging up on her. Two would appear less threatening. "Sue and I could just head up there," Fiona suggested.

Partial Sue shot Fiona a look, slightly annoyed that Daisy had been let off the hook while she'd been roped into confronting the Bulldozer in Barbour, as Malorie was known.

Daisy scrunched up the spent piece of kitchen roll she'd been using to wipe the counter, now worn ragged, and tossed it in the bin. "No, no. I don't want to let the side down." She shrugged on her coat and slung her bag over one shoulder, clearly wanting to get this over and done with. "Shall we go?"

Simon Le Bon led the way, impatiently tugging on his lead, then stopping every so often to investigate some intriguing smell or another, his nose twitching as it evaluated who had been past here and whether it merited the addition of his scent. Some spots made the cut, while others were not deemed worthy of a lift of his leg.

The community centre, Malorie's domain, loomed above them like a flat-roofed fortress of salmon-pink brick and very few windows. A seventies carbuncle among the Victorian splendour of Southbourne Grove.

"Gird your loins everyone." Fiona shouldered the door open followed by Partial Sue and Daisy, but not Simon Le Bon who pulled in the other direction, not liking the aroma of the place. Fiona couldn't blame him. It smelled like a school and had the ambience of a prison visitor centre with its migraine-inducing fluorescent lighting and cracked vinyl floor that had seen too much multifunctional action. Marked out with lines of withered tape, it served as a space for everything from badminton to bring-and-buy sales, as well as its day job as a meeting place for older, retired folk.

As they entered, it became clear why Simon Le Bon had been reluctant to take point on this one. The committee of Christchurch Dog Club were gathered, their dogs by their feet. Malorie sat at the head, quite an achievement as they were arranged in a circle and there were only four of them, but she'd managed it by utilising the big leather chair from her office, while the rest had to make do with lowly orange plastic chairs, the ones that made your behind sweaty.

Fiona recognised the faces of each member from their profiles on the club website. Kenneth Prendiville, the ratty-faced club secretary who had assisted Malorie adjudicating the Best Biscuit Catcher competition. A scary Doberman stood by his side, ready to spring into action at the first sign of trouble. Delia Hawkins, the vice chair and Jilly Cooper lookalike, sat opposite with her more docile golden retriever dozing on the floor. Next to her, the cereal-haired treasurer David Harper, had a small fluffy Pomeranian perched on his lap that resembled an indignant slipper. Malorie appeared to be winning in the most impressive dog-owner stakes, with not one or two, but three massive Alsatians sprawled around her — a visual but not particularly subtle clue as to who called the shots.

Collective dogs and owners turned to regard the three visitors with outraged expressions. Then the dogs did what dogs did best. They barked their heads off at the intrusion, jaws rapidly clacking open and shut. Even Simon Le Bon joined in. It took a while to quiet them down, each owner employing different tactics, some calmly shushing them, stroking their heads, sensibly indicating that everything was okay, while others, David Harper in particular, shouted at their pets to be quiet, which only egged them on.

When the excitement had died down, despite several dogs still grumbling with their hackles raised, Malorie spoke, although it was more of a scold. "What are you doing here? We're discussing private matters."

"The matter of the death at the dog show," added Kenneth Prendiville.

"Well, it's not private anymore, is it Kenneth," Delia Hawkins chided, her golden retriever now fully awake, grunting its assent. Kenneth scowled back, although it was difficult to tell, as his face had spent so much time scowling that it had possibly stayed that way permanently.

Fiona ventured further into the space, flanked by Daisy and Partial Sue, glad of their moral support, apart from Simon Le Bon who struggled to go in the other direction. "We're so sorry to barge in on you like this, but it's the murder that we've come to see you about."

"Do you have information?" Malorie's face hadn't softened, neither had anyone else's.

"It's the other way around," Partial Sue said.

The members of the dog club committee exchanged confused glances.

Fiona clarified, "We were wondering if you could give us some information."

"What sort of information?" Kenneth Prendiville asked.

"We'd like a list of all the people who entered the dog show," Daisy said. "If it's not too much trouble."

"Out of the question," David Harper snapped. His Pomeranian yapped twice, as if to say, "Yeah, that's right."

"Only the chairperson has the final say on what decisions will be made," Malorie reminded him, but then agreed anyway. "Out of the question. Those are confidential documents."

Fiona really wanted to point out that they were entrance forms for a fun dog show where canines competed to catch biscuits and whose eyes were prettiest, not the nuclear launch codes, but she held her tongue.

Delia Hawkins put up her hand. "May I raise a question?"

Malorie glanced at the other two committee members who nodded their agreement. "You may."

"Can I ask what you'd use the information for?" Delia asked.

"We're doing our own murder investigation. It would really help us if we knew who'd entered."

"You think one of them might be a suspect?" Delia Hawkins asked.

"We don't know at this stage," Partial Sue replied. "It just helps us form a picture."

"We can't have you harassing our entrants, accusing them of murder." At the sudden change in Malorie's tone, her Alsatians' ears pricked up.

"We wouldn't dream of accusing anyone," Daisy said. "Not unless we had a good reason."

"Still out of the question," Malorie snapped.

"Have you given that list to the police?" Fiona asked.

"Of course," Malorie replied.

"Then what's the difference?"

This stumped Malorie but only temporarily. "Well, because they're the police. It's their job."

"Yes, but there's a possibility, actually a very real possibility, they might also accuse one of your entrants," Fiona replied. "So what's the difference?"

Before she could think of a justified response, Kenneth Prendiville spoke. "Well, I think we should do everything we can to help catch the murderer. This terrible tragedy happened at our show and if it means giving these ladies the list of entrants then so be it." His reasonable words seemed at odds coming out of such an unreasonable face.

Malorie threw him a filthy look, presumably because he had undermined her stance. "You always get a bit Zen at this time of year, don't you, Kenneth?"

"I don't know what you're talking about," he replied.

Malorie didn't give him a chance to continue. "You must excuse Kenneth. We have the AGM coming up. He's paranoid he's not going to get voted back in, so he becomes all Zen and one with the earth, so that members will like him and vote for him. We call it his Karma Ken routine."

Delia joined in. "He's been really going for it this time. Even sent them Christmas cards."

Kenneth's face flushed with anger and embarrassment. "I am not getting Zen and stop calling me Karma Ken. Okay, maybe I do that a bit. But this is different. Someone was killed at our show. We want to find out who did it, don't we?"

Strangely, the remaining committee members managed a reluctant and barely perceptible nod.

Kenneth Prendiville shook his head in disgust at his colleagues. "You don't look too enthusiastic. Don't you want to find Sylvia's killer?"

"Course we do," David Harper replied. "It's just that these people aren't the right ones to do it. They're not the police. They could do a lot of harm poking their clumsy noses into something that's very sensitive." His Pomeranian yapped twice.

"Is it possible for a nose to be clumsy?" Daisy whispered.

"You sound like you have something to hide," Partial Sue said. A remark designed to goad, and it did just that.

David Harper clicked his fingers rapidly, as if he were summoning a waiter, then pointed to Delia. "Let the record show I resent that remark — with a great deal of resentment."

"Minutes aren't being recorded," Delia pointed out. "It's an impromptu, emergency meeting not a scheduled one. Only scheduled meetings require a transcript of our words. Remember we're here to discuss whether we should rerun the show at a later date or if that would be inappropriate."

Kenneth said, "Er, I thought that was private committee business, not to be discussed in front of outsiders."

"Well, it was until you mentioned it for all to hear," Delia replied. "Horse has bolted. Galloping to Ferndown, trampling across people's gardens and splashing through their koi carp ponds like the start of *Black Beauty*."

"Oh, I loved the start of *Black Beauty*," Daisy gushed. "But Follyfoot always gave me the creeps."

Bickering ensued between the committee members, none of them listening to what each had to say. Malorie's eyes blazed with fury, or was it despair? Picking up on her mood, her Alsatians simultaneously stood to attention, growling. Eventually, she'd had enough. "Order! Order! I will have order!"

Silenced by her rage, the other three members were instantly humbled, eyes lowered. Likewise, their dogs cowered a little too, apart from David Harper's Pomeranian who stared arrogantly, looking down its wet nose at everyone. Through gritted teeth, Malorie said, "There is a simple way to resolve this. We put it to the vote. All those in favour of handing over our list of entrants to these ladies raise their hands."

Kenneth and Delia lifted their hands in the air.

"And all those against."

Only David's hand went up. "You haven't voted, Malorie," he sneered. His dog yapped twice.

"Chairwoman is allowed to abstain if she sees fit. Read the rules, which means you're outvoted two to one. As you handled all the entry forms and fees, David, I'd like you to furnish these ladies with the information they require."

David Harper stood upright, clutching his fluffy dog under his arm like a rugby ball. "This is ridiculous." He marched off and tried to slam the aluminium door on his way out, but it was too stiff, catching on the uneven floor and squeaking to a halt just before it would have struck the frame.

"What's his problem?" asked Partial Sue.

"Well, you know how dogs are like their owners," Delia replied. "His dog's spoilt and thinks she's in charge of everyone."

Fiona made a mental note that David Harper really didn't want them seeing that list. Possible suspect box ticked.

"You will have the information in the morning," said Malorie. "I'll make sure of it. Now you've taken up too much of our time. We have other matters to discuss. Good evening."

The three ladies thanked her, turned and left, affording themselves little self-satisfied grins. Victories, no matter how small, were still victories.

CHAPTER 12

Next morning Malorie was as good as her word. An email awaited Fiona in her inbox. Not the list of entry forms as she'd hoped, but an agreement of sorts, a pre-emptive, hurried-together NDA typed in Malorie's bolshy, calling-a-spade-a-spade tone rather than legalese. It stated, in no uncertain terms and with copious quantities of exclamation marks, that the details of the dog show entrants were not to be shared or passed onto anyone else and should be deleted once they'd finished with them. And if a strong suspect arose, Malorie wanted to be the first to know. If Fiona agreed to these terms, then Malorie would oblige her and forward on the list. Fiona couldn't fathom just what she thought they were going to do with the details of several dozen dog owners, and just who would be dying to get their hands on them, unless it were a marketing company who had decided to embark on some very limited and highly targeted leafleting in the Christchurch and Southbourne area.

Fiona wasted no time pinging back to say that she agreed to her terms, even adding a few exclamation marks of her own, just to show how serious she was. Five minutes later, Malorie replied, with all ninety-seven dog show entrance forms. She also informed her that the committee had decided to rerun the show, and were in the process of picking a date after Easter.

Fiona forwarded on the list to Partial Sue and Daisy. The trio of ladies began trawling through them to discover if Sylvia Steadman was among the entrants. Malorie had informed them that, for convenience, all entries had been made online via the dog club website. Each form was a simple affair: name of dog, name of owner, date, address, email and telephone number, plus a tick box for which category they wanted to enter — they could enter as many as they liked, at a cost of five pounds per category. Some categories were more popular than others, Sweetest Eyes had the most entries while Best Biscuit Catcher had the least, being a more specialised discipline.

"Hey, just thinking about Best Biscuit Catcher, what about the guy who accused Ewan Fitch of cheating. You said he appeared pretty angry. Could he have killed Sylvia?"

Fiona remembered the bearded man with the cocker spaniel all too clearly, his face burning like a medieval beacon. "Yes, he was very angry, but it was directed towards Ewan Fitch, not Sylvia, and he was in the main arena the whole time, well, until he stormed out of the marquee."

"Bingo!" shouted Daisy. "Found her! Sylvia Steadman entered Charlie for the Golden Oldie category on March the fourth, one week before the show. It's got her new Christchurch address."

The other three ladies gathered around her screen. "Good work, Daisy," Fiona said. "That gives real weight to our jealous competitor theory. Let's keep looking, see if any Staffordshire bull terriers had entered — it might lead us to our neck-tattooed suspect."

The ladies continued searching the remaining entrants. Partial Sue reached the end first. "Well, I haven't found any Staffies, have you?"

Daisy scrolled some more, then shook her head, followed by Fiona. "Okay, so no lead there. We'll have to think of some other way of tracking him down." Fiona paused, deep in thought. "You know, Christchurch Dog Club is big, over six thousand members, according to their website. That's a lot of dog owners."

Daisy smiled. "Well, this area's made for having a dog. You've got the beach, the forest, St Catherine's Hill. People look at you weird round here if you don't have a dog."

Fiona frowned. "But only ninety-seven people entered in total."

"Not everyone will think their dog is good enough to enter," Daisy replied.

"Yeah, that's true. But the show was busy, very busy, but there weren't six thousand people there, two or three hundred I'd say. How come it's such a big club? I mean, membership isn't free. It costs twenty-six pounds a year."

Partial Sue, ever sharp-eyed when it came to money, spotted the answer. "Because of all the perks you get. Says on their website, you pay twenty-six quid a year, but you get twenty percent off all sorts of things: pet insurance, dog food, pet shops, accessories, local groomers, dog walkers, local vets — Julie Sheers is one of them. That's a great deal, Fiona. Works out only fifty pence a week."

It made sense. Owning a dog was expensive and Fiona's yearly vet's bills nearly topped two hundred pounds. The saving she'd make on that alone would more than justify the membership fee. Although she would have to put up with regular emails from Malorie. It was bad enough hearing from her in the real world let alone the virtual one.

"Speaking of Julie Sheers, any news from the Kennel Club about her being a vet at the same shows Sylvia entered?"

"Oh, yes," Partial Sue replied. "I'm glad you reminded me. They emailed me back. According to their records, Julie and Sylvia's path never crossed at any dog shows where Julie was on veterinary duty. No connection between the two, I'm afraid."

The bell above the door tinkled. The Wicker Man made a grand entrance, producing a deep medieval bow as if he were basking in an encore at the Globe Theatre. "Good morrow, dear ladies."

"Hello," they chorused.

His eyes soon lost their mischievous twinkle, as they fixated on the table, and the absence of any baked delights. "Is there perchance any cake that I have hitherto not spied?"

Cake had slipped everyone's mind. They'd been so preoccupied with waiting for Malorie's email, they hadn't even put the kettle on. A troubling and unfamiliar state of affairs at Dogs Need Nice Homes.

"We forgot the cake," Partial Sue gasped, as if she'd driven home after leaving a small child in Asda.

"And the tea. We haven't had so much as a drop," Daisy said, almost feverishly. "What is becoming of us?"

"No tea, no cake. Are you ladies feeling okay?" the Wicker Man asked, genuinely concerned.

Molly, the newest member of Dogs Need Nice Homes appeared at the door. "Did someone mention cake?" She approached the table and placed a large white box in the centre. "I got this from an artisan baker in Penn Hill. A little treat for you all. I hope everyone likes Vicky sponge."

"Vicky sponge?" asked Daisy.

Molly flipped open the lid to reveal a plump, freshly baked Victoria sponge.

Daisy rubbed her hands with delight. "Oh, Vicky sponge! I've never heard it called that before. From now on we'll always call it Vicky sponge."

"Thank you, Molly. You didn't have to do that," said Fiona.

"Well, I'm very glad you did," said the Wicker Man, eyeing up the cake. "We were lost at sea a moment ago. I'm Trevor from next door, but everyone calls me the Wicker Man."

"Hello." Molly smiled.

"Molly's our new member of staff," Fiona said.

The Wicker Man used this as an excuse to give another theatrical bow. "Felicitations on this joyous occasion."

"He always talks like that," Partial Sue informed her. "You'll get used to it."

Fiona pulled out a chair for her. "Welcome to Dogs Need Nice Homes, Molly. I think you're going to fit in here very well."

Simon Le Bon leapt out of his basket, tail wagging at the newcomer followed by a brief sniff of her shoes. That was all the greeting he could spare, as he turned his attention in the direction of the cake, nose twitching away.

The kettle was boiled, plates dished out, and slices of cake were wedged into mouths, accompanied by various groans of satisfaction.

"That was the nicest Vicky sponge I've ever had." Daisy prodded sticky crumbs on her plate with her forefinger and popped them in her mouth. The Wicker Man, who'd usually make his excuses at this point and leave, stayed on for a few minutes.

Fiona got to her feet. "Well, I suppose I better show Molly the ropes."

"Don't worry," Partial Sue said with a smile, "there's not much to it."

"I can show Molly if you like," Daisy said.

It hadn't escaped Fiona's attention that Daisy had taken a shine to Molly. She was roughly the same age as Daisy's daughter Bella, a daughter she never saw and missed so much that sometimes it made her body physically sag. Bella was like her mother, a gentle soul but ill-equipped for the rigours of life, not helped by Daisy having doted on her. When Bella had lived at home she'd held Daisy's marriage together, acting as the glue between her and her toxic husband. The fracture between them occurred when Bella met a man who was just like her father — a completely selfish arse. Daisy didn't want her to marry him and make the same mistake she had. They subsequently fell out and now she never saw her. Daisy's marriage fell apart soon after, leaving her with nothing but an aching loneliness. In Molly, Daisy had obviously found a surrogate daughter.

"Yes, why not." Fiona said. "Start with the sort."

"The sort?" Molly asked. "Sounds like a daytime game show."

"It is." Partial Sue grinned. "Except there are no prizes and it never ends."

Daisy stood up. "Honestly, it's not as scary as it sounds." Molly followed her into the storeroom to begin her training, a trial by fire or more accurately, bin liner, bag for life and cardboard box — the favoured methods of bequeathing donations.

Fiona snatched up her phone and delved once more into the list of dog show entrants, eager to pinpoint potential suspects. "We need to narrow them down somehow. Find out who was Charlie's closest competition and therefore who'd most likely want Sylvia out of the way."

"Well, for a start, there's last year's Best in Show winner, Barbie the Maltese. Owner is Pippa Stroll. She entered again this year. I saw her name when we were scrolling through the list of entries. It's not a name you easily forget. She must have been trying for a second win."

"Good work, Sue. She goes to the top of our suspect list."

"The winners of all the other categories are also going to be suspects — they'd all get instant qualification to enter Best in Show, and would therefore be Charlie's rivals."

"But apart from Best Biscuit Catcher, none of the other categories got to run so how are we going to know who they are?"

The Wicker Man who had been earwigging their bizarre conversation and helping himself to a third slice of cake, muttered, "You investigating the death at the dog show?"

Fiona and Partial Sue nodded.

"And you need to know who was favourite to win each category."

They nodded again.

"Then you need Reg Anagram."

Fiona wondered who or what was Reg Anagram.

CHAPTER 13

They crossed the road with the Wicker Man, immediately wishing they hadn't. A dangerous activity in his company, not unlike Russian roulette except played with speeding cars and double-decker buses instead of a bullet and revolver. He either hadn't paid attention to the green cross code when he was little or just didn't care, as his technique involved stepping blindly into the road, oblivious to whatever vehicle happened to be hurtling towards him. The method behind this road-crossing madness became clear, as they made it to the relative safety of the central island, accompanied by a chorus of blasting horns and screeching brakes. "What's vexing them?" he demanded to know. "Don't they know the law's changed? They have to stop for pedestrians now."

"I don't think it means you can step straight into the path of an oncoming car." Fiona was glad she'd left Simon Le Bon with Daisy and Molly. Car horns made him nervous, as they did most creatures and people, apart from the Wicker Man.

"Pah! They'll just have to learn the hard way." He continued his suicidal walk across to the other side, forcing a Toyota Corolla to swerve around him.

Fiona and Partial Sue stayed put, sensibly biding their time for a gap in the traffic. When they safely reached the other side, they continued up Southbourne Grove then took a left down a small side road with several narrow shop units. One of them was called Reg's Dry Cleaning.

"Dry cleaning?" Fiona questioned.

"That's Reg's main stock in trade, but he runs a nice little earner as a backstreet bookie." The Wicker Man had ditched his Shakespearian lilt and was becoming more of a geezer with every syllable. "He takes bets on the sly for anything local, Sunday football league games, horticultural shows and the Christchurch Dog Show. Now you can't mention this to anyone, first rule of Fight Club and all that."

"Our lips are sealed," Partial Sue said.

"Good. Now the second rule of Fight Club . . ."

"We get it," said Fiona. "Don't talk about it."

"No. Not that. Second rule is don't call him Reg Anagram. Reggie or Reg is fine, but he doesn't like being referred to as Anagram. Gets a bit sensitive about it. Actually, I probably shouldn't have even mentioned it."

"Er, okay." Fiona wondered what had earned him such a nickname. "Dare I ask why people call him Anagram?"

"Is it because he likes doing anagrams?" Partial Sue suggested. "I am partial to a good anagram."

"His name's Reggie Geiger," the Wicker Man replied.

It took Fiona and Partial Sue a few seconds to rearrange the last letters of his name. Then they both laughed in delight.

"See, that's why he doesn't like being called Anagram. He doesn't like people laughing."

"I think it's a great nickname," Partial Sue said. "I wish I had a nickname."

Fiona wondered whether this was a good time to point out that she already did. Unsure at how she'd take it, Fiona decided not to reveal her moniker, in case she had the same reaction as Reg. Names were sensitive things. In Fiona's experience it was always best to call a person by what they wanted to be called, not what you felt they should be called. That was just common decency. "If he likes Reg or Reggie, then that's what we'll call him."

"Good. Follow me." He pushed open the door to the chemical kingdom of Reg's cleaning emporium. A simple space, hygienic and sparse, with a smooth blue Formica counter running across the width of the shop and a cash till at one end. Behind this were racks of clothes on wire hangers sheathed in plastic, waiting to be collected. Every inch of wall space had been covered in panels of various sizes, listing the individual price of every conceivable item of clothing that might need to be washed, everything from a slip to a kilt and a wedding dress to a cummerbund. Reg was clearly a details man.

Reg appeared from the back, a small, compact and rotund fellow. His knuckles were covered in gold rings and his poorly dyed, short-cropped hair, a little too solid in its tone, made it appear as if he were wearing a svelte, close-fitting crash helmet.

"Trevor! To what do I owe the pleasure?"

"Reg! Me old mucker!" The Wicker Man had gone into full-on bloke mode now. They slapped their palms together for a hearty handshake. "I'd like to introduce you to two very good friends of mine. This is Fiona and Sue."

"Hello there." Reg grinned warmly.

Partial Sue and Fiona returned the greeting.

The Wicker Man lowered his voice to a whisper. "I'm guessing you heard about the death at the dog show."

Reg bowed his head. "Shocking, just shocking. Poor woman losing her life. Who'd have thought it?"

"Actually, that's what we wanted to ask you about," Fiona said.

Reg threw a worried glance at the Wicker Man, as if to say, just who are these people?

"It's okay, Reg. Sue and Fiona are alright."

Fiona thought it best to play straight with the bookie. "We're investigating Sylvia Steadman's death. We have a theory that the murderer might be one of the other competitors, a rival who didn't want her to win."

"Makes sense but what's that got to do with me?" All trace of warmth had fled Reg's face.

"We need to know who her biggest competition was," Partial Sue added. "The favourites to win the other categories and get a place in the Best in Show final."

Reg shook his head. "I'd rather not get mixed up in that."

"You're not getting mixed up in anything, Reg," the Wicker Man reassured him. "All you're doing is giving a list of odds. Same thing you'd do for any punter placing a bet."

Reg chewed it over in his mind, then said, "Alright, fine." He moved over to the left-hand wall and began pulling back the panels advertising his prices. They appeared to be mounted on hinges, like little doors, revealing a hidden blackboard on the reverse side. Fiona caught a brief flash of one. Covered in chalk writing, it appeared to be odds for how many times Christchurch Quay would flood this month.

"Now which one was it?" Reg opened and shut panel after panel, searching for the right one, as if the whole wall were a giant advent calendar. "Ah, here we are." He stopped at one and opened it wide. "Christchurch Dog Show. Odds for Best in Show. Charlie is the favourite at two to one, or should I say, was odds on favourite until his owner died." He picked up a cloth and rubbed Charlie's name out. He continued, ramping up his bookie patter. "Next is Barbie the Maltese, last year's Best in Show winner, and this year's second favourite to win behind Charlie at ten to one."

"But now Charlie's out of the way, this would make her the favourite," Fiona said.

"That's right." He moved down the list. "Then there's Rolo the Chocolate Lab, twelve to one, always a crowd pleaser is Rolo with the Waggiest Tail. Next, we have Max the Weimaraner, last year's winner of Sweetest Eyes, fifteen to one. Then we have the legendary Lord Bob who's won Best Biscuit Catcher three years in a row. Could he take Best in Show this year? Sixteen to one says he's in with a shot. Last but by no means least, we have Nellie the Cockapoo and Haggis the Havanese, joint outsiders at twenty to one. But don't discount them. Show's not over until the Pope's a Catholic." He gave a dirty Syd James laugh.

Partial Sue whipped out her phone. "Would you mind if I took a picture?"

Reg's cheeky grin dropped again. "I'd rather you didn't. But you can write them down."

"Fair enough." She opened the Notes app on her phone and thumbed them in with the deft speed of a teenager.

"How do you arrive at these odds?" asked Fiona.

"Er, I'd rather not say." Reg closed up the panel.

"Thing is," Fiona said, "if we're going to investigate any rival owners who might have had it in for Sylvia and Charlie, we need to be sure these names aren't pulled out of a hat before we start pointing fingers."

Reg appeared offended. "I may do this on the sly, but I pride myself on giving value for money."

Value for money wasn't a term Fiona would normally associate with backstreet gambling, or any sort of gambling where people willingly threw their money away, but she kept her thoughts to herself, choosing instead to rephrase the question. "If you could just give us an idea of how, for instance, Barbie ended up on top of Lord Bob." This was turning into the most bizarre conversation ever.

Partial Sue put her phone away. "Or is it just random? Gosh, imagine if your punters found out that all these odds were made up." She had a knack for goading people, handy when they needed information, especially when it came to asking someone to explain their working out of a mathematical nature.

Reg huffed. "It's not random. I have someone who gives me the inside line."

"Who?" asked Fiona. "Is it someone at the dog club?"

Reg hesitated, just a smidge, but enough to confirm it.

"It has to be," Partial Sue joined in. "Who else would know which dogs were most likely to win?"

Fiona remembered the meeting they had with the dog club committee and how one particular member threw his toys out of the pram. "Is it David Harper, the treasurer? He handles all the online entries. He'd know every dog and owner who would've entered that show."

Partial Sue backed her up. "And he stormed off when we asked him for the list of competitors. Got a guilty conscience, if you ask me."

Reg's shoulders hunched and his face reddened. "Hey, David's got nothing to do with the murder. I mean, yes, he gives me the low-down on all the dogs, but that's all. He has a pretty good take on who's likely to win, but it's Malorie who's the judge. She has the final decision."

Fiona stepped up to the panel Reg had closed moments ago. "May I?" She didn't wait for his permission, reopening it to examine the odds, much to Reg's distress. "Someone putting a bet on Charlie isn't going to make much of a return at two to one. The odds for all these other dogs are far more favourable. If they took Charlie out of the picture, they'd stand to make a lot of money if they'd bet on one of these other dogs. I mean, how does it work since the show got cancelled? Have you refunded people who've made bets? I take it you know the show is being rerun after Easter."

Reg nodded his head slowly. "So I've heard. I've refunded anyone who bet on Charlie, but I'm honouring all the other bets, holding on to them for when it's rerun."

"At the same odds?" asked Partial Sue.

He nodded his head again.

"Well, there you go," Fiona said. "Maybe someone wanted Charlie out of the way so they could make a packet by betting on a dog with better odds. Fixing the show."

Reg closed up the panel and glared at Fiona. "I think your imagination's got the better of you. I'm a little backstreet bookie. For punters to have a little flutter. A couple of quid here, a fiver at the most. I couldn't take a big bet even if I wanted to."

The Wicker Man came to his defence. "Reg is small time. A little service to locals in the know. Nothing worth killing someone over."

Reg began opening and closing other panels on the wall, revealing the numerous bets he had on the go. "Look at this. Odds for the WI's baking competition." He crossed the shop to the opposite wall. "The Southbourne fun run, Tuckton Classic car show, Iford regional BMX final. I'm small time, anyone will tell you."

Fiona had to admit it, Reg's operation was the betting equivalent of the village hall rather than the Albert Hall. Although, Fiona couldn't help but be impressed with the sheer variety Reg offered his clients. BMX racers rubbed their protected shoulders with the earnest baking folk of the Women's Institute. The array of parochial gambling on offer was dazzling. "So it's possible to bet on anything then."

"Oh, yes," Reg replied. "Absolutely anything. As the old saying goes, if you can think about it, you can bet on it. But I'm strictly the little local stuff as you can see."

"Do you ever have a flutter?" Partial Sue asked.

Reg shook his head firmly, possibly because over the years he witnessed a steady stream of punters losing more money than they made, even if it was only small change. "I prefer to invest my spare cash."

Not heeding his words, the Wicker Man began discussing a bet he wanted to place on which pump at the local petrol station would be the next to have an out of order sign slung around its nozzle.

They thanked Reg for his help and left him and the Wicker Man to hash out his petrol-pump predictions. They had what they came for — a list of possible rivals who might have wanted Sylvia out of the way, and they'd explored an avenue of investigation that they hadn't previously thought of, that it might be a local betting scam, only to immediately cross it straight off their list. No matter, mission accomplished.

Walking back to Southbourne Grove, Partial Sue rapidly swiped at her phone. "So we have a juicy list of promising rivals we can work our way through, jealous suspects who'd want Sylvia out of the way. As we thought, number one is Pippa Stroll and her dog Barbie, now they're the new favourites to win. A-ha." She paused her scrolling. "Found her entry form. According to her address she's just a stone's throw away. Should we pay her a visit?"

"No time like the present."

The address didn't lead them to a home but a shop in a side street similar in size to Reg's but far swisher. Painted in pastel pink, it was a beauty parlour, called I Feel Pretty. Treatments on offer were listed on the shop sign below its name: *hair, facials, makeup, dermal fillers, eyebrows, lashes, nails, waxing*. Through the window they could see a row of floor-to-ceiling mirrors, framed in pink with matching chairs, each one empty. At the back, above a trio of vacant but gleaming hair-washing basins, a giant mural dominated the wall — an inverted green champagne bottle tipping bubbling froth everywhere, accompanied by the words *Live. Laugh. Love.*

"That is so not the sort of place where I would get my hair done," Partial Sue remarked.

"Me neither." Fiona self-consciously raked a hand through her streaked grey hair in an attempt to smarten it up.

As soon as they pushed the door open, they were hit by a pungent waft of fragrant shampoo and perming fluid. Heels clacking away, a smiley, short-statured woman strutted towards them, a creamy white long-haired dog tucked under one arm, presumably Barbie. Dog and owners' hair matched perfectly, as if it had been dyed from the same bottle. As soon as Pippa Stroll caught sight of Fiona and Partial Sue, her cheesy grin swiftly turned to a scowl. They recognised her instantly. She was none other than the snotty woman whom Daisy had accidentally barged into at the dog show, knocking coffee all down her.

CHAPTER 14

Pippa placed Barbie on the floor. "Go to your happy place, sweetie." Her Maltese immediately scuttled off towards the till. Like Fiona's dog, Barbie had a little spot reserved for her beside the salon's reception desk, except unlike Simon Le Bon's, it wasn't a dog bed that had seen better days. This was a plush, pink, velvet throne with sparkling gold painted legs and claw feet, and Barbie's name embroidered on the backrest in gold thread, no less. Barbie ignored it and snuffled around the desk, hoping to find crumbs. "Go to your happy place, sweetie," Pippa repeated, impatience creeping into her voice. The tiny dog ignored her again. Pippa tutted, picked up Barbie and placed her on the throne, and told her to stay. She obeyed but a low growl rumbled at the back of her throat, signalling she wasn't happy about this.

Pippa turned back to Fiona and Partial Sue, and snapped, "I hope you've come to pay for my dry cleaning."

"Funnily enough we've just come from the dry cleaners," Partial Sue replied with a smile.

Pippa Stroll didn't find the coincidence amusing in the slightest. She marched back the way she came, disappearing behind a door just below the upended champagne bottle painted on the rear wall.

Partial Sue quickly turned to Fiona and whispered, "She's that stuck-up cow who was horrible to Daisy."

Pippa returned clutching a receipt, which she thrust in front of them. Fiona took it and examined the cost. Pippa's jumper dress hadn't been cleaned at Reg's, or any dry cleaners in Southbourne or Christchurch, for that matter, but a place called Premium Dry Cleaners in the highly desirable hamlet of Canford Cliffs, known for its posh shops and bars, and highly undesirable prices. After getting a good look at Reg's costs, which were impossible to miss, it appeared that this outlet charged triple what he did. Fiona hadn't come here to haggle. They needed to question Pippa, and keep her sweet, if such a thing were possible. Best to comply with her demands.

Fiona pulled out her purse and offered to pay on Daisy's behalf, more than the cost on the receipt. But before she handed over the money, she wanted information. "Can I just ask, at the dog show, before the coffee spillage, had you entered the marquee through the small entrance at the rear?"

"Why do you want to know?" Pippa regarded her suspiciously.

"Just curious."

"Had you been to the Portaloos to spend a penny?" Partial Sue asked.

Pippa winced as if she'd had lemon juice squirted in her eye. "God, no. I wouldn't be caught dead in a toilet TARDIS. I went to the kiosk on the quayside to get coffee."

"Why did you go there? Bit out of the way, isn't it? The dog club was serving tea and coffee." Partial Sue liked the tea and coffee served at the show, mostly because it only cost pence rather than pounds.

"Oh, please. I'm not drinking that muck. I wanted a proper coffee. Literally just bought it when your friend knocked it all down me. Hadn't even had so much as a sip."

"Her name's Daisy," Partial Sue remarked. "And she didn't knock it down you. A guy with a Staffie bumped into her."

"Well, I didn't see any of that. All I knew was my jumper dress was ruined."

"You didn't see the guy with the spider's web neck tattoo?" Fiona asked.

"No, all I saw was your clumsy friend, Maisie . . ."

"Daisy," Partial Sue corrected.

"Whatever. She was on a collision course with my latte."

"Apologies, on our friend's behalf." Fiona handed her several notes. "Keep the change."

"I'm not a mini-cab driver." Pippa snatched the money and went over to the till where she popped one of its buttons. After extracting a selection of coins she returned, slapping them into Fiona's hand. "You're lucky I'm not charging you for the distress or the coffee I never got to drink. I had to go home and change. I couldn't stay at the show stinking of stale coffee."

"But the show was cancelled. You heard about Sylvia Steadman dying?" asked Fiona.

Without a trace of sympathy Pippa said, "Oh yes. By the time I got back the ambulance was there, and Malorie was telling everyone to go home. I needn't have bothered coming back. Complete waste of time, causing Barbie all that stress for nothing. She gets very anxious just before a show."

The two ladies stared at her, shocked at Pippa's callousness. A woman more irked by the slight inconvenience of having to go home and change than by a woman losing her life.

Pippa returned a poisonous, perma-pout stare. "What? You want me to feel sympathy for a dead person I've never met. Well, I'm not going to pretend to be upset over a dead stranger. That's hypocritical, if you ask me. Do you know one person dies in the world every second." She glanced at her watch, her words coinciding with every tick of the second hand. "Someone's just died . . . someone's just died . . . someone's just died. I bet you don't feel sorry for any of them, so why should I feel sorry for Sylvia Steadman?"

"But weren't you shocked that she was murdered?" Fiona asked.

Pippa's rosebud lips formed a fine and delicate 'O' and her skin became ashen. "M-murdered? I thought it was a heart attack."

"That's what they thought at first. But later they realised it was murder."

Pippa steadied herself, not helped by her skyscraper heels. "Murdered? Are you sure?"

Partial Sue and Fiona nodded.

Pippa did have a soul after all. Her perfect skin contorted into a painful mask or would have done if it hadn't been Botoxed up to the nines. "Oh my gosh. That's terrifying. Why would anyone want to kill her, and at a dog show?"

"That's what we're trying to find out," Partial Sue said. "I take it the police haven't contacted you yet?"

"No, not yet."

"They will," Fiona replied. "It's probably taking a while to track everyone down and question them."

Pippa swallowed hard.

"Had you heard of Sylvia Steadman?" Partial Sue asked.

"I mean, I didn't know her personally, as I said, but everyone's heard of Sylvia Steadman and Charlie. Well, in dog show circles."

"Did you know that Charlie was favourite to win Best in Show?" Fiona asked.

Pippa's sympathy was short-lived. Her shock transformed slowly into a small, but polite quivering smile, verging on irritated. "Er, I think you'll find that Barbie was the favourite to win Best in Show." She clip-clopped over to Barbie, hoisting her from her throne. Barbie didn't concede to this and grumbled as she was squeezed and nuzzled. Pippa affected a squeaky voice for her precious pet. "That's right. Mummy's little fluff-aloo was all set to win Best in Show, wasn't she?"

"Not according to . . ." Fiona nearly forgot the first rule of Fight Club and was about to mention Reg's name. "We heard from a reliable source that Charlie was favourite to win, but Barbie was a close second."

Pippa stared up from her furry embrace with fury in her eyes. Her affection fled and she abandoned Barbie, dumping her unceremoniously back on her throne, then fixing Fiona with eyes like black holes sucking the hope out of life itself. "Barbie was the favourite, everyone knows that. She won Dog Most Like Its Owner and Best in Show last year. She would've done the double again this year. Charlie wouldn't have stood a chance."

"But Charlie is an ex-Crufts winner," Partial Sue pointed out.

Pippa swung her blacklight stare at her. "So what? That was four years ago. Charlie's old, must be at least seven or eight. No one would have stood a chance against Barbie. I mean just look at her coat. No dog's in better condition than Barbie. I do all my own grooming. I'm the best beautician in the area. I'm better than any grubby dog groomer. I'm actually going to branch out into dog grooming. Ever tried getting a dog grooming appointment? They're always booked up and they're not even that good. With my superior standards I'm going to clean up. I'm opening a chain of four to start with. Going to dominate dog grooming around here. I've got the investment and everything. Anyway, Barbie would've beaten every dog there. No doubt about it. Even an ex-Crufts winner like Charlie. But I suppose we'll never get the chance to prove that now Sylvia's dead. Such a shame."

Fiona and Partial Sue left Pippa Stroll to her ambition and bitterness, and made the walk back to the charity shop.

Partial Sue shook her head, half disgusted, half disappointed. "Well, that was a waste of time. She was standing right next to us when the murder happened."

"Yeah, and she's not exactly trying to cover up her rivalry with Sylvia. If she's the killer she hasn't really grasped the idea of misdirection. She's practically shouting about how she wanted Barbie to beat Charlie, at all costs. Only thing she regrets is that her dog never got to prove its superiority over an ex-Crufts winner."

"I don't think I've ever met anyone so arrogant and full of themselves, and that's saying something — we know Sophie Haverford for crying out loud."

Fiona chuckled. "At least Sophie pretends to be nice some of the time. Pippa's just plain horrible."

"Yeah, probably why her salon's empty if she's like that to customers."

"Come on. Let's see how Molly's doing on her first day. I sort of feel we've abandoned her."

"Oh, I wouldn't worry. Daisy will take good care of her."

The moment they returned to the shop they could sense it. Something had changed, as if they'd stepped into a parallel universe and into an alternate version of the shop. The same but different. A subtle shift, almost imperceptible and tantalisingly just out of reach. To add to the surrealness, Daisy was nowhere to be seen. At least Simon Le Bon hopped out of his bed with welcoming wags, although these abruptly stopped when he smelled Fiona's clothes and detected the scent of another dog. The pet equivalent of cheating on someone. He turned up his nose in disgust and went back to his bed.

Molly emerged from the storeroom, a stack of clothes in her arms. "Oh, hi, Fiona. Hi, Sue."

They silently nodded, their minds preoccupied, eyes flicking around the shop attempting to identify what had changed. Fiona put her curiosity to one side. "How's it going, Molly? Everything okay?"

She beamed. "Oh, yes, indeed. I'm getting stuck in, as you can see."

"Where's Daisy?" Partial Sue asked.

"She took an early lunch."

Partial Sue was not happy about this. "Well, she should be looking after you, not nipping out for a sandwich."

Molly began hooking clothes onto hangers. "Oh, it's fine. I insisted she go. Like you said, there's not much to it, so I started making some rearrangements, I hope you don't mind. I've grouped the clothes together in colours rather than sizes. I thought it makes them more visually appealing, especially if you're trying to match outfits. But I can put them back if you don't like it." She gestured to a rotary display to the right of them.

That was it. The shift they had both perceived. The clothes which had previously been a multi-coloured jumble, were now an orbital rainbow of garments, clustered together in greens, reds, blues, whites and yellows. But Molly wasn't done yet.

"I've also done something similar with the books. Instead of placing them in alphabetical order, I've made them genre specific, like they do in Waterstones."

Partial Sue's OCD kicked in. Not liking change, her head juddered as she spoke, and her hands shook. "Everyone expects alphabetical order. That's how it's done. We've always done it like that."

"We did try it in genres once," Fiona said. "But some genres are a lot smaller than others and we ended up with sections that only had a couple of books in them."

Molly led them over to the hallowed ground of the bookshelves, the shop's pride and joy. "Yes, but I've combined smaller genres with bigger ones, horror with crime for instance."

Fiona could sense Partial Sue tensing up. Horror was horror and crime was crime, and never the twain should meet, well, it did in some books, but they were rarely donated to the shop, apart from the odd Thomas Harris novel. Genres weren't the equivalent of the old Woolworths pick 'n' mix. You couldn't throw different flavours together. Or could you? Fiona had to admit that the shelves were far more pleasing on the eye, especially as Molly had made little signs for each genre in felt tip with her swishy copperplate handwriting.

"There's a simple visual shorthand to book covers to inform the customer of what they're getting." Molly guided them through her new colour-coded literary landscape. "For instance, horror and crime novels usually have dark or black covers, while at the other end, chick lit has bright pastel yellows and pinks, while literary and historical fiction go for dark blues, greens and burgundies."

"Yes, we had noticed. Me and Fiona have read the odd book in our time." Partial Sue said it in a light-hearted tone that had a serrated edge to it.

"I'm sorry. I'm telling you how to suck eggs," Molly apologised.

"Not at all. I think it looks lovely," Fiona gushed. "Don't you, Sue?"

"You've done all this since we've been out." Partial Sue didn't say it in a praiseworthy way, more of a shocked and disturbed way at how quickly one's world could be turned upside down.

Molly didn't pick up on her distress. "Yes, and I managed to sell a few items. A woman's camel hair coat, a tennis racket, a game of Hungry Hippos — I pity the family that's getting that, noisy isn't the word — and some books. New system's working already."

Fiona clapped her hands. "Well, I think this deserves a cup of tea to say job well done."

Partial Sue didn't share her enthusiasm, instead choosing to grind her teeth. Thankfully, Molly didn't notice, delighted that her shop modifications had been well received. Her face suddenly became serious. "Oh, there was one other thing. A man came in asking for all three of you, just now."

"What man?" Partial Sue asked.

"Nervous chap. Didn't say his name. Didn't stay long enough for me to ask."

"What did he want?" Fiona asked.

"Said he had information. About the dog show."

Fiona took a step closer. "What sort of information?"

"Crucial information, he said."

Fiona and Partial Sue had clearly picked the wrong time to leave the shop.

CHAPTER 15

After returning from an early lunchbreak, Daisy had not ceased berating herself for 'abandoning her post', as she put it. She'd been absent when someone had come in with vital information about the case, and in her mind that was unforgivable.

Partial Sue tried to console her. "Daisy, we were out too."

"Yes, but you thought I would be here, holding down the fort. The second I step out of the shop, a valuable witness shows up. I've made a right mess of things."

Fiona gave her a warm smile and placed a reassuring hand on her. "You had no idea that would happen. None of us did."

"I'm sure he'll be back," Molly reassured her. "Why don't I make us all a nice cup of tea."

"That sounds like a great idea," Fiona said.

They took seats around the table while Molly disappeared into the storeroom briefly, reappearing with the large, brown teapot, placing it in the centre. After leaving it a minute or two she poured them each a cup, but sensibly let everyone see to their own milk. Tea was a highly sensitive and personal pastime, as individual as a fingerprint. Many a decent cup of tea had been ruined by dairy presumptuousness. Add the wrong measure of milk and it could be weeks before the recipient would forgive you.

Daisy sipped hers first. "Oh, my gosh. That is a lovely cuppa."

Fiona slurped hers and gave a satisfactory sigh. "You make a good cup of tea, Molly."

Partial Sue followed suit, but her reaction was less enthusiastic. "Not bad, I suppose."

Molly ignored her. "I find the trick is not pouring boiling water on the leaves. After the kettle's boiled, I let the water cool down a touch. Otherwise, it burns the tea and kills the flavour."

"Well, I never." Daisy's face lit up at this life-changing revelation. "That's the way I'm going to do it from now on."

"I think I'll stick with boiling water. I am partial to a piping hot cuppa. Nothing worse than when it's lukewarm." Partial Sue clearly had tea-making envy.

"Oh, I don't mean leave it so long that it's lukewarm," Molly explained. "Just a minute or two."

The debate would have continued, and although the correct way to produce the perfect cup of tea was a valid one, Fiona wanted to steer the conversation towards more pressing matters. "The chap who came in with information, how would you describe him?"

Molly thought for a second. "Short, grey hair. Middle-aged. Medium build."

That described the majority of the male population in Southbourne above the age of forty-five.

"And he definitely wanted to speak with us?" asked Partial Sue.

"Yes. He asked to speak to Fiona, Sue or Daisy. I said you were all out at the moment. I asked if he wanted to leave a message. His face went blank. Then he told me to tell you that he had information about the dog show. He said he knew who did it, then he panicked as if he'd said too much. He said, he'd be in touch. Next second, he was gone."

"And you said he was nervous."

"Oh yes, really antsy. Kept looking over his shoulder all the time he was here, which wasn't very long."

"So, what now?" asked Daisy.

Fiona didn't answer straight away, until she'd worked through the logic in her head. "Well, there is nothing we can do but wait for him to make contact. We don't know who he is or where we can find him. So we'll have to sit tight. In the meantime, we keep working through our list of Charlie's rivals and question their owners."

After Molly had left to pick Dina up from school, they took turns calling potential suspects, using the contact details on the entry forms. All their calls went unanswered or straight to voicemail. Possibly because, being early afternoon, people were busy working, running errands or, like Molly, doing the school run. But the most likely explanation was that they didn't like answering a call from a number they didn't recognise. Fiona certainly didn't. She'd had her fill of scammers on the other end of the line telling her that her internet was about to be cut off or that she had a package she'd never ordered that need to be redelivered.

Fiona resigned herself to the fact that they would have to resort to calling on these people in person. Showing up unannounced on someone's doorstep didn't always put them in the best frame of mind to answer questions. Pippa Stroll a case in point. Although, to be fair, their very first encounter with the beautician had resulted in Daisy pouring coffee all down her. She was never going to be pleased to see them. However, Fiona got the impression that Pippa Stroll would be in a bad mood even if they'd given her prior notice of their intention to visit, quilled in ink on a piece of vellum resting on a velvet cushion delivered by a footman in a powdered wig.

They'd give it until the end of the day to give their potential suspects time to listen to their voicemails and get back to them. If no one responded they'd start knocking on doors and demanding answers — in the nicest possible way, of course.

CHAPTER 16

Next day, not long after the cake had been sliced and the tea had been poured (it was Partial Sue's turn, who told them in no uncertain terms of her intention to stick defiantly to her original tea-making technique of scorching the tea leaves with boiling water, resulting in a strong serviceable cuppa but not nearly as nice as Molly's), the Wicker Man burst through the door. For once he didn't head straight for the cake, leading Fiona to wonder if he were feeling okay.

"Ah, good. I see you're all here," he bellowed. "This is most fortuitous." He pulled several grubby, folded-up pieces of paper from his pocket and unfurled them. "I was wondering if you may lend me your lugholes. I have some new material to bestow upon you."

Molly looked puzzled. Daisy leant over and enlightened her. "Trevor here is a stand-up comedian."

The Wicker Man blushed. "Well, I'm trying to be."

"He's going to be in an amateur talent show at the Regent Centre," Daisy added. "We're all going. Would you like to come?"

"Yes, I'd love to if I can get a babysitter for Dina. What sort of stand-up comedy is it?"

"I do observational stuff. Kind of Michael McIntyre mixed with Victoria Wood."

"Oh, I like both of those."

"Well, without further ado may I offer up a modicum of my mirth?"

Molly became puzzled again.

"He wants to tell you some jokes," Partial Sue explained.

"Oh, yes please." Molly nodded eagerly. The others did not, bracing themselves for what was to come, possibly an ordeal of awkwardness. Fiona hoped and prayed more than anything that his routine had improved. She desperately wanted him to be funny. It was painful enough having to listen to someone who thought they were amusing, but torture having to then explain to them why they weren't funny.

The Wicker Man cleared his throat, forgoing his bizarre voice warm-up ritual. He glanced at his sheets of paper, then looked up. "This is a good one." He shook himself out a little, getting into character. "Why has everyone started writing the date round the wrong way. Take Nine Eleven, for instance. What's that all about? Nine eleven is the ninth of November, not the eleventh of September. Don't they know that the day comes first then the month? What's that all about?"

Nothing. No reaction from any of them.

"Okay, tough audience. I like it. Putting me to the test, eh?" Undeterred, the Wicker Man persevered, shuffling through his notes, seeking out something that would strike their funny bones. He giggled as his eyes lit up, alighting on a suitable gag. "You'll like this one. Have you ever noticed how no one ever says the word 'hark' anymore. That's because it's old-fashioned, isn't it? We never use the word hark for anything these days. Except when it's raining. Yes, for some odd reason, whenever it pours, the word hark gets dusted off and dropped into conversation. 'Ooh, hark at that rain.' What is it about heavy precipitation that makes us want to speak like an Elizabethan weatherman? 'Ooh, hark at it coming down.' Why only rain? You never hear anyone say hark at that car alarm or hark at that that JCB."

It raised the briefest of smirks from all four. A fleeting tug at the corner of their collective mouths but not enough to be classed as a smile, and certainly not accompanied by a chuckle or even a titter. He waited for any further reaction. None came.

"Seagulls," Partial Sue said randomly.

"Seagulls?" the Wicker Man questioned.

"I sometimes say hark at those seagulls when they're squawking too much."

"Yeah, I sometimes say that too," Daisy added. "And thunder. Hark at that thunder."

"Wind." Fiona joined in. "Hark at that wind. Maybe change it to weather. Why is the word hark only used to describe extreme weather?"

"And seagulls," Partial Sue added.

Whipping out a pen from his back pocket, the Wicker Man scribbled furiously on the paper, amending his act. "Good, yes. Now the million-dollar question, was it funny?"

This was the bit Fiona dreaded. Clearly it wasn't by the fact that none of them had laughed. Everyone simultaneously shrank in their seats and hung their silent heads low. She half hoped the Wicker Man would be satisfied with a titbit of constructive feedback and be on his way. No such luck. He wouldn't take their lack of laughter as an answer. Standing in front of them expectantly, he awaited their honesty, and they owed him that much. However, honesty was like food — a lot depended on how it was presented. Fiona prepared to let him down but with plenty of garnish and fancy trimmings. "It's getting better."

Suddenly they all agreed, heads bobbing enthusiastically, even Molly who had not been subjected to the Wicker Man's humour before.

His face brightened, taking this as a small but decisive victory. "Really? Am I getting better?"

"Oh, yes." Fiona's affirmation was accompanied by more enthusiastic nods from her colleagues.

The Wicker Man took this as a win, a big, gleeful smile splitting his face. "Oh, you don't know how much that means to me."

Guilt punched Fiona in the gut. It would be irresponsible and downright reckless to let him go on stage with that material, believing that it would create a room full of laughter. Fiona had to set him straight. "But I don't think it's quite ready for an audience in its present form." She winced inside as she'd spoken every word.

The Wicker Man took it the wrong way. "You mean it needs a polish. No problem. I shall put some elbow grease into my routine and have it gleaming like a chrome crash helmet."

This diplomacy lark was a tricky business. Fiona attempted to rephrase her words while treading with featherlike steps. "I don't think it needs a polish, not yet, anyway. I would say there's, erm, what's the best way to put it . . . ?" She could feel dots of sweat popping up on her forehead. "Er, I suppose there's lots of room for improvement." Fiona cringed for daring to utter that phrase. A phrase she loathed but it was the only one that came to mind. Patronising and detestable, she'd disliked it ever since it'd first been thrust on her at a school parents' evening. An insult disguised as a compliment, her sadistic sports teacher had offered it up to her mum and dad as a sop when really what he wanted to say was that Fiona was hopeless at sports and would always be the last one picked for team games.

The Wicker Man's glee turned sour. "How do you mean, room for improvement?"

Partial Sue's legendary rusty iron-bar bluntness came to her rescue. "It's still not funny."

"What?"

"Sorry, I'm just being honest. It's definitely better, but it's more . . . I dunno. Something you would agree with rather than something you'd laugh at."

The Wicker Man's saddened eyes darted around his mini audience seeking the refuge of a differing opinion. They alighted on the one person guaranteed to be nice and kind. "What do you think, Daisy?"

"Me?" She scratched around for the right words. "You're definitely an entertainer. It was definitely entertaining. I can honestly say, I felt entertained."

His face brightened a little until Partial Sue bludgeoned him back to where he had been before. "But it's still not funny. It needs to be funnier."

His face plunged into a mask of depression. "Right. Make it funnier. Okay, how do I do that?"

Before any of them had a chance to deliberate on what direction his stand-up routine should go, they were saved by the bell, or more precisely, a ping from Fiona's phone. "Sally Wilde, owner of Rolo the chocolate lab and Waggiest Tail favourite, has just replied. She's agreed to answer our questions about the dog show. She'll be here in a minute."

"That sounds promising," Partial Sue replied.

"A chocolate lab, you say." The Wicker Man smiled mischievously.

Sensing that a joke was coming, the ladies waited patiently, collectively worrying how bad it would be. The grinding cogs in his mind where almost audible, and the strain on his face made them uncomfortable. No matter how hard he tried, no joke came forth and the Wicker Man slumped into a chair, defeated and disappointed that he could not conceive of anything remotely funny about a chocolate lab.

CHAPTER 17

The shrill of a slipping fan belt alerted the ladies and the Wicker Man to a van clunking to a halt outside. It could've done with a wash but through the grime they could clearly see the clip-art graphic of a sandwich with a smiley face riding a surfboard with the words *Sally's Sandwiches* emblazoned above.

"That'll be Sally, then," Partial Sue remarked.

They watched as she tumbled out of the van, dressed in a kaleidoscope of colours, clashing so violently that they appeared to be having all-out war. With large, red-rimmed glasses, garish leggings and baggy layered tops, there was something of the Su Pollard about her. In one arm, she grasped the handle of a deep basket piled high to the brim with pre-packed sandwiches. A few of them toppled out onto the pavement. She snatched them up before Rolo, who'd bundled out behind her, could sink his teeth into them. He missed his chance as he was too busy bouncing around with erratic excitement like a dropped firework. She held onto his lead tightly, attempting to control him. "Heel, Rolo. Heel." He ignored her command, head darting everywhere to take in his new surroundings, while at the other end, that famous tail whipped back and forth like a possessed metronome on the highest setting.

"Oh, look how waggy his tail is," Daisy declared.

Sally and Rolo blasted through the front door like a hurricane making landfall. Rolo's tail whirled around devastating everything in its path, toppling hatstands and knocking over displays. Sally apologised non-stop. "Oh, my gosh. Sorry, sorry. I am so sorry." The Waggiest Tail favourite would've been the least favourite to win Best-Behaved Dog, if there was such a category, making Fiona and, no doubt the others, wonder how he would stand still long enough to be judged at the dog show, or perhaps get disqualified for being so boisterous, knowing how ordered Malorie like things to be.

Abandoning her basket of sandwiches on the counter, Sally attempted to tidy up Rolo's devastation with her free hand while heaving on his lead with her other, preventing any more destruction. He didn't knock anything else over, but he did wee up the hand-sanitising station by the door. "Oh, my gosh, I'm so sorry. I'll clean that." But before the words were out of her mouth, cleaning ninja Daisy had pounced on the dribble with disinfectant spray.

Rolo's snuffling nose locked on a new target, as he reared up on his hind legs, attempting to get within snatching distance of the cake on the table. After a sharp tug from Sally, he switched direction and noticed he wasn't the only dog in the shop. Simon Le Bon cowered in his bed as Rolo thundered towards him, wrenching Sally behind him. He proceeded to dance around in front of him, those thick floppy paws drumming on the floor without any discernible rhythm, clearly wanting to play. Simon Le Bon was not in the mood for fun and bared his teeth.

"Stop it, Rolo. Stop it. I'm sorry he just gets excited at new places and people. He'll calm down in a minute." Sally pulled what looked like a piece of red plastic from a pink bum bag. Catching the scent of it, Rolo wheeled around, hypnotised. "This is the only thing that will distract him." Rolo dropped to his belly, eyes fixated on the snack.

"Is that a sundried tomato?" asked Partial Sue.

"Yes." Sally tossed it and Rolo caught it first time, hungry for another. "He likes olives too but not the black ones, and only in moderation. Honestly, I should've called him Tapas, not Rolo."

Everyone giggled except the Wicker Man, annoyed that Sally's jokes, though unintentional, were better received than his. She tossed Rolo another one. He snaffled it then remained fixated on Sally's bum bag, hoping that another might appear. "That's better. Good boy. Honestly you must think I'm a terrible dog owner. But I've tried to train him and he's just too excitable. I'll pay for anything broken."

"Oh, don't worry," Fiona reassured her. "I don't think any damage was done, apart from a little damp patch by the door."

Gradually Rolo calmed down, as if his batteries had drained. Exhausted by all the chaos he'd caused, he flopped onto his side. Sally helped tidy up, righting hatstands and returning items to their proper places. However, he sat up the moment Sally retrieved her basket of sandwiches, as did Simon Le Bon, hoping for any stray morsels. "Now, to make up for all the mess, who'd like a free sandwich? And secondly, who would like to see my superpower?"

"Free sandwich?" the Wicker Man enthused.

"Superpower?" Partial Sue questioned. "What superpower?"

Sally beamed. "I can guess people's favourite sandwich. I'm usually spot on, well, nine times out of ten."

"What fun," said the Wicker Man. "Can I go first?"

"Ah, you're an easy one." She plucked a sandwich from her basket and tossed it to him.

The Wicker Man caught it with both hands. "Cheese and pickle! Spot on! What wizardry is this? Sand-wizardry, if you will. How did you know?"

"It's my superpower, I mean I would've preferred super speed or invulnerability, but I'm good at reading people, their personalities, and because of my job, I sort of honed it into guessing their favourite sandwiches."

She threw one to Fiona, who caught it and gazed upon it open-mouthed. "Camembert and cranberry. I love Camembert and cranberry. Sally, how did you do that?"

Sally shrugged. "It's a gift."

"Do me next. Do me next." Daisy bounced up and down. She caught her sandwich and held it to her chest like a precious object.

"What did you get Daisy?" asked Partial Sue, jittering with curiosity.

"Only the best sandwich in the world. Prawn with Marie Rose sauce."

"And for you." Sally lobbed a bacon, lettuce and tomato sandwich towards Partial Sue.

She caught it in one hand. "Oh, I am partial to a BLT. How did you know?" They couldn't stop asking that question, amazed at Sally's low-key but inexplicable superpower.

"Oh, Molly doesn't have one," Daisy noticed.

Sally became horrified that she'd overlooked someone. "Gosh, I am so sorry. Don't worry, I can fix that." Sally reached into her basket then hesitated, turning her gaze on Molly, eyeing her from head to toe and rubbing her chin. "Mm that's strange I'm not getting anything from you. Either you're tricky to read or you're hiding something," she joked.

Molly blushed, shifting in her seat uncomfortably. "Oh, er. I don't like sandwiches."

"How can you not like sandwiches?" A baffled Wicker Man asked with a mouthful of cheese and pickle. "It's like people who don't drink tea. What's wrong with them?"

Partial Sue disagreed. "Not everyone has to like the same sort of thing, Trevor. We're all different. Molly doesn't have to like sandwiches."

"I'm more of a sushi type of person," Molly said.

"Really?" Sally replied. "Cos I've got sushi wraps in the van, but I wasn't getting that from you. Would you like me to get you one?"

Molly declined the offer with the wave of her hand.

"Oh well, like I said, nine times out of ten I get it right." She stared at Molly intensely, as if searching for something she'd lost. "Hey, don't I know you from somewhere?"

Molly blushed.

Sally snapped her fingers. "Oh, I know I've seen you before. It's on the tip of my tongue." Sally's face lit up with recognition, then immediately darkened, her voice becoming subdued. "Oh, your parents were in the news for that, er, thing they did . . ." Sally struggled to find an ending to the uncomfortable sentence. Molly bowed her head.

Sally's face reddened. "Oh my gosh. I'm so sorry. I didn't mean to embarrass you."

Molly waved it away. "It's quite alright."

Fiona jumped in to change the subject. "Sally, we were going to ask you about the dog show." Relieved at being pulled from the wreckage of a conversation, Sally brightened. Fiona invited her to sit down at the table. "We're sort of doing our own investigation, and we were wondering if you saw anything?"

Sally took a seat. "I can do better than that. I can show you." She pulled her phone from her pocket and cued up a video. "I filmed the whole of the Best Biscuit Catcher, right from the beginning."

"That started at eleven," Partial Sue said.

"Yes, that's right."

They gathered round the screen and watched. From the angle, it appeared that Sally had been near the trade stands, on the opposite side where Fiona stood. They watched as dogs and owners took their places in the main arena, drilled by Malorie, as if they were on a parade ground. Starting off with around ten or twelve hopefuls, the competition soon whittled down to the last two, and then the cheating scandal unfolded.

"Look," Sally pointed out, "you can see Ewan Fitch swapping his biscuit for a sausage." She had sharp and steady camera skills, and focused on his hand reaching behind into a pouch attached to the back of his belt when he thought no one was looking, caught in the act.

"Ah, a tactical advantage if ever there was one," the Wicker Man commented.

Sally had kept her camera focused on Ewan Fitch while accusations of *cheat* rang around the marquee, the crowd gasping and groaning that something so controversial could occur at such a genteel event. By contrast, Ewan Fitch remained cool and calm, as did his dog, both of them standing as if they were waiting for a bus. The camera blurred as the view switched to the committee members gathered around Malorie, hoping to resolve the matter.

"Hey, there's Fiona," Daisy said, but it was only the briefest of glimpses.

After much conferring, Ewan Fitch and Lord Bob were declared the winners. Sally captured the trophy being awarded to them, accompanied by hearty cheers and applause from around the arena, although some people were clearly not happy about the decision and refused to clap. Soon after people began to disperse, an audible commotion could be heard off camera. Not people grumbling about competition rules and rulings but cries of shock and shrieks of genuine concern. Sally swung the camera round and caught the swelling crowd. From the left-hand side Julie Sheers entered the frame, shouldering people out of the way. The crowd closed around her, blocking Sally's view of what happened next. The footage ended abruptly.

A few nervous swallows occurred around the table, reliving the shock of someone dying unexpectedly at an event that was supposed to be fun. The people in the footage at that point not aware that worse was to come. It was murder. Nobody spoke.

Fiona broke the silence. "I know this is probably a silly question, as you were filming the whole time, but did you see a guy with a spider's web neck tattoo at all? Maybe before you started filming."

"He had a Staffordshire bull terrier with him," Partial Sue added.

Her eyes widened. "No, definitely not." Her words were accompanied by vigorous shakes of the head. "No, I don't know anyone like that. No, sorry."

Fiona didn't know Sally, but she could tell when someone was lying. The gifted sandwich maker was definitely over-egging her denial.

"I saw something," Molly said.

Not what any of them had been expecting, all eyes switched to Molly. "Could you rewind the footage back to where you point the camera at the commotion?"

Sally obeyed, and pressed play.

"What are we looking at?" Partial Sue asked.

"There. Pause it," Molly commanded.

The image freeze-framed on the crowd. People swarming to get a closer look while others drifted away. Molly pointed to a blur of a man, rushing off to one side. Hard to make out any discernible features apart from his grey hair and the grey top he wore. "That's the man who came in the shop, saying he had information about the murder."

CHAPTER 18

After Sally and the Wicker Man had left, and Molly had gone to pick up Dina, the three ladies gathered around a computer screen examining Sally's footage. She'd kindly sent it to the shop's laptop, and they'd hoped that viewing it in a larger format might help them identify the individual who'd visited their shop with tantalising information about the murder. The increase in screen size did nothing to enlighten them. The Grey Man, as they'd nicknamed him, appeared for the briefest of moments, then disappeared off camera. Despite replaying it over and over, and slowing it down, he defied description. Extremely average, if there was such a thing, as bland as mist and just as hard to grasp.

"If only he'd turned his head slightly to the side, we'd be able to see his face," Daisy said.

Partial Sue had become more cynical with every viewing of the footage. "I can't see how this helps. How are we going to use this? We can't exactly show it to people and say do you know this man? It could be anyone. How is Molly so sure it's him?"

"She's adamant," Fiona replied. "Just the way he carried himself, I suppose."

"It's next to useless, is what it is."

Fiona sighed in agreement. "Well, I guess nothing's changed. We have to wait for him to make contact as before."

A grumpy atmosphere swilled around inside Dogs Need Nice Homes, as it often did when the three of them thought they were making progress, only to find they hadn't moved forward at all. Although Fiona did have something that needed further investigation, or perhaps discussion. "Did you think Sally was lying?"

"What about?" asked Partial Sue.

Fiona was surprised that Partial Sue, being a dyed-in-the-wool cynic, hadn't picked up on it, which made her doubt herself. "Well, when I asked if she saw the tattooed lad with a Staffie, she denied it a bit too much. Which sort of implies the opposite. Maybe she did see him or even knows him."

"I sort of remember," Partial Sue said. "Mind you, I was still gobsmacked by her ability to guess my favourite sandwich. Then I got distracted by Molly saying she saw something."

"Me too," said Daisy. "But come to think of it, I do remember her shaking her head a lot."

Fiona shut the laptop. "Yes, and she said she didn't know him three times to be exact."

"A case of Sally doth protest too much, methinks." Partial Sue screwed up her face. "Urgh, I'm starting to sound like the Wicker Man."

"Yes, I mean no," Fiona said. "But yes, she was a bit over the top with her denial."

Partial Sue had a more rational answer. "She could've been getting all snobby about knowing anyone with a Staffie because of the stereotype. Like I did until you set me straight."

"We only asked her if she saw someone with a Staffie," Daisy replied. "Not if she knew him. And she didn't strike me as a snob. I liked her."

"Me too," Fiona agreed. She couldn't imagine anyone not liking Sally. The sandwich-guessing sorceress had a genuine air about her. She was fun to be around, apart from having to tidy up after her dog. She was also extremely generous and had probably given away over twenty quids' worth of free food this morning alone, just for entertainment value. This thought made Fiona stop in her tracks. Who does that just for fun? Especially someone who runs a small business selling sandwiches. She couldn't imagine that the profit margins were huge. Did Sally have an ulterior motive for her frivolity? Had it all been part of an act to soften them up? There was no such thing as a free lunch, as they said, literally, in this case. Had they paid for theirs with a spot of misdirection to distract them? Enamoured by her parlour tricks, Daisy and Partial Sue had certainly bought into it until Fiona had pointed out that Sally denied seeing the lad a bit too much. However, try as she might, she couldn't imagine Sally being so devious. She wore her heart on her sleeve, hence, not being so good at telling fibs. But despite all that, Fiona was sure Sally was lying for some reason.

"I think we should get her back in," said Partial Sue. "Press her for answers."

"Well, it's only a hunch." Truthfully, Fiona thought it was more than that, but her gut was telling her to tread carefully.

"I could do some digging." Daisy whipped out her phone and was already nose-deep in cyberspace. "Sally had all the social media logos on her van. She must be pretty active on them for her business. If she does know him, there's a slim chance she might have a picture of them together."

"It's worth a try," Fiona said. "Find some evidence before we start firing accusations. Failing that, we question her again." Her phoned pinged. "Oh, I've just got a text from Ewan Fitch. Says he's at Southbourne Beach, right this moment, walking Lord Bob and can spare five minutes. Will you two be okay if I nip down there?"

"Of course," Partial Sue replied. "But what if he's the killer and he's luring you there to do you in?"

"Well, if he is, he's just incriminated himself by saying he'll meet me there in a text, plus the beach is covered in security cameras and there are always people taking their dogs for a walk, even in March, so not the brightest murderer in the world."

"But the dog show was packed with people and look what happened," Daisy cautioned.

"True. I'll make sure he doesn't get too close."

Simon Le Bon's ears had popped up at the mention of the 'W' word. He hopped out of his bed and sat in front of her with his big brown eyes pleading in the manner of a starved orphan, tail oscillating behind him. "Okay, come on then." He spun around in excited circles, like a furry Catherine wheel, not even stopping to have his lead attached.

It only took a matter of minutes to walk down to the beach, the enviable benefit of living and working in Southbourne — everywhere was near to the sea — although Fiona wouldn't have classed it as a walk, more of a desperate canter. She had been given a small window of opportunity to question Ewan Fitch and she didn't want to squander it. Not that she was holding out much hope. Ewan was a suspect in the loosest sense of the word. He had literally been ringfenced from the crime in the main arena, where he'd been competing. However, it was always worth prodding people for information when you had the chance. You never knew what might come of it.

Fiona cut down a long, zig-zagging path that led to the beach. There were several of these sliced into the cliffs along Bournemouth Bay. Steep with hairpin turns, they played havoc on her knees going down and were hell on her calf muscles on the way up. Thankfully, this was one of the gentler ones, allowing her to drink in the view of the wide, majestic, sweeping bay. Today it was sheathed in monochrome grey light, the sea merging with the sky, impossible to distinguish where one started and the other ended. She spotted a couple of surfers out to sea, sitting on their boards, bobbing as they waited to pick off waves breaking far beyond the battered wooden groynes. Fiona shivered and did up a few more buttons, wondering if she should've put a coat on Simon Le Bon. He seemed happy enough, trotting importantly towards his favourite place.

They'd arranged to meet at the Lifesaving Club. A small and featureless cubelike building at the base of the zig-zag. True to his word, Ewan Fitch stood beside it, his wide muscular back to her, wearing nothing but a polo shirt and chinos, despite the stiff breeze. A doggie pouch clung to his belt, the same one he had worn at the show. Lord Bob sat obediently beside him, watching dogs and people walking past but not daring to react or move. Clearly trained to his owner's exacting standards, the boxer was the opposite of Rolo.

Fiona sidled up to the pair of them. "Are you Ewan?" she asked, knowing full well he was. "I'm Fiona." Before meeting him, she would have put him in his early forties, but on closer inspection he was definitely in his fifties. He kept himself in shape, which had thrown her slightly, and his dark, well-maintained hair had only a few flicks of grey at the temples. The result of good genes and discipline.

He didn't offer up any greeting, instead launching straight into some random small talk. "See those surfers, they probably don't know it, but the waves they're catching are breaking over an old, submerged sea wall. That's where the coastline used to be — makes you think, doesn't it?"

Fiona surveyed the waves marching towards the beach in well-ordered lines. About a hundred metres offshore, they'd rear up suddenly, spilling their power in a large frothing mass. "I never knew that."

"That's how much the coastline's receded in the past hundred years. But it pales into insignificance when you realise this whole place was inland during Neolithic times. The sea in front of us would have been pastureland with the sea a mile or two beyond."

Normally, being a local history nut, Fiona would have been chomping at the bit to hear more, and she was all for preserving the coastline and hated seeing it fall into the sea. However, the clock was ticking. Her five minutes were fleeting.

Before she could attempt to steer the conversation to more pressing matters, Ewan Fitch must have sensed her urgency. "But we're here to talk about dog show matters." He began walking and clicked his fingers. Like a statue come to life, Lord Bob moved off his spot and immediately went to investigate Simon Le Bon who was happy to oblige. Fiona let him off his lead and the two dogs immediately went into a bum-to-nose formation, checking each other out and twirling around like a living yin and yang symbol, although a very unequal one, Lord Bob dwarfing the little terrier cross.

Fiona was about to launch into her questions when Ewan Fitch began informing her of his whereabouts on the day of the show with military precision. "I arrived at the Priory car park on Sunday morning at ten twenty-six. Paid by parking app so you can check that if you wish. I bought a takeaway flat white at the Boathouse restaurant next to the car park using a credit card. That would have been ten thirty-six. I have the credit card receipt. You might think that ten minutes between parking and buying a coffee is a long time, but there was a queue, and I didn't want to risk buying a coffee at the show. You do that once then never again," he chuckled.

"Yes, I've heard that."

"And the Boathouse does make a cracking flat white. From there I'm afraid I'm a bit vague on timings as I don't have any points of reference. But it's a good five-minute walk along the quayside to the marquee at the other end. Then it took me maybe a minute or two to get inside. It's free for competitors but there's always a logjam of people, caused by curious passers-by peering in and wondering if it's worth the modest entry fee. Rough guess, I'd say I was inside between ten forty and ten forty-two."

The two dogs trotted ahead, Lord Bob assuming the role of the alpha, Simon Le Bon following diligently behind, the wind parting his fur in a neat line along his back. They took it in turns investigating smells in an almost civilised fashion.

Ewan Fitch continued. "I mooched around the show for a bit. Said hello to some familiar faces. I can give you their names if you like. Browsed a few of the stands. It's always the same ones each year. I think they only let in traders approved by the club. Nothing I haven't seen before. Although, I did see some strange vacuum thing that sucks up dog dirt. A bit over-engineered, if you ask me. What's wrong with a bagged hand? Anyway, at ten to eleven I was by the main arena, as instructed by Malorie, to wait for the start of the Best Biscuit Catcher category. She runs a tight ship. Would put some of my COs to shame, that one. Then we started competing bang on eleven. By the time it was over and I was leaving with my trophy, I believe Sylvia Steadman was gasping her last."

Fiona changed tack. "How much did you want to win?"

Ewan Fitch appeared surprised by the question. "To win?" He waved the comment away. "Ah, well it's just a bit of fun, isn't it?"

He didn't strike her as the sort of person who did anything for fun. "That business with switching the biscuit for sausage. That was quite serious. You must have wanted to win at all costs."

Ewan Fitch attempted to play it down. "I feel it's more about entertainment. The crowd loves seeing Lord Bob do his thing. I didn't want to disappoint them, and that bit of sausage broke the show's record. It was worth it."

Fiona wasn't buying it — the idea that he was doing it to please the crowd. Ewan Fitch had been a soldier, possibly a high-ranking one. An officer she'd guess by the way he held himself. Victory was in his DNA, whether he was behind enemy lines, vastly outnumbered, taking fire, or under a sagging marquee at a dog show. It was all the same to him. Possibly ruthless, would he want to win by any means necessary? Hence why he cheated. "But you must have wanted to win Best in Show?"

"I won't lie to you. It's flattering making it to the main event. But Lord Bob's no oil painting. He wouldn't stand a chance against Barbie or Rolo."

She watched the athletic dog trotting beside her own. A handsome animal with a silky bronze coat and a pleasing gait. She wasn't buying Ewan's modesty. He wouldn't be satisfied with just winning his category. He'd want Lord Bob to go the whole way and take Best in Show. Had he killed Sylvia to up his chances of winning? Trouble with that theory was it still sounded absurd in Fiona's mind, to kill someone over a dog show. And if it were true, there were still two other dogs Lord Bob would have to beat, Barbie and Rolo, if the odds were to be believed. Admittedly, having met Rolo in the flesh, his chances would've been greatly reduced if Sally couldn't control him on the day. But that still left Barbie, who had more chance of winning than Lord Bob. But this all became academic. Ewan Fitch was in the arena when Sylvia was murdered.

Ewan glanced at his watch. "I'm afraid I'll need to be making tracks soon. Got a meeting with a property developer who wants me to part with my cash so he can knock down a house on the cliffs and put up flats."

"You're a busy man."

"Yes, I have several businesses. Fingers in lots of pies."

"What sort of pies?" asked Fiona.

"Property, mostly. But also IT security and fitness. I own a handful of gyms in the area." He took a piece of sliced-up sausage and slung it towards Lord Bob, who caught it without hesitation. Simon Le Bon looked hopeful. "Can he have one?"

"Of course," Fiona replied.

Ewan gently tossed the snack towards the terrier. Not the most athletic or alert dog in the world, it bounced off Simon's head. While he frantically glanced around to locate where it had gone, Lord Bob had already snaffled it off the ground. Ewan pulled another morsel from his pouch and allowed Simon Le Bon to retrieve it from his fingers.

"I take it you were in the army," said Fiona.

"That obvious?" A charming smile danced on his lips.

"You mentioned COs earlier. I guessed you meant commanding officers." Truth be told she knew long before he'd let that slip. The forces radiated off Ewan Fitch like strong aftershave. Made of the right stuff, squared away and not a hair out of place on either him or his dog.

"Right, yes. I was a lieutenant in the Royal Marines based in Poole. Saw action in Iraq."

"Do you miss it?"

Ewan thought for a moment. "Yes and no. I miss the camaraderie of the lads. The purpose. The challenge. The action. But I don't miss people trying to shoot me," he laughed. "That can be quite tedious."

"Did you ever kill anyone?" Fiona knew you weren't supposed to ask a soldier this, but then this was a murder case.

Ewan Fitch didn't seem to mind and answered without hesitation. "Oh, yes. Part of the job description, I'm afraid."

They were looking for a killer and one was standing right beside her. A professional, no less, whose job it had been to take lives. He certainly wouldn't lose sleep killing an ex-Crufts dog owner. But that still didn't answer the question of how he'd done it while he'd been ensconced in the arena the whole time, all eyes on him. Unless he'd killed her by telekinesis. Inside, Fiona berated herself for going off at such wild and elaborate tangents, but her mind wouldn't stop theorising. Another one popped into her head — he could have had an accomplice in the crowd with a syringe. That would be difficult to prove and pull off. And just who would be prepared to murder someone on behalf of a jealous dog competitor? It'd have to be someone extremely loyal. "Is there a Mrs Fitch?"

"No wife, I'm afraid. I'd like one, but I fear they'd leave me. I'm too selfish with my time."

"Any brothers or sisters?"

"Nope. Only child. Parents passed away. It's just me and Lord Bob." At the sound of his name, Lord Bob turned to look at his owner, as did Simon Le Bon, but for quite different reasons. He was hoping another snack was forthcoming. Ewan didn't disappoint them and pulled a couple of sausage slices from his pouch, flinging one to his dog and one to Fiona's. Simon caught it this time, looking very pleased with himself.

"Did you know Sylvia Steadman at all?"

"No."

"But you'd heard of her."

He shook his head.

"Not from her Cruft's win or those TV ads?" Fiona asked.

"I don't watch TV. Thief of time. Got better things to do."

Running out of reasons to question him, Fiona felt like she had backed into a private cul-de-sac, stalled her car and now the neighbours were nosing out of their windows wondering just what the hell she was doing. She could sense her own desperation, attempting to make Ewan Fitch fit the crime — just because he was a trained killer didn't make him a murderer.

He glanced at his watch again. "I'm sorry, Fiona. I really must go."

"Just one more question. Did you see someone with a neck tattoo and a Staffordshire bull terrier at the show?"

Ewan Fitch exhaled through his nose. "Gosh, there were hundreds of dogs and owners there. All a bit of a blur." He mulled it over. "A lad with a neck tattoo? Possibly, possibly not. Sorry, I can't recall anyone like that."

Fiona thanked him and watched him marching towards the zig-zag, Lord Bob at his heel.

Ewan Fitch had referred to the owner of the Staffie as a lad. She hadn't mentioned his gender or referred to him as a lad. How had Ewan Fitch known this? Luck? Coincidence? Or was he lying?

CHAPTER 19

"I think you're reading too much into it, Fiona," Partial Sue reassured her. The three of them had gathered around the little table, slurping their tea while Fiona shared her suspicions about Ewan Fitch.

"He referred to the Staffie owner as a lad," she explained. "I never said he was a lad. How would he have known that?"

"Could be Staffie stereotyping again," Partial Sue replied, shrugging. "Mention a Staffordshire bull terrier to anyone and they instantly conjure up a dog on a chain held by a hard young bloke on a council estate with tattoos."

Fiona bit her lip. Partial Sue was right. Like it or not, most people had a preconceived image of Staffies and their owners, and she would guess Ewan Fitch would be no exception.

"Did you find out anything else?" asked Daisy.

"Not really. Apart from him having several local business interests in property, IT and gyms. Oh, and there's an old, submerged sea wall off Southbourne beach. But I did find out that Ewan Fitch used to be a lieutenant in the marines."

"No surprise there," said Partial Sue. "He looks military."

"And by the pouch on his belt," Daisy added. "I noticed it when he came past our stand. He didn't buy anything, though."

"Why does having a dog pouch give him away as military?" Partial Sue asked.

"Well, you know, soldiers always have stuff on their belts, little pockets for ammunition, hand grenades and little snacks squirrelled away — in case they get peckish when they're on manoeuvres — I imagine packets of crisps would fit quite nicely into those little pouches."

Partial Sue blew on her tea. "I'm not sure they'd have crisps in them."

"Why not?" Daisy asked.

"All that crunching would give their position away. Slice of Battenberg would be better, sugary and stealthy, and it would fit nice and snug. But it's an interesting point. Not about their choice of snacks, but about his dog pouch — very handy for concealing a small but lethal injection."

"Yes, and he's a trained killer." Fiona wanted it to be Ewan, had tried to make it him, but the undeniable facts of the situation always dragged her back to reality. "There's one big problem. He was stuck in the arena, competing. I saw him there, as did loads of other people."

Partial Sue and Daisy became silent, appearing a little disheartened by the fact that Ewan Fitch couldn't have possibly done it.

"We'll put him to one side for the moment," Fiona said. "Daisy, how did you get on with Sally's social media? Any sign of our tattooed lad?"

Daisy shook her head. "Nothing. Although it's quite possible she deleted any shots of them together. But it made me hungry looking at pictures of her sandwiches on Instagram. She does a mean cheese, ham and coleslaw. I might have to make one when I get home."

"I thought prawn was your favourite," Partial Sue said.

"Yes, but cheese, ham and coleslaw is my backup sandwich."

"Oh, really," Fiona said. "My backup sandwich is tuna and sweetcorn."

"B-backup sandwich?" Partial Sue queried.

"Yes, you know. Your backup sandwich," Daisy explained. "The one you choose when your favourite's not available. You must have a backup sandwich."

Partial Sue had an expression of mild panic in her eyes. "I don't. I mean, I've never encountered a situation where a BLT isn't available."

Daisy gasped. "Foolish words, Sue. What happens when you go to Boots for your meal deal?" She knew how partial she was to a meal deal. "You get to the sandwich section and they've sold out of BLTs. What happens then?"

Flummoxed and confused, Partial Sue stared back. "Jeez, I don't know. I suppose I've been lucky up until now."

"It's not a question of if but when," Fiona warned. "You need to get that sorted before you're staring at an empty shelf in a chiller cabinet with a sandwich dilemma on your hands. Now, where were we? Oh, yes. Let's park the social media search for now. We still have a few other rival competitors we need to question. The ones who haven't made contact yet."

Daisy put her tea down, as a thought occurred to her. "That makes them more suspicious if they don't come forward, doesn't it?"

"Yes, it does," Fiona agreed. "It's a great way of filtering out anyone who's hiding something. But it's not always an admission of guilt. Sometimes people are scared to come forward. They get timid, which is understandable, especially in a murder case. So we might have to track them down and winkle some answers out of them. Make a nuisance of ourselves, knock on doors." She pulled out her phone and sifted through the dog entry forms. "Starting with Dean Atkins, owner of Max the Weimaraner, last year's winner of Prettiest Eyes. Odds of fifteen to one to win Best in Show."

CHAPTER 20

After work the following day, the three ladies locked up the shop and strolled to the end of Southbourne Grove, led by Simon Le Bon, straining on his lead, eager to scout out new smells. They followed the road until it snaked its way down into Tuckton, a sweet little hamlet by the River Stour. Replete with little patisseries, and the odd microbrewery, best of all, it had a tea garden straight out of the 1940s, where you could sip tea with an iced bun under sun umbrellas and watch the river slide past, while marvelling at the stunning cottages lining its banks, apart from one — the home of Dean Atkins. If he had been too timid to come forward and speak to them about the murder, then nothing about his property reflected that. It was brash, showy and just a little bit tasteless.

"How did that get past planning?" Partial Sue gazed up at the fortress clad in glass and grey stone, dwarfing the sweet little houses around it. "That balcony is big enough for a gun emplacement."

Fiona had to admit, the boxlike building did have the aggressive stance of a Second World War fortification designed to take out stray Messerschmitts. "This guy must know people in all the right places. I wonder what cost more, the building or the backhanders to get it approved?"

Just in case passers-by hadn't cottoned on to how incredibly well-off the occupants were, three cars filled the driveway: a Bentley, a Range Rover Evoque and a small, two-seater sports car that Fiona didn't recognise but it looked exotic and expensive, and a nightmare on the knees to get in and out. To complete the full set of posh toys, a handsome Sunseeker motor yacht sat in the river at the back of the house, lashed to a narrow wooden jetty.

Of course, being such an exclusive residence, access to the front door was barred by a couple of high electric metal gates and a matching fence with railings that prodded the sky like a rack of spears. Fiona spotted an intercom panel set into the stone gatepost. She pushed the button, expecting to have to persuade a garbled voice on the other end to allow them in.

Without so much as a word exchanged, the gates clunked, then silently swung open. The three ladies exchanged shocked glances. Just in case the person operating them changed their mind, they hurried in and made a beeline for the front door, a solid slab of hardwood, possibly illegal to harvest in this day and age. Their feet had barely touched the front step when it opened.

A large man took up the whole of the doorway. This must be Dean Atkins. A swathe of thick golden hair topped his head, and he dressed not unlike Ewan Fitch, wearing a polo shirt with beige slacks, except he bulged in all the wrong places, perhaps the result of too many business lunches. "Hold up a minute," he snarled.

Fiona thought he was talking to them until she noticed his head kinked at an awkward angle, and the phone wedged into the crook of his neck. He beckoned them in with a wrist that jangled with gold, as if he were expecting them. The ladies didn't hesitate and stepped into the hallway, dominated by an outlandish chandelier, glittering like a galaxy above their heads and just as large. Fiona regarded it, wondering how long it would take to clean. Daisy also gazed at it longingly, probably wishing she could be the one to clean it.

They followed Dean Atkins along the hallway, as he continued gabbling away on the phone. "Yeah, yeah. Transfer's gone through. It should show your end. Yeah, yeah."

He showed them into his kitchen while he finished up his conversation, giving the three ladies time to survey the vast cubelike space. The back wall was completely glass from floor to ceiling, while a sleek granite worktop ran along the entire length of the adjacent wall. This was accompanied by a central island, long as a landing strip with wide drawers beneath that didn't appear to have any handles, and there didn't seem to be any cooker. Perhaps they didn't cook, or it had been designed to be invisible. Either way, they definitely hadn't bought it from Wickes and almost certainly had it built bespoke in somewhere like Germany or Scandinavia. On the other side of the room stood a flat screen TV, as big as a shop window, facing an emerald green sofa that could probably accommodate a whole football team, plus their coach and several training staff. This evening, the only people who occupied it were two small children. The ladies could only see the backs of their heads, as they were engrossed in playing Minecraft on the mammoth screen. They appeared to be having a good stab at building the Tower of Babel, except in this particular version of the doomed monument from the ancient world they'd added a roller coaster around the outside.

A door opened to the left. A dark-haired, vampish woman in her late forties swished out of what looked like a snug, complete with modern wood burner and more traditional furnishings. She padded barefoot across the flagstone floor, her silk dressing gown open, revealing a slender polished body dressed in a satin pink pyjama shorts set. Presumably this must be Mrs Atkins. Fiona wondered if her feet were cold, but a place like this would probably have underfloor heating. She resisted the temptation to reach down with her hand and test her theory.

"Hello," the three women greeted her politely in unison as she slunk past them. Throwing them a brief glance, she didn't utter a word, then pulled a bottle of wine from a built-in fridge, poured herself a large glass then slunk back the way she came.

"Bit rude," Partial Sue mouthed.

"Can't buy class," Fiona mouthed back.

A dog's face lazily flopped over the back of the sofa next to the children, its snout pointing down, a perfect recreation of the 'Kilroy was here' doodle. Its nose twitched curiously at the strangers in the house, but it was the dog's laser-like eyes they all found hypnotic — the colour of an orange sunset.

"That must be Max the Weimaraner," Partial Sue said.

"No wonder he won Sweetest Eyes last year," Daisy said. "They're beautiful."

Simon Le Bon's tail wagged enthusiastically, hoping that he'd made a new doggie friend. But like its mum, Max deemed him not worthy of even getting off the sofa for further investigation. Nonchalantly, he turned his head away and disappeared behind the sofa's back rest.

Dean Atkins began pacing up and down in front of them, his telephone conversation turning into a verbal wrestling match, becoming louder and more aggressive with each syllable. "Yeah, but you said you didn't need paperwork . . . we made a verbal agreement . . . oh, you can't remember that . . . how convenient . . ."

The waiting became more awkward, the more heated the discussion became. The trio of ladies found themselves edging away from him. Views have a natural gravity about them, and their feet instinctively took them towards the window wall, and the promise of what they would see beyond. They weren't disappointed. Streetlights glowed orange in the darkness, tracing the footpath beside the gentle curves of the river. Peppered with boats, it silently meandered its way past the stone tower of Christchurch Priory, spotlit in all its glory.

"Don't look at what you can't afford," a voice said behind them. They all turned to see that Dean Atkins had finished his conversation and smugly grinned at them. He'd said it as a joke but hadn't managed to mask the condescension behind his words. "Sorry about that. Doing money deals abroad. Buying and selling currency. Had to catch Kuala Lumpur before they turned in for the night. Bunch of crooks, making out a transfer hadn't gone through. Must have thought I was born yesterday."

Fiona wasn't going to let his condescending comment go unchecked. "How do you know we can't afford it?"

"I know people, and you're from that charity, ain'tcha?"

They hadn't called ahead or given him any indication of the nature of their visit. Were they that obvious?

He grinned. "Sorry, but nobody I know who works for a charity is rolling in it. No disrespect. I mean, I'm just like you."

Fiona doubted very much he was like them. He had all the trappings of success and wasn't afraid to show it. The big, vulgar house, the trophy wife and probably one of those funny drawers in his wardrobe that wobbled his expensive self-winding watches when he wasn't wearing them. If Fiona had money, she wouldn't live like this.

"I started out doing shift work," he explained. "Shift this, shift that," he guffawed at his own wordplay. "Nah, but seriously. I did start off shifting stuff. Buying and selling second-hand trucks. Made my dosh that way. Where there's muck there's brass. Or where there's trucks there's brass." More guffawing. "Everyone needs to move stuff, am I right? Anyway, I'll be back in a second with your gear. Now what did I do with it?" He disappeared through a door to a utility room, then came straight back out. "Nope, not in there." He crossed the kitchen to peer in another room where they got a glimpse of a pool table. "Not in there, either."

The ladies exchanged puzzled glances. What did he think they were here for?

"Hon!" he called out at the top of his voice. "Where's the bag of donations?"

From behind the snug door they heard Mrs Atkins bellow. "In the utility room!"

"I looked in there."

"Well look again."

Before Fiona or anyone else could point out that they weren't here to collect any charity donations, he slipped into the utility room and returned with a bulging white plastic sack in his fist. "Was there all the time. Blind as a bat, I am."

He held it out to them, the logo of the Cats Alliance clearly visible. "There's some good stuff in there. You'll be able to fetch a few bob for my old dinner jacket and trousers. It's Gieves & Hawkes, no less. Course, don't fit me no more." He patted his stomach with his free hand.

"I'm sorry, Mr Atkins, we're not here to pick up donations." *Especially not ones destined for the Cats Alliance*, Fiona wanted to add, but she held her tongue.

"But we are from a charity shop," Partial Sue added.

"Eh?" was all Dean Atkins could say.

Fiona enlightened him. "We're from Dogs Need Nice Homes but we also solve crimes in our spare time. We're investigating the death of Sylvia Steadman. You know, the woman who was murdered at the dog show."

His face relaxed, as the penny dropped. "Oh well, you've come to the right place. Because it was me who killed her."

CHAPTER 21

Dean Atkins looked at them, unflinching, unblinking and expressionless. A face you'd describe as deadpan. The face of a cold-blooded killer.

He'd confessed to murder, came straight out with it and not a trace of guile. The shock of his unprompted revelation seized up Fiona's brain, and no doubt, that of her colleagues who stood there dumbfounded, but only momentarily. He'd made his confession in front of his kids, who continued to click away on their controllers. A fact that was not lost on her. Either he was the worst psychopathic, heartless killer and his children were all in terrible danger, or he was winding them up.

The latter became apparent as Dean Atkin's face split into a massive grin, then into huge roars of laughter, the kind that originate from deep within the belly. "Your faces! You should see them! What a picture. Oh, I should've been an actor."

Fiona couldn't see the funny side of joking about killing someone. "So you didn't kill Sylvia Steadman?"

"No! Of course not."

"Er, should we be having this conversation in front of your children," Daisy pointed out.

Without turning around, one of his kids said, "Dad's always playing tricks on us. We're used to it."

"Well, that's to keep you on your toes," he called over to them.

"Dad made us late for the dog show," said the other sibling, with that brutal childhood honesty. "Doing his dodgy deals."

If Dean was embarrassed, then he didn't show it. Not that he struck Fiona as someone who'd be embarrassed about anything. "Let's get some privacy." He led them into the room with the pool table. Thankfully there were no pictures on the walls of dogs playing billiards. He had some taste, at least, but not much. The room was a man cave with a set of three old arcade games blinking away against one wall, Pac-Man, Frogger and Space Invaders, beside a green-topped poker table and a life-size cut out of David Beckham from his England days. Another mammoth TV screen, bigger than the one in the kitchen/diner, dominated the far wall. Of course, it did.

Dean Atkins slotted himself behind a bar with padded leather swivel stools lined up in front of it. He gestured for then to sit down and began fixing himself a whisky. "Want one?"

The three ladies declined.

Fiona came straight out with it. "Just for the record, you're not the killer and your confession was all done for comic effect."

"Well, it made me laugh." He took a sip of his drink, winced, then added more club soda. "But yes, I mean no. I didn't kill Sylvia Steadman. I was nowhere near her when it happened."

"But you attended the show?" Fiona asked.

"Yes, but not until after the murder. Max is really the kids' dog. Set me back two grand, he did. Had him from a puppy. Course, it's muggins here who takes him for walks now they're bored with him. But they still wanted to enter him into the Sweetest Eyes category. You know what kids are like. Love winning things, and he won it last year, so they wanted to try again and get another trophy, maybe see if they could do the double and get Best in Show."

Dean Atkins drained his drink and poured another. "So, anyway, we were all set to leave when I get this call from Shanghai about a deal. Takes me a while to sort out. By the time I get off the phone, it's eleven twenty-eight. Official start time of Sweetest Eyes is eleven thirty. There's no way we're going to make it, especially as Malorie is a stickler for time. Kids are disappointed, getting all upset. So I call up the number on the website. Just my luck, it goes straight through to Kenneth Prendiville, dog club secretary. Do you know him?" Dean Atkins didn't give them time to answer. "He's a ratty, uptight prick, 'scuse my French. I used to take the kids to his dog obedience classes when Max was a puppy. Strict, he is." Dean Atkins made a fist. "I nearly had to have words with him one time, for snapping at my kids. But this time I was prepared to sweet-talk him, maybe give him a bung, see if I could persuade him to postpone the start of Sweetest Eyes. But surprise, surprise, he's all nice, laidback about it. Right unexpected. He's like, 'Oh don't worry. It's fine. We can move it to twelve, I'll just let the other competitors know, leave it with me.'"

Karma Ken, Fiona thought.

"I didn't have to bung him any cash or nothing, saved a few bob. Kids are happy but when we get there it's all irrelevant. Ambulance is there and people are leaving. Show's called off. Anyway, that's the same story I told the police."

"Police have interviewed you?" asked Fiona.

"Yep," Dean replied. "Sat right where you're sitting. They didn't have anything to drink, neither."

Fiona searched her mind for anything else she could ask him. She would check his story, but it all seemed a bit pointless if he showed up after the murder, and his kids had backed him up. Of course, he could've briefed them to wheel out that story should anyone ask. But they did let one little nugget slip. "Your kids said you did dodgy deals."

"Oh, pay no attention to them. They like winding up their old man. Probably get it from me. No, it's all kosher, but I do have someone who gives me a nudge now and then, when to get in on something good."

"Sounds like insider trading," Partial Sue said.

"Not if a company discloses the information. I pay a guy to keep an eye on big players in the corporate world, company directors. The second they start buying or selling stock, or announce something big, he tells me and I jump on it. All totally legit."

It sounded like a line, a well-rehearsed line, kept in reserve just in case anyone asked, which, judging by the way he rattled it off without thinking, he'd spun to a great number of people. Either that or he'd practiced it a lot in the mirror.

Dean took another slug of his drink. "Don't worry, I told DI what's-her-face the same thing."

"DI Fincher."

"That's the one, and her scruffy sidekick. Didn't say much."

"DS Thomas," Partial Sue replied.

"On your way to the show, did you pass anyone running away with a neck tattoo?" Fiona asked.

"With a Staffie," Daisy added.

Dean Atkins didn't hide his prejudice. "He your main suspect? Doesn't surprise me. Bet he thinks he's hard."

"I didn't say it was a he," Fiona said.

Dean Atkins smirked as if she were being naive. "Come on, it's got to be a bloke if he's got a dangerous dog like that."

"Actually, Staffies are very friendly dogs," Daisy said.

Dean shook his head. "Well, I don't like 'em. Keep 'em away from my dog and my kids but to answer your question, no I didn't see anyone like that."

They left Dean Atkins to his whisky and his stuck-up wife, thanking him for his time. He'd wanted something in return and had foisted the bag of donations on them, the one destined for the Cats Alliance. Initially Fiona had refused to take it — they already had more donations than they knew what to do with — until Partial Sue pointed out that they could leave it outside Sophie's shop overnight, which would annoy the hell out of her.

There was no way they could confirm his story, not without verifying everything with DI Fincher. Gone were the days when the young police detective would give them the odd crumb from the table. She'd shared slivers of information in the past, and had regretted it ever since, vowing never to do it again. However, there was one piece of the puzzle they could confirm.

"What are you doing?" asked Partial Sue.

Fiona thumbed her phone as they ambled up the hill back towards Southbourne. "I'm on the dog club website. There's a mobile contact number on there, the only one. It's Kenneth Prendiville's number. I'm going to message him, see if Dean's story is true about showing up late." Fiona hit send. The walk back took a great deal longer than the walk there. Interruptions were plentiful, as they met dogs coming in the other direction, stopping to perform their doggie greetings, forcing their owners to engage in awkward chit chat. This usually went along the lines of a nervous chuckle and comment about how funny it was that dogs said hello with a quick sniff of their behinds, or one of the owners asking about what type of dog the other had.

After they'd completed the third canine engagement, Fiona had an idea. "You know our elusive lad and his Staffie? Well, I was thinking, all dog owners stop and natter, as we've just experienced . . ."

Fiona was interrupted by a ping.

She pulled out her phone and examined it. "That was Kenneth Prendiville. He's just confirmed. Dean Atkins did call him to ask if he could postpone the Sweetest Eyes category."

"So he was telling the truth." Partial Sue didn't appear too happy about this. "Darn it, another suspect with an alibi."

"Anyway, sorry, where was I?" asked Fiona.

"Dog owners stopping and chatting," Daisy reminded her.

"Oh, yes. Dog owners stop and chat and always walk dogs at the same spot. I know I do. See the same faces, human and canine. It got me thinking, this lad and his Staffie must do likewise. Have a local dog walking spot. Someone somewhere must have seen him out walking his dog."

"Very true," Partial Sue added.

"So we visit local dog walking spots and ask around," Daisy suggested.

"Exactly," Fiona replied. "This weekend, we hit all the popular places in the local area and put out feelers."

The three ladies smiled under the glow of a streetlight. It felt like a plan. It felt like progress. After their recent lack of any success, surely this was bound to yield results. Fiona didn't want to be presumptuous or big-headed, but she thought the idea had potential.

Simon Le Bon didn't think so and lifted his leg up the lamppost.

CHAPTER 22

After a weekend traipsing around every park and green space frequented by dog walkers, or in fact, anywhere that had a nearby poo bin, an onslaught followed. After putting the word around about the tattooed lad and his Staffie, first thing Monday morning, a never-ending procession of dog owners and odd people entered the shop to report that yes, they'd seen him. At first, Fiona and the ladies had congratulated themselves. Their plan had worked. Worked better than they could have imagined. The shop's doorbell had never rung so much on a Monday morning. But as they listened patiently to every account and sighting, it soon became clear that most of the information that landed in the ladies' cake-crumbed laps was nothing more than a cascade of tittle-tattle and tale-telling. A chance for uptight individuals to vent their Staffie prejudice.

"His dog bit my dog."

"He doesn't pick up his dog poo."

"His dog has attacked several children."

"His dog barks all night."

And some of it not dog-related.

"He's actually a drug dealer."

"He dented my car."

"He plays his music too loud, and the council won't do anything."

And some, most bizarre.

"He stole the gnomes from my front garden."

"He took an Amazon package in for me and won't give it back."

Stories came from far and wide, some people making the journey from Poole to log their complaints. That was the one thing that they had in common; none of them originated from the same place. The locations were disparate, spread out, which led Fiona to believe they weren't about the same person. Unless the tattooed lad was walking his dog in a different spot every day to avoid detection — which was quite possible, but highly unlikely. None of it got them any closer to finding his regular walking spot.

The snitching continued well into Tuesday morning. The doorbell tinkled for the fifth time in so many minutes. However, a face appeared that Fiona and Partial Sue recognised. Reg Anagram, the dry-cleaning backstreet bookie, wandered in, his eyes flitting around at the multitude of multifarious goods on offer.

"Good morning, sir," Molly called out.

Taken aback at being referred to as a sir, or maybe dazed in the headlights of Molly's unflinching enthusiasm, Reg appeared unsure of himself and knocked into the hat stand and then the shoe rack. Not on the same scale as Sally Wilde and Rolo, but enough to broadcast he didn't entirely feel comfortable being here. He peered past Molly, locking eyes with Fiona.

"Hello, Reg," Fiona said.

After some swift introductions he managed a forced reply. "Oh, yes. Er, hello."

Reg stood in the middle of the shop, twisting the gold rings on his fingers. It didn't help that everyone stared at him expectantly.

"Can I help you with anything?" Molly asked.

"Er, no. Sorry." He took a step forward in Fiona's direction, glancing around before speaking. "Look, I'm not one for grassing anyone up, but the Wicker Man told me you was looking for a bloke with neck tattoos and a Staffie."

"You know him?" asked Partial Sue.

"No, but I know where he goes, well, someone who sounds like him. There's a café next to Pokesdown station. A greasy spoon. I drive past it on my way to work. Seen him outside, vaping with his dog."

"What's it called?"

"The Flying Teapot." Reg started his retreat out of the shop, uncomfortable that he'd spilled the beans, especially as the place he'd mentioned would probably let you have beans with everything.

"Won't you stay for a cup of tea?" asked Daisy.

Reg shook his head, not wanting to outstay his welcome. Like a cheap cockney informant he muttered, "You didn't hear this from me, okay." He turned and was gone.

"Well, that was an unexpected surprise," Partial Sue commented. "What do you think?"

"He sounded genuine," Fiona said.

"And he didn't mention anything nasty about Staffies or their owners." Daisy smiled.

"Yes," Fiona said. "Which means he doesn't have an axe to grind like everyone else so far. I think we look into this one. Plus, it's really close." Fiona looked to Molly. "Would you mind if we nipped up the road to follow up this lead?"

"Not at all," Molly replied.

"It's so handy having you here." Partial Sue was already pulling on her coat. "Don't know what we'd do without you."

Fiona clipped on Simon Le Bon's lead. The three ladies left the shop and set off at a brisk pace, Simon Le Bon tugging them along, always busy, always in a hurry to get where they were going even though he had no idea where that was.

The shops fizzled out into houses, as they reached the end of Southbourne Grove where it met Pokesdown high street cutting across it to form a T junction. While Southbourne was all independent shops and quirky tea rooms, Pokesdown was more bohemian with emporiums devoted to dusty antiques, vintage clothing and the odd tattoo parlour where an afternoon could easily be lost purely by having a jolly good mooch, or getting your skin inked.

While they waited at the crossing for the little man to turn green, their eyes were pulled in the direction of Pokesdown's many antique shops and the intriguing items piled up in their windows. "Is there anything better," Fiona said, "than an antiques forage?"

"Antiques forage, that sounds like the name of a Sunday evening reality TV show," Daisy suggested. "I'd definitely watch it."

"Yes, it does, with Alan Titchmarsh and Carol Kirkwood," Partial Sue suggested. "You ought to copyright that, Fi. Before someone steals it. I did some foraging here the other day. Got myself a nice horse brass for the downstairs loo."

The crossing beeped. They hurried over to the other side, greeted by the entrance to Pokesdown station and the modest frontage of the Flying Teapot café next door, a traditional British café, if ever there was one, complete with steamed-up windows and a chalk A-board standing to attention outside, advertising all-day breakfasts for a fiver.

"That's good value, that is," Partial Sue gushed, ever one for a bargain.

A mismatched selection of tables sat on the pavement, presumably where this tattooed lad sat and vaped with his dog. Above the door hung a sign, not unlike one you'd find outside a pub, bearing the name of the café and a piece of snazzy 1930s-style artwork.

"Oh, will you look at that." Daisy pointed to the sign. "When Reg said it was called the Flying Teapot, I thought it would be of a teapot with wings. But it's like a train." The dark green teapot in question had wheels and sped along some tracks at an oblique angle, grey smoke streaming from its spout, hauling carriages behind it.

Partial Sue took a picture on her phone. "It's what the Flying Scotsman would look like if it were a teapot. It came through Pokesdown station once."

"What, a teapot?" Daisy asked.

"No, the Flying Scotsman. My dad saw it. Train didn't stop but he stood on the platform with lots of other people to watch it fly past. Said it gave him goosebumps."

"Someone should make train teapots like that," Daisy suggested. "They'd make a fortune."

"Come on. Let's see if we can get some answers." Fiona pushed the door open. Pungent wafts of burnt toast and cooking oil confronted them. Not that it was supposed to smell any other way. This was a proper 'caff' where the tables were plain and hardwearing, clustered with bottles of sauce, caked dry around their lids, although, strictly speaking, the ketchup should've been decanted into giant, squeezy tomatoes made of red plastic.

A gang of four builders sat in the corner, shedding brick dust from their overalls, or maybe it was plaster. In the past, they would have been arguing about football or been lewd and lairy, but nowadays they sat in silence, mesmerised by their phones. An older couple sat on the opposite side, not talking to each other. They didn't appear to be in a mood but perhaps they had simply run out of things to say.

Behind the counter, a middle-aged cook handed two plates loaded with food to a waitress in her late twenties wearing a tabard with a large pocket on the front. She transferred the plates to the older couple who offered their thanks then went back to their vow of silence. On her way back the waitress smiled at the ladies. "Sit wherever you like."

Fiona was about to say they weren't here for food when Partial Sue blurted, "I'll have a full English and a mug of tea. Can't turn down a full English for a fiver."

The waitress retrieved a pad from her tabard pocket and scribbled down her order. She looked at the other two expectantly.

"Looks like we're eating." Fiona snatched up a nearby menu, as did Daisy, having been forced into ordering something by their colleague. Top of the list was the full English then variations on that theme, which mainly consisted of its constituent parts paired with toast: beans on toast, fried egg on toast, scrambled egg on toast, sausage and toast, bacon and toast, all except cheese on toast which wasn't in the full English family but certainly could be. Below this they offered a surprisingly comprehensive list of freshly made sandwiches. You could even add smashed avocado for an extra pound; a recent addition, judging by how it had been written in biro. Partial Sue got rather uppity at this, whispering within earshot of the waitress that they were just cashing in on current culinary trends and that she could buy her own avocado for a pound. Fiona shushed her and told her that wasn't the point.

"Fancy sharing cheese on toast?" asked Daisy.

Unlike Partial Sue, calories clung to Fiona and Daisy like confetti on a wet pavement. Fiona nodded. "Definitely, and two mugs of tea."

"Very good." The waitress bustled off with their order.

The three ladies slid themselves into a table by the window. Fiona tied Simon Le Bon's lead around one of the legs, leaving it nice and long so he could hoover up stray bits of bacon and sausage.

"I thought we'd come here for information," Fiona said. "Now we're having full-on brunch."

Partial Sue grinned. "Brunch never did anybody any harm. Plus, it softens them up for questioning if we order something. Makes them more likely to talk."

"Not if you're going to criticise their menu," Fiona pointed out.

"I was just saying, I can buy a whole avocado for a pound and smash it myself."

"Well, that's just it. You don't have to make it yourself. They do the smashing. That's why they charge a pound. But to address your other point. It's the first time I've ever heard of a full English being used to pump someone for information."

Partial Sue held her cutlery upright in clenched fists which rested on the table, as if she were a hungry Dickensian gentleman awaiting a feast. "Now that would be a novel approach to interrogation. I'd happily talk if someone offered me a full English."

Daisy wiped her knife and fork, never trusting the cleanliness of any establishment to be as thorough as her own. "Depends if that person likes a full English or not. I'm not a massive fan of all that food so early in the morning, makes me sleepy the rest of the day."

"Full English is good any time," Partial Sue replied. "I sometimes have a cheeky one in the evening for supper."

The debate continued until the waitress returned with their food.

As she was about to walk away Fiona asked, "Sorry, is the dog allowed in here?" Fiona knew he was and had noticed the little dogs-welcome sign by the door, but it served as a useful segue.

"Oh yes. We're dog-friendly." She knelt down and scratched Simon Le Bon's ear. He was more interested in sniffing her fingers, that had recently been in close proximity to egg and bacon.

"Do you get many dog owners in here?" Fiona asked.

The waitress got to her feet. "Oh yes, we have lots of regulars. Not many cafés let dogs in. I think it makes for a nicer atmosphere, as long as they don't start barking at each other."

"Does a lad with a Staffie ever come in here, has a spider's web neck tattoo?"

The waitress thought for a moment. "Not that I can remember. I mean we get a lot of lads in here with tattoos."

"He's a regular," said Fiona. "Sits outside, vaping with his dog."

"The dog doesn't vape," Daisy quickly pointed out. "Just the lad."

The waitress plunged both hands into the front pocket of her tabard. "Yeah, we get a lot of them too. We do allow dogs but the owner" — she nodded her head towards the cook — "doesn't like vaping, so they sit outside."

Fiona scribbled her mobile number down on a napkin. "Would you do me a favour and call me if you do see someone like that?" She slipped a tenner out of her purse and handed it to her with the napkin. "For your trouble."

The waitress smiled and accepted it. "Of course."

CHAPTER 23

After regrouping back at the shop, they gathered around the table to think about their next move.

The tip-off about the lad and his Staffie hadn't been a dead end exactly, more of a wait-and-see situation. Sometimes enquiries had to be left to bear fruit. Sometimes you just had to be patient. They still had Molly's mysterious shop visitor, the Grey Man. Hopefully he'd pluck up the courage to return to the shop with his tantalisingly 'crucial' information, but they couldn't get complacent, couldn't rely on this. If the Grey Man did show up, who's to say what the quality of his intel would be like? Similar to X marking the spot to buried treasure, informants rarely turned up saying, "I know who the killer is and here's the evidence which I've arranged in a folder with coloured-coded subdividers and DNA samples." In Fiona's experience, the best you could hope for was another piece of the puzzle that might help you fit a few others in place.

"What now?" asked Daisy, sipping yet another cup of tea.

"We press on. Continue interviewing Charlie's rivals," Fiona stated.

Partial Sue took a slug of tea and made a face. "I'm still not sure about this letting-the-kettle-cool-after-it's-boiled malarkey. I feel like I have to drink it down quick before it goes cold." Molly had gone home for the day, allowing Partial Sue to speak her mind.

"That's a bit of an exaggeration," Fiona said. "It's hot, just not burn-your-tongue hot."

"I like it," Daisy said. "It's just the right temperature. No need to blow on it."

"Oh, yes. Blowing on your tea is such an inconvenience." Partial Sue had become uncharacteristically sarcastic.

Fiona looked at her, surprised. "What's the matter with you?"

"Sorry. I apologise. I'm just frustrated. I want something to happen and feel like we're not getting anywhere. We're still no closer to finding out who Neck Tattoo is, and this Grey Man doesn't look like he's going to show up any time soon."

Fiona attempted to reassure her. "It's a slow process. Can't force it. In the meantime, we work the list of Charlie's rivals. Be methodical."

"Keep on keeping on," Daisy agreed.

Partial Sue became quiet.

"You okay?" Fiona asked.

"There's something else we should be doing before that. But you're not going to like it." Partial Sue stared at Daisy, unblinking.

"Why are you looking at me like that?"

Fiona joined in. "Yes, why are you looking at her like that?"

"I think we've been too preoccupied with the theory that it's a rival at the dog show."

"It's a good, solid theory," Fiona disagreed. Partly because it was true and partly because it was the only theory they had.

Partial Sue shook her head. "I'm not saying that it isn't, but we've neglected some investigative basics."

Fiona was clueless, as was Daisy by the look of her. What was it they had forgotten?

Partial Sue put them out of their misery. "We need to get into Sylvia's house. Have a quick shifty around. Look for clues. Anything amiss."

Daisy folded her arms in protest. "Oh, no. I'm not doing that. I'm not breaking and entering. You can do it without me."

Truth was, they couldn't do it without her. Like a midnight elf in a fairy tale about a poor cobbler, she had legendary nimble fingers. Her skilful digits had crafted umpteen doll's houses, furnished with insect-sized rocking chairs and coffee tables, finely detailed in every way imaginable. Those same steady hands also made her one hell of a lock picker, albeit a reluctant one.

Fiona didn't like the sound of it any more than Daisy, but she had to admit, having a nose inside a murder victim's gaff would be extremely advantageous. "Daisy. I understand your reluctance . . ."

"It's not reluctance." Daisy jutted her chin out defiantly. "It's criminal, plain and simple. Plus, the police would've already searched the place and taken anything interesting so why bother?"

"You never know what we might find," Fiona replied. "Something they've overlooked."

Daisy tightened her folded arms. "I can't see how."

"Plus, is it breaking and entering if no one lives there?" Partial Sue asked.

Daisy glared at her. "Yes, it is. I want to catch the killer as much as you do, but not by getting arrested, thank you very much."

Partial Sue tried a different angle. "We won't get arrested if we're careful."

"I'm always careful and the answer's still no." Daisy sat back in her chair to signify an end to the matter, then she leant forward with another thought. "Why don't we question her neighbours instead?"

Fiona helped herself to more tea. "It's not the same as getting a look inside her house. And Sylvia had only been there two weeks. Her neighbours probably knew her about as well as we do."

They eventually struck a deal with Daisy, based on the school of thought from one of Partial Sue's favourite films, the classic crime-heist *Heat*. She showed them the iconic speech on YouTube of Robert De Niro's bank robber facing off against Al Pacino's hard-nosed cop. She didn't really need to, but it was an excuse to watch the legendary exchange. In the movie, De Niro's mindset formed the basis of a get-out clause for Daisy, that should she 'feel the heat coming around the corner,' or got the jitters as Daisy preferred to call it, then they walk away, abandon the mission. No questions — her call. After fine-tuning the terms, she agreed.

CHAPTER 24

Finding Sylvia's new home in Christchurch was easy enough. Her address was on her dog show entry form. After closing up the shop, they waited until the evening to head out into the damp air, when people would be too busy in front of their TV or phone screens to notice three ladies creeping around outside in the darkness.

Partial Sue's Fiat Uno came to a halt at the side of the road, its tyres grinding against the kerb. Not quite opposite Sylvia's house but positioned so that it gave them a diagonal view across the quiet street. Knocked up cheaply, it was one of a development of four identical redbrick houses where the builders had opted for that made-to-look-old style in an attempt to fit in with the wizened houses around them. It hadn't worked and they weren't fooling anyone with plastic leaded windows and concrete Doric columns holding up flimsy porches. But the real kicker sat square in the middle of Sylvia Steadman's home, just below the eaves. A thoroughly modern burglar alarm.

Daisy slid her lockpicks back into her coat pocket. "That's it. I'm feeling the heat around the corner. Start the car, Sue. I want to go home."

Partial Sue snatched the keys out of the ignition. "Well, let's not be too hasty. I bet that alarm's not switched on. Not if the police have been in there."

Daisy, normally a calm and mild-mannered soul, fidgeted in her seat. "How do you know? They're the police. It's their job to keep things safe. They're bound to have switched the alarm back on."

Fiona had no idea about this side of police procedure. They would have certainly been in Sylvia's house to collect evidence and brought a technician with them to deactivate the alarm, but would they have switched it back on after they locked up and left? It seemed more than likely. Fiona came to the only realistic conclusion. "We can't risk it."

Partial Sue pointed towards the house. "But look, it's not even blinking. Don't burglar alarms blink when they're on?"

"Not all of them. Daisy's right. There's too much heat." Fiona was beginning to sound like a Hollywood gangster.

Partial Sue still wanted in, at all costs. "It'll be fine. We have to try."

Daisy planted her pouch of lock picks on Partial Sue's lap. "Well, you can try without me."

Partial Sue handed back her lock picks. "Oh, come on, Dais. You know I can't pick locks with my quivering fingers." She held out her hand just to show how much it shook in case she didn't believe her.

Daisy opened her mouth to reply when Fiona interrupted. "We'll compromise."

"What?" Daisy's voice quivered with worry at where this might be going.

Fiona attempted to reassure her. "We'll have a quick look around the outside of the property. Shine our torches in any windows. See if anything's amiss."

"But what if someone sees us?" Daisy asked.

Fiona thought for a moment. "Sue, do you still have the collection tins in the back of your car from the dog show?"

"Sure do," she replied, getting excited. "They've been emptied, though."

"Doesn't matter. We'll pop some change in them. Take them with us. Anyone challenges us. We rattle our collection tins under their nose and say we're charity collectors, which is true, but we act like particularly pushy ones, and say we didn't get an answer at the front door and are trying around the back."

Partial Sue grinned. "Nothing kills people's curiosity like being asked for money."

Daisy didn't share her enthusiasm. "I still don't like it. We're trespassing."

Fiona gave her a gentle smile. "I tell you what, Sue and I will have a nose. You stay here. There's no point in the three of us going in — it'll just look weird."

"But that makes me feel like I'm being a coward."

Fiona shook her head. "Not cowardly at all. As I've always said, I don't want anyone doing anything they're uncomfortable with. Plus, we need a lookout. You stay here and keep watch. I'll put my phone on vibrate. Ring it if you see anyone coming."

Daisy shoulders relaxed. "Okay, I can do that. Sorry. I feel I've let the side down."

Partial Sue made a face. "Don't be silly, Dais."

"No need to apologise. Ready, Sue?"

"Let's do this." Now they were both sounding like gangsters from a crime-heist movie.

Checking the street was clear, they exited the car and went around to the boot to retrieve a couple of collection tins. After filling them with loose change, they crossed the road and headed for Sylvia Steadman's house. It was only when they were within spitting distance that they realised it had a gravel drive.

"Uh-oh. I am not partial to gravel drives. Nothing noisier."

"It's fine. We're just a couple of charity workers collecting for homeless dogs. We're supposed to be here."

Easier said than done. Stepping onto the drive, Fiona's wincing intensified with every crunching footstep, each one loud enough to rival a giant munching on cornflakes. Making it to the safe haven of the front doorstep, they paused in case a concerned neighbour came careering onto the driveway, accusing them of being somewhere they shouldn't. Nothing happened. Fiona checked her phone. Nothing from Daisy. She nodded to Partial Sue who wasted no time peering into the little window set into the front door.

"What can you see?" asked Fiona.

"Not a sausage. It's too dark."

Fiona switched on her phone torch and held it up to the glass. "What about now?"

"That's better. Still not much to see. Here, you have a look."

They swapped places. Fiona squished her face up against the glass, not a good idea as her breath immediately steamed it up. She cleared it with her cuff and peered in. There wasn't much to look at. A fairly bland hallway with several pairs of shoes neatly arranged below the stairs, and above, a selection of coats on hooks. "It's a bit sparse. But then I suppose she only moved in a couple of weeks ago."

Moving to the left, they trod across a small but soggy front garden to a modest bay window and repeated the same exercise. A little more to see this time but nothing unexpected. A compact lounge with a flat screen TV, far too large for the room it inhabited. Two matching sofas sat at right angles to each other, but it was the cabinet in the corner that caught their attention, their torchlight blinking back at them as it flicked over shelves full of gleaming trophies.

"Wow," Partial Sue gasped. "Would you look at that."

"That is a lot of trophies." A sadness thumped Fiona hard in the chest. This was a woman's life, her achievements and hard work, all encapsulated in glass and wood. More like a tomb now that she had passed on. Had this been the reason for her death? A jealous rival who wanted to deny her and her dog one last trophy? To Fiona it seemed a trivial thing, not worthy of taking a life. But she knew not to be so naive. Envy could be a poison and when laced with the desire for glory, it was a lethal combination, burning like acid in one's veins. She wondered to whom these trophies would go, seeing that Sylvia had no family. And what about poor Charlie? He'd lost his mum. Poor thing would be traumatised. She made a mental note to check in with Kerry Pritchard and see how his foster care was going.

"Come on. Let's see if we can get around the back," Partial Sue whispered. Fiona followed her down the side of the house where a tall gate blocked them from going any further. She tried the handle. Locked. Below it was a keyhole to a latch lock.

"This is where we could really do with Daisy," Partial Sue said quietly.

"Maybe not. The gate shuts against the neighbour's fence. Which means that the little metal box that the latch fits into must be screwed to it." The fence was a simple affair, made up of slender overlapping slices of wood held together in a thin frame which was then screwed to thin wooden posts, no thicker than a person's arm and not particularly robust. "Here, hold this." Fiona handed her phone to Partial Sue and pressed her shoulder to the fence. It flexed slightly but not enough to dislodge the latch from its housing. Partial Sue joined in, giving it a shove. This time the fence bent at a much greater angle, freeing the latch, allowing the gate to open.

"God bless shoddy builders," Partial Sue said.

Quietly, they moved through the gate, down a narrow passageway where they found a half-glazed kitchen door. Shining their torches through the window, they observed a clean uncluttered kitchen, apart from a plate with a sparse covering of toast crumbs with a butter knife resting on it and what appeared to be a smear of jam. A shiver inched down Fiona's spine. Most likely Sylvia's breakfast before she headed off to the dog show. A simple meal that would be her last. In the corner on the floor was a large china double dog bowl with Charlie's name on it. It looked like a one-off, perhaps made for Sylvia by a friend. Water still sat in it. To the left of this were three brown packing boxes stacked one on top of the other, waiting to be opened, perhaps full of Sylvia's crockery that she hadn't got around to putting away, and never would.

Further down, the passageway led to the back garden, a surprisingly large square of grass. Not vast but bigger than expected compared to the compact house. Perhaps why Sylvia chose this particular property. Discarded dog chews were strewn across the grass. A kitchen window faced the garden next to a narrow set of French windows, a chessboard of paving slabs in front, a little uneven in places.

Moving silently around up to the French windows, they shone their torches inside to find an unfurnished bare room. Nothing.

Partial Sue killed the light on her torch. "Well, that's that."

"Let's get out of here before we're seen."

They made their way back out stopping briefly to shove the fence panel so they could close the gate, leaving it the way they found it. They were just about to creep across the gravel driveway when Fiona took a diversion back to the front door.

"What are you doing?" Partial Sue hissed.

"You go on. I'm just checking something." Fiona bent down to peer through the letterbox. Switching her phone light on once more, she could see some post hadn't been pushed all the way through. Sylvia had one of those letter boxes that had been lined with brushes to stop drafts. Sometimes, they also stopped letters from completing the final leg of their journey to the doormat.

With her other hand, Fiona retrieved a tissue from her pocket and reached in and pulled them out. She shuffled through the letters with the tissue, careful not to get fingerprints on them. It was all junk mail. However, the one at the bottom of the pile wasn't addressed to Sylvia Steadman. It was addressed to Ewan Fitch.

CHAPTER 25

Next day, Molly poured them all tea. Snatching hers up first, Partial Sue didn't want to risk it cooling down any further and guzzled the brew down fast. She slammed the empty cup on the table, as if she were downing shots at a bar, just in case Molly and the others hadn't got the message that she preferred her tea to be the temperature of molten lava. "Why would Ewan Fitch be getting mail at Sylvia's house?" she demanded to know.

It was a question they'd been repeatedly asking all morning.

"I don't know," Fiona replied. "But I specifically remember asking him if he knew Sylvia Steadman, and he denied it. Said he'd never heard of her."

"He did it, without a doubt," Partial Sue replied.

Daisy clapped her hands together. "This is the breakthrough we've been waiting for. This proves that Ewan Fitch is the killer!"

Fiona didn't share their enthusiasm. "It only suggests that he was lying about knowing her. Not that he did it. We need to establish his motive, and some evidence would be nice, before we start throwing accusations around. I mean why would he kill Sylvia Steadman?"

"I think it has to be our jealous-rival theory, surely?" Partial Sue poured herself another cup. "Has to be. He wanted to go the whole way at the dog show. Win Best in Show."

Fiona selected a bourbon from a plate of biscuits and started deconstructing it, prising the thing apart to get to the chocolatey middle. "That's possible, but it doesn't take into account the information we've just learned. Somehow, Ewan Fitch is connected to the property that Sylvia Steadman moved into, and he lied about knowing her."

"Maybe it was a love letter," Daisy said.

Fiona shook her head. "It was junk mail offering him twenty per cent off a new exhaust."

Partial Sue's eyes lit up. "Twenty percent? That's not a bad deal, actually. But maybe Daisy's on to something. Perhaps they were having an affair."

Daisy gasped. "Perhaps Sylvia was his fancy woman. They had a secret affair, had a falling out and then he killed her. The jealous lover."

"Ewan Fitch isn't married. Neither was Sylvia. Why hide it?" Fiona asked.

Molly had kept herself out of their little investigative debates so far but decided to make a suggestion. "Sounds like a long-distance relationship. I remember you said she lived in Bristol. He lives here. She retires and he's keen for her to move down. Maybe they're not at that moving-in-together stage. He owns an empty property, which is why it gets his stray mail. I'm always getting mail for the previous owners. Anyway, he suggests she can live in it so they can be closer but without the commitment of living together."

"She can walk away if she feels the heat coming around the corner," Daisy suggested.

"Exactly," Molly agreed.

"Entirely plausible," Fiona agreed. "Ewan Fitch invests in property, but it still doesn't explain why he lied about knowing her."

"But didn't Sylvia buy that place? We saw the pictures." Daisy thumbed her phone then scrolled through the pictures on Sylvia's social media. She stopped at the one with her holding up the keys to her new home.

Molly leant in to have a look. "Doesn't say anything about her buying it. She could be renting from him."

They'd assumed she owned her new place. A rookie mistake. Never assume anything. "We need to find out who owns that property," Fiona suggested. "Her or Ewan Fitch."

No sooner had she said it than Partial Sue had her phone out and tapped away on it. "I'm going on the government website. Do a land registry search. That will tell us who the current owner is." She halted in her tracks. Face alarmed. "Uh, oh. That's not good."

Fiona wondered what prohibitive spanner had fallen into their investigative works this time. "What's the matter?"

"It costs money to look at the title register."

"How much?"

"Five pounds."

"Is that all?"

Partial Sue grimaced. "I could get a full English at the Flying Teapot for that."

"I'll treat you next time we're there," Daisy offered.

Partial Sue martyred herself by pulling out her credit card. "No, no, it's fine." She filled in her details. A second later the information popped up on her screen. "Sylvia's house is owned by Sparshack Holdings Limited." She flicked onto the government's Companies House website and searched for the name. A property and real estate business with no mention of Ewan Fitch among its list of directors. They all got stuck into their phones, searching and cross-referencing Ewan Fitch's name with the name of the company for any possible connections. Nothing appeared.

Partial Sue put her phone away. "She must've rented it from Sparshack Holdings. Maybe he did too, sometime in the past."

"Bit of a coincidence if he did," Daisy said. "How would we find that out? Would it be on that government registry thingy?"

Partial Sue shook her head. "That only tells you who owns the property. Not who rented it in the past. I imagine, we'd have to ask Sparshack Holdings for a list of all their previous tenants if we wanted to know that. Which, I'm pretty sure they wouldn't give us."

"Maybe he used to own the property," Molly suggested. "Then sold it to them. Could you find that out on the land registry?"

Partial Sue looked sheepish. "We could. But it's another fiver."

"You know what? Forget that," Fiona said. Partial Sue's shoulders relaxed. Her credit card was safe for now. "Whether he owned it or not, Daisy's right. There's too much coincidence going on here. Someone's been murdered at a dog show who moved into a house that a rival competitor lived in or possibly owned at some point. This is big. We can't keep it to ourselves. We need to tell DI Fincher and DS Thomas about this, so they can get to the bottom of it."

"Isn't it possible that they already know this?" Molly asked.

"Definitely." Fiona smiled. "But never assume anything. As we've learned to our cost. I think we should text DI Fincher what we've uncovered."

Daisy became worried. "But then she'll know you've been snooping around Sylvia's house, trespassing."

"Strictly speaking, being on private property is not a crime," Partial Sue replied. "It's only trespassing if you don't leave the property when asked."

It worried Fiona a tad that Partial Sue knew the intimate details of trespassing, and possibly at what point had she'd been on someone's land and been asked to leave. Fiona put it to one side for the moment. "We don't have to tell her how we came by this information. We just tip her off that Sylvia Steadman and Ewan Fitch lived at the same address, perhaps at different times. So, are we all in agreement?"

They all nodded.

Fiona thumbed a message to DI Fincher and hit send.

They waited for a reply. None came. But that was to be expected. DI Fincher hardly ever replied immediately to anything Fiona sent her. She was a busy lady.

Once Molly had gone, a lethargy crept over the shop. After the initial thrill of what they uncovered had subsided, the ladies pottered around the shop, not really doing a lot. Sending that text to the detective had taken the investigative wind out of their sails. This was the strongest lead they'd had so far, eclipsing all others but it also created a stalemate. They couldn't move on until they had answers. Until they'd heard that either Ewan Fitch had been arrested or had been cleared.

Fiona had a thought. "Oh, I've just remembered what I needed to do."

"What's that?" asked Partial Sue.

"To call Kerry Pritchard. She's fostering Charlie. I just wanted to see how he's doing."

"Er, I wouldn't make that call, just yet." Daisy had been cleaning the inside of the front window but had stopped abruptly. Something had caught her eye. It must have been important because nothing normally deterred Daisy from her favourite pastime. "You are not going to believe what I can see over the road."

CHAPTER 26

Partial Sue and Fiona rushed to the front of the shop, crowding around Daisy to witness what had interrupted her obsessive cleaning. Across the road, at the Cats Alliance, a bizarre sight unfolded before their eyes. Sophie Haverford, manager and self-confessed cat lover and dog disliker, was struggling out of her shop, preceded by a handsome standard poodle with a thick black glossy coat. Feigning calm, she pretended to be in control, when clearly she was not. Flustered would better describe her demeanour. Dogs were emotionally smart creatures and highly sensitive. It could probably detect her uncertainty and perhaps her fear.

"Is that who I think it is?" Partial Sue asked.

Fiona blinked several times to make sure she wasn't dreaming. "That's Charlie. What the hell is Sophie Haverford doing with Sylvia's dog? She doesn't even like dogs."

"Are you sure that's Charlie?" Daisy asked. "I thought a show dog like him would be better behaved."

Partial Sue chuckled. "Dogs can sense weakness. He's assuming the position of the alpha in the relationship."

"Or Charlie's grieving the loss of Sylvia, which is why he's misbehaving," Fiona said.

That certainly appeared to be true as Sophie cavorted along the pavement, tugged awkwardly this way and that by the rebellious animal determined to investigate every smell that took his fancy, regardless of what she wanted to do. Behind them, Sophie's mild-mannered assistant, Gail, emerged from the shop. Turning briefly, she pulled the door closed and locked up. She caught up to her boss but kept a safe distance.

"Why is Gail walking behind them?" Daisy asked. "Oh, that's why."

Charlie stopped to do his business. Gail immediately pulled out a roll of green poo bags from her coat pocket, tore one off, then crouched down to bag up the mess, while Charlie pulled Sophie onwards, seeking out his next odorous engagement.

Partial Sue harrumphed. "Well, that doesn't surprise me. Sophie getting Gail to do her dirty work. Same old same old."

Fiona's mind wouldn't make sense of the sight in front of her. "What on earth is Sophie Haverford doing with Charlie though? She's a cat person through and through."

"She must have adopted him," Daisy suggested.

Fiona pulled out her phone. "I'm going to call Kerry and find out."

But she didn't have a chance to make the call to the dog fosterer. While their collective befuddled gaze had been held by the odd trio of two women and an ex-show dog shambling up Southbourne Grove, an unmarked police car pulled up on the road outside. DI Fincher and DS Thomas stepped out and approached the shop.

The three ladies instinctively moved back from the window and stood, quite by accident, in a deferential line near the shop's front door, as if they had been waiting to receive the two police detectives like foreign dignitaries.

"This must be about Ewan Fitch and that text I sent," Fiona whispered. "I bet he's been arrested."

DI Fincher pushed the door open, followed by DS Thomas. Quite used to the officers' intrusions, Simon Le Bon left the comfort of his basket, made two waggy-tailed circuits around them, then took himself back off to bed. DI

Fincher glanced at the three of them, lined up before her, as if awaiting inspection. "At ease, ladies."

It was only then that Fiona realised that they were still standing in a line. They broke formation and gathered at the round table, inviting the officers to sit. The DI joined them, but DS Thomas took up his usual spot, leaning against the front door.

"Would you like tea?" asked Daisy.

They both declined.

"Let me guess," Fiona said. "This is about Ewan Fitch. You got my text."

"Yes, I did. But no, this isn't about Ewan Fitch." DI Fincher's face became serious. Not that it could ever be described as jovial or light-hearted, her face only operated in degrees of gravitas, but on this occasion her expression had been set to the highest level of grimness. "Sally Wilde has been found dead in her home."

CHAPTER 27

There was a short pause. A delay in their reactions. Bad news has a habit of stalling one's brain temporarily, so the neurons don't fire for a second or two. But with unfeasibly bad news it can seize them up completely, the mind refusing to accept what it was hearing.

"I'm sorry — what?" asked Fiona.

DI Fincher attempted a sympathetic expression to soften the blow. "Sally Wilde, owner of Rolo the dog, another contestant at the dog show, was found dead at her home in Southbourne. We believe she was murdered."

Now they were all caught up, the tragic news hit them like a freak wave on a beach. It would have swept their feet from under them had they not been sitting down. Gasps all around. Hands slapped over mouths in disbelief. News of any murder would shock anyone to the core but what made this one so terrible was that they all liked Sally. Though they had only met her once, she was a bright ray of sunshine, albeit a clumsy one. A light that someone had decided to snuff out. The same killer as Sylvia Steadman? Almost definitely.

"I can't believe it." Daisy struggled for breath and reached for her inhaler.

Partial Sue shook her head. "But she was just in here the other day."

"That's what I wanted to talk to you about," DI Fincher said. "I have an eyewitness who claims to have seen her van parked outside your shop."

"Wait, you don't think we did it, do you?" snapped Partial Sue.

"I'm just gathering information. Building a picture of her last movements."

"How did she die?" Fiona asked.

"I can't say anything at this point."

"Do you think it's the same person who killed Sylvia?" Partial Sue asked.

"As I said, I can't say anything at this point. But I do need to question you about what she was doing here."

"We asked her to come," Fiona answered. "As part of our own investigation."

"I see." There was a trace of cynicism in the DI's voice. "Go on."

Fiona swallowed, shock still catching in her throat. "We asked her if she saw anything at the dog show, specifically around the time Sylvia died."

"And what did she tell you?"

"She did better than telling us," Partial Sue interrupted. "She showed us a video of the Best Biscuit Catcher competition."

"Yes, I've seen that video," the DI said. "She passed it on to us. Then what happened?"

"We watched it all the way through," Fiona explained. "It didn't really reveal much—"

"Except at the end of the video . . ." Partial Sue interrupted.

Fiona panicked and kicked her under the table, worried she would blabber about the Grey Man Molly had pointed out in the crowd. Not that there was much to see, but Fiona wasn't ready to share that information with the detectives just yet. Not until they'd heard from him first and learned what he had to say. They had to protect his anonymity because nothing scared away an informant like being on the police radar. She managed to salvage the situation, just. "Er, we saw the commotion. People rushing over to where Sylvia had collapsed. But then you already know that if you've seen the footage."

Fiona could feel the weight of Partial Sue's radioactive stare on her.

"Anything else?" asked DI Fincher.

"There was one thing," Daisy said. "We asked Sally about the tattooed lad, the one we saw running away. She denied knowing him — three times," Daisy added.

"You think that was significant?" the detective asked.

"Well, it's the same number of times Saint Peter denied Jesus."

"Exactly," Partial Sue agreed. "She made a big deal of denying it, which means she is, sorry, was, hiding something. And we think we know . . ."

Fiona tapped Partial Sue with her foot again, for the same reason as before. She was worried her colleague would reveal the tip-off they'd received from Reg Anagram, that the tattooed lad hung out at the Flying Teapot café. If the police knew this, then they'd descend on the place, spook the waitress who'd promise to keep an eye out for him and then they might never get a lead on who he was.

Partial Sue glared at her after her foot received another impromptu kick. Fiona did her best to look apologetic, then turned to the detective. "We think she knew him. Ninety-nine percent sure."

"Okay, interesting." DI Fincher made a note of it.

"How did Sally Wilde behave when she was here?" DS Thomas piped up. "Scared? Anxious?"

"Kerfuffled," Daisy said.

Everyone turned to stare at her.

"Kerfuffled?" the DI asked.

Daisy apologised. "Sorry. I'm not sure that's even a word. You know, she was a bit dizzy, all fingers and thumbs. In a nice way, of course."

"What? Agitated?" asked DS Thomas. "Did she mention if she'd had a falling out with anyone, a disagreement?"

Fiona shook her head. "No, nothing like that. We only met her the once, but I'd say that was her normal state of affairs. She was a bit clumsy and so was her dog at first but then he calmed down."

"After he'd had a sundried tomato," Partial Sue clarified. "She was very nice. We liked her a lot. She guessed all our favourite sandwiches. Gave us free ones."

A lopsided smile twitched at the side of the icy female police officer's mouth. "Yes, we experienced Sally Wilde's superpower when we questioned her."

"Oh, what was your favourite sandwich?" asked Daisy. "Did she guess it right?"

"She did. Roast beef and horseradish."

Partial Sue licked her lips. "Oh, good choice. What about you, DS Thomas?"

"He doesn't do carbs," the DI replied on his behalf. "Which she also guessed right." No surprise there. The lean and muscular detective lived in sportswear and hit the weights whenever he could.

"Poor Sally." Daisy sniffed. "She was such a lovely person. Muddled but lovely. Who would want to kill her?"

DI Fincher rose to her feet. "That's what we're going to find out. Then put them behind bars."

"Do you think it's the same person who killed Sylvia?" Partial Sue asked again.

"Did she die in the same way? Lethal injection?" Fiona asked.

DI Fincher sighed. "You know I can't reveal anything about an ongoing case."

They did but that didn't stop them firing questions at the young detective like an ack-ack gun, hoping one would hit the mark. They bombarded her non-stop until her patience ran out. "Okay, stop! Enough! I am not giving you information about a murder case!"

"But we just want to help catch Sally's and Sylvia's killer," Daisy pleaded.

"It's the same person. Has to be," Partial Sue muttered.

DI Fincher raised both palms to assuage the audible assault. "No more questions because I will not answer any of them."

"We ask the questions," DS Thomas reminded them.

"Yes, thank you, DS Thomas. We ask the questions. You give us answers. Understood?"

The three ladies nodded.

"Just because I slipped up once by giving you information does not mean I will do it again, so please don't ask. Now, as I've reminded you before, I can't stop you performing your own investigation, but if you do find something significant you must inform us immediately."

"Like we did with Ewan Fitch," Fiona offered.

"Exactly."

"And has he been arrested?" Partial Sue asked.

DI Fincher glared at her. "We are satisfied that Ewan Fitch is not part of this investigation."

"But he lived at the same address as Sylvia," Fiona said. "There has to be something in that."

"Believe me there is not."

The three ladies stared expectantly, clearly not satisfied with her answer.

DI Fincher sighed. "Right, I am only saying this because I don't want you pestering someone we've eliminated from our enquiries. Ewan Fitch is into property. The house Sylvia lived in and the others next to it were one of his first developments. He sold three of them but had a job shifting the fourth. His profits were tied up in that last house. To stop himself going bankrupt, he sold his own house and moved into it until he could sell it to a holding company, who later rented it to Sylvia Steadman."

"Only thing he's guilty of is building crappy houses," DS Thomas smirked.

"Oh," was all Fiona could say. It had never occurred to her to look into who had built the houses in the first place.

A rookie error, especially as Ewan Fitch had told her he was a house developer, and would have had absolutely no idea that Sylvia was renting one of his old properties.

DI Fincher rose to her feet. "We'll be on our way now."

"Just one other question," said Fiona. After the telling off they'd been given, Daisy and Partial Sue shuddered and braced themselves for DI Fincher's wrath.

The detective didn't explode. She sighed wearily. "It better not be about the murders."

"No, I just want to know if Rolo, Sally's dog, is okay?"

"Yes, he's fine. Staying with a friend."

"Okay, thank you."

After the two police officers left, the three ladies slumped in their seats, devastated, disheartened and disorientated. Death was always an unexpected and unwelcome guest, murder even more so. They'd only met Sally once but knew she would've become a good friend of the shop. Forget buying Boots meal deals, they would have looked forward to Sally barrelling through the door just before lunchtime with her big basket of delicious homemade sandwiches and even bigger grin. Something told Fiona that Sally would've insisted on giving them away, and they would have had a right old ding-dong battle foisting their cash on her, while Sally wouldn't hear of it, and would've pushed their money away. She pictured the scenario as clear as if it were happening before her, a scenario that would sadly never have the chance to become real. It made Fiona's insides feel hollowed out. Mourning the loss of a friend they never had.

CHAPTER 28

A gloom settled over the shop. One that didn't appear likely to budge for some time. For the rest of the afternoon, rather than brooding about what had happened, Fiona decided that they should turn that negative energy into something positive, continuing to delve into who the killer might be. Sally's sad demise had at least provided them with new information — a fledgeling pattern of sorts had emerged, reinforcing their main theory of the rival killer coveting the Best in Show title. It made more sense now. An obvious connection, Sally had been third favourite to win. The killer was gradually taking out the biggest threats, starting with Sylvia and now Sally. However, there was a competitor between these two — Pippa Stroll with Barbie, second favourite to win. Either she was the killer, eradicating her two closest rivals, or she was next.

"But I spilt coffee all down her when Sylvia was dying," Daisy pointed out. "She can't be the killer. Which means she must be next. Her life's in danger. We have to tell the police."

"Surely, they would have figured this out," Partial Sue replied. "It's so obvious."

Fiona pulled out her phone. "As we've learnt to our cost, never assume anything." She called DI Fincher. It went straight to voicemail, as it always did, so she left a message, informing the detective that they thought Pippa could be next. Then, she dialled Pippa Stroll's beauty parlour, I Feel Pretty.

She answered first time with a saccharine-sweet pre-arranged patter. "Good afternoon, Pippa speaking. How can I help you feel pretty today?"

"Hello, Pippa. It's Fiona Sharp. We came in the other day to ask you about the death at the dog show." She put the call on speaker phone so the others could hear.

Pippa dropped her sunny tone. "Oh, what do you want?"

"We don't know if you heard, but another contestant at the dog show has been found murdered — Sally Wilde. We thought we'd better tell you . . ." Fiona struggled to broach the subject of her possible impending fate.

"You can save your breath," Pippa replied. "I already know."

Her curtness surprised Fiona. "You know about it?"

"Yes. Police have already told me. You're a bit late to the party, dear." Pippa was aware of Sally's murder but mustered no sorrow or sympathy or even shock over the murder of a fellow contestant. Nor even fear that she might be next.

Fiona clenched her jaw. Nothing annoyed her more than being referred to as dear, even if the person who'd uttered it was a potential murder victim. She was trying to help Pippa, to warn her, although the police had got there first by the sound of it, but all she was getting back was condescension — *no good deed goes unpunished*, Fiona thought. "What did the police say?"

"I don't think that's any of your business. The matter's in hand."

"Oh, I see."

"Is there anything else you wanted?"

"No, that's it. We just wanted to make sure you were alright."

Pippa paused, then softened her tone slightly. "Er, thank you. For thinking of me."

"That's okay. Stay safe now."

"I will." Pippa hung up.

Partial Sue tutted and folded her arms. "Well, she's a cold-hearted so-and-so. If anyone's the killer, it's her. She didn't seem to be bothered in the slightest about Sally's death or worried about the fact that someone could be out to kill her. I'd be frightened if it were me, and if she's not, it can only mean one thing — she's the one doing the killing."

"She did sound grateful towards the end," Daisy noted.

"Much as I'd like her to be the killer, and I don't want to sound like a broken record, but it's a physical impossibility, unless she's figured out how to be in two places at once. Plus, she's far too antagonistic to be the murderer. As we said before, not exactly keeping a low profile."

Partial Sue's eyes widened. "What if it's a bit of reverse psychology? Act bolshy and over the top because no killer in their right mind would act like that if they'd just killed two people. It's a double bluff."

"Gosh," Daisy said. "You'd have to be very cocky and arrogant to pull that off."

"Exactly!" Partial Sue exclaimed. "Cocky and arrogant. That's Pippa Stroll to a tee."

"Apart from the fact that I was tipping coffee all down her when Sylvia was dying," Daisy said.

"Okay, yeah. There is that problem," Partial Sue muttered. "Unless she has an accomplice."

An accomplice would solve a lot of their problems. Fiona had also thought this when she'd questioned Ewan Fitch. Like Pippa Stroll, he too had the impenetrable alibi of being nowhere near Sylvia when she was murdered. But an accomplice could have pulled off the murder while either Ewan or Pippa were elsewhere, forging an air-tight alibi. However, that theory was tricky to turn into practical reality. Motivation being the biggest problem. Just what accomplice would have feelings so strong for someone else's dog that they would be motivated to kill? Of course, there was the prize money. But two hundred pounds split two ways wasn't exactly worth the risk. The only way Fiona could make it fit was if the pet had two owners who were in a relationship, who'd have equal affection for their beloved dog, coupled with a shared and ruthless ambition to see it win. Ewan Fitch had stated he was single, a fact that had been up for debate with their discovery that he had lived at the same address as Sylvia Steadman, until DI Fincher revealed that he'd built the house. But what about their hot-headed beautician? "Is Pippa Stroll married or in a relationship?"

Daisy was on it in seconds, sifting through social media sites in a trancelike state, thumbs a blur. After a few minutes, she came up for air. "As far as I can tell, Pippa Stroll's online status is single. I mean, she could be lying."

Partial Sue became jumpy and enthusiastic. "We could keep an eye on her. Tail her wherever she goes."

"Aren't there laws against that sort of thing," Daisy said.

"Yes, it's called stalking," Fiona reminded her.

"Not in our case," Partial Sue replied.

Fiona really didn't want to go down the road of pursuing a suspect all over town, but she could see that Partial Sue did, hiding behind a newspaper like an old-school gumshoe. Even if this course of action bore any fruit, just what would they say to the police if they got caught? "We've been stalking Pippa Stroll for several days both in the real world and online, and have discovered she has a partner that she's never mentioned." Rather than haul Pippa Stroll in for questioning, it would be more likely that the police would slap a restraining order on them, forbidding them from coming within 500 feet of her. She decided to shift the focus away from Pippa and onto Ewan Fitch, specifically their little tip-off to the police. "What do you think about Ewan Fitch? DI Fincher said he wasn't part of their enquiries. What do you make of that?"

"I noticed that," Partial Sue remarked. "They didn't seem too worried about him living at the same address as Sylvia Steadman."

"And then there's Sophie Haverford and Charlie, of course," Daisy remarked.

Fiona received a jolt. A bucket of cold water thrown by the hands of reality. For some reason, her mind had blotted out the fact that her rival from across the road at the Cats Alliance was the new owner of a murdered woman's dog. Why Fiona's mind had chosen to erase this from her short-term memory was as big a mystery to her as the murder itself. Perhaps, because the very notion itself was so preposterous that it had rejected it. Thrown it out as an impossibility.

"Surely that makes her a suspect." Partial Sue sounded hopeful. "Sophie killed Sylvia so she could get her hands on Charlie."

Though a logical conclusion, it also made no sense whatsoever. Sophie disliked dogs, whom she regarded as little more than hairy dustbins on legs. And as far as their owners were concerned, they were just like their pets — mucky, unsophisticated and easily distracted. So why ever would she want to be a dog owner? In Sophie's opinion, cats were pet royalty. Smart, self-sufficient and, most importantly, self-grooming. Far superior companions than dogs in every way.

"Well, I think we're about to get the chance to find out." Daisy pointed out of the window. "Here she comes."

They watched as Sophie paraded across the road preceded by a more controlled Charlie, his coat, almost as glossy as Sophie's perfectly coiffured bob of black hair.

CHAPTER 29

Bursting through the door of the charity shop to create a tad-dah moment, Sophie threw both hands in the air, including the one clutching Charlie's lead. If it had been any shorter it would have garrotted the poor animal. "Ahoy, fellow dog lovers!"

Simon Le Bon jumped up to greet him. For a brief moment the two dogs stood nose to nose, tails wagging, until Sophie smartly wrenched her dog away from Fiona's mongrel, as if he might sully his pedigree status.

"So, you're a dog owner now?" asked Fiona.

"That's right. I've joined your happy breed, and this is my beloved dog, Sebastian." Sophie ruffled the curls on the top of his head, then cleaned her hand with a squirt of disinfectant gel.

"Sebastian?" Partial Sue questioned. "Oh, for a moment we thought it was Sylvia Steadman's dog, Charlie."

Sophie grinned. "Oh, he is. I've adopted him, but he's now called Sebastian."

"Won't that confuse him, having a different name?" Partial Sue asked.

"Sometimes it's good to change an adopted dog's name," Fiona explained. "If they've been abused in the past, so they can make a fresh start. But I don't think that's the case with Charlie. Why have you renamed him?"

"Because the name Charlie reminds me of that ghastly perfume housewives wore in the seventies because they thought it was sophisticated. No, Sebastian is a much better name."

Fiona decided to address the elephant in the room, head on. "Sophie, what are you doing with a dog? You said you didn't like dogs or their owners the other day."

Sophie feigned shock and hurt, recoiling at the accusation. "Did I? Well, that's news to me."

Partial Sue backed Fiona up. "Yes, you said dog owners were scruffy and wore grubby gilets. Then, you asked what poo bags were called and we told you they were called poo bags."

Sophie wrinkled her petite nose. "Oh, well, no, I can't remember that."

Fiona took a different line of questioning. "And what does Jenkins think of sharing his home with a dog?" Jenkins sounded like Sophie's personal butler, but was in fact her stunning Siamese cat, whom Sophie worshipped and adored as if he were an Egyptian deity.

She waved away her concerns. "Oh, Jenkins is fine with having a dog."

"Really? I can't imagine that. Poor thing's going to be stressed having to worry about a dog in the house. Wasn't Kerry bothered about you having a cat when she was considering you for adoption?"

"Oh, it's fine," Sophie replied. "I made sure he was out when she came to inspect my place. As long as Jenkins and Sebastian are kept in separate rooms, it's all going swimmingly well. Besides, Kerry was more interested in the secure, communal garden out the back, so Sebastian can do his you-know-whats before bedtime. Plus, I made a sizable donation to help with her dog fostering."

"Are you allowed to have dogs in your flat?" Daisy asked.

Sophie glared at her. "It's not a flat. It's a beachfront penthouse. And it's fine."

"You mean you haven't checked the rules," Partial Sue said.

"Rules, schmules. When you pay the sort of money I did for a beachfront penthouse you don't expect to quibble over such silly matters. Anyway, I love having a dog. Love the camaraderie between us dog owners. I feel as if I've joined a big, happy family. Getting out in the fresh air, the friendly chats with other like-minded people . . ."

"Picking up the dog poo," Fiona said.

"Oh, yes. Well, apart from that."

"Er, you don't actually pick up his poo," Partial Sue pointed out. "Gail does that."

Sophie scrunched up her face. "How do you do it? It's vile. I mean, carrying around another animal's doings."

"Like a lot of things in life, it depends on how you look at it," Daisy said. "Is it a dog poo or is it an organic handwarmer? I've started reading *Zen and the Art of Motorcycle Maintenance.*"

Fiona pressed Sophie further. "There are so many dogs that need rehoming, why did you choose Charlie, I mean Sebastian?"

Sophie became flustered. "Gosh so many questions. It's beginning to feel like an interrogation. I suppose we bonded straight away. You just know when you've made a connection. When your eyes meet theirs. There's nothing like it."

Fiona wasn't buying what sounded like a load of rehearsed PR spin. She knew her rival from across the road was fuelled by celebrity and was perpetually desperate for kudos, even if she had to stoop to owning a dog. "So it had nothing to do with Charlie being an ex-Crufts winner?"

Sophie staggered backwards, as if the question had knocked her off balance. "Oh, my gosh, no! What do you take me for? I'd quite forgotten about that."

"So you have no plans to enter Charlie for any dog shows?" Partial Sue asked.

"Well, now you mention it, I might enter the odd one. Not the silly little local ones, of course. Maybe something a bit bigger, more prestigious. I mean, who knows, maybe Charlie could win Crufts again?"

And there it was. Sophie Haverford was as shallow as she was transparent. In under a minute, she'd gone from supposedly forgetting Charlie's show-dog credentials, to possibly entering him into the odd show, and on to claiming another victory at Crufts, and all the attention that would come with it. Parading around the main arena, basking in all the adulation and glory.

Partial Sue shook her head and folded her arms. "You haven't made a connection with Charlie. You just want to make yourself look good."

"I have made a connection with him," Sophie insisted. "But so what if I enter him into shows?"

"Because that's the real reason you adopted him." The tinnitus in Fiona's ears hissed. She'd had enough of this woman. They gave up their time in the charity shop to raise money for dogs who'd been abandoned by people who had acquired them for all the wrong reasons, or didn't understand the long-term commitment of having a dog. "What happens when he stops winning competitions? What are you going to do, hand him back?"

Sophie became indignant, fisted hands on hips. "Excuse me? How dare you lecture me about abandoned animals. May I remind you that I work for a pet charity."

Fiona stood up, faced her. "Then you should know better. Doesn't matter whether it's a dog, a cat, or a goldfish, a pet is for life, not just for propping up your over-inflated ego."

"I can assure you, that's not why I adopted him. I adopted him because we have a bond." Sophie bent down and threw her arms around the poodle's neck, nuzzling her head into his. Although it didn't escape Fiona's attention that she winced very slightly at being in such close proximity.

While Fiona and Sophie argued, Partial Sue did some rapid scrolling and speed-reading on her phone. She cleared her throat dramatically. "Just thought I'd point out. According to Kennel Club rules you need to have raised a dog from a puppy to enter it for competitions. Not the little fun shows like Christchurch, but the major competitions you're talking about. But obviously that doesn't matter because you've made a connection with Charlie."

Sophie's mouth guppyed open and shut. "Wh-what?"

Partial Sue continued, "Yeah, you can't just buy and sell show dogs. Show-winning dogs have to be born and raised, not bought on eBay."

"That makes sense," Daisy remarked. "Otherwise, every Tom, Dick and Harry would be doing it."

The ladies all stared at Sophie for her reaction. Then something happened that they had not experienced since they had the misfortune of knowing Sophie Haverford.

She was lost for words.

This new revelation must have taken up the whole of her brain's processing power, as she swayed slightly, presumably weighing up her options. There weren't that many to be fair. If she kept Charlie, she'd be saddled with a dog that had no use to her, now that it had been revealed that she couldn't enter him for competitions. If she got rid of him, it would prove they were right. Sophie's face gurned into odd shapes as her plans of being a dog show champion crumbled before her eyes. Of sashaying through the crowds and being stopped every second to have selfies with admiring fans and, of course, holding best-in-show trophies aloft. All that praise and kudos that she dreamed of, that she craved like a vampire craved blood, would never happen.

Fiona decided to make it easy for her. Not that she was worried about Sophie's feelings, but she was concerned for the welfare of Charlie. "Why don't we take Charlie for a bit. Look after him, while you have a think about what you want to do."

Sophie's eyes flicked rapidly between the three women. Possibly attempting to detect if this was some sort of trap to catch her out. That if she stepped into it, they would suddenly all point their fingers and cry, "A-ha. Caught you."

But Fiona knew Sophie all too well. They were offering her a means of escape, without any catches. She knew they wouldn't rat her out, that they would keep this whole debacle to themselves. Not that it mattered. If it did get out that Sophie had adopted a dog just so she could stick some silverware on her mantelpiece, she would just deny everything using that wretched slippery tongue of hers.

Sophie stopped swaying. Her confidence rebooted. "You know, as someone born to be altruistic, I find it hard to say no to anyone, or indeed, any creature who needs my help."

"Uh-oh," Partial Sue muttered. "Here comes the holier-than-thou speech."

Sophie either didn't hear or chose to ignore her. "I act selflessly before I think, which means I say yes to too many things. My fingers are in a lot of charity pies."

"I like the sound of charity pie," Daisy said.

"What are you trying to say, Sophie?" Fiona asked.

She knelt down and cradled Charlie's head in her hands, her head level with his. "I'm sorry, old chap. But these ladies have made me realise I don't have the time to devote to you. It wouldn't be fair on you, and it wouldn't be fair on all the other people who rely on my precious sacrifices. I'm only one person and I can only do so much. I realise that now." She sniffed back a tear at the end for good measure.

Partial Sue rolled her eyes so hard they almost came back on themselves.

As Sophie stood up and handed Charlie's lead to Fiona, her face went from one of angelic sorrow to outright nausea. "Does their breath always smell that bad?" she asked as she cleaned her hands with more disinfectant gel.

"Yes, I'm afraid so," Fiona replied. "All part of the fun."

Sophie swiftly regained her regular default expression of smug superiority. Reversing out of the shop, she blew kisses towards Charlie, who didn't seem too bothered about her departure. "Farewell, my gentle friend. Take good care of him."

Fiona reassured Sophie. "Don't worry. We'll keep him here until Kerry can . . ."

Before she could finish, Sophie had turned tail and fled while the going was good.

"So much for making a connection," Fiona remarked. "She couldn't wait to drop him like a hot potato the second she knew she couldn't compete in shows."

They gathered around Charlie and made a fuss of him, rubbing under his chin and giving his fur a good stroke. Simon Le Bon came over to join them, not wanting to be left out of any affection up for grabs.

"Did that nasty lady only want you so she could show off?" Partial Sue rubbed Charlie's ears. He liked this and leant into it.

"Well done for spotting that rule," Fiona said.

Partial Sue's face became ashen, then she grinned devilishly. "Er, there is no rule. I made it up. You can enter a dog if you've bought it from someone else, as long as the change of ownership is registered with the Kennel Club. But she's not a details person. I knew she'd never check. It was a bit of a test to see what she would do, to flush her out, although, I think we all knew she'd want nothing to do with him the second he wasn't useful to her."

"Well, I never, Sue!" Fiona snorted. "Devious but downright useful. Good thinking. You probably saved Charlie from a life of misery."

Charlie had obviously had enough of all the attention. Fiona took his lead off so he could have a snuffle around the shop followed by the little furry shadow of Simon Le Bon, who'd taken a liking to the very large and very well-groomed poodle.

Fiona called Kerry Pritchard to tell her things hadn't 'worked out' between Charlie and Sophie, omitting the gory details, and that he'd need picking up. Fiona briefly considered adopting Charlie herself as a companion for Simon Le Bon, as she watched them do their doggie tag team thing around the shop, investigating every corner, even though her dog already knew it like the back of his paw. But taking on another dog was a big commitment. She had to be realistic.

Charlie wasn't like Simon Le Bon. He was a big, strong dog who'd need a lot of exercise to keep him healthy. He really needed to be with a family or a young couple who had the energy to devote to him. No, she had to face facts that Charlie would have to be orphaned a second time.

CHAPTER 30

They'd spent the rest of the day seated around the table, while they waited for Kerry Pritchard to pick up Charlie, sipping tea and stopping to serve the odd customer, while they debated the likelihood of Sophie being the murderer. Had she killed Sylvia just to get her hands on her prize-winning dog?

"I think it's unlikely," Fiona said. "She's an awful person, capable of anything, but not murder. It's a lot of risk and effort just to get hold of a dog that you're going to abandon at the first sign of an obstacle."

"She felt the heat coming around the corner." Daisy was becoming fond of quoting the line from the famous bank heist movie. Although, it did jar with her parochial paraphrasing. "So she scarpered sharpish."

"Or she's just plain stupid," Partial Sue added.

Fiona shook her head. "I don't think Sophie is a murderer or stupid. However, she is an opportunist. A quick-thinking narcissist who spotted a situation she could turn to her advantage, until Sue put the kibosh on it with a well-timed white lie. Besides, if she is the murderer, what reason would she have for killing Sally Wilde? Unless she'd planned to adopt Rolo as well."

"That's true," Partial Sue agreed. "Let's put a pin in it for now."

Fiona's phone pinged. A text from Sophie.

Fi, be a darling and ask the dog fosterer if I could have my five pounds donation back, seeing as I'm returning that dog.

Forget that, and so much for her sizable donation. Five pounds wouldn't even cover a sack of dried dog food. Did that woman have no shame? She didn't even refer to him as Charlie or even Sebastian but as 'that dog'. To Sophie, he was merely a piece of merchandise that hadn't fitted her needs and could be returned for a refund like something bought online that didn't live up to its reviews.

At a shade before five thirty, Kerry Pritchard arrived to take Charlie back home. She made a fuss of him the moment she entered the shop, and he responded with plenty of licks and wags of the tail. She gave him a treat from her doggie utility belt strapped across her chest and offered one to Simon Le Bon. As she straightened up to face the ladies, her cherubic face glowed red, and it wasn't just because she'd been bending over to receive all that doggie attention. "I feel like a proper wally."

"Whatever for?" asked Fiona, surprised.

"I'm usually a pretty good judge of character. You have to be when you're sending a dog to a new home. But I've properly cocked this one up. I thought Sophie would make a good dog owner."

"Listen," said Fiona. "I wouldn't lose a minute's sleep over Sophie Haverford. She's a silver-tongued siren who can charm the birds down from the trees."

"And then get them to peck you," Partial Sue added.

Daisy giggled. "She's right. Why don't I make you a nice cup of tea."

Kerry declined. "No, thank you. I better get this one back with the others. Start trying to find him a new home."

Fiona smiled sympathetically. "Shouldn't be too difficult. What with him being an ex-Crufts dog."

Kerry pulled a face. "I try not to mention it. Otherwise, it attracts the wrong people."

"People like Sophie Haverford," Partial Sue said.

"I never mentioned it to her," Kerry said, looking guilty.

Fiona thought back to the conversation they'd had with Sophie on the morning they'd discovered Sylvia had been murdered. "Er, I think that might be our fault. We let it slip."

"Don't worry," Kerry replied. "To be honest, everyone knew the day after the show. It's going to be pretty hard keeping it a secret."

"Tell me," Partial Sue asked. "Did you manage to find new homes for any of your other foster dogs at the show?"

"I wasn't there. Bit of a busman's holiday being at a dog show. I'm surrounded by dogs every day."

"Fair enough," Partial Sue replied.

Kerry clipped Charlie's lead on his collar, thanked the ladies, then waved her goodbye.

Daisy watched the pair of them out the window as they walked up Southbourne Grove. "Poor old Charlie's going around the houses at the moment."

"Do you think it's odd that Kerry wasn't at the dog show?" Fiona asked.

Daisy turned around. "Not really. I thought it made sense what she said. If dogs are your work, sometimes you want a day off from it."

"I suppose . . ." said Fiona. "But the dog show was full of dog lovers. Isn't it the perfect place to find new homes for her foster dogs?"

"Like I did with that couple and Bovril," Partial Sue said.

"Exactly. It's a prime opportunity to find homes for dogs. It doesn't make sense."

"How did she actually acquire Charlie, I mean, did the police drop him off, or did someone from the dog club do it?"

Fiona felt another potential line of enquiry emerging. "I think we need to find out."

CHAPTER 31

Next morning, Fiona opened up the shop for the day and found an envelope waiting for her on the doormat. She picked it up and went inside, shutting the door behind her. Switching on the shop lights for a better look, she turned it over in her hands. Plain and white, it bore a sticky label printed with her name in Helvetica. There was no sign of a postmark, leading her to deduce that this had been hand delivered, not posted.

She was about to run her fingers under the flap when the hairs on her neck stood up. She had the peculiar feeling she was being watched. Sure enough, she glanced up to see that a small crowd had gathered by the door. She recognised the woman waving vigorously through the window.

Malorie Granger let herself in, even though the shop's sign was still turned to closed. The full complement of the dog club committee trooped in after her: Kenneth Prendiville, club secretary, David Harper, treasurer, and Delia Hawkins, vice chair. They had all left their dogs at home. This must be serious.

Simon Le Bon waddled up to them, tail wagging, nose sniffing keenly, sensing the smell of other dogs on the committee members' clothes. They ignored him. This must be very serious indeed, and Fiona guessed that it was no accident they'd showed up en masse when she was alone, outnumbered and perhaps a little docile first thing in the morning. The dog club committee equivalent of a police dawn raid.

"Mind if we barge in?" Malorie blurted.

Fiona slipped the unopened envelope in her pocket. "Looks like you already have. Can I make you all a cup of tea?"

"Oh, yes please," Kenneth Prendiville said eagerly. "I'm parched."

Malorie shot him a look that wiped the ratty smile off his face. "This is not a social jolly, Kenneth. We're here on club business."

"May I have the floor?" David Harper stepped forward.

Malorie moved to the side to let him pass. "The committee recognises this was your idea. You have the floor, David."

This was all too formal for Fiona, especially this early in the day. They were in her shop and on her time, not in one of their pompous meetings at the community centre. "No one's taking any floors or recognising anything until I've had my cup of tea. Now, does anyone else want one?"

Two hands gingerly rose, belonging to Kenneth Prendiville and Delia Hawkins.

Malorie caved in too. "Oh, might as well then."

David Harper's mouth downturned further at being interrupted, not that Fiona had ever seen it upturned. Last time she'd encountered the club treasurer he'd thrown his toys out of the pram when they'd asked for a copy of the show's entry forms. Had he been hiding something or was he just being a pompous arse? Right now, he was clearly miffed at being upstaged by the offer of tea. He really shouldn't have been — everything stops for tea, without exception.

After boiling the kettle and placing steaming cups in their hands, all except David Harper who stubbornly refused refreshment, as if to do so would detract from the gravity of the situation, Fiona proposed that they sit around the table. They declined, preferring to stand. Fiona wondered if this was to give them the psychological advantage. But she soon realised there was a far more innocuous explanation; the committee members, with the exception of David Harper, dispersed around the shop, browsing its shelves as they slurped their drinks. Fiona smirked to herself. In her experience there were two things British people couldn't resist — the offer of tea and the temptation of snagging a bargain.

David Harper stood in the middle of the shop, rigid and, from what Fiona could tell, seething.

"Go on, David," Malorie barked, as she shuffled through a rack of coats. "Don't mind us."

David Harper cleared his throat. "Thank you, Chairwoman Granger. As Treasurer of the Christchurch Dog Club, I have, as do we all, a duty of care. Indeed, our guidelines clearly state that we have a degree of responsibility, safeguarding, if you will—"

"Do get on with it, David." Delia Hawkins spoke while scanning the shop's considerable collection of second-hand crime books. "I have to be in Lymington at ten."

"Well, if you didn't interrupt me then maybe I could," he snapped. "As vice chair, I recognise and respect your authority, but that does not give you the right to talk over me. Please be respectful."

"Go on, David, no one's going to interrupt you," Malorie reassured him.

"As I was saying . . ."

The clatter of metal falling to the floor interrupted him for a third time. Everyone's gaze swung in the direction of a guilt-ridden Kenneth Prendiville. "Sorry." He put his tea to one side and swiftly bent down to gather up a selection of wooden-handled saucepans he'd been examining until they'd crashed to the floor.

"Is anyone taking this seriously?" David Harper's face had now become the colour of simmering jam. He huffed while Kenneth Prendiville shoved the saucepans and their lids loosely on top of one another, creating a precarious stack. When he was sure of no more interruptions, David Harper attempted to resume his speech, but Malorie hijacked it.

"What David's trying to say is, how's the investigation going?"

David Harper looked ready to explode. Whether that was because Malorie had commandeered his little speech or condensed all his verbosity into a neatly packaged question, Fiona couldn't tell.

"We have some leads," Fiona replied cautiously.

"Leads? What sort of leads?" asked Kenneth Prendiville.

Now she knew how DI Fincher felt when being pressed for information about an ongoing case. She could see why the detective was reluctant to give out details when everything was still up in the air, and nothing was certain. "Just leads at the moment. People of interest."

"May I ask who?" Kenneth Prendiville said.

David Harper jumped in on the conversation to avoid being spoken over. "Yes, just which people of interest are you, er, finding interesting?"

Malorie's eyebrows knotted together. "You see, the problem we have is that our members are scared, terrified now that Sally Wilde has become the second victim. They're all wondering if they will be next and are eager for details. The police are characteristically tight-lipped, which has led us to you. Are there any reassurances you can give us?"

"Not really. It would be wrong and irresponsible to point any fingers at this stage."

David Harper folded his arms and furrowed his brow. "So, am I right in saying that you have suspects, of whom, it could be said, potentially, that if someone were to point fingers at a later stage, when more valid evidence has been gathered, that said fingers might be pointed in their direction."

Fiona struggled to untangle his words. "Er, ye-es. Actually, I'm, sorry, what?"

Malorie sighed. "What David is trying to say is . . ." David huffed dramatically, as Malorie once more had to clarify his words, as if he were incapable of lucidity. "How close are you to finding the killer?"

Fiona took a deep breath. She didn't want to paint a bleak outlook, but neither did she want to give them false hope. "Whether it's us or the police, we will catch him, or her, or them. But I can't put a timescale on it. Sorry, but that's the best I can offer."

Kenneth Prendiville stepped forward without knocking anything else over. He smiled and clasped both hands in front of his chest. The expression didn't sit well on a face that seemed more suited to sneering. "Well, I for one would like to thank you for your efforts. Keep up the good work."

Fiona thanked him back. At least he was trying to show his appreciation, which was more than could be said for the rest of them who seemed aloof and indifferent.

However, Kenneth had been clearly softening her up in readiness to make his main point. "Now, have you considered joining the dog club? It has so many benefits — twenty percent off lots of local suppliers. It's a great way to save money."

Delia Hawkins groaned, "Jeez, Kenneth, you're really going for it this year with the Karma Ken routine." She turned to Fiona. "He wants you to join the club, so you'll vote for him in the upcoming AGM. Come on, Karma Ken, it's time to go."

"I am not Karma Ken. I'm merely pointing out what a cost-saving it is."

Delia began shooing him out of the shop, along with David Harper. "Come on, time to go."

Normally Malorie would be the first to cajole Fiona into signing up to something, but she looked as if she had other things on her mind. Hanging back from the others filing out of the shop, she pulled Fiona aside and quietly asked, "Would you do me a favour?"

"What sort of favour?" Fiona tensed.

"Sylvia Steadman was murdered at our event, and Sally Wilde was a competitor. I feel terribly responsible for what happened to them. Would you let me know as soon as you have any breakthroughs?"

Fiona's shoulders relaxed. "Of course." Malorie turned to leave and join the others outside, but Fiona held her back with a request of her own. "Can I ask you a question?"

"Of course."

"Kerry Pritchard, the dog fosterer."

"What about her?"

"I was surprised to hear that she wasn't at the show."

Malorie waved the comment away as if it were trivial. "She never comes to our shows."

"Why not? Wouldn't it be the perfect place to find new homes for her foster dogs?"

"Not in her opinion," Malorie replied. "She says it's preaching to the converted. Most people there are already owners. Harder to persuade people to adopt dogs if they already have them."

Fiona could sort of see the logic in that. Maybe Partial Sue had got lucky with the couple who wanted to adopt Bovril — they weren't yet dog owners, and Fiona herself had briefly considered adopting Charlie, but had dismissed the idea, mostly because she already had Simon Le Bon to care for. "How did Kerry acquire Charlie?"

"I called her. She came and picked him up."

"At the show?"

Malorie nodded.

"But she told us she didn't come to the show."

Malorie huffed. "Well, technically I suppose she didn't. This was after we'd sent everyone home. I'd left too. I had a ton of things to sort out, what with the show being cancelled, but David Harper waited with Charlie in the empty marquee until Kerry came to collect him. Obviously, this was long before the police informed us that Sylvia had been murdered."

David Harper, the temperamental, fastidious fusspot. She watched him outside the shop as he waited on the pavement with the others for Malorie, growing impatient, his pinched face glaring like an angry QR code. Was there a connection between Kerry Pritchard and David Harper?

"Anything else?" asked Malorie.

Fiona shook her head.

"Remember, I'd like to be the first to know as soon as you have anything solid about these murders, and I mean unequivocal evidence."

"Of course," Fiona replied.

Malorie left to join the others outside. Fiona watched as she swiftly debriefed them before they went their separate ways. They were an odd bunch. Officious and authoritarian to a point where it was difficult to take them seriously. But she could appreciate the importance of their visit and Malorie's little request. The club members would all be panicking. Worried about a murderer stalking dog owners. Was this killer simply targeting the favourites to win or was the general membership at risk too? She was sure it was the former but that wouldn't stop every club member biting their nails and snatching glances over their shoulder, worried that it was their turn next. The committee wanted reassurance and results — they wanted to find out who did this to one of their own. More importantly, could it actually be one of their own — David Harper possibly in cahoots with Kerry Pritchard, especially as she'd lied about not being at the show, or was Fiona reading too much into it? She would wait and get a second opinion from Partial Sue and Daisy.

CHAPTER 32

After the tea had been poured, Fiona informed Daisy and Partial Sue of the dog club committee's impromptu early-morning visitation, and Malorie's revelation that Kerry Pritchard had been to the dog show to pick up Charlie.

"A-ha," Partial Sue cried. "So, Kerry was lying to us. She said she wasn't at the show."

Daisy disagreed. "Well, hold on a second. From what Fiona said, the show had ended."

"What do you think, Fiona?" Partial Sue asked.

"I think it's worth discussing."

The debate continued, but after thirty minutes of hard deliberation, they all agreed that Kerry Pritchard was a dead end. A question mark still hung over David Harper, due to his obstructive nature at the start of their investigation, but as far as the dog fosterer was concerned, they'd been jumping to conclusions, desperate to make connections where there weren't any. She had no motive to kill Sylvia or Sally. She wasn't even at the show at the time of the murder, not until everything was over, and since then had been trying to rehome Charlie. All she'd got out of it, as far as they could see, was a measly five-pound donation that Sophie was in the process of trying to get refunded. Hardly a reason for murder.

Molly appeared out of breath and flustered. "Sorry I'm late. I discovered a letter in Dina's school bag from last week, asking her to bring in bits and pieces this morning to make an Easter garden. I've been rushing around trying to find lolly sticks and picking flowers from the garden."

Daisy chuckled. "Oh, I remember those days. Finding dog-eared letters at the bottom of Bella's bag from weeks before . . ."

At the mention of a letter, Fiona remembered the envelope in her pocket that had appeared on the doormat first thing this morning. She'd completely forgotten about it, distracted by the appearance of the dog club committee. She pulled it from her pocket, prised it open and unfurled a surprisingly thick, plain, white piece of paper that had been folded three times. More adrenaline flooded her system. Printed in Helvetica was a simple message.

I have information about the dog show murder.
I cannot return to the shop.
I am being watched but will contact you when it's safe.

"Oh, my gosh." Fiona held it out for her friends to see. "This was left on the doormat when I came in this morning."

There were gasps all round, big melodramatic ones. They smoothed the letter out on the table, weighing it down at the corners with an assortment of objects that were close at hand — a salt shaker and pepper mill (not matching), Fiona's empty tea cup and a quarter pound bag of sherbet lemons that Daisy had procured from the traditional sweet shop on her way to work, which was swiftly losing its ability to function as a paperweight due to everyone helping themselves because of the excitement, so they swapped it for a carved woodpecker from the shelf nearest to them. They had to hold the note down somehow, as the hefty paper kept creeping back into its folded form, making it difficult to examine. Partial Sue said she reckoned it was 120 gsm, the good stuff, not that toilet paper most people fed their printers. Not that there was much printed on it.

"You think it's from the Grey Man?" Daisy asked Molly.

The ladies looked to her for clarification. "Er, yeah, I suppose. It pretty much says what he said when he popped in. Apart from the bit about him being watched, but I could've guessed that by the way he kept nervously glancing out of the window. So yes, ninety-nine percent sure it's him."

Partial Sue's eyes lit up. "Hey, if he thought he was being watched and kept looking out the window, maybe he was worried about being seen by Maleficent across the road."

"You mean, Sophie." Fiona smirked.

"Who else would he be worried about?" Partial Sue replied. "She could still be a suspect after all that nonsense with Sylvia's dog. Maybe he didn't want her to see him because he thinks she's the murderer."

"Well, if that's the case then he wouldn't have chosen the shop to make contact," Fiona pointed out. "He'd have done it elsewhere."

Daisy popped a sherbet lemon in her mouth. "Southbourne Grove is a busy road. Lots of people come through here. Could've been anyone he was worried about."

"Anything else you notice about the note?" Fiona asked Molly.

She bent down for a closer look. "I mean there's not much to see. It is what it is."

Daisy crunched away on her sweet. "He's started every sentence with 'I'. Is that relevant?"

"Not really," Fiona said. "Varying sentence structure probably wasn't high on his agenda."

Partial Sue snatched up the note, sending the impromptu paperweights everywhere. She weighed the heft of the paper in her hand. "Why's it printed on such high-quality paper? Maybe he works in a hotel."

"Why a hotel?" asked Fiona.

"I don't know it's just the first thing that came to mind. But I suppose it could be any business where they want to impress someone with the quality of their correspondence."

"Wouldn't it have a letterhead if it were from a business?" Fiona asked.

"Oh," said Partial Sue, disappointed. "That's true."

"Should we be touching it?" Daisy asked. "What about fingerprints?"

"This is someone with information, not the murderer," Fiona replied. "Well, at least, I don't think it is."

Partial Sue waved the note around. "But we still need to know who this person is."

Fiona took the note from her and examined it carefully. "I don't think so. This person's clearly frightened. I think we continue our current strategy — let them come to us, not go looking for them, otherwise we might scare them off. And we won't share anything with DI Fincher and DS Thomas until we know more."

"I think that's a smart idea," Molly agreed.

The Wicker Man burst through the door. Fiona stuffed the note into her pocket.

"Fancy a cuppa, Trevor?" Partial Sue asked.

"Thought you'd never ask. Any cake going spare?"

Without thinking, Daisy patted herself down, checking if she had a spare one on her. Bereft of any baked delights squirreled away in her garments, she held out her bag of sweets. "Sherbert lemon?"

"Now you're talking." The Wicker Man delved into the bag, popped one in his mouth, then settled into a chair, rolling the lozenge around with his tongue. Partial Sue went off to make tea.

"I'm glad I've caught you all." He pulled out his own folded piece of paper. For a moment, Fiona wondered if he'd also received a note from the informant. "I've got some new material to run past you."

Fiona relaxed. "Oh, yes. We could do with cheering up."

Partial Sue halted her tea-making, rushed back out and retook her seat, eager to hear his new routine.

Crunching up his sweet and swallowing it to clear his mouth, the Wicker Man got to his feet and held out the sheet of paper in front of him. "Okay, the new stand-up material shall now commence." He didn't bother with his convolutedly bizarre warm-up, but did pause for effect. He waited a beat or two then launched into his routine. "You know, I do love a good zombie movie. But have you ever noticed how no one ever dresses appropriately. I mean, the heroes in these films know they'll get infected if they get bitten, so what do they wear? The most flimsy T-shirts and blouses that offer no protection from a zombie bite whatsoever. Now if it were me, I'd be wearing at least three very thick, sensible jumpers, and not any old jumpers. I'd wear the polo necks my nan used to knit me for Christmas. Those things were as thick as Brillo pads. No zombie could ever bite through your nan's home-knitted jumpers. Although it would change the nature of zombie movies. Instead of scavenging for food, medicine and weapons, they'd all be sitting around purling and bobbling, which has fringe benefits of relaxing them. Because surviving a zombie apocalypse can be extremely stressful."

His eyes tentatively peeked over his sheet of paper to gauge their reactions.

"I don't really watch a lot of zombie movies," Partial Sue remarked. "In fact, I don't think I've seen any."

Daisy winced. "I don't like them. Too much blood."

"I guess we're probably not the right target audience," Fiona said.

His eyes darted over to Molly, who being in her thirties, might be more of a fan. "Yeah, I mean, sorry. Zombie movies aren't my thing either. I prefer a good romcom."

Daisy wobbled with joy. "Oh, yes, I love a good romcom."

"But you get that zombies bite people and . . ." The Wicker Man's words were lost as the ladies became sidetracked by recommending romantic comedies to each other.

Eventually, Fiona said, "Oh, sorry, Trevor. We went off on one. Do you have any other stuff you want to run past us?"

"If it's not too much trouble."

"Of course not, fire away."

After having his confidence knocked, his mouth quivered as he spoke. "This is only a short one. Here goes. When I was little, I used to think that there was a type of meat called ends meat, and that my mum wasn't very good at cooking it, because she was always saying she didn't know how to make ends meet."

A snigger prickled at the back of Fiona's throat. The other ladies gently tittered.

"I quite like that," Fiona said.

The others agreed.

"You do?" asked a shocked Wicker Man.

"Yes," Fiona replied. She thought it wise to pour a little tepid water on proceedings before the Wicker Man booked a slot at the Edinburgh Fringe. "It's not sidesplittingly funny but I like the wordplay."

"Yes, the wordplay. It's funny — punny, you might say." Partial Sue chuckled to herself.

"Exactly."

This energised the Wicker Man. He fidgeted on the spot, presumably from all the new possibilities and ideas that fizzed and fireworked in his brain. "Well, I never. I believe you've proffered a new land of mirth for me to explore. I am in your debt, fair ladies."

"Not at all," Partial Sue replied. "We did nothing. We just found it amusing."

Once again, Fiona thought it wise to temper his enthusiasm with some realism. "This new land you're going to explore — it may need some cultivating."

The Wicker Man nodded his head eagerly. "Yes, yes, of course. Virgin territory always requires taming, and this one will, no doubt, need my comic husbandry. But it is brimming with fecundity."

Daisy raised her eyebrows at his last word.

"It means fertile," he clarified, then gave a dramatic bow, thanked them once more and left.

"Well, I think that's a nice start to the day," Daisy said. "Nothing like giving someone encouragement."

"Yes," Fiona agreed. Although, deep down, she hoped that he wasn't going to go off and pen a string of awful puns and one-liners to subject them to. Last time she watched any comedy, puns seemed out of fashion. An unwelcome image of an audience groaning at the Wicker Man's wordplay popped into her head. Not something she wished on him.

Later, after lunch, when Molly had left to pick up her daughter from school, Daisy suddenly cried out, as if she'd trodden on an upturned plug. "Oh!"

Fiona and Partial Sue rushed to her aid.

"Are you okay, Daisy?" Fiona asked, worried that she'd done herself a mischief.

"Yes, yes. I'm fine. I completely forgot, what with the excitement of that note and everything." She pulled out her phone, searching through it while she spoke. "I don't know if you remember but I set myself the task of checking Sally Wilde's social media posts."

Fiona and Partial Sue nodded.

Daisy continued. "This was back before she'd been murdered. At the time we thought she could be a suspect, could've been hiding something. But then, after she died, I changed my searching to look for anyone who might've had it in for her, checking the comments on each of her posts. It's taken ages."

"Did you find anything?" Fiona asked.

"Yes and no. She set up her sandwich business about two years ago, announcing it on social media. There are hundreds of comments wishing her luck, and congratulations. However, there's this one comment from this chap, which says, 'Good luck with your new business. I'll miss you serving me my favourite sandwich (which as you guessed is a bacon sarnie!) before catching my train every morning.' He's got his location down as Southbourne. His nearest station would be Pokesdown, right next to the Flying Teapot."

Daisy handed Fiona her phone. She examined the post, with Partial Sue peering in.

"You think she worked at the Flying Teapot?" Fiona asked.

Daisy nodded. "That was my first thought."

Partial Sue wasn't convinced. "Lots of stations have cafés next door, or inside them."

Fiona scrolled through the other comments. "Let's assume she did work there. Surely there would be a few more posts from her old customers wishing her luck."

"I think she deleted them," Daisy replied.

"Why would she delete them?" asked Partial Sue.

Daisy swallowed hard. "Okay, I'm making some big leaps here, and this might be just my over-active imagination, but remember how we were convinced that she was lying about knowing the tattooed lad?"

Fiona and Partial Sue both nodded.

Daisy continued. "We know for a fact that he was a regular at the Flying Teapot, thanks to Reg Anagram's tip-off. Now, let's assume Sally Wilde did work there. The tattooed lad would certainly be one of her customers. But for some reason, she doesn't want anyone to know this — she denied him three times. Now we don't know why this is, but to make it convincing, she needs to cut ties with the Flying Teapot, to cover up that she worked there, because people might discover it was the tattooed lad's regular hang out, and make the connection with her. So she has to go through all her social media posts and delete the ones which mention the Flying Teapot. This would take ages, so she probably just did a search using the Flying Teapot as keywords then hit delete, that's what I would do. But she missed this one because it doesn't mention the café's name."

Fiona handed back her phone. "Okay, I can see the logic in that."

"But why would she want to keep it quiet?" Partial Sue asked.

Daisy drew another deep breath for dramatic effect. "What if she knew he was the killer?"

Fiona didn't want to jump to conclusions, but it sounded like a very plausible theory. "Daisy, I think you could be onto something. Maybe he threatened her to keep her quiet, so she denied knowing him. Then she hurriedly deleted any connections to him online. But maybe he wasn't satisfied with this and silenced her for good."

Partial Sue decided to play devil's advocate. "Hold on a minute. The police would have interviewed anyone who knew Sally after her death, including people she used to work with."

"Maybe," Fiona replied. "They might not have got round to interviewing her old employer yet — it's two years since she last worked there. They don't have the benefit of our little Reg Anagram tip-off — that the tattooed lad is a regular customer."

"But we still don't know if Sally Wilde worked there for sure."

Fiona smiled. "There's only one way to find out."

CHAPTER 33

Daisy had insisted on going with Fiona. It had been her lead and she was eager to visit the Flying Teapot to see where it might take them, hopefully to the doorstep of the killer — the tattooed lad who was now top of the leader board in terms of suspects. They all agreed and Partial Sue stayed behind to look after the shop. Before they left, she warned them to be on their guard. They could be getting close.

Simon Le Bon was also eager to get to the Flying Teapot, but for a completely different reason. Long before the café came into sight, he began heaving forward on his lead, almost choking himself. Normally he was a well-behaved dog, but he had a good memory, as most dogs did when it came to food. He knew they were heading in the direction of that place that smelt of cooked meats, some of which fell to the floor. Because of that, deep guttural snorts from the little mongrel accompanied them the rest of the way.

After crossing the main road, they were about to enter the café as a customer was just leaving, flipping up the hood on his sweatshirt before he stepped outside. Fiona and Daisy politely moved to one side to let him out. However, Simon Le Bon didn't know about the correct etiquette for letting someone exit a building first, and thrust forward, nearly tripping the poor guy up. Fiona apologised. He smiled at Simon Le Bon, bent down and rubbed his head affectionately. "He's keen. Smells must be driving him mad."

As he straightened up, Fiona noticed him clock Daisy. A barely perceptible tick of recognition flicked across his face, swiftly turning into surprise. His face looked familiar to Fiona, although she couldn't place it. He brushed past them and carried on his way. The two ladies stepped inside, Simon Le Bon leading the way.

A second later, Fiona's memory cells caught up and lit up like Blackpool Tower. "It's him! The tattooed lad. He recognised you."

"I didn't recognise him."

"His hood was covering his neck tattoo, and he's left his dog at home. Come on!" Fiona turned and bundled out of the café followed by a bewildered Daisy.

Outside, they caught sight of him, hurrying towards the corner of a side road. "Excuse me!" Fiona shouted. "Wait!"

He didn't stop to answer or risk a glance back at who'd called after him. He made a run for it. Darting around the corner, he disappeared into the back streets of Pokesdown.

Daisy and Fiona gave chase, making it to the corner where they'd last seen him. It led to a maze of narrow streets lined with tightly packed terraced houses, which all looked the same. There was no sign of him.

"We'll never catch him in there," Daisy said, gasping for breath. "Not with our knees."

She was right. He had a head start on them and was easily twice as fast. Plus, they had no idea which way he'd gone. Fiona admitted defeat. "Come on. We might be able to get some answers at the café."

They headed back inside the Flying Teapot, which appeared to have exactly the same clientele as the last time. One table was occupied by a similar set of dusty builders and another by a different couple of pensioners, silently sipping on mugs of tea. Although, today, there was the addition of a group of listless students who appeared worse for wear, stuffing forkfuls of all-day breakfasts into their mouths, presumably hoping to cure their hangovers.

There was no sign of the waitress, so Fiona and Daisy sidled up to the counter at the back, where the cook busied himself over a gargantuan frying pan the size of an upturned dustbin lid, deep with oil and covered in a flotilla of eggs, bacon and sausages.

Over the deafening sizzle Fiona asked, "Excuse me, there was a young lad just in here a minute ago. He's got a neck tattoo and usually has a Staffie with him. I don't suppose you know who he is?"

Without looking up from his pan the cook said, "Oh, Adrian. Yeah, he's always in here. What's he done this time?"

"Nothing that we know of. Why'd you ask?"

The cook flipped over half a dozen eggs, which hissed disapprovingly. "Always getting into trouble that one. Actually, he's a lot better now. But he used to be a right so-and-so."

"What sort of trouble?" Daisy asked.

"Not for me to say. You should ask his sister."

"Who's his sister?" Fiona asked.

The cook nodded towards a door at the side of the counter. "Here she is now."

The waitress in the tabard appeared, a fresh stack of napkins in her hands, ready to replenish the dispensers on the tables.

The cook looked up from his frying. "Faye, these ladies were asking about your brother."

"Hello again," Fiona said.

An unconvincing smile troubled Faye's lips.

Fiona smiled back. "Do you remember, last time I was in here I asked you if you could keep an eye out for a lad with a neck tattoo who came in here with a Staffie? I gave you my number, said to call me if you saw him. Turns out he's your brother, Adrian."

"Could I take my break now?" Faye quietly asked the cook.

He nodded.

Faye led Fiona and Daisy to a table in the corner, the one farthest away from the other customers. When they had sat down, Faye leaned over the table and hissed, "Why are you asking about my brother?"

"First off," Fiona replied, "why didn't you tell us he was your brother?"

Faye sat back in her seat. "I don't know who you are. He's my little brother. I'm going to protect him."

"What are you protecting him from?" Daisy asked.

Faye became silent. Cast her gaze down at the crumbs on the tabletop.

"Protect him from what?" Fiona repeated the question.

Faye looked exhausted. "After my dad left us, my mum was a wreck. I sort of stepped in to look after him. Even though he's no longer a teenager, I still feel responsible for him."

Daisy decided to change the subject. "Did Sally Wilde used to work here?"

She nodded.

"Have you heard that she's dead?" Fiona asked.

Sadness tugged at the edges of Faye's mouth. She nodded again.

"Thing is, we also asked Sally if she knew anyone with a neck tattoo and a Staffie. Like you, she denied it."

"And we think she deleted any mention of working at the Flying Teapot on her social media," Daisy added. "Why would she do that?"

Faye didn't look up. "I asked her to do that, to protect Adrian."

"What are you protecting him from?" Fiona asked.

Again, Faye refused to answer. Loyal to her brother, she was reluctant to reveal his secret.

Fiona decided to change tack. "Did Sally Wilde have any enemies?" Fiona asked. "Anyone she'd had a disagreement with?"

Faye glanced up, shocked. "Sally was the nicest, most generous person ever. I can't imagine anyone disliking her."

Fiona couldn't either. From the brief time they met her, Sally appeared to be a little ray of light. "Any problems she mentioned to you? Anyone threaten her?"

Faye shook her head. "Not that I know of. Her sandwich business was ticking along nicely. I mean, she had to work hard, but Sally loved it, and her customers adored her. Told me that working for yourself didn't feel like work. That's what I want to do, eventually. Be my own boss."

Fiona girded her loins, readied herself to ask the question they'd come here for. "Did your brother have anything to do with her murder, and the death at the dog show?"

Faye's eyes became fierce. "No, no way, and Sally was our friend. Why can't you just leave him alone. He's done with getting into trouble."

"What sort of trouble has he been in?" Fiona asked.

Faye appeared on the edge of tears. "He didn't have anything to do with any murders, I know he didn't. You've got the wrong person. Hundred percent."

"Then why does he keep running away? First at the show and then, just now."

Faye said nothing.

Fiona let the silence hang in the air for a bit, until it became uncomfortable, then asked, "Have the police been in to question you yet?"

She shook her head.

Fiona could have threatened her at that point. Told her in no uncertain terms that they were about to go straight to the police, to inform them that they knew the tattooed lad's identity. But playing hardball wasn't Fiona's style. In any case, she wasn't even sure she could pull it off. Laying out a logical argument to help Faye see sense was more her style.

"Thing is, the police will eventually come here to question you. It's only a matter of time before they learn that Sally Wilde used to work here. They might already know. Just haven't got round to it yet. Probably interviewing all her sandwich customers first. I imagine she had quite a few. But when they do come calling, they'll undoubtedly ask you if you know a lad with a spider's web neck tattoo and a Staffie, who was seen running away from the murder scene. At that point, you will have a choice. You can tell them about your brother, or you could lie to them. You could get in serious trouble if you lie. Equally, if you do tell them the truth, they aren't going to be very happy that you withheld this information. But if you come forward or, ideally, Adrian comes forward, sooner, rather than later, it'll be a lot better all around."

Faye sniffed back a tear. "He'd never do that."

"Why not?"

Faye didn't answer.

"Everything will be alright, Faye." Daisy attempted to comfort the young waitress while keeping things realistic. "But he needs to come forward and clear his name. If he doesn't it's just going to make it worse. Make him look more guilty. Let us talk to him. Maybe we can help?"

"How can you help?"

"We need to hear his version of events," Fiona explained.

"I can't promise anything, but we know the two detectives in charge of the case."

Faye sat with her hands in her lap. Her tired and sad eyes revealed the strain of covering for her brother. She was in a no-win situation. There was only one decision she could make.

She took her phone from her pocket and called Adrian.

CHAPTER 34

A cautious Adrian pushed open the door to the café. Worry had drained the colour from his face, and he looked as if he hadn't been sleeping. He poked his hooded head inside and scanned the room to make sure this wasn't some kind of ambush. His sister immediately rushed over to greet him and presumably assuage his fears, or perhaps stop him from losing his nerve and running out of the door. She led him inside, over to where Fiona and Daisy sat. His dog trotted beside him, a toothy grin on his face, tail wobbling back and forth at the other end. The Staffie stretched forward on his muscular legs, eager to make Simon Le Bon's acquaintance, and Fiona's little terrier was happy to oblige, emerging from underneath the table, equally waggy. After a few introductory sniffs, the Staffie rolled over on his back, an invitation to play. Simon Le Bon wasn't quite ready for that level of intimacy yet, but continued to have a good nose of his new friend.

Adrian took a seat, flipping the hood of his sweatshirt back, while his sister introduced everyone. "I have to get back to work, but you need to listen to these ladies, Adrian. They speak a lot of sense."

"Alright," Adrian replied, trying to maintain his aloof, tough-guy image, but Fiona wasn't fooled. He was camouflaging his fear.

Fiona and Daisy said hello.

"What's your dog called?" asked Fiona.

"Red Bull." Adrian reached down and rubbed the Staffie's chin.

"Is that because he's energetic?" Fiona queried.

"Yeah, he never stops. Always on the go, he is. And 'cos he's a bull terrier. What's your dog called?"

"This scruffy fellow is Simon Le Bon."

"Bit long for a dog's name, innit?" Adrian said.

"Yes, I suppose. But he's named after the New Romantic singer. They have the same hair."

Clearly Adrian had no idea who Simon Le Bon was. He whipped out his phone to Google it. "Oh yeah, so he does." He reached down and stroked Fiona's dog. "He's a cute little fella."

There was a short silence. Adrian looked across to Daisy. "Sorry for knocking into you at the dog show."

Daisy waved it away. "That's quite all right. Just an accident."

"You were in quite a rush," Fiona remarked.

Adrian's face became guilt-stained.

"Who or what were you running away from?" Fiona asked.

His anger flared. "You think I did it, don't you? I knew this was a mistake. This always happens." Screeching his chair back, Adrian stood up. "I'm out of here."

From across the café, Faye looked over, concerned.

Without Adrian noticing, Fiona held up a hand to signal that everything was okay.

"Before you go, why don't we all have a nice cup of tea and some cake?" Daisy suggested. "What do you say, Adrian? Our treat."

Adrian paused. Halted his swift exit.

"I don't know about you," Fiona said. "But I'm gasping for a cuppa and a bite to eat. Do you want tea, Adrian, and something to eat?"

Slowly, Adrian sat back down. "Yeah, that sounds good."

They didn't need to put in an order. Faye had been earwigging the whole conversation from across the room. She brought over three mugs of tea. The café didn't serve cake, but they did have hot cross buns, freshly toasted and dripping with melted butter. Adrian wolfed his down and gulped his tea. They ordered the same again for him. The refreshments did the trick, calming his temper.

"Can I give Red Bull a treat?" Fiona asked.

"Sure," he replied.

Fiona pulled a bone-shaped meaty biscuit from a little Tupperware box she kept in her coat pocket. The Staffie reached up and took it gently from her fingers. She also gave one to Simon Le Bon, otherwise he'd give her the cold, furry shoulder for the rest of the day.

Contented crunching came from below the table. "I think they like that," Daisy remarked.

Fiona smiled. "Happy dogs, is there anything better?"

"Nothing better," Adrian replied.

Fiona decided to capitalise on Adrian's improved mood. "Listen, Adrian, we're not judging you or anyone, we just want to build up a picture of what happened at the dog show, that's all. Why don't you tell us your version of events? What led up to you bumping into Daisy?"

He hesitated, then said, "Yeah, okay. But I'll have to go further back than the dog show to explain that."

"Oh?"

"I'm sure my sister's already told you, I used to have a bit of a reputation for getting into trouble."

"What sort of trouble?" Fiona asked.

"Fighting, vandalism, nicking bikes, shoplifting. Petty crime. But I could see where it was heading. Gateway to the bigger stuff. Seen loads of older lads round here go that way. And I didn't want it."

"So what did you do?"

"I couldn't talk to any of my mates about wanting to change. They were on the same path. So, I took some advice that's helped me stay out of trouble. First, from my sister. She's not like me. She's sensible. Smart. Far too smart for this place. You know, she saves up her tips and invests it. She's going to be really successful, I just know it. Anyway, she told me to turn and head in the other direction whenever I sensed trouble."

"Walk away when you feel the heat coming around the corner," Daisy enthused.

"Exactly. That's from *Heat*, innit? Yeah, I love that movie. Anyway, I listened to my sister, and that's what I do now. First sign of trouble, and I'm out of there. It's like an automatic reaction. Second bit of advice I got from Sally. She used to work here, you know? When I heard someone had killed her, I wanted to go out looking for whoever had done it and make them pay. But I didn't. I listened to the first bit of advice, walk away from trouble."

"What advice did Sally give you?" Fiona asked.

"She told me to get a dog. She said dogs keep you calm. Keep you positive. They distract you. Give you a reason to get out every day in the fresh air. I got Red Bull here and never looked back." He leaned down and made a fuss of his dog, rubbing his floppy, moist muzzle with both hands. In return, Red Bull slathered his tongue all over Adrian's face. He straightened up. "Best two bits of advice I've ever had. Changed my life. Been out of trouble ever since. Thing is, I still look like a troublemaker. I'm always getting stopped by the police, and I still get followed around in shops by store detectives. You know, people cross over the road when they see me and Red Bull coming. But Red Bull wouldn't hurt a fly, and neither would I, well, unless someone was really asking for it."

"So how did you end up at the show?" Fiona asked.

"Okay, so now I'm staying out of trouble, and I'm done with hanging around with a bad crowd. So, I thought I'd have a butcher's at the dog show, maybe get to know some other dog owners. Make some new friends. I'm looking around the place, minding my own business when I see this woman with a big poodle thing. People are crowding around her. I'm curious, wondering if she's a celebrity. Then she starts having trouble breathing, holding her chest and that. And then she collapses. I panicked. My gut reaction to get away from trouble kicked in. I know it sounds harsh, but what was I going to do? And there were loads of people already around her, so I headed for the exit. But on my way there, I pass this vet in her uniform, chatting to a dog owner. I thought, maybe she could help her. I butted into their conversation and told her there was a woman in the crowd who'd collapsed. Once I'd pointed out where she was, that was it. I legged it out of there. That's when I knocked into you. That's the truth, I swear it."

Adrian sat back and folded his arms.

"Before Sylvia collapsed," Fiona said. "Did you see anyone near her? Near enough to inject her?"

"There were loads of people near her. But I didn't see anyone inject her."

"Could you describe any of them?"

"Not really. It was all a bit of a blur."

"Did you see anything suspicious or out of the ordinary?"

Adrian shook his head. "Nah, nothing. Apart from everyone taking pictures of her dog."

"Did you see Sally at the show?" Daisy asked.

"Yeah, of course. We chatted for a bit. She can talk, that one. I made my excuses, said I wanted to have a look around the show."

"And where was this?" Fiona asked.

"Near the main arena. She wanted to film one of the categories."

"Did she seem scared?"

"No, usual, cheerful self." His face became downcast. "I can't believe she's gone."

Fiona took a moment to get her next words in the right order. She didn't want to spook Adrian, provoking him into running away again. But equally she needed to outline the seriousness of his predicament, while also providing him with a solution. A solution she was sure he'd be reluctant to take. Perhaps a bit of positive praise might do the trick. "Well, Adrian. I think you've been very smart in taking your sister's advice, and Sally's."

"You do?" He sounded surprised.

"Absolutely. Not everyone would have the foresight to ask for advice and then have the self-discipline to follow it. So, yes, you've been incredibly smart."

"Oh, er, cheers. No one's ever called me smart before."

"Well, you are. And it's worked out, hasn't it? Kept you on the straight and narrow."

"Definitely."

"And you got Red Bull."

Adrian beamed. "Best thing to ever happen to me."

Fiona took a deep breath. "Thing is, you're going to need to be smart again and take some more good advice. Right now, the police are looking for a guy matching your description, running away from the scene of a murder. The longer they're looking, the worse things are going to get. It'd look much better if you come forward. Tell them exactly what you told us."

"No, no way. I know you mean well. But you're not me. They'll take one look at this." He pointed to his face and made circles around it. "And decide I did it."

Fiona leant forward. "Not without evidence they can't, and you alerted the vet. Why would you do that if you'd just murdered Sylvia Steadman with a lethal injection? And we've already spoken with Julie Sheers the vet, and the police have too — she backs up your story. You panicked, that's all. That's not a crime. Lots of people do."

"And what reason would you have for killing Sylvia Steadman?" Daisy asked.

"I didn't even know her."

"Exactly," Fiona replied. "There's no connection between the two of you, is there?"

Adrian shook his head.

"Have your paths ever crossed?" Fiona asked. "Had any disagreements with her. An argument in a coffee shop. Did she steal your parking spot?"

"No, nothing. First time I'd clapped eyes on her was at the show."

"Then you don't have any motive. Nothing to gain. Whereas there were a lot of people at that show who wouldn't have minded if she suddenly dropped out of the competition."

"Really?" Adrian furrowed his brow in disbelief. "You think a rival dog owner killed her?"

"That's the theory we're working on," said Daisy.

"And you can bet if we are, then the police are too," Fiona added. "You hadn't entered Red Bull into the competition, had you?" They already knew this from scanning the online entries, but it didn't hurt to double check.

"No way. I love Red Bull, but let's be honest, he's no oil painting."

"Ah, he's got a sweet face," Daisy said.

"If you weren't in the competition, what possible reason could you have for killing Sylvia Steadman?" Fiona smiled. "What do you say, Adrian? Fancy clearing your name?"

Adrian sighed. "No. I get where you're coming from but there's no way I'm rocking up to no police station on me tod."

"What if we come with you?" Daisy suggested.

CHAPTER 35

Daisy and Fiona couldn't accompany Adrian into the interview room, so they waited patiently in the lobby of the police station. After DI Fincher and DS Thomas had been notified that the neck-tattooed lad was in the building, they'd appeared immediately, and showed no emotion as they led him through the security door. Did the two detectives feel foolish that they hadn't found the main person of interest in the case, but a couple of charity shop volunteers had? Possibly. But Fiona hoped and prayed that this wouldn't count against him. She was sure they would be professional and after hearing Adrian's story, would see that he hadn't done anything and had simply been in the wrong place at the wrong time.

Fiona became anxious, nervously playing with her hands, wondering if she'd done the right thing. She was sure she had but it was the outcome of the interview that concerned her most. Would they see him as innocent as she and Daisy had, or would this be a chance for them to fit someone up? They'd certainly be under pressure to make an arrest. It didn't help that Red Bull cried the whole time they waited, a constant whimpering for his absent owner. Simon Le Bon decided to show solidarity with his new four-legged friend and joined in.

The desk officer didn't seem to mind the stereo sobbing or the fact there were two dogs in his lobby, so Fiona assumed it was okay. He'd probably seen far worse in here than a couple of lovelorn dogs. Fiona and Daisy employed every trick they knew to keep them calm — rubbing under the chin, gently scratching around the neck and massaging the ears. In the end it was Fiona's box of doggie treats that was the best distraction, highlighting a dog's main priorities: food first, owner second.

After an hour and a half, Adrian emerged through the security door, his face beaming.

They'd released him without charge.

Relief is the most wonderful tonic and Adrian had transformed into a new being. Light and sunny, all that fear and stress he'd been holding onto had melted away. His spirit had been lifted and there was an unquenchable light in his eyes.

The second Red Bull caught sight of his owner, he sprang forward and leapt up on his hind legs, tail whipping back and forth. Adrian crouched down to embrace him, his face getting drenched with licks. Not to be outdone, Simon Le Bon joined in.

"What did they say?" Daisy asked.

"Oh man, they asked me a ton of questions. I was so nervous. But I took your advice and answered as honestly as I could."

"What sort of questions?" Fiona asked.

"It was details they were after. Loads of them. I guess they were trying to trip me up. Kept asking me about my movements at the show. Exactly where I was and when things happened. I suppose, like you said, to see if it tallied up with what the vet had said. Which I'm guessing it did because they stopped asking about that and moved on to asking me where I was yesterday."

Daisy gasped. "When Sally was murdered!"

"What did you tell them?" Fiona asked.

"I was shaking all the time. But I held my nerve. I was in Chichester all day. I do house clearances. It's not regular work but it suits me because I can take Red Bull with me in the cab, and it's cash in hand. It was an early start. Heading up the M27, I stopped at Rownhams services for a quick slash and a coffee. They asked me for every detail — the address of the house I was clearing, the reg of my van, what time I stopped at the service station. Anyway, so the big, older copper writes this all down, then goes out the room. Half an hour later he returns and gives the woman copper a tiny nod of the head. Then she said I was free to go. Released me without charge."

"He must've gone out to do an ANPR search to verify your story," Fiona said.

"What's ANPR?" asked Adrian.

"There are special cameras on the motorway and on a lot of main roads that can read the number plates of vehicles as they pass. If your van had been on the motorway, the ANPR cameras would've picked it up. The police would've been able to pinpoint exactly where it was on the day in question to back up your story. They might have also got access to CCTV footage of you going into the service station to buy coffee. If all that happened at the same time as Sally's estimated time of death, then you couldn't be her killer."

"Your house clearance gave you a watertight alibi." Daisy smiled.

Adrian puffed his cheeks out. "Wow, that's the last time I complain about work. I got lucky there. I mean, the coppers don't want me skipping town or nothing, in case they need to ask me some other questions, but apart from that, it's all good. I'm free!" Adrian couldn't help himself and gave them both huge hugs. "Thank you so much. I owe you one. If there's anything you need. Anyone you want sorting out, I'm here for you."

Fiona gave him a nervous smile. "You're welcome, Adrian, and we appreciate the offer. But I'm sure you wouldn't want to get in any more trouble."

"Yeah, yeah, of course. Ignore what I just said. I'm just excited, that's all."

At that moment, Faye appeared in the lobby, her face desperate for answers about her brother. "Adrian. What happened?"

"It's all fine. No charges. I'm free to go."

Faye shuddered and almost collapsed on the spot. When she'd recovered, she launched herself at her brother and wrapped her arms tightly around him.

"Steady on, sis," Adrian gasped. "You're gonna crack a rib."

She loosened her grip and wiped a tear away. "Sorry, I've been so worried about you. Been feeling terrible about all this. So guilty."

"What have you got to feel guilty about?" Adrian asked.

"I feel responsible for you. You're my little brother."

"Well, everything's okay, thanks to these ladies."

Faye released Adrian and turned to shake Fiona's and Daisy's hands. "Thank you so much. You've taken a weight off my shoulders."

"Our pleasure. Happy to help."

Adrian checked his phone. "It's well after teatime, and I'm starving. Who's up for some celebratory pub grub?"

Daisy's eyes lit up. "I can never say no to a pie."

"Me neither," Fiona agreed.

"And this is on me," said Faye.

CHAPTER 36

Next day, Partial Sue had been grumpy all morning. She hadn't told them why, but Fiona could guess. It was because she'd missed out on a slap-up meal in the pub — her third favourite place after a tea shop and a car boot sale. That was bad enough, as she was extremely partial to a freshly pulled pint of conker-coloured ale accompanied by a steaming steak and kidney pie with chips cut thick enough to use in Jenga, but even more disappointing was that someone else had paid for it. For a person who watched their pennies, that was the Holy Grail for Partial Sue, especially if said Holy Grail had been full of piping hot gravy to dip her chips in. With hindsight, Fiona knew that she should've called and asked her to meet them at the George (where the gravy was particularly spectacular) but with all the excitement of Adrian being eliminated from enquiries, it had slipped her mind.

Apart from Partial Sue feeling left out, there was another small downside to Adrian clearing his name. Fiona guessed that the police, like them, had probably pinned their hopes on him being the killer. He'd been seen by multiple witnesses, running away from the scene of the crime, which usually put you top of the list of suspects. Sure, there were other people of interest, the other competitors, but so far, the ones they had talked to had yielded nothing. They all had alibis. And the ones they hadn't spoken to yet, well, Fiona knew they'd be following in the footsteps of DI Fincher and DS Thomas, who'd already interviewed them. It was unlikely they'd uncover anything new. Fiona had to face facts. Now Adrian was out of the picture, they were back to square one. No closer to finding out who the killer was. To make matters worse, now that Sally Wilde had also been murdered, they were possibly looking at a fledgeling serial killer who might have designs on taking out the whole of the competition. Another life could be taken at any moment. They needed to take a different path, untrodden by the police. One that would give them a breakthrough. Fast.

Molly placed a pot of tea in the centre of the table, next to a neatly sliced cake cut into perfect eighths. "Help yourself to Vicky sponge."

Partial Sue snatched up the pot first and filled her mug, fearing the tea would be lukewarm because of Molly's kettle-cooling tactics.

Fiona helped herself to a wedge of cake. "I think we should take a new angle on this case."

"Why should we do that?" Partial Sue snapped, clearly still upset.

"Have you got pie envy because we went to the pub yesterday?" Daisy asked innocently.

"No, I have not got pie envy," Partial Sue answered in a tone that implied the opposite. "Fiona, please continue."

Fiona thought for a moment. "I think we should spend a bit of time looking into who Sylvia was as a person."

"Do you mean asking her friends?" Daisy asked. "Because she liked keeping people at arm's length, according to her social media."

"I was thinking more about the people she used to work with." Partial Sue plated a slice of cake. "What, at Bristol City Council?"

Fiona shook her head. "That was my first thought, except the police would have already been there and done that and have nothing to show for it, seeing as they've made no arrests. I was thinking of something more left field. More dog-related. Something that the police might not have cottoned onto yet."

"What's that?" Partial Sue asked.

"The Good Companion dog-food ads. Specifically, the production company who made them. They'd have a pretty good idea of what Sylvia was like, she made enough of them. I've heard film shoots are quite gruelling. Early starts, late finishes, even for little thirty-second ads. It can bring out the worst in people. Maybe she was demanding, a bit of a diva on set. Made an enemy of one of the crew, and they'd decided to get revenge."

Daisy finished her tea. "But if that's the case, what about Sally? Why would anyone on that film crew want to kill Sally?"

"As cover," Partial Sue suggested. "Say, someone on the crew had it in for Sylvia. Maybe Sylvia mistreated them. Bullied them on set. There's a chance others saw it too. To avoid suspicion, this person kills Sylvia somewhere totally unrelated, at a dog show. Then kills another competitor just to be on the safe side, to make it look like it's a jealous rival bumping off the competition and nothing to do with the world of film production."

"That's an excellent point, Sue," Fiona remarked.

Molly looked doubtful. "Those ads were made ages ago. That's a long time to wait for revenge."

"Or the killer's bided their time," Partial Sue replied. "Waited on purpose so their actions wouldn't be connected with the dog ads."

"Yeah, and there's no sell-by date on revenge," Daisy said. "It's like the green beans in Waitrose, they don't have sell-by dates on them anymore. You just have to use your common sense now."

"There's no such thing as a sell-by date," Partial Sue said. "It's use-by or best before . . . Sorry, Fiona, we're getting side-tracked. So what should we do next?"

"Well, first we need to do our research. Find out who made the ads — the production company."

Daisy thumbed away on her phone. "They're called Trelane Film Productions."

Molly sat stunned at Daisy's technological prowess. "Jeez, how did you do that so quickly?"

"It's Daisy's superpower." Fiona went onto her phone to fact-check Daisy's findings.

"That and being very good with extremely fiddly things." Daisy wiggled her fingers in the air. "I have small pixie hands. Perfect for making my doll's houses. Would you like to see some of them, Molly?"

She didn't look too thrilled at this prospect. Before Daisy had a chance to inflict Molly with photographic evidence of her vast collection, Fiona interrupted. "Yep, Trelane Film Productions are the ones who made the ads. Owned by Greg Trelane. Based in Soho, London."

To Molly's obvious relief, Daisy suddenly lost interest in showing off her doll-house craftsmanship. "Ooh, can we have a trip to London? Can we? I love going to London. We could go up on the train and after talking to this company we could watch the buskers in Covent Garden. It's really close to Soho, and they're very good. Then have dinner at the Ivy followed by a spot of shopping and then a show in the evening. Oh, please, it would be lovely."

In the briefest of moments, Daisy had mapped out a whole itinerary for a day in the capital. The rapidity of her planning made Partial Sue's head wobble. "Steady on, Dais. We haven't even spoken to these people yet."

"Let's see if we can get an appointment first," Fiona said. "Then if there's time afterwards, maybe we can take in some sights. But if we discover something significant, we may have to come straight home."

Gleefully, Daisy clapped her hands together. "Would you like to come, Molly?"

"No. I can't," Molly replied. "I have to pick up Dina from school."

"Oh, that's a shame."

Molly smiled. "Honestly, it's fine, and you'll need someone to man the shop while you're away."

"Oh yes, would you mind?" Fiona asked.

"Not at all. Although I'll have to close up while I collect Dina, but I can bring her back here afterwards. She can help out. She'll love that."

"Are you sure you don't mind, Molly? You're doing us a big favour."

"No, I'll be fine."

Fiona took a deep breath. "Right. Let's see if we can get some answers." She dialled the number on their website and put it on speaker phone. The call was answered after the first ring.

"Hello, Trelane Film Productions, Tanya speaking. How may I help you?" said a young, monotone voice that wasn't particularly friendly or helpful, and was probably watching TikTok on her phone while speaking on the company's landline.

Fiona thought it best to start at the top of the company and work her way down. "Oh, hello. Can I speak to Greg Trelane, please?"

"Who's calling?"

"My name is Fiona Sharp."

"And what is your call regarding?"

"I'm phoning about Sylvia Steadman. She was murdered."

"Oh, yes. Did she play a dead body in *Line of Duty*?"

"No, she's not an actress. Er, well, I suppose she is, I mean she was. Her dog Charlie won Crufts. They starred in several ads your company made for Good Companion dog food. But she really was murdered. We're investigating her death, and we really need to ask Greg Trelane some questions."

Tanya didn't react or show the slightest emotion or comprehension. Perhaps she'd only just joined the company. "Oh, okay. Let me just try his extension."

She clicked off. Fiona got a dose of banal, royalty-free dance music played in her ear while she waited. A second later Tanya came back on again. "I'm afraid he's not available at the moment. But I can leave him a message. Get him to call you back."

"Is there anyone else we could speak to?"

Tanya spoke rapidly. "No, no one's available at the moment. They're all very busy, I'm afraid. All I can do is pass on the message. Very sorry. Have a nice day."

She hung up before Fiona had a chance to ask her anything else.

A cynical Partial Sue said, "She's giving you the fob off."

Fiona was still hopeful. "Let's give her the benefit of the doubt. We'll try again after lunch."

Lunch came and went and despite trying again and again, and asking to speak to different people, from production assistants to admin assistants, no one at Trelane Productions would take their calls. Without mentioning anything about Sylvia Steadman, Partial Sue even pretended to be from the tax office and used some of her accountancy jargon, which comprised of using threatening codes starting with 'P' and 'S', but Tanya would not put her through to anyone, not even the company accountant.

If Fiona didn't know better, she'd say Trelane Productions were hiding something.

CHAPTER 37

Fiona was first to arrive at the shop on Monday morning. After unlocking the door, she unclipped Simon Le Bon, who scuttled off inside to have a sniff around. On her way to work, Fiona had been psyching herself up for another round of calling Trelane Productions, hoping to catch Tanya off guard first thing in the morning. That came to an abrupt halt when she glanced down at what was waiting for her on the doormat.

Her verbal clash with the receptionist would have to wait. In front of her feet, sat another plain envelope. Same as before, bearing a sticky label printed with her name in Helvetica. Except this time, it also included Sue's and Daisy's names.

Without thinking, she bent down and snatched it up. Carefully prising open the adhesive flap, she reached in and plucked out its contents. As before, it contained a single, heavyweight sheet of paper folded in three. She unfurled it and read:

I know who did it.
Meet me at 11.00 today at these coordinates:
50^{0} 49'40" N 1^{0} 44'25" W
Do not tell anyone.

A surge of adrenaline swelled in her chest. Turning over the note in her hands, she checked there was nothing else on it. Same as before. Just three lines. Simple, clear and stark. Presumably from the Grey Man, but this time he wanted to meet and hopefully share vital information, knowledge he'd previously been too scared to impart. More and more hits of adrenalin caused Fiona to judder. Part excitement and part intrigue, this was what they had been waiting for. They would finally meet the elusive and rather timid Grey Man, and hear what he had to say. Would Sylvia Steadman's and Sally Wilde's killer be revealed at eleven o'clock? Fiona caught herself before she got overly optimistic. It might be too good to be true. Things like this often are. She had no idea how good the quality of his information might be. It might not even be accurate or true. But she couldn't help quivering with anticipation. Besides, this person had gone to great and cautious lengths to cover his tracks. No one would create that much secrecy unless it was of great importance, or they were deluded, which could also be a possibility.

Fiona's hands shook as she carried the note inside. Simon Le Bon stared at her from his basket with a pair of curious chocolate-drop eyes, sensing Fiona wasn't quite her normal self. She needed a cup of tea to calm her. Several to say the least.

She'd just filled the pot and set it down on the table when Partial Sue bundled in, a wiry ball of energy. "Morning Fi." She spied the steaming pot, as she shrugged off her coat. "That's what I like to see, the tea all ready and waiting."

"If you think that's good. Wait until you see this." Fiona held the note aloft.

Partial Sue snatched it out of her hands, her eyes scanning along the small lines of text, while her mouth hung open. "He wants to meet you."

Fiona handed her the envelope, addressed to all three of them. "Not just me."

Partial Sue's eyes became wider. "What shall we do?"

Daisy came in with Molly behind her. "Morning," they chorused.

Partial Sue held out the note and the envelope. "We got another message from the Grey Man. He wants to meet us. Well, you, me and Fiona."

The pair of them hurried over to the table. "You're kidding," Daisy said. "Let me see." Gingerly, she took the note and the envelope, carefully examining their brief content while Molly glanced over her shoulder.

"Looks like he's plucked up the courage to spill the beans," Molly said. "Must be important if he's gone to all this trouble."

"My thoughts exactly," said Fiona.

Partial Sue poured herself some tea. "Are we going to meet him?"

"Yes, I think we should. I want to find out what he has to say."

Daisy became anxious. "Are you sure it's safe? Maybe he's the killer and wants to make us his next victims."

"I don't think a murderer would want all three of you there," Molly said. "He'd be outnumbered."

Daisy remained doubtful.

"Where's this place he wants to meet?" asked Partial Sue. "Have you found it online?"

Fiona produced her phone and showed them a map. "It's here. In the New Forest. Bagnum Garden Centre, just outside Burley."

Everyone's shoulders relaxed. The Grey Man wanted to meet in a public place. Not just any old public place, but a garden centre.

Daisy's demeanour instantly softened at this news. "Nothing bad ever happens in a garden centre."

The intoxicating mix of well-ordered horticulture and associated products made garden centres the epitome of calm, attracting the most genteel clientele. The only place safer would have been a police station.

"Why didn't you say that in the first place? I am partial to a good garden centre."

Daisy's eyes gleamed at the prospect. "We could go to the restaurant for lunch afterwards. I've always said garden centres do the best food. Such good value for money."

"Maybe he wants to meet you in the restaurant," Molly conjectured.

Daisy's face lit up. "Do you think?"

Fiona had to agree. "That would make sense."

Daisy went online and Googled Bagnum Garden Centre. "Yes! They've got a restaurant!"

"Do they do roast dinners?" asked Partial Sue.

"Only on Sundays. But I'm sure they'll be serving something scrummy like cauliflower cheese or shepherd's pie, and I wouldn't mind browsing the plants afterwards. I'd love to get a lemon tree. Make my own lemonade."

Partial Sue huffed cynically. "Would it survive in our climate?"

"They covered this on *Gardeners' Question Time*. As long as you bring them inside during the winter and put them in a sunny spot during the summer, they're fine."

"Well, I never. I like the sound of growing my own lemons. I am partial to homemade lemonade."

In the space of a short conversation, it had gone from being a risky mission to meet a shady informant, to the ladies going out for a jolly: a hearty meal, followed by a potter around to stock up on garden goodies. Fiona had to agree that it sounded like the perfect way to spend a long lunchbreak, but she had to remind them and herself of the real reason they were going. "I don't want to sound like a bore. But let's just remember, we're there to find information about the killer."

Daisy blushed. "Sorry. I got a bit carried away."

"No need to apologise," Fiona replied. "Garden centres have that effect. I once went in to get some twine and came out with a pair of fleece-lined slippers, secateurs and two-for-one on some hanging baskets." She turned her attention to Molly. "Would you mind holding down the fort while we're gone?"

"Of course, no problem," Molly replied.

"We'll be back before you have to pick up Dina. If not, call the police," Partial Sue joked.

"I think you'll be fine." Molly grinned. "It's only a garden centre. Not a dark alleyway at midnight."

They all giggled.

CHAPTER 38

There were two main roads through the New Forest. The A31 and the A35. They'd picked the A31 because they thought it would be quicker, being a dual carriageway. But not today. In their haste to get there, they hadn't checked the traffic reports. Roadworks had strangled the two carriageways into a single, sluggish line of vehicles at Poulner Hill just outside Ringwood. Partial Sue's Fiat Uno crawled up the endless incline, stuck behind a large lorry with a sticker on its bumper that read: *How is my driving?* There was an 0800 number underneath it. Fiona wondered if anyone actually called it to say, yes, it's actually rather good.

Partial Sue slumped forward on the steering wheel and groaned. "We're going to be late. We should have gone the other way."

"Well, it's easy to say that with hindsight," Fiona replied. "I should've checked the traffic before we left. I hope the Grey Man will still be there."

Two minutes after turning off the main road into the forest proper, they hit another, slightly smaller delay, although a much cuter one. Up ahead, a New Forest pony stood in the middle of the road like a four-legged statue.

These adorable creatures with their pretty eyes and swishing tails roamed free in the forest, which meant they could take their sweet time going where they pleased. This one currently straddled the white lines, holding up cars in both directions, fixated at the weird humans sitting in their strange little boxes on wheels. You could get irritated about roadworks and broken-down lorries holding you up, but it was impossible to shake your fist when it was an adorable chestnut-coloured pony causing the delay. Lucky that Simon Le Bon had been left behind with Molly, as he'd have his front paws up on the dashboard, barking his head off by now, thinking it was some oversized dog with strange-shaped paws. Eventually, the pony had had enough of people-watching and decided that the verge on the other side of the road looked more interesting.

Once they were safely past, and had said their collective 'ahs,' Partial Sue put her foot down, accelerating hard but keeping the vehicle under the forty mile an hour speed limit.

They were just about to hit the outskirts of the village of Burley, when Fiona spotted the sign for Bagnum Garden Centre. Partial Sue nearly overshot the turning, braking at the last minute. Taking a hard right, she pointed the car down a narrow, noisy gravel lane, flanked by dense woodland. After a while, the lane opened up into a car park and they found themselves in front of a wide, single-storey garden centre. They'd made it with a minute to spare.

Resembling a traditional American prairie house only lower and wider, it was clad in horizontal dark wood planks. A deep veranda ran the entire length of its frontage and beneath overhanging eaves racks of metal shelving enticed visitors with bargains before they'd even set foot in the place. But there would be no enticing today. The shelves were cold and empty, as was the car park.

"It looks closed for the day," Daisy said, disappointed.

"I'd say it looks abandoned," Fiona added.

"But it had a website and everything." Daisy was clearly upset that there would be no purchasing of any lemon trees today and certainly no noshing on cauliflower cheese or shepherd's pie.

"Depends," said Partial Sue. "Place could have gone bankrupt, but the website is paid up for the year. Still running because no one's bothered to take it down."

"What shall we do?" Daisy asked.

Fiona rubbed her chin. "Well, seeing as how our informant is the cautious type, maybe he's chosen this place because it's secluded, and no one's here."

"I don't like the look of it," said Daisy.

"Me neither," Partial Sue agreed.

"We should at least see if he's here."

"It doesn't look like anyone's here," Partial Sue replied.

"Think of it from his point of view," Fiona explained. "He's scared to reveal who he is, so he's not exactly going to stand outside with a welcome banner. He's going to stay out of view."

"Okay," Partial Sue agreed. "We'll have a quick look for him together. But no splitting up like those idiots in films. I hate it when they do that. It's so obvious something bad's going to happen."

"Right, we stick together," Fiona said. "No wandering off."

"I still don't like this." Daisy trembled.

Fiona reassured her. "We won't be long. We'll stay close to the car in case we need to get out of here fast."

Daisy reluctantly agreed. After they'd all exited the vehicle, she left the passenger door wide open, then went around the other side to open the driver's door.

"What are you doing?" asked Partial Sue.

"Leaving the doors open. Like Fiona said, in case we need to make a quick getaway like Starsky and Hutch."

"Are you planning on doing a bonnet slide, as well?" Fiona asked.

"Well, maybe. If needs be," Daisy replied without a hint of irony.

"I've always wondered where the police learn to do that," said Partial Sue. "Do you think there's a course?"

Fiona smiled. "Come on, let's see if we can find our Grey Man."

They headed up the shallow ramp to the main entrance of the building. Fiona gave the double doors a try, but they were firmly locked. Edging along the veranda behind the racks of vacant metal shelves, they took it in turns peering through the darkened windows. All they could glimpse was the empty interior of an abandoned garden centre, the silhouettes of more empty shelves.

They reached the end, where the veranda met a high fence enclosing an outside area which would've normally been full of racks of large decorative pots and benches of hardy, outdoor plants, and possibly, during the summer, one of Daisy's sought-after lemon trees. The area was empty, apart from a discarded bucket on its side and a length of hosepipe snaking its way over the ground, the other end still attached to a tap poking out of a wall.

"Hello!" Fiona called out, in case the Grey Man was concealed behind one of the racks. She tried again but there was no response. "Let's try the other side."

They headed back past the double doors to another outdoor area on the right-hand side of the building, this one less secure. More of a display area, it contained a variety of small wooden buildings arranged in a hotchpotch layout. Some stood on artificial grass, while others had their own decking and patios out front. It was an assortment of sheds and garden rooms, and as they wandered between them, they glimpsed through the windows to find that each one had been modelled to show different uses. One was a home gym. There was a yoga room complete with those giant bouncy balls, although they had deflated somewhat, and another was an art studio. Another had been decked out like a miniature pub complete with bar, hand pumps and stools. Fiona tried a couple of doors. Same story. Locked up tightly.

"Hello," Fiona called out. "Hello."

They waited. Again, no response.

"I don't think anyone's home," said Daisy.

"Well, that's that," said Partial Sue. "We tried."

The place appeared to be deserted. There didn't seem to be any other option. Fiona conceded, "Okay, let's go."

As they turned around to head back to the car, from behind them they heard a shrill, "Pssst!"

Startled, they spun around to see the doors of a garden room slightly ajar, the farthest one away from where they stood. Through the small gap in the door, a woman desperately beckoned for them to come inside. A woman they recognised.

"Molly?"

CHAPTER 39

"Quick, inside," Molly urged them in a whisper bordering on a shout.

"Molly what are you doing here?" asked Fiona. "I thought you were back at the shop."

She put her finger to her lips to shush her and frantically waved them inside.

The three women rushed towards the garden room, glancing left and right, as if some villain might leap out and grab them at any moment. As soon as they stepped inside, Molly slammed the door behind them. A cluster of small spotlights lit up the windowless garden room, which had been mocked up to resemble a music studio. A guitar was propped up in the corner next to a keyboard and a small sound desk. On closer inspection they were fakes, made of hollow, moulded plastic but realistic none the less. However, the walls and ceiling were lined with thick and squishy acoustic foam, with a repeating pattern of geometric protrusions to soak up any unwanted noise.

"Molly, what's going on?" Fiona's words sounded odd and unsettling, echoless. "What are you doing here?"

"I'm the Grey Man," she announced.

They exchanged puzzled looks.

"What? I don't understand."

"You will in a minute."

Partial Sue had a more practical question on her mind. "If you're the Grey Man, why have you dragged us all the way out here? Why couldn't you just say what you had to say back at the shop?"

Molly chuckled to herself. "Because I needed a ruse to get you all out here."

Fiona felt her stomach drop down a lift shaft and tinnitus ringing in her ears. Something was very wrong. Standing in front of the door, blocking the exit, Molly produced a stun gun from her pocket. Fiona had seen one of these before, in the hands of Molly's parents.

Molly swayed, giddy with her own smug superiority. "Let me just say, you three are so easy to play. Some amateur sleuths you are. Make up some mysterious Grey Man with information about the killer and arrange to meet at a garden centre, and you're anyone's. I knew you wouldn't be able to resist my trap."

"But we saw the Grey Man on the video Sally played to us," Daisy said. "You pointed him out."

Molly sniggered, derisively. "I have no idea who that was. Just some blurred guy in the crowd. I saw an opportunity to embellish my story and you fell for it."

Fiona had had enough of all her self-congratulatory claptrap. "Why are you doing all this?"

Her mood suddenly switched, voice prickling with anger. "You know why? Did you really think you'd get away with putting my parents behind bars? That there wouldn't be consequences?"

Partial Sue folded her arms. "Er, they weren't put away because of us, they were put away because they're murderers. We just happened to catch them."

Molly glared at them. "My parents would do anything for me. They did it so I could give Dina the perfect childhood — the one that I never had. I guilt-tripped them into it."

This was news to Fiona. News to all of them. "Wait, you put them up to it?"

"Of course I did. It was all my idea. Planned it all along. They just put it into action. They do whatever I tell them to do."

Fiona's stomach plummeted some more, while the tinnitus whined a little louder. All along, everyone thought Molly had been the innocent one. The sweet, quiet, single parent who was unlucky enough to have a psychopathic mother and father prepared to kill for their darling daughter behind her back. The ladies had felt sorry for her. But she had been pulling the strings all along. The spoilt brat who'd bullied her parents into getting what she wanted. "I told them, under no circumstances were they to say anything if they got caught. Keep me out of it."

"Oh, that's thoughtful of you," Fiona replied. "So, you made them take the fall."

Molly tutted, as if it were so obvious. "Of course. Who'd bring up Dina if I was in prison? She'd be in care. I couldn't have that. But now my little girl is growing up without any grandparents thanks to you, and I've got no support. No one to look after Dina if I want to go somewhere."

"You could leave her with social services," Partial Sue muttered. "She'd be better off away from you."

"I'm a good mother!" She waved the stun gun in Partial Sue's face.

Partial Sue kept her cool. "Did you kill Sylvia Steadman?"

Molly sighed. "Course I didn't. Nothing to do with me. Why would I want to kill her? And before you ask, I have no idea who did. But I did kill Sally Wilde."

The three ladies gasped.

"Why did you kill Sally?" Fiona demanded.

"What did she ever do to you?" Partial Sue added.

Molly thought carefully, furrowing her brows. "She was on to me. I know she was. Said she was good at reading people. Did that thing with the sandwiches, guessing your favourites. But when she came to me, she stopped, said I was hiding something. She recognised me. Knew what my parents did. She knew what I was up to. I could see it in her eyes. I had to get her out of the way, or she would've blown my cover, ruined my plans to deal with you lot."

Molly was clearly paranoid and delusional as if they hadn't guessed already.

"You nasty so-and-so," Daisy snarled, stepping forward, surprising all of them, not least Molly. "She wasn't on to you. She just couldn't tell what sandwich you liked, that's all. And your story's been all over the news. She had no idea what you were up to. You killed her for nothing."

"Get back!" Molly warned. She shoved the two prongs towards Daisy, forcing her back. "You know, out of the three of you, you're the one I despised most."

Fiona wondered how anyone could dislike Daisy. There was nothing to dislike.

Molly continued her bitter monologue. "You. With your fiddly fingers and bloody doll's houses, and always talking about food and cake and what you're having for tea."

"Now that's not fair," Partial Sue interrupted. "We all do that."

"Shut up." Molly turned her venom on all three of them. "You're all so irritatingly twee and nice. Apart from when you were discussing the murder, I had to listen to your inane conversations about sell-by dates and who has the best bags for life, M&S or Waitrose, or your favourite car park. Honestly, I thought I was going mad. It was like being trapped inside a bad sitcom, the ones that aren't funny. The sort you watch on a Sunday night because there's nothing else on."

"I happen to like Sunday night TV," Daisy said defiantly.

"So do I," Partial Sue agreed. "*Countryfile* to kick off, then *Call The Midwife*, followed by a solid police drama like *Happy Valley*."

"Oh, I do like Sarah Lancashire," Daisy added. "She used to be in *Corrie*, you know."

"Was she?" Partial Sue sounded pleasantly surprised. Molly's face became inflamed. "See! This is what I'm talking about! I'm standing here holding a stun gun, threatening your lives, and you're discussing the telly!"

"You're the one who brought it up," Partial Sue countered.

Molly shook with an anger that she'd been bottling up all this time. Fiona had to change the subject fast, or she feared Molly might use her weapon on them, possibly starting with Partial Sue and then Daisy. "How did you know what to inject Sally with, to make it look like the dog show murderer? Police haven't revealed that yet."

This halted Molly in her tracks. A chance to boast was always certain to distract murderers. "I didn't know. I just used window cleaner. Close enough. Did the trick. But the police bought it, I think, and so did you. Very convenient having another killer out there to take the blame."

"Are you going to kill us with window cleaner?" Daisy asked.

"No, I've got something special lined up for you three, which is why I brought you here. My parents will be locked away for good, so you're going to suffer the same fate. I'm locking you in here. And don't bother shouting for help, as you can see it's nicely soundproofed and no one ever comes here. There's no signal or Wi-Fi either, but just to be on the safe side, throw your phones on the floor then kick them to me."

The ladies did as they were told and sent their mobiles skidding across the floor. Molly scooped them up and slipped them into her coat pocket. "That's why I chose this place. No signal, deserted with a ready-made soundproof prison."

"Wait," Partial Sue said. "After we left the shop, how did you get here before us?"

She flashed a self-satisfied grin. "I waited for a day when both main roads through the forest had roadworks on them, so it didn't matter which one you took, you'd still get held up. That allowed me to take the quiet back roads, get here before you. They also have the added bonus of no traffic cameras, so my car wouldn't be detected. I left it out of sight and snuck in across the woodlands."

"You won't get away with this," Fiona said.

"I think I already have. I'm just smarter than you. Thought of everything. I'll be the one who raises the alarm when you don't come into work tomorrow morning, making myself look innocent. And when the police come calling, I'll say I had no idea where you were going because you kept it a secret. The note they find on your dead bodies will back that up. The police will put two and two together and pin it on the dog show killer posing as an informant to lure you into a trap to silence you. I mean, that's if they find your dead bodies. Who's going to know you're here?" Molly grinned.

"Er, hold on," Partial Sue said. "Won't they get suspicious that Sylvia's killer hasn't used the same method of murder — lethal injection."

Molly shrugged. "Doesn't matter. Different circumstances. You know what police are like. They'll come up with a loose theory to make it fit. Injecting three people at once is tricky for one person. I mean, I briefly considered it but found this was easier, and more poetic. You get to rot in here just like my parents in prison. Although having said that, with all this acoustic foam, it's pretty airtight. You'll probably die from lack of oxygen first."

"Wait," Fiona exclaimed. "What's going to happen to Simon Le Bon?"

A sadistic smiled played on Molly's face. "Oh, don't worry, he's tucked up in bed, back at the shop. I'm going to adopt him. Dina's always wanted a dog."

"He's my dog. Not yours!" Fiona shrieked.

The end of the stun gun sparked violently. "Behave or I swear, I'll use this!"

Fiona flinched.

"Now it's time I was going." Molly reached behind her and yanked the door open. "Oh, I've got one more surprise for you." Slipping out quickly, she closed the door and locked it.

A second later. The garden room plunged into darkness.

CHAPTER 40

"She's left us in the dark!" Partial Sue exclaimed, almost as if this were worse than being imprisoned.

"I can't see a thing!" Daisy shrieked. "What are we going to do?" She began panting, not coping with this situation at all. "I don't like it."

Fiona ignored the deafening ring of tinnitus in her ears. "It's okay, Daisy. We're going to be alright."

"We're locked in an airtight, soundproof box. How is this going to be alright?" Partial Sue asked.

Daisy gasped for air. "I feel odd, like I can't breathe."

Fiona needed Daisy to be calm. She was key to getting out of there in every sense of the word, but not if she was on the verge of a panic attack. "First things first. Take your inhaler."

They heard Daisy rummaging around in her bag, then two sharp puffing sounds.

"Better?" Fiona asked.

"Yes, a bit."

Fiona ran her hands along the thick and bumpy, sponge walls, searching for the door or what she presumed was the door. Every inch of the interior felt identical. Eventually she located a handle embedded in the soft foam. She gave it a try.

Locked solid. She shouldered the door several times. Beneath the foam, the solid door didn't budge. "That's not going anywhere."

"What are we going to do?" Daisy asked, still fearful.

"Do you have your lockpicks?"

"No, but I think I've got some hairpins." Daisy sifted through her bag once more. "Got them."

"Great, now can you make them into lockpicks in the dark?"

"I don't know," Daisy replied.

"You can do it, Dais," Partial Sue encouraged her.

"Normally I could, but my hands are shaking so much. I'm worried we're going to die."

"Don't think about that," Fiona reassured her. "One step at a time. All you're doing at the moment is bending some thin metal to make the, er, what are they called again?"

"The tension wrench and the pick."

"Focus on that, and that alone, and take your time."

The room became silent, apart from the odd grunt now and again in the darkness. It didn't take Daisy long. "Done it." She sounded more confident now.

"Fantastic," Fiona said. "Now, can you pick a lock in the dark?"

"You don't need your eyes," Daisy explained. "It's all about feeling your way."

"Thank goodness for that," Partial Sue said with a sigh, "because I can't see a thing in here."

"Head over to where I am," said Fiona. "Follow my voice."

The floor creaked ominously as delicate footfalls approached Fiona in the dark. When Daisy was standing next to her, she took her by the hand and gently guided it to where the handle was. "Think you can pick it?"

"Piece of cake. Just need to get down on the floor." They heard Daisy shift position, then groan, "Uh-oh, that's not good."

"What's the matter?" asked Partial Sue. "Is it your knees? Crouching down plays havoc on my knees."

"No, there's no keyhole."

"There must be."

"Well, see if you can find it, because I can't."

In the darkness, Fiona and Partial Sue scrabbled around below the door handle in an attempt to locate the elusive keyhole, their fingers desperately searching among all that foam.

"You're right. There isn't one," Partial Sue concluded.

"Maybe it only locks from the outside," Daisy suggested.

Partial Sue became anxious. "If it does then we're stuffed. Stuck here, and I'm starting to get a headache. Lack of oxygen does that."

Fiona had to divert the conversation away from the awful conclusion. Keep them positive. Keep them calm. "You wouldn't have a door that can only be opened from the outside, not in a public place. It's probably been covered over by the sound insulation. We need to remove it."

Instantly, the ladies clawed away at the foam. Hands attempting to tear away big lumps of the stuff. It was tougher than expected and wouldn't yield to their efforts, springing back into place.

"Must be glued on. We need something sharp," Fiona suggested.

"I know just the thing." They heard Partial Sue clomp across the room, knocking into the only objects in there: the mock musical instruments. Next came a stamp of a foot and a shattering of plastic. Partial Sue returned, placing large shards of broken plastic into their hands. "This should do the trick."

Armed with makeshift tools, the three of them attacked the foam, stabbing and raking it.

"Ow!" Daisy cried.

Partial Sue apologised. "Sorry, that was me."

"You know, I think just one of us should do this," Fiona suggested. "We're going to end up cutting our hands to ribbons, and we need Daisy's intact."

"You do it, Sue," Daisy said.

Partial Sue didn't need asking twice. In the pitch black they heard a mixture of hacking and scraping and panting as she went at the foam. "Jeez, this stuff is strong." About five minutes later, the noise ceased, replaced by a different one. They heard her picking at the door with her fingernails. "I think I've found it. Just got to clear the hole."

"Good work, Sue."

"There, all ready for you, Daisy."

Feet shuffled, as the two ladies swapped position. The room descended into a dense silence. Then, louder than they'd ever heard them before, came the scratching of Daisy's lockpicks inside the tumbler. There were clicks and clacks and heavy breathing, and although they couldn't see her, they could sense her concentration, intense and focused. A few groans and sighs followed. That was to be expected. Fiona knew from experience of watching Daisy that every lock had its own personality. Until you got to know it intimately, it was a trial-and-error exercise in which you could get so far only to have the pins inside the lock fall back into place and have to start again.

Fiona had no idea how much time had elapsed. Though she tried to remain coolheaded, she couldn't prevent the slow creep of paranoia, its cold hands encircling her throat. Why was Daisy taking so long? She never normally took this long. Unhelpful thoughts turned to distressing what ifs. What if Daisy couldn't pick the lock? What if they couldn't escape? How long would it take them to die? Surely lack of oxygen would kill them before dehydration. Her breath snagged in her throat and her lungs tightened.

Daisy's lockpicks continued clicking away. A metallic Morse code. But then came one click deeper and more solid than the rest. It was accompanied by the delicious rotation of machined metal inside machined metal.

Brightness blinded their daylight-starved eyes as Daisy flung the door wide open.

CHAPTER 41

Fiona had decided to play it safe. They all had. After what they'd just been through — a near-death experience — there was no point in tempting fate, poking it with a sharp stick and asking if it would like to have another go. Molly was armed and dangerous and none of them fancied getting several thousand volts from a stun gun. Plus, Fiona had Simon Le Bon to think about. He could become an unwitting hostage in the whole situation, and she was not prepared to take that chance, no matter how satisfying it would be to see Molly's smug face drop when they strolled back into the shop. Instead, they waited outside on the pavement, keeping a safe distance, while the professionals went in and did their thing.

It didn't take long.

Four uniformed officers marched Molly out of the charity shop in handcuffs, the last one clutching an evidence bag containing the stun gun. They led her to one of their cars parked outside. Before placing her in the back, Fiona couldn't resist the deliciousness of showing Molly that they were alive and well. She called out to her, "Not bad for some twee older ladies."

Molly caught sight of them, her face horrified and bewildered. "What the . . . ? How did you . . . ? That's impossible."

Daisy held up her hairpins in her fist. "Never underestimate someone with fiddly fingers."

Partial Sue rubbed it in some more. "And now we're going to discuss sell-by dates and bags for life, then we're going to watch *Call The Midwife*."

Before Molly could answer, the police officer plunged her head inside the back of the car.

DI Fincher appeared from out of the shop with DS Thomas behind. The young female detective held Simon Le Bon by his lead. "This little fellow was desperate to see you."

Overwhelmed and bubbling with excitement, Simon Le Bon bounced and yelped his way towards Fiona, nearly losing his balance his tail wagged so much. She scooped him up in her arms and received a barrage of licks and kisses. "Did that nasty woman want to take you away from me?"

"Thank you, ladies," DI Fincher said. "You've done a good job. Now I have to ask, after your ordeal, do you need any medical attention or counselling?"

"We're fine," Partial Sue replied.

"Well, support's available if you need it."

"Did Molly admit to killing Sally?" Fiona asked.

"Not yet but we've got you three as witnesses to her confession, and we've definitely got her for false imprisonment, threat to kill and possession of an illegal weapon."

"She told us she didn't kill Sylvia Steadman."

"That's the same story she told us," the detective replied. "She said she has an alibi. That she was in a soft-play area with her daughter at the time. We'll verify that."

Fiona was sure Molly was telling the truth about not killing Sylvia Steadman. She had no quarrel with her. Had no motive and nothing to gain from her death. She'd merely used it as an opportunity to enact a slightly flawed copycat killing of Sally Wilde, fuelled by a crazed paranoia that the sandwich maker was onto her.

"What will happen to Molly's little girl?" Daisy asked. "She's the one I feel sorry for."

DI Fincher sighed. "Yes, as is often the case, it's the children who suffer. Social workers will pick her up from school, but Molly informed us she has family in Cornwall on her father's side, and family on her mother's side in Somerset. Social services are trying to get hold of them now."

"She told us she had no family apart from her mum and dad," Partial Sue said.

"Another lie, I'm afraid. Now, we'll need to take statements from you."

"Of course," Fiona replied. "Would you like to do it in the shop?"

DI Fincher nodded.

"I think we all deserve a cup of tea." Daisy smiled.

* * *

A few days later, they were still reeling from the trauma of the garden centre. Fiona didn't know which was worse, being imprisoned and nearly dying, or the fact that they'd been betrayed, a murderer in their midst this whole time, and hadn't even noticed. They'd taken Molly under their wing, and she'd well and truly played them to perfection. Though they'd put on a brave face when the police marched her out of the shop, Fiona got a shiver whenever she thought about what might have happened, and she felt sure her colleagues did too. After such a close brush with death, she'd suggested they all take time off. But no one, herself included, had any real desire for that. The best therapy was being in each other's company. They were stronger together, and there was no better support than the security of their friendship.

However, there was one small upside to all this. The ladies had each bought a new phone, seeing as Molly had smashed theirs. Daisy and Fiona upgraded to something sleeker, faster and shinier. The chance to swipe a virgin screen, play with new camera filters and explore the latest bit of kit, fresh out of the box, was always a thrilling prospect.

Partial Sue, on the other hand, did not see it like this. She'd had her phone for nearly ten years and had not planned on changing it any time soon, until Molly had stepped in, literally driving her heel through its screen. In any case, why would she need a new phone, when she had a perfectly serviceable old Nokia 3310 sitting in her kitchen drawer, gathering dust? It would do just fine as a replacement, and she proceeded to extol its virtues, attempting to justify her decision to the other two. She pointed out that it was a proper phone, not like these namby-pamby ones today that break if you sit on them. A Nokia 3310 could withstand being hit by a mortar round and had a battery that lasted until the sun went cold. Okay, it might be a bit basic, but she could make calls and send texts. What more did she need? Daisy pointed out that instant, superfast access to the internet, which the Nokia did not have, might come in handy, especially for detective work, searching for clues and verifying facts on the go. In the end, Partial Sue caved in, but disappointingly, bought exactly the same phone she'd had before from eBay.

To help put thoughts of Molly behind them, they threw themselves back into the investigation, resuming their attempts to get through to Trelane Film Productions.

Fiona hung up her new phone. "Greg Trelane is still not taking our calls. No one there is."

They were going on the assumption that Molly didn't kill Sylvia and would continue to pursue that it was a separate killer, unless they heard otherwise. So far, whether by phone or email, all attempts to contact anyone at Trelane Film Productions had hit a brick wall. Through a bit of online jiggery pokery, Daisy had also managed to find Greg Trelane's mobile number but that went straight to voicemail every time they called it.

"You know what?" said Partial Sue. "It's clear this guy's avoiding us, which makes me think he's got something to hide."

Fiona frowned. "Either that or it's one of those pretentious companies where they don't talk to the likes of us because we're not famous or don't have money. I'm beginning to think the only way we're going to get in front of him is by confronting him in the street."

Daisy who'd had her head deep in her phone, tinkering with its new features, suddenly poked her head up with a face full of hope. "Does that mean a trip to London?"

"Yes, I suppose it does."

Daisy pogoed up and down in her seat with excitement. "Oh, my gosh! We're going to London! We're going to London!"

"To question someone," Partial Sue reminded her. "Not just for a jolly."

Daisy continued bobbing up and down. "Yes. But if there's time afterwards maybe we could, you know, go to Covent Garden at least."

Fiona nodded. "I'm sure that will be possible. However, bear in mind it's a stakeout of sorts. We need to wait outside Trelane Film Productions, to intercept Greg Trelane going into work, and that could take all day."

"What if he's away filming?" Partial Sue asked. "Or on holiday."

"Then we keep coming back until he's there."

"I like the sound of that." Daisy grinned.

"That could get expensive." Partial Sue frowned.

Fiona ignored her. "What time should we leave? It'll need to be quite early I'm guessing if we want to catch him before he gets into work."

Daisy was desperate to maximise her time in the capital. "If it's his company, he'll be first in. We should go as early as possible."

"Or he'll swan in when he pleases. You know what these creative types are like. Probably doesn't get 'inspired'" —Partial Sue made air quotes —"until he's had his skinny latte and sourdough toast. What's wrong with normal toast?"

"Well, I don't know about that," said Fiona. "But to be on the safe side I think we need to be there early. Leave about five thirty in the morning. That should get us there by seven thirty if we get the fast train."

"Yes!" Daisy cried. "I mean, that's sensible."

Partial Sue groaned, dragging her feet. "But we'd have to close the shop if we all want to go. Maybe I should stay behind."

"Oh, no. I think we should all go," Daisy protested. "It won't be the same without all of us."

Fiona couldn't tell whether Partial Sue's reluctance was because she wanted to avoid paying for a ticket or because the thought of catching a train at that time filled her with dread. With the energy of an enriched uranium rod, she couldn't imagine Partial Sue had a problem getting up in the morning, so it had to be the former. But she did have a point. Now Molly was gone, who'd look after the shop when they went out as an ensemble? Perhaps they were worrying unnecessarily. "You know what? We've just had a nasty experience. Imprisoned by a murdering psychopath. If anyone asks, the shop's closed because we all need a day to get over it."

"That sounds fair," Daisy agreed.

"Okay, I suppose," Partial Sue agreed reluctantly.

Fiona pulled her credit card out. "I'll pay for the tickets. My treat."

Partial Sue brightened up somewhat.

CHAPTER 42

Early morning light began to assert itself, taking charge of the darkness. It did nothing to stir Fiona who sat on a cold metal bench in the station, forcing her eyes to stay open. Daisy, next to her, was similarly comatose with lack of sleep, snuggled up in her thick duffle coat and scarf, resembling a hamster going into hibernation.

Partial Sue, by contrast, had been antsy from the moment they'd arrived at just a little after quarter past five. She paced up and down the platform, sometimes glancing at her phone, sometimes at the time displayed above them. Maybe she should have stayed behind. Their outing, though it had barely started, revealed an obsessive side to her personality that they never knew existed. Fiona wondered if Partial Sue liked being in control when it came to travelling, which would explain why they always took her car whenever they needed to go anywhere. Maybe she had to be in the driving seat, deciding where and by what route they went. Having someone else at the wheel, whether it was a car or a train, didn't suit her at all.

Partial Sue marched over to them. "The second we get on board, we must get a table. I am partial to having a table."

Maybe it wasn't obsessiveness at all. She just had a thing for sitting at tables on trains.

Partial Sue outlined the severity of the situation, as if she were briefing a squad of special forces about to be dropped behind enemy lines. "It's a fast train. Comes from Weymouth. Stopping at only the main stations along the way. But we can't be complacent. Those tables will go like hot cakes." She snapped her fingers. Indeed, the platform was full of people wanting to hit the capital early, mostly suited commuters but there were also a few casually dressed day-trippers. Partial Sue continued her rant. "Those commuters think they have a right to a table because they're commuters. Well, we have as much right as they do, especially seeing how much these tickets cost. We should be in lie-flat beds at that price."

"Mm, lie-flat beds," Daisy muttered dozily.

Fiona didn't want to point out that Partial Sue hadn't actually paid for her ticket. "Why is it so important to have a table?"

Partial Sue glared back at her in disbelief. "Because it just is. More space to spread out and we can face each other, have proper conversations. Lay out evidence for analysis. Documents and the like."

"I don't have any documents," Fiona said.

"Neither do I." Daisy sounded hoarse.

"Okay, well, we need it to spread out our food, and our tea. You can't do that with those silly little fold-down trays."

Fiona gulped. "Er, in my rush to get here I forgot to bring anything."

"Me neither," Partial Sue replied. "It's fine. We can get something from the buffet car."

At the mention of food, Daisy's eyes, which up to this point had been small slits, opened wide. "They don't have buffet cars anymore. When did you last go on a train?"

"Gosh, I don't know, possibly pre-millennium."

"Don't worry," Fiona said. "They'll have a buffet trolly."

Daisy cleared her throat. "You're lucky if you get a buffet trolley. They don't always have them."

A mild panic set in, rising up Fiona's throat which had suddenly become dry as oven-baked sandpaper at the thought of no tea to drink or anything to eat for the entire journey. Partial Sue gulped hard, clearly feeling the same dread.

Daisy stirred into life, albeit in slow motion. "Don't worry, you can share some of mine."

"Do you have enough?" Fiona asked.

Daisy hoisted up a Tesco bag for life that had been by her feet, in her opinion the most superior bag for life out of all the supermarkets, due to the number of items you could fit into it, and its strength-to-weight ratio. Demonstrating its TARDIS-like qualities, she plunged her hand into the cavernous bag and listed its inventory. "I have a large flask of tea. It's a one-and-a-half litre jobbie so it should last us to London. Separate small bottle of milk, so you can have it your own way. One pack of croissants and those little jars of jam and marmalade, and a bag of pains au chocolat. Oh, and I got sausage rolls as a savoury alternative. I thought we could have a mini breakfast on the train."

"Another reason for a table," Partial Sue pointed out.

Daisy continued, "I've got a whole Vicky sponge. Sorry, I mean Victoria sponge." The ladies had made a vow never to call it Vicky sponge ever again, after Molly had coined the phrase and tried to kill them. "There's a bag of cheese twists, freshly baked, well, they were yesterday. I have a six-pack of Walkers. A family bar of Dairy Milk and a box of Quality Street, as I know Sue is partial to a green triangle and Fiona likes the purple one. For drinks, apart from the tea, I've got a selection of juice cartons: orange, mango and cloudy apple. Oh, and a packet of Hobnobs and jam donuts. I tried to get strawberry, but they'd sold out, so we have to make do with raspberry. I hope that's okay. I know not everyone likes the seeds in raspberry jam, what with them sticking in your teeth. My cousin once got one stuck between his tooth and his gum, so far down the dentist had to cut it out. But don't let that put you off. And I've got another one of Sue's favourites, a packet of Penguins."

"I am partial to a Penguin." She was, except Fiona knew she never splashed out on them, preferring to save her pennies and buy the cheap imitation Puffin bars at the twenty-five-pence shop.

But Daisy wasn't done yet. "Oh, and a packet of Strepsils, in case the smog gives us sore throats."

"We're not going to Dickensian London, Daisy," said Fiona. "They don't have pea soupers anymore."

Before Daisy could reply, a recorded announcement played over the public address system, warning members of the public to be on their guard for any suspect packages, instructing them to, "See it. Say it. Sorted." The voice sounded eerily familiar.

"Why did that announcement sound like Audrey Hepburn?" Partial Sue asked.

"Well, I suppose they don't want to alarm people," Fiona replied. "Audrey Hepburn is the voice of calm."

"And sophistication," Daisy added. "They can do anything with computers these days. I saw an advert for chocolate once that had Audrey Hepburn in it. They'd brought her back to life with computers."

"They can do that with any dead actor, the CGI's so good," Partial Sue remarked.

"I'd like to see Richard Gere," Daisy said.

"Er, I think he's still alive," Fiona replied.

"Oh okay, then I'd like to see Cary Grant. He could play opposite George Clooney as two brothers who fall in love with the same woman. Or how about James Dean playing opposite Robert Pattinson as two hitmen who are hired to kill the same woman, but both end up falling in love with her." Daisy continued pitching movie ideas centred around the same theme of love triangles, featuring resurrected stars playing opposite their modern-day counterparts.

The PA bing-bonged. This time, a far less glamorous, more world-weary voice came over the public address system, blandly announcing that the train now approaching platform two was the 5.30 to London, calling at Southampton, Winchester and London, Waterloo.

Like automatons coming to life, the hitherto motionless commuters automatically clustered into groups, converging on spots equally spaced along the platform. They were battle-hardened daily travellers, who knew instinctively where the train would stop, and where the doors would open. By comparison the three ladies were slow off the mark and joined the back of the queue of the group nearest, led by Partial Sue, whose eager body language would suggest it was taking all of her willpower not to push to the front.

The train slid into the station and as it decelerated, Partial Sue's head flicked back and forward like a meercat, unsuccessfully attempting to spot a free table in the passing carriages. Once they'd clambered on board, she made them traipse the length of the train in search of one. The train moved off, causing them to sway and stagger forward as they searched, as if they had been on the sherry.

"Can't we just sit in the normal seats," Daisy complained, struggling with her bag. "There's plenty of them."

"No, I want a table." Partial Sue would not be deterred from her mission.

Shuffling awkwardly up the narrow aisle, bumping into seats and being thrown forward every now and again, they reached the last carriage. Partial Sue let out a whoop of joy. "Free table ahead."

As they bustled towards the table, it became clear this had been an over-optimistic assessment. One seat was occupied by a suited gentleman who'd strategically placed various bags and his overcoat on the remaining three seats to discourage anyone else from sitting there. To really push home his message, he'd transformed the table into a temporary office, his nose deep in his laptop and every inch of the tabletop covered in papers and documents.

"Er, that doesn't look free," Daisy said.

But Partial Sue wouldn't be deterred. "I know his game. That's just a ruse to put us off. Excuse me?" she asked him. "Could you move your bags so we can sit down."

Without looking up, he said, "These seats are taken."

"By whom? I don't see anyone."

The man muttered something under his breath then said, "My colleagues will be joining me soon. I'm saving them a seat. Now if you'll excuse me, I have a lot of work to do." He tapped rapidly on his keyboard, signifying the conversation was over.

"Come on, Sue, we can sit over there." Fiona had spotted three empty seats a few rows behind. Two together and one across the aisle. Partial Sue took the one on its own, because of its strategic position, diagonally across from the table-hoarding suit. She could keep two beady and somewhat murderous eyes on him, something that Fiona could tell she would be doing the whole journey.

After settling in, Fiona whispered to Daisy, "I think we need to distract her." Daisy looked across at Partial Sue, rigid as a statue, her eyes throwing invisible daggers at the man. Fiona knew what Partial Sue was like, once she got something in her head, she wouldn't let it go, not until they'd been thrown off the train.

CHAPTER 43

The pair of them had tried everything to distract Partial Sue, mostly involving food from Daisy's Fingal's Cave of a bag, wafting things in front of her to tempt her away from her surveillance mission. Without taking her eyes off the guy, Partial Sue refused everything. Nothing would deter her. Not even the offer of a Penguin. Throughout the journey, she watched, hawklike, as new passengers got on and tried in vain to sit at the man's table only to be put off by the same excuse. Each time, Partial Sue's jaw clenched tighter.

Daisy tried once more to distract her. "I had a brain wave when we were getting on the train. A business idea."

"Oh, what's that, Daisy?" Fiona over-egged the enthusiasm for Partial Sue's benefit.

"I think I could make a fortune."

The mention of money got Partial Sue's attention. She tore her bitter gaze away. "What's the idea?"

"Well, you two were worried because you hadn't brought anything. It got me thinking. I bet a lot of people find themselves in the same position. They've gone out without any provisions, or maybe they've gone for a walk. It's a nice day and they decide to go further, you know, make a proper day of it, but they haven't brought anything. What do they do? So my idea is a sort of waistcoat-style thing made of a thin plastic, similar to what crisp packets are made of, so it's disposable. It would have four or five pockets like a fisherman's vest, but each pocket would be a sealed bag of different nibbles. One would be crisps, another nuts, another wine gums or something sweet, maybe the last one, a top pocket, would have orange squash and a long straw so you could take sips while you walk. You could buy it at newsagents and convenience stores."

"And you wear it?" asked Fiona.

"Yeah, I call it the Snack Jacket."

"The Snack Jacket," Fiona repeated. "That's a good name, catchy. The buttons could be made of sweets, like gob stoppers."

"Oh yes, or even real chocolate buttons, although I suppose they'd melt if it's a hot day."

"What a great idea. What do you think, Sue?"

Sue harrumphed. "Why don't you just buy the things you need at the newsagents and put them in your pocket or ask the newsagent for a bag?"

"I suppose you could do that," Daisy replied. "But what if you don't want to carry a bag and you don't have pockets."

"What clothes don't have pockets?" Partial Sue sighed. "Unless you were going out for a walk in a ball gown."

While they were debating the merits of wearable snacks, the train stopped briefly at Winchester, took on more passengers, then pulled away from the station. As if compelled by some invisible force, Partial Sue rose to her feet and was about to approach the suited man once more, until Fiona said, "Sue, why don't you just leave it. We're nearly halfway there now."

"I can't."

"It's fine," Daisy added. "Let him have his stupid table."

But Partial Sue wouldn't relent. "Didn't you hear what he called me?"

Daisy and Fiona both shook their heads.

"He muttered the D-word at me."

Fiona and Daisy gasped. To a female retiree, nothing was more insulting than someone dropping the D-word.

"That's not all," Partial Sue exclaimed. "He added the C-word and the other D-word at the beginning."

"Oh, my gosh!" Fiona was outraged on her behalf. "Not calm down, dear?"

"The very same."

"How dare he." Daisy flushed with anger.

"You should've told us."

"I thought you heard him."

"No, but now I can see why you were so annoyed at him. Completely justified." Fiona stood in solidarity with Partial Sue, joined by Daisy. "Let's give him a piece of our minds."

They followed Partial Sue across the aisle to confront the condescending table hogger. "We'd like to sit at this table, so please can you move your stuff."

The suited man, still nose-deep in his laptop, repeated his well-worn table-blocking excuse. "I'm saving these seats for someone."

"No, you're not," Fiona said.

At her brusque tone, he glanced up, recognising that he'd seen off these three once before, back at Christchurch.

"We've just passed Winchester," Partial Sue growled. "Train doesn't stop now until it reaches Waterloo. So there aren't any friends that will be joining you. Unless they're imaginary."

A few people in the carriage sniggered.

"Look here," said the man.

"No, you look here. You've hogged that table the whole way. Had it all to yourself. I'm sure lots of people in this carriage would've liked sitting with their friends, but they couldn't because you think you're better than everyone else. Now please move your stuff off the seats so we can sit down. And, for the record, don't tell me to calm down, dear." There were mutters of assent from the other passengers. If she didn't have their support before, she certainly had it now.

"No," the man refused.

Daisy held her phone in front of her and pointed it at the suit. "I hope you don't mind me filming you and sticking it on YouTube."

"That's a good idea," Fiona said. "You could call it Selfish Commuter Doesn't Like Sharing."

"So if you don't want to be table-shamed on social media, I suggest you make some space for us," Partial Sue replied.

The man glanced around the carriage, weighing up his odds. They didn't look good. Every head was turned in his direction, eager to see how this would play out. Several other phones came out. The prospect of becoming one of those videos that got shared online of poor public behaviour would not end well. "You know what, I'm going to sit somewhere else!" He slammed his laptop shut, scooped his papers and documents into his briefcase, then huffed and puffed as he gathered up his things. The three ladies sidestepped out of the way as he left to find a seat in another part of the train.

A woman nearby began to clap. Another man followed and then the whole carriage was applauding. Partial Sue smiled self-consciously then nodded to her friends who slid into the hard-won vacated seats. "I think I'll have that Penguin now, Daisy."

CHAPTER 44

Daisy's giant food bag was a fair bit lighter when they stepped off the train at Waterloo. A short tube ride later and they were on a park bench in Soho Square, opposite the offices of Trelane Film Productions, perfectly positioned to spot Greg Trelane, either coming or going. He'd certainly picked a prestigious business address for his company in a swish, narrow, six-story Art Deco building with tall glass windows and a grand entrance. All four sides of the square were clustered with an eclectic mix of equally glamourous buildings, some gothic and pointy, others in the traditional Georgian style with their perfect proportions, while a few were clean and modern.

"Look at all the cool and trendy people." Daisy jittered with excitement. "I bet they're going off to do important jobs."

"You're not wrong there," Fiona said, watching the hordes of flat-white-sipping fashionistas passing by. "Traditionally, Soho is where all the ad agencies and film companies have their offices. It's a great place to celebrity spot."

Daisy couldn't contain herself. "Do you think we'll see someone famous, like Elizabeth Curlew?"

"Who?" Partial Sue asked.

"You know, Elizabeth Curlew. She used to go out with Hugh Grant."

"Oh, you mean, Elizabeth Hurley."

Daisy giggled at her name mix-up. "I can't believe I called her Elizabeth Curlew."

"I doubt we'll see her or Elizabeth Hurley," Fiona said. "I think she designs bikinis now."

"Oh, really?" Daisy sounded disappointed. "What about Claudia Winkleman?"

"You can dream bigger than that." Fiona smiled. "I was thinking more Brad Pitt or Emily Blunt."

Daisy nearly fell off the bench. "You're joking. What, big Hollywood superstars come here?"

"Sometimes."

"Although, they're more likely to Zoom these days," Partial Sue muttered cynically.

Fiona looked at her phone. "Just after eight o'clock. I hope we haven't missed him. Shall we remind ourselves what he looks like again." She dabbed at her screen and pulled up a profile picture she'd downloaded from LinkedIn to help them identify him. In his late fifties, the silver fox had a thick mass of grey hair that had been gelled across his head, clippered at the sides, leading down to a neatly trimmed similarly coloured beard. The shot had been professionally taken, lit from a flattering angle, highlighting a nice set of cheekbones.

"He's a handsome fellow," Daisy commented.

Partial Sue leaned in. "You have to be careful with those profile pics. People are reluctant to update them. That could be what he looked like ten years ago."

Daisy nudged Fiona in the ribs. "Er, that looks like him, coming this way."

Across the road, as Partial Sue predicted, an older, more dishevelled version of the person in the profile picture hurried along the busy pavement, head down, thumbing his phone. Leather courier-style bag over one shoulder and scarf knotted around his neck.

"That's him. Come on."

The three of them leapt off the bench, crossed the road and headed in his direction.

"Yoo-hoo, Mr Trelane?" Fiona called out, worried he might slip into his office before they reached him. Greg Trelane popped his head up, and glanced about, slightly puzzled, as did a few others on the pavement, curious at who would be using the phrase yoo-hoo in London, especially Soho. His eyes immediately locked on the three ladies heading towards him. Pretending he hadn't seen them, his head jerked back down, and he continued on his way.

"Mr Trelane? Greg Trelane?" Fiona asked, as they caught up to him.

"Who wants to know?" he replied, slightly terrified at being cornered by three older women at this early hour.

Fiona ignored his question. "I was wondering if we could ask you a few questions about Sylvia Steadman."

"No, sorry. I don't have time." He increased his pace, accelerating away from them.

Fiona, Daisy and Partial Sue rushed after him. "It won't take long," Fiona pleaded.

"I'm too busy." He reached the doors to his office and was about to push them open when Partial Sue said, "Did you know she's been murdered?"

Greg Trelane stopped in his tracks, spun around and faced them. "Sorry, what did you say?"

"Sylvia Steadman was murdered at a dog show in Christchurch," Partial Sue replied.

"We're trying to find her killer," Fiona said. "It would really help if you could answer some questions."

Greg Trelane stepped away from the building, his eyes full of alarm. "Are you serious?"

"Absolutely."

He ran a hand through his thick, silvery hair. "I can't believe it. I had no idea."

"I'm sorry you had to find out this way," Fiona replied.

"There's a café around the corner. Let's talk in there." Greg Trelane led them to a tiny Italian that appeared to be the genuine article. Battered wooden tables and chairs lined the pavement outside, while its window was filled with bright, ornamental little cakes and savoury pop-in-the-mouth pastries, almost too pretty to eat. Inside was cramped in a cosy sort of way, dominated by a coffee machine the size of the *Titanic*, steaming, puffing and grinding out espressos to a never-ending procession of customers eager for takeouts on their way to work.

A waitress brought over an espresso for Greg, accompanied by three lattes for the ladies. He briefly removed his hand from his mouth, to neck his drink. It had been there, clamped in shock, ever since Fiona had begun recounting the brief story of how Sylvia had died.

"I still can't believe it." Greg waved his cup in the air, signalling to the waitress that he needed another. "And someone injected her? What with?"

"We don't know," Partial Sue replied. "Can I ask what Sylvia was like, as a person?"

"I liked her. She was smart. We worked well together."

"What about everyone else?" Fiona asked.

He studied the wall which was covered in gorgeous black and white photos of famous Italians: Pavarotti, Gina Lollobrigida and some footballers. He hesitated before answering. "Other people weren't so fond of her."

"In what way?"

"She didn't suffer fools gladly. Being a Crufts winner with Charlie, she had very high standards, and that went for everything. Trouble is, film shoots are chaotic, messy places. Not sure that it suited her."

"Anyone in particular take exception to her high standards?"

"I'll be honest, the whole crew didn't like her. She became very demanding. Refused to do certain things. It got a bit awk-ward between us towards the end."

"Did she annoy anyone enough to make them murderous?" Fiona asked.

"God, no. I use an experienced crew. They've worked with people a lot more demanding than Sylvia. Divas come with the territory in this business. It's just expected that you have to put up with spoiled film stars on set. They're tolerated if you pull in big audiences, but not if you're a Z-list celebrity like Sylvia doing little dog-food commercials. If you get too big for your boots, word gets around. The client didn't renew her contract. No one wanted to work with her — except Dylan Fraser."

"Who's Dylan Fraser?" they chorused.

The waitress placed another espresso in front of him and took away his empty cup. Greg downed the coffee as if it were a vodka shot. "He's her dog groomer. She had it written into her contract that he had to be there for every shoot to prepare Charlie — a hangover from her dog show days. Dylan prepared Charlie before every dog show — she wouldn't trust anyone else."

"Do you know where we can find him?"

"Yeah, he's right here in London. Has a dog grooming salon in the Seven Dials. Supposedly the best in the country."

"One more quick question," Fiona asked. "Was Sylvia diabetic at all?"

Greg Trelane shook his head. "No, I don't think so."

London was proving to be very fruitful indeed, and it was still only breakfast time.

CHAPTER 45

They threaded their way along Charing Cross Road, its pavements thick with people relentlessly bustling past its famous picturesque bookshops, piled high with teetering towers of rare and sought-after first editions. There would be no stopping to browse today, not even a quick peek. Fiona knew what she and her friends were like. Once they ventured inside one, they'd have to look in all of them, and it would take more than a daytrip to explore Charing Cross's cavernous bookshops.

Despite the lack of shopping, Daisy couldn't hide her joy at being in the capital, luxuriating in the buzz that only London offered. "Oh, it's just like being in a giant Monopoly board."

"Charing Cross isn't in Monopoly," Partial Sue pointed out.

"Isn't it? I was never very good at Monopoly, probably why."

"I am partial to a game of Monopoly, mostly because I always win." Partial Sue giggled.

"You know, that doesn't surprise me," Fiona said.

Before she could challenge them all to a game when they got home, they crossed Shaftesbury Avenue, and then into the area known as the Seven Dials, where seven narrow streets converged like the spokes of a wheel. At the centre of this urban hub stood a column bearing six sundials, with the seventh dial being the column itself — hence the name.

"You can tell the time no matter which direction you come from," Fiona remarked.

"Only if it's not cloudy." Partial Sue's cynicism never let them down.

Daisy almost exploded with glee, pointing to a large building at the apex of two streets. "Look *Matilda*'s on!" The Seven Dials was also home to the Cambridge Theatre and Roald Dahl's *Matilda*. "Can we watch it! Oh, please."

"I imagine you'd need to book tickets well in advance," Partial Sue said.

"Maybe next time we're here." Fiona sounded like a parent.

And Daisy acted like the child. "Oh," she moaned, but was soon distracted. "Look at all the lovely little shops." The network of narrow lanes around the Seven Dials was lined with what used to be nineteenth-century slums and warehouses where, back in the day, it was best not to venture, or you'd end up mugged with your throat cut. Nowadays, there were more subtle and nicer ways to fleece you of your money. Around every cobbled corner were delightful boutiques and quirky shops with swanky apartments and trendy offices above.

"Didn't Agatha Christie set a murder mystery here?" Partial Sue asked.

"Yes, I think she did." Fiona spotted the road they were looking for. "That's where Dylan Fraser's grooming salon is. Come on."

A brief walk down Monmouth Street and they came to a slick white shop with large silver block letters above the door, spelling a simple but memorable name: FUR. Through the front window, it resembled an Apple store, clean and sparse. From front to back, two rows of large plain tables were separated by an aisle down the middle. A groomer stood at each table fussing around a dog secured by a harness. Some were being clipped, fur flying off in every direction while others were further along in the process, receiving a blow dry, their coats rippling in waves. A young apprentice busied himself around the legs of each table, sweeping up dog hairs the second they touched the floor.

Down the centre of the aisle strode a distinct but slight figure of a man. Dressed in a baggy black boiler suit with a slick black man bun, he looked like a Liquorice Allsort — the one that's always left at the bottom. Every now and then he would stop at a table, where the groomer would immediately stand back while he scrutinised their work and gave his direction. This must be the famous Dylan Fraser.

Fiona wished she'd brought Simon Le Bon, instead of leaving him with her neighbour. Perhaps they could've squeezed him in for a quick tidy up. Although, it didn't seem like the kind of place that would accept walk-ins. No, you'd probably need to book a slot a month in advance or be referred by an existing client before they'd even consider you. She made a mental note to book him in somewhere as soon as they got home.

"It looks too posh for the likes of us." Daisy gulped.

"Nonsense," said Partial Sue. "It's where they cut dog hair, it's not the flaming Ritz."

"Yeah," Fiona said. "But I bet those dogs have Highland spring water in their bowls, not tap water. Come on, let's see what this Dylan Fraser knows."

Fiona pushed open the door. Almost as if on cue, every dog's head simultaneously swivelled in their direction, curious to see who'd entered. She supposed they were all hopeful that it would be their owner, come to collect them. A handsome Siberian husky on the table nearest shook with excitement despite them not being his owner, making the groomer's job considerably harder.

The man in black spun around to see who had disrupted his well-drilled realm of flying fur and wagging tails. Surprisingly, he gave them a warm and charming smile of perfect white teeth. "Ladies, welcome to FUR. What can I do for you?"

Fiona approached him. "Are you Dylan Fraser?"

"I am the very same."

"Greg Trelane, the film producer, gave us your name and said you might be able to help us."

"I'm afraid we're booked up two months in advance."

Fiona tried to look sympathetic. "Er, it's not grooming we're after. I don't know if you've heard but Sylvia Steadman passed away recently."

Dylan Fraser's perfect smile dissolved instantly, his face downcast. "Yes, I still can't believe it. Still haven't got over it. Did you know her?"

Fiona shook her head, then drew closer, speaking in hushed tones. "Er, did you also know that Sylvia's life was *taken*?"

"I'm sorry. What?"

Fiona waited a beat. Delaying the words that sat precariously on her lips. "She was murdered."

The phrase, though gently uttered, appeared to devastate the diminutive dog groomer. He swayed, almost staggered sideways and had to reach out a hand to steady himself on a nearby table.

"We're so sorry," Daisy offered.

"And sorry you have to hear it from a bunch of strangers," Partial Sue added.

"Are you sure?" His eyes were rimmed with dread.

"Positive," Fiona replied.

"Oh, my gosh. This is awful, just awful. I need a drink."

CHAPTER 46

Dylan Fraser led them past a couple of deep, stainless-steel wash stations with overhanging shower heads on flexible hoses, where a small chihuahua was being shampooed. The dog glared at them with two black marble eyes as they passed, not enjoying the experience.

They were shown into an office at the back. Like everything in the salon, the office was slick and sparsely furnished with only a desk and a tall glass-fronted fridge, stacked mostly with champagne. Fiona wondered where he kept the hoover. Dylan removed a can of G&T from the fridge. "Would anyone like one? I'm afraid it's ready-mixed as I've run out of tonic and lemon and ice, but when needs must."

The three ladies shook their heads and took a seat in front of the desk, a minimalist Scandi number with tapered, almost spiked legs. Judging by its immaculate finish Fiona would bet it was extremely expensive, and definitely not available in the Ikea catalogue. Dylan collapsed in his office chair, cracked open the ring pull and drank straight from the can. "Forgive my vulgarity for not using a glass but it's not often you get shocking news like this."

"That's quite understandable," Daisy said.

"Don't mind us," added Partial Sue.

Dylan Fraser cast his eyes downward at his drink and brushed a tear from his eye. "How was she murdered? I thought she had a heart attack."

Fiona outlined how Sylvia had lost her life at the Christchurch Dog Show, while Dylan listened in stunned silence. When she finished, he drained the can and retrieved another from the fridge, his hands shaking and his skin pallid. "Have the police arrested anyone? Any suspects?"

Fiona shook her head. "We're doing our own investigation, and were wondering if you knew anyone who had anything against Sylvia, enough to want her dead?"

Dylan sniffed back another tear. "No, not really. She kept herself to herself. Didn't really have any close friends. Preferred the company of dogs to people."

"We have a theory that it might have been a jealous dog show rival who killed her," Partial Sue said.

Dylan swallowed a big gulp of his G&T. "That's a good theory. All dog show competitors are jealous, even at a local level. Dogs are like their children, everyone thinks theirs is the best and the most beautiful and, like parents who get annoyed if their child doesn't get the lead in the school play, they get most upset if they don't win."

"What about when Sylvia won Crufts?" Fiona asked. "Could one of the other competitors who lost out have killed her? Just bided their time until now?"

Dylan shook his head. "If that was the case, Sylvia wouldn't have been the target, that would have been the judge. It's the judge who decides who wins or loses. They're the kingmakers."

"What about before a dog show? What if someone took out Sylvia to eliminate the favourite to win?" Partial Sue asked.

"Possibly," Dylan replied. "But then Charlie would have been the target, not Sylvia. Of course, a dog can't enter without an owner. But it's far easier to remove a dog from the competition than their owner."

Fiona shrank in her seat at this horrible revelation. But it made sense. If someone didn't want Charlie to win, why go to the risk of killing Sylvia when there was a far simpler alternative? Being a dog lover, Fiona simply couldn't fathom that a fellow dog lover, even the bitterest rival, would ever harm someone else's dog so theirs could win. "Surely another dog owner wouldn't do that."

Dylan frowned. "Though it's rare, there are rumours floating around the dog world of favourites being poisoned right before a show to prevent them from competing."

As well as shocked, Fiona began to feel amateurish. They'd been so wrapped up and enamoured by the theory of a rival owner, that they'd overlooked the obvious. Killing Sylvia would still leave her dog alive — a rival's biggest threat to winning. As they'd witnessed with Sophie's questionable adoption of Charlie, he could still legally enter competitions once change of ownership had been registered. It didn't make sense for a rival to go to all the trouble of killing Sylvia when they would still be left with the same problem: an ex-Crufts winner still at large and able to compete.

Dylan exhaled. "But it's all irrelevant because Sylvia didn't enter the Christchurch Dog Show."

Fiona exchanged confused looks with Daisy and Partial Sue, then turned to him. "She did, we've seen her entry form."

"I think I've got it saved on my phone." A second later Daisy had it up on screen. She leant across the desk to show him.

Dylan examined the form, his eyes flicking back and forth. He shook his head. "It has to be a fake."

"What makes you think that?" Fiona asked.

"I groomed Charlie before every event he entered, big and small. For every advert he was in, bar none. She wouldn't trust anyone else to do it and would book me months in advance. If Sylvia had entered the Christchurch Dog Show I would have known about it. Been there to groom Charlie, without question."

"But it's just a little local dog show," Daisy pointed out. "Maybe she didn't think it was worth bothering you."

Dylan smiled. "I know Sylvia. It would be a matter of personal pride for her. She was a perfectionist and had a reputation to keep up. If I wasn't there, then I can assure you, she wasn't competing. Besides, I think Sylvia had had enough of entering competitions. It's a lot of work, and she'd already reached the peak with Crufts. Can't get better than that. Maybe she went there to help out."

"No," Fiona said. "As far as we know, she turned up like a regular punter. Well, apart from everyone crowding around to take pictures of Charlie."

"But why would anyone fake her entry form?" asked Partial Sue.

Dylan shrugged. "I have no idea."

The room fell silent, then Fiona said, "Tell me about the film shoots for the dog food ads. You accompanied her for each one."

"That's right." Dylan's face brightened a little. "They were a lot of fun. Always jetting off to some exotic location, put up in a good hotel and they paid very well. Nice work if you can get it."

"Greg Trelane told us Sylvia was a bit of a diva on set, and got fired for it," Partial Sue said.

Dylan sighed. "That's partly true. As I said before, Sylvia wasn't a people person. She could be blunt and offhand if things weren't done right. I was used to it, others weren't. A few noses were put out of joint. But that's not why she got fired. In fact, she didn't get fired at all. Greg Trelane's not telling you the whole story."

"What's the whole story?" Fiona asked.

"Everything was going fine with the campaign, despite Sylvia having the odd tantrum now and then. Nothing that would merit being fired. But then things began to change. I'm sure you've seen the ads. Charlie on a chaise, Charlie in a health spa, Charlie on a beach. Harmless stuff, but then the client wanted him to do sillier and sillier things, extreme sports like water skiing and bungee jumping. Sylvia refused, said it was humiliating for Charlie, and I supported her. The client refused to budge on the new direction, so Sylvia walked away. It was her decision, not theirs. But Good Companion dog food didn't want to look stupid or lose face, so I guess they put the rumour around that she'd been fired because she was difficult to work with. Still, it was fun while it lasted. We had some great times on those photo shoots." Dylan went quiet, then began to sob. "I can't believe she's gone."

Fiona wanted to give Dylan a hug, soothe his pain, but felt awkward in a very British sort of way. She'd only just met the guy. Would it be too intimate to start wrapping her arms around him? Instead, she got to her feet and handed him a clean tissue. He thanked her, wiped his eyes and blew his nose.

When his sobs had subsided, Fiona asked, "Do you think the client, Good Companion, could have had anything to do with her death?"

He shook his head. "Despite Sylvia quitting, I think they were glad to see the back of her. It gave them an excuse to do something different, and by that, I mean cheaper. Those ads were expensive — foreign locations, big crew and cast. The ads that replaced them were studio based. Infomercial style. Far cheaper." He paused. "You know, thinking about it, maybe that was the plan all along. Make unreasonable requests. Ones they knew she'd refuse so she'd be forced to walk, so they could save a ton of money. They got what they wanted."

"That's highly likely," Partial Sue said. "I know in the corporate world, companies will do that to an employee whose salary has become untenable. To avoid a costly redundancy, they shift their role, just enough so it's still part of their job description, but different enough so they'll either hate it or fail. A poisoned chalice to get them to leave."

"What happened to Charlie?" Dylan asked. "Is he okay?"

"Yes, he's fine. He's with a very good dog fosterer we know. She'll find him a good home soon. I'm sure of it." Fiona thought it best not to mention the disaster with Sophie Haverford. She didn't want to add to this man's already distressing morning.

CHAPTER 47

After leaving Dylan Fraser's salon, the ladies made the short stroll down to Covent Garden to fulfil at least one of Daisy's wishes. London's old fruit and veg market appeared resplendent in the mid-morning light, its cobbles gleaming, thronging with a fresh crop of tourists and shoppers. However, after a morning spent breaking the tragic news of Sylvia's death to two people completely unaware of her murder, their hearts weren't really in it.

As they shuffled around the central square, the bad taste in Fiona's mouth intensified. She didn't envy the police one bit. Breaking the news to someone that their friend had been murdered, well, it didn't get much worse than that. It had robbed them of their appetite to indulge in retail therapy, of which there was a great deal to be had in Covent Garden. Not even the talented street entertainers could drag them out of their moods. Although an act that recreated the attack on the Death Star from *Star Wars* in full costume performed on unicycles did come close.

They wandered over to the Ivy to see if they could book a table for lunch. The only one available was in the no man's land of dining at four thirty. Perfect for afternoon tea but too late for lunch and too early for dinner.

"We should have booked in advance," Partial Sue said, as they dawdled away.

"It would have been tricky," Fiona replied. "We didn't know when or if we'd catch up with Greg Trelane. We could have been waiting for him all day."

"There are plenty of other places to eat," Daisy pointed out. Covent Garden was a foodie heaven, offering every style of cuisine imaginable.

"I don't feel that hungry," Partial Sue said.

"I'm not in the mood, either," Fiona replied.

"Truth be told, I feel a little sad," Daisy said.

They all agreed. While tourists and shoppers fizzed around them, marvelling at the vibrant sights, sounds and smells of Covent Garden, the three ladies stood disheartened, unsure about what to do next.

"Why don't we head home," Partial Sue suggested. "Get the next train. Remember, we've had a traumatic few days, what with Molly imprisoning us and having to break bad news to two different people. Maybe we should give the investigation a break for today. Give our brains a rest. Let this new information sink in. Then start again tomorrow."

Though they'd learned something profound, the idea that Sylvia might not have actually been in the competition and her entry form may have been faked, Fiona's head was in no shape to start unpicking it all. Not just yet. Not while she and her colleagues felt emotionally fatigued. The early start hadn't helped either. "That sounds like a good idea."

"But what will we do about lunch?" asked Daisy. "We're bound to get peckish at some point on the train. I have a few snacks left but not much."

"We can get our favourite sandwiches from the M&S at the station," Fiona suggested. "Then eat them on the train when we feel hungry."

"I like that idea."

It seemed like such as straightforward plan, until they reached the M&S at Waterloo. Partial Sue stood in front of the chiller cabinet, fixated at the vast array of sandwiches on offer, unable to decide for the simple reason that they had temporarily run out of her favourite. She stared at the empty space where the BLTs should be, almost willing them into existence.

"I don't want to hurry you, Sue, but the next train leaves in five minutes," Fiona warned. She and Daisy had already selected their sandwiches and were ready to pay.

"Don't rush me," Partial Sue snapped.

"See, this is why you need a backup sandwich," Daisy said.

"That's not helping, Dais," Partial Sue replied.

"What about bacon and brie, or chicken and bacon?" Fiona suggested. "They're like a BLT."

Partial Sue screwed up her face. "They're nothing like a BLT. It's all about the textures. The contrasts. Tangy tomato, crunchy lettuce, salty bacon. That's why a BLT is the greatest sandwich in the world. Bacon and brie doesn't cut it, neither does chicken and bacon."

Fiona wasn't about to be drawn into a debate about whose favourite sandwich was superior. "What about ham and coleslaw?"

"I only like freshly made coleslaw, otherwise it's too slimy. I can't decide."

"Now, if you had a backup sandwich this wouldn't be happening," Daisy stated the obvious again.

"Still not helping, Daisy," Partial Sue hissed.

"Sorry." Daisy disappeared around the next aisle.

"Oh, no. I think I've offended her."

Rather than be offended, Daisy returned with a large grin on her face and something large behind her back. "Fiona, would you mind putting your favourite sandwich back and having your backup sandwich instead. It's tuna and sweetcorn, isn't it?"

"No, I wouldn't mind."

"Ta-da!" She presented a vast sharing platter of classic sandwiches cut into quarters, usually bought for impromptu board meetings. "I knew they had these somewhere. We can put our sarnies back and share these. There's prawn for me, tuna and sweetcorn for Fiona, plus a few other flavours, but most importantly . . ."

Partial Sue gazed at the selection and her eyes lit up. "BLT."

"Come on," said Fiona. "We can still make the next train."

By the time they passed Woking, Partial Sue had demolished all the BLTs and had moved on to egg and cress, that fidgety metabolism of hers burning calories like an incinerator. She held another up in front of her. "I think this will be my backup sandwich from now on. You can't go wrong with egg and cress."

"And they sell them everywhere," Daisy pointed out.

"It's a solid backup sandwich. But it's no match for tuna and sweetcorn," Fiona boasted.

A debate ensued about who had the best backup sandwich, which lasted until they reached Christchurch. There were no clear winners in this fight.

CHAPTER 48

The following day, normal service resumed. Fiona got in first, as she always did and opened up, happy to have Simon Le Bon back by her side. She unclipped him and he did his usual snuffling circuit, checking everything was as it should be before giving himself permission to curl into his bed, his unkempt fur almost merging into the fabric. He needed smartening up, especially after seeing the posh London dogs in Dylan Fraser's salon. Fiona called the nearest groomers to see if they could fit him in. Best they could do was three weeks from now. She tried another and got the same response. She was about to try a third when an ear-splitting squeal from outside interrupted her. Glancing out of the window, Fiona saw Partial Sue grind the gears of her car, as she crowbarred it into an unfeasibly tight space.

After the usual morning pleasantries, Partial Sue made for the storeroom to put the kettle on, eager to slot back into the comfort of their routines, all, that is, except for one. Ever since Molly had been arrested, they'd returned to pouring boiling water straight into the pot, abandoning her technique of letting it cool slightly. Her colour-and-genre-coordinated book-arranging system had also been reverted to hardworking alphabetical order, and the clothes were hung in any old fashion. If

Fiona were honest, it looked worse, but they didn't care. Their comfort zone was back to being as it should be — a Molly-free, chaotic, cosy mess, and that's the way they liked it.

Daisy came in, a cake tucked under her arm in a slightly battered box.

"Is that the one from yesterday?" Partial Sue placed the steaming pot in the centre of the table.

"It is indeed. This hardy little fellow has been up to London and back. We didn't get around to eating it so I thought we could have it today. Although I have no idea what state it's in."

"I'm sure it'll be fine," Fiona said.

Daisy slid the cake out of its crumpled box. Apart from being a little lopsided, it was perfectly serviceable. As the familiar sounds of babbling tea being poured and a knife slicing through soft sponge echoed through the shops, everything was right with the world, aside from the fact that they still had a murderer to catch.

Fiona sipped her tea, burning her tongue. The intense spike of pain caused something to nag at the back of her mind, a flicker of something so fleeting it was impossible to comprehend. She shrugged it off. "Yesterday's revelation was quite a big one."

Daisy spoke with a mouthful of cake. "Yes, Dylan Fraser believing Sylvia's entry form was faked. That changes everything."

Partial Sue played devil's advocate. "There's still a chance Sylvia just didn't think Christchurch dog show was a big enough deal to bother him."

"True," Fiona replied. "But he knew Sylvia better than we did, and she was a perfectionist. Perfectionists don't do things by halves. If she'd entered the show, she would've entered it to win, in which case, she'd have hired Dylan Fraser to groom Charlie."

Partial Sue sighed. "Okay, let's say that Sylvia hadn't planned to enter the dog show, who would fake her entry form and why? Unless she faked it herself but that makes even less sense."

"I don't know about the who or why," Daisy said. "But we might know the how."

"What do you mean?" Fiona asked.

"Well, if her entry form's been faked, surely it'd be by someone who has access to the Christchurch Dog Club website. All entries were made online, so it has to be one of the committee members."

Fiona nodded. "That would be David Harper, the treasurer. He handled all the entry forms and payments. He could have easily faked her entry form. Plus, he's in cahoots with a dodgy backstreet bookie. Perhaps he and Reg Anagram are in it together."

"But why would they fake her entry form?" Daisy asked.

"What if it was a betting scam?" Partial Sue replied. "Like those big Far-Eastern syndicates that bet on a football team to lose because they've bribed the goalkeeper a ton of money to let goals in."

"That's it!" Fiona blurted. "Forget fake entry forms and jealous dog show rivals. What if Sylvia did genuinely enter the show, but she had no intention of winning, hence why Dylan Fraser was not hired to groom Charlie. She'd been bribed to throw the show. Lose it on purpose, knowing that Charlie was favourite to win, thereby making someone a lot of money, because they'd bet against her."

"It seems a bit far-fetched for a local dog show," Daisy remarked. "And Reg Anagram is a little backstreet bookie, taking small bets, just pennies and pounds."

"Forget Reg Anagram." Fiona was eager to prove her point and began scrolling on her phone. "I'm thinking big international betting rings. But remember what he said, that old saying, if you can think about it, you can bet on it. Look at this betting site. The weird stuff you can place bets on: cheese rolling in Gloucestershire; the Annual Wife Carrying Contest in Ireland; even Elvis coming back to do another concert. You can literally bet on anything, no matter how small or silly."

"Would Sylvia want to get mixed up in something like that?" Daisy asked. "I mean, she'd just retired. Wanted the quiet life and was looking forward to walks on the beach and spending her pension."

"Who knows? Perhaps she had debts. I mean, she was living in a rented house. Maybe these people made her an offer she couldn't refuse. Charlie is an internationally renowned ex-Crufts winner, a big draw. The favourite and a dead cert to win, especially against a bunch of local dogs. We know that's true because he had odds of two to one to win Best in Show. Not a great return on your money. But if they bet on him to lose, they'd have been quids in."

"But then she dies, gets murdered. How does that fit into it?" Daisy asked.

"Okay let's assume Fiona is right," Partial Sue said. "There's a lot of money riding on this deal. Millions maybe. What if at the last moment Sylvia gets cold feet, tells this betting ring she can't go through with it. They're some powerful and dangerous people. They bump her off for going back on the deal."

Fiona got excited. "I think we're onto something."

Daisy wasn't convinced. "If that's the case, why didn't she cancel her entry, or withdraw."

"Well, because she was scared and didn't want to tip off these people that she'd reneged on the deal until the last minute."

Daisy still wasn't buying it. "Okay, but would she really turn up to a competition she'd been bribed to throw and had then got cold feet. If it were me, I'd be on my way to hide in a caravan in Norfolk."

"Daisy's got a good point," Partial Sue said. "I'm not sure how all the pieces fit together but I think it's worth pursuing. So if it's not David Harper and Reg Anagram, who should we be looking at?"

"We need a much bigger player," Fiona said. "Someone with Far Eastern connections."

They all had the same person in mind. "Dean Atkins."

CHAPTER 49

Fiona didn't like to stereotype people. It was unhelpful and, in her experience, never an accurate reflection of who someone was, and very rarely an indication of whether they were guilty or not. Some of the nicest, most charming people she'd met in her life had also been the most devious. She only had to look across the road to Sophie Haverford for proof of that — Sophie could turn on the charm at the drop of a hat. Similarly, killers rarely acted or looked like killers, for the simple reason they didn't want to attract attention to themselves. They usually hid what they were up to behind a mild-mannered persona and an average lifestyle. The last person you'd expect. Molly was a perfect example of this.

However, in the case of Dean Atkins, she found it extremely difficult to separate the man from the stereotype. If someone were to draw a villain with a blank sheet of paper and some crayons, they'd probably end up scrawling something resembling Dean Atkins. The owner of Max the Weimaraner, current holder of the Sweetest Eyes award, was a loud, brash geezer with a flashy house and cars, gold bracelets and the gift of the gab. Straight out of the villain's playbook, he was almost a walking cliché. She had to put that to one side for a moment. Try her hardest to stop it influencing her judgement. But it wasn't just the way he looked and how he spoke, it was also what he'd said that had alarm bells ringing in her head, giving her tinnitus a run for its money. "Do you remember when we visited him, he was on the phone making a deal in Kuala Lumpur?"

"That's not a crime," Daisy pointed out.

"Didn't he sell trucks or something?" said Partial Sue.

"Used to sell trucks," Fiona pointed out. "He was buying and selling currency, if I remember rightly."

"He made a joke about killing Sylvia Steadman. I remember that," Partial Sue remarked.

Daisy grimaced. "That wasn't very nice, but would he make a joke about killing her if he really did kill her?"

"I think that was just his blokey sense of humour," Fiona replied. "It was the language he used that caught my attention. He talked about bungs and paying people off. It seemed like that was the way he got things done, by bribing people. He was even prepared to pay Kenneth Prendiville to delay the Sweetest Eyes category because they were going to be late for the show."

"Not a million miles from bribing Sylvia Steadman," Partial Sue said.

"Exactly."

Daisy drained her cup, then poured another. "But if Sylvia had been bribed, surely the money would've showed up in her bank account. Don't the police check that sort of thing?"

"Money can be hidden electronically, these days, untraceable," Partial Sue explained. "But if Sylvia didn't go through with it, no money would've been deposited into her account."

"I think we need to question Dean Atkins again," Fiona suggested.

Daisy and Partial Sue nodded in agreement.

Safety in numbers rather than discretion seemed the better part of valour, so they decided to visit him en masse, which meant closing the shop again. A reluctant decision after it had been shut all day yesterday, but it had to be done. They had no idea how dangerous Dean Atkins could be. Whether he was the mastermind behind an international betting scam or just a small cog, or if the whole theory was stretching the realms of credibility for a little fun dog show that the local paper didn't even regard as important enough to cover. There was the strong possibility they were wrong about everything, and Dean Atkins simply had a bit of money and liked showing it off.

After buzzing the intercom at Dean Atkins' outlandish home, the impressive gates swished open. All three flashy cars were in the driveway and the Sunseeker bobbed beside the wooden jetty at the rear — a good sign that Dean Atkins was home. However, it was his wife who answered the door, still in her dressing gown, her cheeks hot and puffy. Fiona wondered if they'd woken her up. If that were the case, she wouldn't be in the best of moods, judging by how standoffish she'd been the last time they'd visited. Fiona attempted to be as pleasant as possible. "I am so dreadfully sorry to disturb you. We were wondering if we might have a word with Mr Atkins. We were here before, about the dog show . . ."

"I remember you." She cut Fiona off. Her voice sounded brittle, on the verge of cracking. "He's not here."

"Do you know when he'll be back?" asked Partial Sue.

She held onto the door for support. Tears began to stream down her cheeks. "I don't know."

"Mrs Atkins, are you okay?" asked Daisy. "Do you need help?"

She faltered at the offer of kindness. A shaking mess. "He's gone."

"Gone?" Fiona asked.

"Come in, please." Leading them through the palatial hallway into the vast kitchen-diner with its breathtaking widescreen views of the Priory and the river, she showed them to the vast sofa where Max was curled up on the end. With a half-hearted wag of his tail, the indifferent Weimaraner barely registered their presence. Simon Le Bon on the other hand, strained to make friends but Fiona held him back. This wasn't the time or the place. Mrs Atkins draped herself around her dog, as if he were a living comfort blanket. She gazed vaguely out of the window.

"What happened, Mrs Atkins?" Fiona asked.

"Please, call me Abbey," she sniffed.

"Can I make you a cup of tea?" Daisy offered.

"That's very kind of you but I'm fine." Abbey cuffed the tears away. "Dean left suddenly without warning. A couple of days after you visited."

"He just left?" asked Partial Sue.

She nodded. "Never said where he was going. Never came back."

"Have you told the police he's missing?"

She shook her head. "He's not missing. His passport's gone and his phone, but it just keeps going to voicemail."

"Oh, my gosh. I'm so sorry, Abbey." Fiona's words sounded useless in the face of this woman's tragic situation.

"The kids don't know. I've just said Daddy's away on business, which he is a lot of the time. But we always know where he is. He's never done this before." The tears were back in full force.

For the second time in so many days, they were in that tricky position of having to comfort someone they barely knew. Once again, Fiona did the only thing she could think of. She handed her a clean tissue. Abbey accepted it, dabbing her tears and blowing her nose.

Fiona braced herself for a line of questioning that she really didn't want to pursue in Abbey's current state, but she had to if they were to get anywhere. She started in the most subtle way she could. "Do you know why he'd disappear like that?"

She shrugged. "I have no idea."

"How were things between the two of you?"

"They were fine. I mean we had our ups and downs but nothing that would make him do something like this."

"I know this is an awful thing to ask but did he ever . . ."

"Play around? Yes, he does, but then so do I. It's kind of accepted in our relationship."

"Is it possible he ran off with someone?"

"I don't think so. He loved his kids too much. Would do anything for them. He might leave me, but he wouldn't leave them. Not like this."

"What about his business?"

"What about it?" was her abrupt reply.

"What was it exactly?"

"You know, I wasn't sure. 'Ask me no questions and I'll tell you no lies,' he'd always say."

"Last time we were here, he mentioned he was buying and selling currency," Partial Sue said.

"Yeah, he'd always say that. His stock answer because it usually shuts people up. He was always making deals though. Phone never stopped ringing."

"Is there a possibility that one of his deals went pear-shaped?" asked Fiona. "And that's why he's disappeared?"

Abbey inhaled deeply, attempting to stall the return of her tears. "You know, I've been denying it, but I think that's what happened. He was on the phone on the morning of the dog show. It was strange because I heard him apologising and he never apologises for anything. He wasn't himself, he was nervous. Something was definitely up. Sounded like some-thing had gone wrong."

"Do you know what?" Fiona asked.

She shook her head.

"When we visited last, he seemed quite cheerful," Daisy remarked.

"Oh, he's good at putting on an act," Abbey explained. "His Artful Dodger, I call it. I know when he's worried because he overdoes it. Gets more cockney sparrow."

"Was it someone at the dog show he was worried about?"

Abbey raised her eyebrows. "I don't know. I think maybe it was one of his far-flung contacts. Sunday morning, he was on the phone to someone for a long time. That's what made us late. After that, he definitely called someone at the dog show, but that was only to get them to delay the Sweetest Eyes category. The kids were getting upset that they were going to miss it."

"Who did he call at the dog show?" Fiona already knew this, but it didn't hurt to see if his wife would corroborate things.

"Kenneth Prendiville. Normally he's very straightlaced and strict, that one. Dean was expecting to have to bung him some cash to get him to postpone the start, but he didn't need to. Kenneth Prendiville was nice, offered to delay our category until after lunch. Kids were happy, that's the main thing. Course, it didn't matter. When we turned up, that lady had died and the show was cancelled."

"Did Dean do that a lot, offer people money when he wanted something done?"

Abbey hesitated and then said, "All the time. 'Palms must be greased', he'd always say. Said he could get anything he wanted for the right price. He knew people who could fix things. Dodgy people who could make things happen."

"He told you this?"

"No, but I overheard conversations when he thought I wasn't listening. I knew when he wanted something dodgy done because he'd ask the person at the other end to, 'apply a little pressure'."

"What do you think he meant by that?"

"I can't be sure, but it sounded like intimidation, using force."

"How did that make you feel?"

"Terrified at first. But gradually you turn a blind eye."

"And did he use that phrase on the phone about the time you noticed him getting worried?"

Abbey didn't answer at first. Her lip trembled. Then she slowly nodded.

"Do you think he'll ever be back?" Daisy asked.

Water pooled in her eyes. "No. Deep down, I've always known something like this would happen. Knew I'd wake up one morning to find him gone. That's what happens when your husband moves in dodgy circles. I've sort of been preparing myself for it. But it's the kids I feel sorry for. I've been putting off telling them that their dad's probably never coming back."

Fiona feared that the tears would come again, but Abbey steeled herself. Sucked them back and held it all in. Found some strength from somewhere. Nevertheless, they felt awful leaving her alone in her big empty house with nothing for company apart from Max and the bleak prospect that her husband had run off. Had it been because he'd been instrumental in Sylvia's death? That was what they needed to find out.

CHAPTER 50

Back at the shop, Fiona fumbled with the keys. They were all hurrying her to get the door open, such was their need for tea. One, because they didn't get any from Abbey Atkins — they were in no position to ask for it — and, two, she was in no state to make it. Her husband had absconded without warning, and the ramifications of this needed to be discussed in great detail. The best and only way to do this was with a calming cuppa in their hands. Tea was conducive to cogitation.

Once they were in, Fiona broke the habit of a lifetime and bypassed the teapot, which would've needed a good rinse out, and tossed three teabags into waiting mugs, then followed it up by sloshing boiling water into them, half of which went over the counter. Fiona's fraught tea-making was a result of the break they'd been handed. Not exactly an open-and-shut case, but on its way there — nothing said guilty like someone doing a runner. Fiona's hands continued to shake as she splashed milk into the tea, which also went over the counter. Despite their collective jitteriness, Daisy hadn't completely lost her faculties and appeared out of nowhere, a fistful of kitchen roll to blot up the spillage.

Next second, they were sitting around the table, gasping with relief as they sipped their tea. It didn't last very long as they began to speak over each other.

"It's Dean Atkins. Has to be," Partial Sue barked.

Fiona agreed but had to be the voice of calm reason to ensure their conclusions were sound, and they weren't jumping the gun. "He wasn't at the show. He couldn't have done it."

"Didn't need to be by the sound of it," Partial Sue retorted. "You heard his wife. He's a fixer. Pays people to do things. He probably hired a hitman to inject Sylvia at the show. It all makes sense. He's on the phone to the Far East. He's not making deals. He's speaking to this betting syndicate. Maybe he's the bringer of bad news. Had to tell them that Sylvia's pulled out of the show, which is why he's all apologetic. They want her punished, killed immediately for losing them a ton of money. He promises to make it happen. Texts a guy he knows. Tells him he has a mark that needs taking care of. Next moment she drops dead from a poisonous injection. That's such a hitman thing to do. In and out quick without being seen. Melting into the crowd."

"The timings are a little strained," Fiona remarked. "If he got the call to kill her on the morning of the show, that's not much time to hire a hitman, brief him on the target, and then for the hitman to get to Christchurch to do the deed."

"Maybe Christchurch has a convenient, neighbourhood hitman," Daisy suggested.

"We're talking about an assassin, not a branch of Budgens."

Partial Sue flapped her hands around. "Okay, okay. We're assuming the call on the morning of the dog show was for him to order a hit on Sylvia. It's possible that happened days earlier. Abbey mentioned she heard him apologising down the phone on the morning of the dog show. What if he had already set up the hit and was simply apologising again and reassuring them that it would happen that day?"

Fiona nodded. "Yeah, that makes more sense, but maybe we can embellish the theory even further. What if he was the architect of this betting scam? Set up the whole thing, pitched it to this powerful syndicate, recruited Sylvia somehow. But it went pear-shaped when she pulled out. The consortium wanted her dead, which he took care of. But he's still not out of the woods yet. They wanted their money back. Maybe he had to raise millions quickly, in the next week or two — you know what these people are like. He's well off but he hasn't got that sort of money lying around. Only option left was to do a runner. Grabbed his passport and phone and disappeared."

"It's beginning to sound very plausible." Partial Sue grinned.

"If he's taken his phone, he can be traced," Daisy said.

"I imagine he's got a new one by now," Fiona replied. "Doesn't matter though, phone company would have records of all his calls to this syndicate, and Sylvia Steadman."

"He won't be able to dodge out of that," Partial Sue said.

Daisy frowned. "There's one thing that still doesn't add up. Like I said before. If Sylvia's been involved in an illegal betting scam, and got cold feet, the last place she'd go would be the dog show that she was supposed to throw."

Partial Sue wasn't going to let anything scupper this theory. "Maybe she thought she'd be safe there. You know, public place — safety in numbers."

"I agree, it is an odd thing to do," Fiona said. "But I think we've got more than enough to get the police interested. What do you think?"

Her two friends nodded.

"Make the call," Daisy said.

CHAPTER 51

A week later, Partial Sue burst into the shop, waving a folded-up newspaper around, as if she were attempting to bat invisible flies away from her head. Dramatically, she slammed it on the table in front of Fiona and Daisy. "You're going to want to read this. Page seven."

Picking up the paper, Fiona leafed through it until she reached the right page. Daisy scooched her chair around so she could read it too. In the top right-hand corner, a headline read: *Local Man Arrested On Suspicion Of Money Laundering.* A small picture accompanied the story. Two police officers led Dean Atkins out of what appeared to be a dilapidated farm building in the middle of nowhere. His hands were handcuffed behind his back. The self-assured cockney geezer didn't look too chirpy. His face was bowed to avoid being caught by the camera, although it hadn't worked. They could see he hadn't shaved or slept, and his shirt was creased and untucked.

Fiona speed-read through the article once then twice. "Says he's wanted for money laundering and had been hiding in the Shropshire countryside."

"That's right." Partial Sue paced up and down. "Money laundering — no mention of betting rings or anything to do with the murder of Sylvia Steadman."

"I suppose it's in the same ballpark," Daisy said. "Big sums of money."

"Well, yes and no," Fiona replied. "They're both organised crime but the outcomes are completely different."

Partial Sue stopped pacing. "Murderers are a big deal for the police. Well, it would be conspiracy to murder in this case plus fraud. It would be good for police PR. Why are they not telling the press about Dean Atkins being a suspect in the dog show murder?"

"Maybe they haven't got enough evidence yet," Daisy replied.

"But the evidence was huge," Partial Sue pointed out. "We outlined everything to DI Fincher in great detail."

Fiona puffed out her cheeks. "Maybe we got it wrong. Maybe we let our imaginations run wild. Made it fit the crime because we wanted it to. It was a theory. We actually had no firm evidence of an international betting syndicate, just a lot of circumstantial evidence we'd made into a narrative."

The ladies grew silent, still stunned. Exactly one week ago they thought they had given DI Fincher and DS Thomas the tip-off of a lifetime. The man who'd arranged Sylvia Steadman's death on behalf of his gambling overlords. It all seemed so watertight. So logical. The suspect had even absconded. What more could they ask for? Though they were a humble trio of amateur sleuths, after tipping off the police, they had afforded themselves a pat on the back in the form of a pie and a pint at the George in Christchurch afterwards. Their impromptu celebration had been premature. They'd been right about Dean Atkins being a criminal but wrong about the crime he was wanted for.

"I can't stand this. We need to know." Fiona pulled her phone out of her bag and called DI Fincher. Fiona hadn't expected her to answer, but she did. Fiona put it on speaker phone.

The detective pre-empted her question. "I know why you're calling, Fiona. I take it you've seen the story in the press."

"I have. Why is there no mention of Dean Atkins' involvement with Sylvia's murder."

"I'm not at liberty to discuss—"

Fiona became impatient. "Yes, yes. I know. You can't discuss ongoing cases. But come on, give us some crumbs from the table. You wouldn't have Dean Atkins in custody if it wasn't for us telling you about his disappearance."

"We'd have got him eventually."

"But what about the murder and the international gambling rings? The pieces all fit, don't you agree?"

"I never agreed or disagreed with that."

"But Dean Atkins ticks all the boxes."

"As I said, I can't discuss that with you."

They went back and forth. Telephone tennis. A game that Fiona would never win. In the end, she resorted to pleading. "Please, you have to give us something. Is Dean Atkins involved with Sylvia Steadman's murder or not? Should we resume our investigation?"

DI Fincher sighed. "Okay, I will say this and then that's the end of the matter. We believe Sylvia Steadman's killer is still at large."

"What makes you think—"

"No, no. Discussion over, Fiona. Now if you'll excuse me, I have a lot of work to get on with." The detective hung up.

An anticlimactic atmosphere settled over the shop. A damp mist of disappointment dulling their confidence and enthusiasm.

"Well, that's a blow," Daisy said.

Partial Sue collapsed into a chair, shaking her head. "I don't understand it. I was convinced he was our man."

"Right person. Wrong crime. That's still a good innings." Fiona tried to make them feel better.

Partial Sue wouldn't be consoled. "So, there's no betting ring. No Far Eastern businessmen sitting around flashy boardroom tables in shiny skyscrapers and expensive suits discussing ways to fiddle the system. Just some seedy guy who cleaned money. I feel like a complete berk."

"Don't you dare," said Fiona. "We have nothing to feel stupid about. We've just helped the police catch a wanted criminal. That's a win."

"It doesn't feel like one."

"What do we do now?" Daisy asked.

"We do what we always do," Fiona replied. "We make tea, eat cake and find the real killer."

CHAPTER 52

A log jam occurred. Not a real one, of course. A mental one. Thoughts became entangled and logic refused to flow with the news that the killer was still at large. Fiona's mind couldn't accept that Dean Atkins had nothing to do with the murder, and because of that, her mind had gone on strike. Lethargy was partly to blame. She'd assumed that the killer had been caught. Job done. Allowed herself to relax. Fiona's detective brain had put its feet up, and liked it, thank you very much, showing no signs of getting back to work any time soon. Daisy and Partial Sue appeared to be having the same problem. Aimlessly, the three of them stared into space, hoping inspiration would hit them, preferably sooner rather than later.

Daisy resorted to their default when things weren't going so well. "I'll put the kettle on."

They'd already managed to down three pots of the stuff and Fiona had surpassed her tea tolerance. "I know this sounds like complete heresy, but I don't think that will help apart from sending us to the loo more often."

"What about more cake?"

"I'm stuffed, and out of ideas," Partial Sue said.

"We still have a few dog show competitors on the list we can interview," Daisy suggested.

"That's a good fallback," Fiona replied. "But I feel like we were onto something before we got distracted by Dean Atkins. Let's take stock. Retrace our steps. Where were we before we got side-tracked by Dean Atkins?"

Daisy's eyes brightened. "Oh, I know. We were in London."

"I think Fiona meant intellectually," Partial Sue said. "Not geographically."

"No, that's good," Fiona replied. "That's when Dylan Fraser told us he always grooms Charlie before a show. He was convinced Sylvia wouldn't enter without him. Therefore, he believed she didn't compete in the Christchurch dog show."

Partial Sue clicked her fingers. "That's it. That's where we got derailed. We didn't believe him because we'd seen her entry form. Then we jumped to the conclusion that she'd been bribed to enter the dog show to throw it."

"That entry form is the key to all this," Fiona replied. "Dylan Fraser thought it must have been faked, but we didn't listen. We went off at a tangent. First step, we need to check if that form is genuine or not."

Partial Sue began to jitter. "If it's been faked it must be David Harper, the treasurer. He had access to the entry forms, and didn't want us to see them, remember? We just need to work out his motive."

"Let's not jump to conclusions again," Fiona said. "We know how that turned out last time. Besides, anyone could've uploaded a faked form."

"Why would someone do that?" Daisy asked.

Fiona shook her head. "I don't know, but first, we need to establish whether it's genuinely been faked before we do anything else."

"What about asking Freya?" Partial Sue suggested.

Freya was the local IT guru who had given up a major position in London to take over her father's computer repair shop when he'd retired. The capital's loss was Southbourne's gain. They had the best tech support in the country, right on their doorstep, although, strictly speaking her shop had another, more adrenaline-fuelled function. One half of it was divided by a hastily built wooden corridor-like construction, used for axe-throwing.

"Yes," Fiona agreed. "She could find out. Hack the dog club website."

Daisy gulped hard, eyes rimmed with worry. "That would be breaking the law."

Partial Sue huffed. "It's a local dog club, not the Bank of England. It'll be fine. And we're not stealing anything, just having a butcher's."

Daisy didn't look any happier. Fiona reassured her, "Why don't you stay here, Daisy? Look after the shop. Sue and I will take Simon Le Bon for a walk up the road to Freya's, see if she can help."

At the sound of the 'W' word, Simon Le Bon's ears flicked up and he leapt out of his bed, a bundle of waggy excitement. Daisy stayed behind, while Fiona and Partial Sue made the short stroll up Southbourne Grove to Freya's computer shop. On entering they found her tearing open a box from Amazon with her muscular, tattooed arms. In her tight zip-up top, black cycling shorts and matching calf-length Doc Marten boots, she looked as if she were about to enter a goth version of the Tour de France.

"Hi, Fiona, hi Sue." Freya smiled at them with a black lipsticked mouth. Simon Le Bon darted forward, wagging his tail. Crouching down to make a fuss of him, she let her face be smothered in doggie kisses. Fiona noticed that the axes and the target had disappeared, replaced by a heavy punch bag hanging from a thick chain.

Partial Sue noticed it too. "What happened to the axe-throwing? I liked that." With her cricketer's bowling right arm, Partial Sue had been frighteningly lethal at splintering the bull's eye.

"There's not much call for it in Southbourne, and I really couldn't get the hang of it. I'm no Lagertha."

Fiona and Partial Sue stared at her blankly.

Freya straightened up. "The Queen of Kattegat."

More vacant stares.

"From *Vikings*, my favourite TV show."

"Unless it involves police procedure or rural settings or both, we probably haven't seen it," Partial Sue chuckled.

"Is the punch bag for keeping fit?" asked Fiona.

"It's for practicing my kick-boxing. I squeeze in a quick training sesh between customers, although it does take me half an hour to undo the laces on my DMs, so I might have to break the habit of a lifetime and invest in some flip-flops." She pulled open the package to reveal a hefty pair of black boxing gloves which she slid out and onto her hands. She bashed her fists together like a boxer before a fight, then threw a few jabs. "Yes, these are perfect! Right, what can I do for you?"

"I have a favour to ask," Fiona said. "I was wondering how you'd feel about doing something for us that's not exactly kosher."

"Depends what it is."

"We need to get a look into the Christchurch Dog Club website," Fiona explained. "Find out whether an entry form has been faked or not?"

Freya laughed.

"What's so funny?" asked Partial Sue.

"You know, I get lots of people asking me to do dodgy things for them. Can I add more money to their bank account or hack their boss's email."

Partial Sue was shocked. "You can do that?"

"Oh, yes. I turn them all down. Make up some excuse or other. But you're the only people who approach me for such innocuous things, like hacking a dog club website. I love it."

"So, will you do it?" Fiona asked. "It's for a good cause — to catch a murderer."

"Yeah, sure. Plus, you're the only people who ask me to do these things for the right reasons. Very cool reasons by the way. Catching murderers."

"We'll make a crime fan of you yet," Partial Sue said.

"I don't doubt that. Follow me." Freya led them behind the counter so they could gather around her weapons-grade computer. She was about to start typing when she realised her boxing gloves were still on. Biting the Velcro fasteners, she tore them open and shook off the gloves. "Right, what do you want to know?"

"An entry form was uploaded to the site to enter the dog show, from Sylvia Steadman."

"The woman who was murdered?" Freya asked.

Fiona nodded.

"Sure, no problem." Freya's fingers dabbed the keyboard like an expert percussionist. Multiple pages opened with dizzying speed. "Okay, got it. Sylvia Steadman, form uploaded on the fourth of March for her dog Charlie to enter the Golden Oldie category. Christchurch address."

"That's the one."

"Okay, let's see what the metadata says."

"Metadata?" Partial Sue asked.

"That's what's really going on behind the curtain. It's the back-end stuff users never see and is almost impossible to fake." She pulled up a file of meaningless computer language. "Okay, says the form was submitted on the fourth of March, so that matches. I've got the IP address of the computer. Let me just check its location. One second. Yep, matches Sylvia's address in Christchurch."

"So it's not a fake?" asked Fiona.

"No, I'm sure of it."

"How sure?" asked Partial Sue.

"I'd say about ninety-nine point nine percent sure."

Fiona could feel her face contorting into a mask of disappointment.

Freya noticed. "Look, this is just a quick check anyone with half an IT brain can do. I could do a deep dive for you, but it will take longer and I'd say it's highly unlikely I'll find anything. This stuff is very tricky to pull off."

"Would you mind?" Fiona replied. "Of course, we'll pay."

"Don't be daft. I do this stuff for fun."

Fiona and Partial Sue dragged themselves back to the shop, their feet heavy. Another disappointment robbing them of mental enthusiasm that reached all the way down to their toes. Partial Sue remained cynical about their chances of catching the killer. Fiona attempted to convince her that it was a temporary setback. Trouble was, she didn't believe that herself.

CHAPTER 53

"Another dead end?" Daisy's eyebrows arched.

Partial Sue tossed her coat down on the nearest chair by the table. "Yep, we've got more dead ends than one of them horrible new housing developments the council keeps building."

"Turns out Sylvia did enter the show, after all," Fiona said. "You were right, Daisy. She probably didn't think it was worth her while getting Dylan Fraser all the way down here to groom Charlie."

"Well, I suppose it makes sense," Partial Sue agreed. "She's retired and I bet he's not cheap." Partial Sue's eyes lit up. "Hey, what if it's Dylan Fraser?"

"Why would he kill Sylvia?" Fiona asked.

"Money, or lack of it. Remember what he said about those ad shoots? Nice work if you can get it, and they paid very well. He must have been really fed up when that gravy train ended. Same went for Greg Trelane. His production company was on to a nice little earner, and Sylvia Steadman put a stop to it all."

Fiona suddenly allowed herself to become excited, but only a smidge. "That would make sense. Both he and Dylan Fraser would've been out of pocket. As you said, they were on to nice little earners."

Partial Sue nodded rapidly. "That's right. Loads of motive there. Maybe it was one of them or both. A collaboration." While Fiona and Partial Sue traded theories about their shiny new suspects, Daisy quietly thumbed away on her phone. Partial Sue's enthusiasm rose with every syllable. "It's so obvious! They stood to lose the most. They were being paid handsomely to jet off to glamorous locations. Why didn't we think of this before?"

"Well, we got distracted by betting scams and Dean Atkins," Fiona replied. "What do you think, Daisy?"

Daisy glanced up from her phone with a face that was about to break bad news. "I hate to rain on your parade of shops, but it's not Dylan Fraser or Greg Trelane."

"It's just rain on your parade. There aren't any shops involved." The hopeful smile that had creased Fiona's face began to falter. "But what's the rain on this particular parade?"

Daisy turned her phone around so they could see. "This is the Instagram account for Dylan's grooming salon FUR." She scrolled through photo after photo of Dylan Fraser clad in a white T-shirt and a white jumpsuit with the top half pulled down and the arms tied at the waist. A microphone headset narrowly avoided his man bun as he addressed a crowd of interested dog owners semi-circled around him. A labradoodle stood on a sturdy metal table, harnessed in front of him, as he demonstrated various grooming techniques. "That's the Harrogate Dog Show," Daisy informed them. "Same day as Christchurch Dog Show. Dylan Fraser did grooming demonstrations all day." Daisy flipped the phone around and tapped into a different Instagram account. She turned it back to show her colleagues. "This is Greg Trelane's personal account. He was in Romania over the weekend of Christchurch Dog Show, filming a promo for a video game called Earth's Last Days."

A suitably bleak and grey, heavy-industrial landscape filled every image with Greg Trelane and his crew setting up cameras and equipment amongst derelict factories and rusting pipework. It told Fiona all she needed to know that

Earth's Last Days was some sort of post-apocalyptic action game, possibly involving people having to hit radioactive zombies with shovels. "Oh," was all she could muster.

Partial Sue attempted to put a positive spin on things. "Well, that would explain why Sylvia didn't book Dylan Fraser. He was already booked. Why didn't he tell us this when we spoke to him?"

"He was in shock. We'd just told him Sylvia Steadman had been murdered. Same goes for Greg Trelane, and we never asked them where they were on the day of the murder — big slip-up on our part." Fiona sighed as another lead went up in a puff of digital smoke. "So, there's no bitter dog groomer or film producer seeking revenge for being out of pocket."

"Looks that way."

"I think we could do with a cup of tea," Daisy suggested.

The kettle boiled and Daisy mainlined boiling water straight onto the teabags in the waiting cups. A minute later she emerged from the storeroom, placing the three steaming teas down in front of them. Fiona snatched hers up at the same time as Partial Sue, both took gulps, rather than sips, and instantly regretted it, burning their tongues and letting out simultaneous ouches.

"Jeez! I keep doing that!" Fiona said. The pain drilled into her tongue, lighting up the nerve centres of her brain.

"Oh, sorry," Daisy said.

"Don't apologise." Partial Sue poked her tongue out and wafted it with her hand several times. "It's Molly's fault. She conditioned us to lukewarm tea with that stupid idea of letting the kettle cool before pouring it." Though Molly had imprisoned them and tried to kill them, Partial Sue held a bigger grudge against her for cavalier tea-making.

Fiona winced in pain.

"Are you okay?" asked Daisy. "Did you burn your tongue really badly?"

"Oh, no it's fine. I've just got this weird sensation in my head. I got it once before when I burned my tongue."

"What sort of sensation?" asked Partial Sue.

"A nagging in my brain. Like I'm trying to remember something important, or I've left the gas on."

"Do you want to go home and check?" Daisy suggested. "I hate things like that. I once went to visit my daughter and had to turn around at Fleet services because I thought I'd left my Velux window open. It wasn't so much the security, it's right up in the roof but it started raining and I was worried my house would be flooded. Of course, when I got home it was shut tight and wasn't even raining down here."

"How is Bella, by the way?" asked Partial Sue. "Is she still not speaking to you?"

Daisy went pale, cast her eyes down and shook her head. She hadn't seen or spoken to her estranged daughter for years. Fiona glanced at Partial Sue who looked like she instantly regretted mentioning it.

Fiona decided to distract them both by resuming their previous conversation. "It's not that I've forgotten to turn the gas off or anything. That's the closest I can relate it to. I'm not sure what my brain's trying to tell me." Often Fiona had times when her synapses fired but the thought or idea they carried couldn't quite reach its destination. The dots were there but they wouldn't join up.

"Well, let's see if we can get to the bottom of it," Partial Sue suggested. "You burnt your tongue — what does that mean?"

Daisy was straight onto her phone to see what the internet had to say. "Dreaming of a sore or swollen tongue means you're jealous."

"I wasn't dreaming."

"You're going off tea," Partial Sue blurted.

Fiona recoiled indignantly. "Never going to happen. Not in this lifetime."

"Yeah, that was a stupid thing to say."

"Let's go back further." Daisy began to speak like a stage hypnotist. "You wanted tea. I made the tea. Then you drank the tea."

Fiona and Partial Sue exchanged puzzled looks as they waited for the rest of her profound observation, but it didn't come.

"Well, what else was Fiona going to do apart from drink the tea?" Partial Sue asked.

"I suppose I could have spat it back into the cup," Fiona said. "To save my tongue but that would have been uncouth."

Daisy made a face. "I once had to do that in a restaurant. Ordered a prawn cocktail but I didn't realise it was in a whisky sauce — I really don't like whisky. I tried to spit it into a napkin but I wasn't fast enough and it went all down my front."

Fiona wobbled with excitement. "That's it! That's it!"

"What, prawns in whisky sauce?"

"No, not that. I need a coffee. Who fancies one?"

Now it was Partial Sue's and Daisy's turn to exchange confused looks.

CHAPTER 54

River boats idled at their moorings while swans slid effortlessly past. A lingering damp settled over Christchurch Quay, as it became that vague and difficult part of the day to define. The end of the afternoon, or the beginning of the evening? The rush hour home for many or teatime for those who liked dining early. Either way, the place was eerily quiet as they swept along the quayside, having left Partial Sue's Uno in the Priory car park. Fiona hugged herself against the cold, looking forward to having a steaming hot cup of coffee in her hands.

"I'm really not sure about having caffeine at this time," Daisy grumbled. "I hope I can sleep tonight. Never after four thirty is my general rule for drinking coffee."

"Daisy, it's only quarter to six," Partial Sue pointed out. "You've got at least another five hours until bedtime."

"I like to have my light off by nine."

"How old are you, eleven? And that's before the watershed, you miss all the good crime telly."

"I can watch it on catch up, but I'm a grumpy goose if I don't get my ten hours."

"Don't worry, Daisy. You don't have to drink the coffee," Fiona reassured her.

"I don't?"

"No, none of us do. This is an experiment." Fiona diverted them off the quayside path and onto the wide, grassy area, much to the delight of Simon Le Bon, his nose zig-zagging in every direction, investigating delectable new smells. Eventually, Fiona found what she was looking for. The dog show marquee had been dismantled, but the trampled grass hadn't completely recovered and provided a large, slightly dishevelled rectangle, indicating where it had been. A particularly worn area in a 'V' shape marked the position of the main entrance. Fiona led them from front to back, until they reached the spot where Malorie Granger had generously given them a stand, thoughtfully placed beside the smaller and somewhat grottier rear entrance, leading out to the Portaloos and generators.

Fiona stopped. "Right, I'd say this is roughly where Pippa Stroll bumped into Daisy, sending coffee all down her front. Pippa claims to have bought a latte from that kiosk over there." Fiona pointed to a small boxlike hut by the quayside. The lights were still on but a man in an apron busied himself over the tables, wiping them down, preparing to close up for the night. Fiona would have to make this quick if she were to test out her theory.

"Yeah, so what?" Partial Sue asked.

"She bought the coffee and claims she came straight in through the rear entrance then the spillage occurred, which doesn't make sense."

"Why doesn't it make sense?" Partial Sue asked. "Sounds reasonable to me."

"Oh!" Daisy nearly burst with excitement as the logic lined up or didn't, in this case. "She spilt hot coffee all over herself! But she didn't squeal or cry out in pain."

"Exactly," Fiona replied. "That's what's been nagging my brain, but I couldn't quite put my finger on it. Like our tongues, the coffee would have gone straight through her jumper dress, and burnt her skin. Why didn't she yelp or squeal in pain?"

"Because she's incredibly thick-skinned," Partial Sue joked.

"Maybe she bought an iced coffee?" Daisy suggested.

"On a cold morning in March, not likely," Fiona replied. "Something's not right there. But I think before we do anything, we need to test our theory. We need to buy a latte from that kiosk, bring it back and see if it's cooled by the time we get here."

"We're not going to tip it all down out fronts, are we?" Daisy quivered.

"No, no need to go overboard. I thought we could just dab a few drops on the backs of our hands, test the temperature."

"Yeah, there's a chance they make coffee the way Molly used to make tea — badly." Partial Sue still wouldn't let it lie.

The three ladies hurried over to the kiosk to put in their order. The man was now stacking up the chairs. "I'm sorry we're just closing."

"Please," asked Fiona. "All we want are three lattes."

The man smiled. "Well, that I can handle." He went inside the kiosk and began preparing their drinks, slotting a cup underneath the nozzle of a slick machine with two rows of brightly lit buttons above.

"Tell me," Partial Sue asked, "can you have different temperatures of coffee?"

"No," he replied, his back to them. "It's all automated. I don't have to do anything apart from remember to press the right button. But it does use freshly ground beans, so it's almost as good as a proper espresso machine."

Partial Sue winked at the others. "That's good to know."

"Were you working on the day of the dog show?" Fiona asked.

"Yep, I'm here every day. I own the place."

"I don't suppose you remember serving a small blonde-haired woman who had a Maltese dog. They look the same."

The man stopped what he was doing, turned around to face them. He paused in thought, then said, "I can't say I remember anyone like that."

"Oh, you would've remembered this one," Partial Sue huffed. "Bolshie, she is. Bit stuck-up. Looks like Dolly Parton but with all the kindness sucked out of her."

The man had another go, trying to recall the woman. He shook his head. "No, sorry." He went back to preparing their coffees. A minute later he turned around and placed three lattes in corrugated paper cups on the counter, whorls of steam rising from them. He swiftly secured their tops with plastic lids.

Fiona paid and thanked the man. They marched back across the grass, to the outline of the marquee where the rear entrance would have been. Taking another few steps, they stopped, roughly where Pippa had bumped into Daisy.

"Who wants to go first?" Fiona asked.

Daisy didn't want to go at all. "I can feel the heat coming through the cup. That coffee's really hot."

"We need to be sure," said Partial Sue.

"Do we all need to do it?" asked Daisy.

"I think we do," Fiona replied. "Some people have different tolerances to heat than others, and your tongue can take more heat than your skin. It only needs to be a few drops. We'll all go together on the count of three."

They held their cups up next to the backs of their slightly quivering free hands, preparing to pour.

"Ready?" Fiona said. "Three, two, one."

"Oh, wait," Daisy interrupted.

Partial Sue huffed, clearly wanting to get this over with. Daisy pulled the cuff of her jumper down over her hand. "For accuracy. To mimic the coffee going through Pippa's jumper dress."

"Good idea." Fiona resumed the countdown. "Three, two, one." They all tipped their cups at once. Thick, frothy coffee appeared from out of the little drinking hole in the top and dribbled over their hands. Not much, just a thimbleful, but that was enough to produce three simultaneous yelps.

"That hurt." Daisy winced. "Even through my jumper."

"Definitely boiling," Partial Sue added.

Daisy produced three cooling wet wipes to douse and clean off the hot beverage.

"Imagine the whole lot going down your front," Fiona said. "So, Pippa Stroll was lying about coming straight from the kiosk to the marquee, otherwise her drink would've scalded her."

"But what does it mean? Why would she lie about that?" Daisy asked.

Over by the kiosk, they noticed the man switching off the lights and closing up for the night, locking the door and testing the handle several times. But rather than heading for one of the two car parks that serviced the quay and driving home to a well-earned evening with his feet up, he walked briskly towards the three ladies. They still clutched their coffees and had no intention of drinking them, except Partial Sue who hated anything going to waste. She took several small sips, not wishing to burn her tongue as well as her hand. "That's not bad coffee."

The man broke into a light jog, as he came towards them. "I just wanted to catch you before you left. You know, I do remember the woman you talked about. Sorry, it took me a while. She was really impatient with me. Told me to hurry up with her coffee."

"Sounds about right." Partial Sue took another sip.

"I told her, it's a machine, I can't make it go any faster. She got really flustered and her dog kept yapping."

"She's a bit rude, I'm afraid," Daisy replied.

The man looked doubtful. "I wouldn't say rude. She came across as worried, stressed."

"Really?" asked Fiona.

"Oh, yes, she was desperate. She kept glancing around, fidgeting on the spot."

"That's strange."

"I tell you what else is strange." He came in closer. "She also bought a bottle of water. I watched her when she left because I thought she was acting a bit odd. She stopped by the back of the marquee, poured half her coffee away on the grass, then topped it up with bottled water. Ruined a completely good cup of coffee."

Something was wrong with Pippa Stroll's behaviour. Whatever the reason for it, one thing was sure. Bumping into Daisy had been no accident. Pippa Stroll had planned it all along, even going as far as diluting her coffee so it wouldn't scald her. She'd been up to something. No doubt about it.

CHAPTER 55

The Charity Shop Detective Agency had a lead. A big, sizable one they'd snatched up with their collective hands and wouldn't let go. Truth be told, they were yanking it in two different directions at this precise moment. All morning, Fiona had found herself adjudicating between the equal and opposing forces of her colleagues' opinions.

"You know, I don't think it's that strange that Pippa poured cold water in her coffee," Daisy said. "People are very particular about their drinks. We like ours strong, but we all take different amounts of milk. Maybe Pippa's one of those people who likes it warm and weak."

"That's true," Fiona agreed. "In Italy they serve coffee with a glass of water."

Partial Sue shook her head vigorously. Something she'd been doing a lot this morning. "That's for cleansing your palette, not watering down your coffee. Pippa's the killer. Plain and simple. She dumped cold water in her coffee to cool it down because she intended to bump into someone and spill it on herself. It was an engineered alibi to place her away from the murder scene. Remember, she admitted to us that she wanted to win Best in Show. Boasted about how Barbie was the best dog there, and she was the best dog groomer. We all heard her. She killed Sylvia to get rid of her biggest rival. Then bumped into Daisy to create an alibi, and I bet she paid for that coffee on her card as further proof. Belt and braces."

Fiona took a deep breath. "There are a few problems with that. Yes, she was Sylvia's biggest competition. But, as we said before, would someone planning on taking out their nearest rival really draw attention to herself by boasting about being better than them? Secondly, I genuinely believe she thought she'd win Best in Show. Call it arrogance or whatever, she was convinced she'd take first place. Someone that confident wouldn't feel the need to take out their nearest rival, not if they thought they were better. She's almost too conceited to be the killer. If she murdered Sylvia, she'd be admitting that Barbie wasn't as good as Charlie."

"Arrogance can sometimes mask insecurity," Partial Sue countered.

"But what about Adrian with Red Bull?" Daisy asked. "He caused the accident. Do you think he was part of it? He had a solid alibi for Sally Wilde's death, but we now know that was Molly. He doesn't have one for Sylvia, well, apart from alerting the vet."

"I think you've answered your own question," Partial Sue replied. "I think his bumping into you was fortuitous for Pippa. I think she would have knocked into you regardless. Do you think it's a coincidence that she involved us in her little pantomime? Three local sleuths. What better people to vouch for her whereabouts at the time of the murder?"

Fiona thought on this and then said, "But that also supports her innocence. We've always said Pippa Stroll was nowhere near Sylvia. You have to be up close to someone to inject them."

Partial Sue nodded. "Okay, I agree but right from the start we've made an amateurish assumption — that Sylvia was injected with something fast-acting, which has given certain people alibis, because they weren't near her at the time."

Fiona frowned. "It wasn't an amateurish assumption. Julie Sheers told us it was fast-acting, and she's a healthcare professional."

"Yes, for pets. Not people. What if Julie was wrong? What if Sylvia was injected earlier, outside the marquee, with something that took a little longer to work?"

"But that's riskier, isn't it?" Daisy said. "Fewer people, more chance of being seen. Pippa and Barbie are a very dis-tinctive couple. They'd have been noticed."

Partial Sue rubbed her chin. "The main entrance was gridlocked with people buying tickets or showing their passes. Plus, you have to remember people wouldn't have been looking at Pippa, they'd have been looking at Charlie. I'm sure he would've been recognised outside, just like he had inside the marquee but to a lesser degree. Pippa could've sidled up to Sylvia, injected her, then got out of there."

The theory began to gain traction in Fiona's mind. "And while the injection is taking effect, she heads around the outside of the marquee, over to the kiosk. Grabs herself a coffee, waters it down then comes in the back entrance, where she bumps into Daisy."

Partial Sue nodded. "At about the same time, Sylvia begins to gasp for breath. Bingo! Pippa Stroll has just bought herself an alibi — a coffee-flavoured one."

"It sounds plausible," Fiona added. "What do you think, Daisy?"

Daisy chewed her lip. "I still don't know."

Undeterred, Partial Sue continued, "We've always assumed the effects of the injection were instant. But if the poison had a delayed reaction, it would give the killer time to be somewhere else. That opens up all sorts of possibilities. Sylvia could've been injected in the car park or walking across the grass."

"I think that's going a tad far," Fiona said. "I agree that Pippa could've injected her outside the marquee, where she had the camouflage of other people and could swiftly jab her with a needle and then disappear, but in a car park or on the grass where there's lots of space it would be tricky to accidentally bump into her. Plus, getting the dosage exactly right so Sylvia dropped down dead inside the dog show, that would be very tricky to pull off."

"Again, we're making assumptions," Partial Sue replied. "We're assuming the intention was for Sylvia to drop down dead inside the marquee. Maybe Pippa didn't know how long the poison would take. Perhaps she thought Sylvia would die before she reached the show. Who knows?" Partial Sue whipped out her phone. "Don't forget, Pippa's a beautician, and if I remember rightly, yes! Here it is." She flipped her phone round for them all to see. The screen showed a web page for Pippa's salon, specifically, a stock image of a woman with flawless skin and pert lips. "Pippa does dermal fillers. Isn't that when they stick jelly in your face or something? She'd know her way around a syringe, that's for sure. I bet she's good at it too. Had lots of practice. Can probably do it with minimal pain. Handy for a stealthy poisoning of your rival."

Pippa Stroll had always ticked a lot of boxes, apart from the most important one — she was nowhere near Sylvia when she died. It had shielded her from being accused, ruled her out of the line-up of suspects, but now that shield had begun to splinter and fall apart.

"She's starting to look a lot like our killer," Fiona said.

"I think she always was, but she's played a very smart game. Made it impossible for the finger to be pointed at her. Manipulated us and used us as her alibi. Ringfenced herself. Very smart, especially boasting about how much she wanted to win. Bit of reverse psychology. She's tried to sell us on the fact that she can't be the killer because a killer simply wouldn't show off about how much they wanted to win. They'd keep a low profile. And we bought it. Very clever."

Daisy squirmed in her seat. "I still have problems with Pippa injecting Sylvia outside the marquee or inside. Like I said before, Pippa and Barbie are very recognisable. They're last year's winners. Very distinctive with all that white-blonde hair. Be impossible for them to merge into the crowd, even if that crowd was distracted by Charlie. Someone would've seen them. Plus, I don't know about you, but no matter how good you are at injecting people, doing it while holding a dog on a lead or in your arms would be difficult. I mean, even though Simon Le Bon is a lovely dog, I doubt I could pick a lock if I had to control him at the same time."

The room went silent. For every promising argument Partial Sue put forward, Daisy had a very convincing counterargument lined up. Whether Pippa had injected Sylvia inside or outside, or on the grass or in the car park, it didn't matter. Daisy's last point had put the kibosh on all of them. Having a dog in one hand and a syringe in the other was not a favourable combination. By the look on her face, Fiona could tell Partial Sue felt the same. You'd have to have the most disciplined and well-behaved dog to pull that off. Dogs were unpredictable, especially when they're surrounded by dozens of other dogs. Barbie wasn't unruly, but she had a mind of her own.

No one spoke for the next five minutes. A long, uncomfortable passage of time by Dogs Need Nice Homes standards, where the gentle chatter never ceased. It felt like an eternity. No one had anything to say or a hefty enough argument that would break the deadlock, so someone else did it for them.

Freya appeared at the door, startling them with a thick laptop folded under her arm. "Hey, got some news for you. You know when I said that Sylvia's form hadn't been faked. I think I was wrong."

CHAPTER 56

The three ladies nearly fell over themselves, leaping out of their seats and ushering Freya inside. Her timing couldn't have been more perfect. They needed a break, preferably a solid one made of hard digital evidence. Fiona tried to keep a check on her emotions, not letting her optimism run away with her. They'd been in this position several times before, only to find it led nowhere.

Freya set up her laptop, not the svelte, delicate, domestic kind you buy from John Lewis, but a heavyweight, custom machine that appeared to be constructed out of discarded parts of a Challenger tank. She flipped it open. The ladies gathered round the counter and stared at the screen, which was like looking into the Matrix — a jumble of nonsensical programming language.

"So what exactly has been faked?" asked Fiona.

"The IP address of the computer that submitted Sylvia's entry form," Freya replied. "First glance, it's all kosher, actually second, third and fourth glance too. I had to dig really deep but there are signs that it's been faked. Probably by a hacker for hire. A very good one."

"You can hire them?" Daisy quivered.

"Oh, yeah. You don't even need to go on the dark web. Regular web has loads of them. All anonymous, of course. They've made it look like the form was submitted from Sylvia's computer, right here in Christchurch."

"Do you know who did it, where it came from originally?" Fiona asked.

Freya shook her head. "They've done a good job of covering their tracks."

"Would police tech officers have detected this?" asked Partial Sue.

"I doubt it. Took me a while to unpick it, and they wouldn't have done such a deep search unless they had a reason."

"So I'm guessing you wouldn't know who hired the hacker?" Fiona asked.

"No, but definitely someone who wanted to make it look like Sylvia had entered the dog show competition."

"Why would anyone want to fake her entry form and then kill her?"

Freya shrugged. "Not my area of expertise. Listen, I better go. Got to open the shop. Mrs Liebling's new hard drive won't replace itself." She winked and closed the lid on her machine. "If you have any questions, just give me a call."

The ladies thanked Freya repeatedly and profusely for her help, as they saw her to the door. Although, to be honest, this new revelation had them more confused than ever. They gathered around the table, sprawling into their chairs, flummoxed.

"So Dylan was right all along," Daisy said. "Sylvia had no intention of entering the show."

"But this doesn't make sense," Partial Sue exclaimed. "Why would Pippa go to the trouble of spilling coffee all down herself to buy an alibi if Sylvia wasn't even in the show?"

"Maybe they're two separate things, unrelated," Fiona proposed. "Maybe Pippa didn't know anything about the hacked entry form and assumed, like everyone else, that

Sylvia was there to enter Charlie in the show. Perhaps this faked entry form is something else, someone else's doing."

"But I can't understand why anyone would fake her entry form?" Partial Sue asked. "What purpose does it serve?"

Daisy was about throw another investigative spanner in the works. "Speaking of Dylan Fraser, I remember what he said about jealous rivals. They'd be more likely to target the dog than the owner. If Pippa did want Charlie out of the competition, why kill Sylvia and have all the risks that come with that?"

"Maybe she just didn't want to harm a dog," Partial Sue said.

Fiona recoiled. "Pippa doesn't seem like the sort who'd be too worried about the welfare of someone else's dog. But that still doesn't answer why she or anyone else would fake Sylvia's form."

Facts and theories refused to make sense of each other, going round and around in Fiona's head like underground trains on the Circle Line at night. They rattled along, mostly empty but crucially, never joining up and always keeping their distance, never stopping, never really going anywhere.

Distraction came in the form of customers and donations. Fiona was glad of it. Huffing and puffing donors bustled through the door, boxes and bulging bin liners in their arms, while customers left with bagged-up items in their hands. The merry to-and-fro monotony of accepting donations and processing payments gave the ladies' investigative brains a much-needed rest.

When the doorbell finally fell silent, the three ladies naturally gathered at the table, where Partial Sue placed a brewing teapot as if it were a deity to be worshiped, which in many ways it was.

They sipped their tea in silence. Minds either occupied, deep in thought or locked up in a state of numbness. Daisy idly thumbed away on her phone.

For want of anything better to say, Fiona asked, "Anything interesting?"

"Not really," Daisy replied, "just glancing through Sylvia's social media posts. Nothing we haven't seen before."

"Which ones?" asked Partial Sue, not sounding like she was particularly bothered about the answer.

"Her retirement do. Everyone looks happy, well, except Sylvia. I mean, she's not exactly sad, just middling, I'd say. Or maybe she's hiding her sadness."

Fiona poured herself more tea. She always preferred the second cup, as it had had longer to brew. She took a thoughtful sip and then said, "Well, leaving your job to retire can be an anxious time."

"What exactly was Sylvia's job?" asked Daisy. "What does a chief administrator do — fill forms in all day?"

Partial Sue baulked. "Gosh, no. It's a heavyweight role, that is. She would have been responsible for the entire running of the Bristol City Council. Organising everything."

Fiona continued, "Going from having all that responsibility to nothing could have been a huge anticlimax when she retired. It might have left her feeling a bit lost at sea. I know it took me a long time to adjust after I finished work." She didn't mention the depression that had haunted her since she retired, appearing now and then to prod and elbow her, reminding her she had no purpose in life. Perhaps Sylvia had had similar fears.

"I miss being a teaching assistant," Daisy remarked, wistfully. "Especially the children. Their antics, the things they came out with and how sweet they could be. Miss Daisy, they used to call me. It did leave a big hole when I left, I must admit. Still makes me tearful if I think about it for too long."

Partial Sue plonked her cup down with a bit too much gusto. "Not me. I couldn't wait to retire. Leave the drudge of the office behind and say goodbye to the boring nine to five."

"But we still work nine to five here," Daisy pointed out. "Well, sort of."

"Yeah, but it's different. It's voluntary. I can walk away from it any time I please. Not that I would want to. I like being here."

"Me too," Fiona agreed. "Working in the shop and solving crimes gives me purpose. Otherwise, I'd feel like a spare part. Maybe Sylvia felt at a loose end too. Didn't know what to do with all that free time ahead."

"I don't think so," said Daisy. "Listen to her post. 'Last day at work. Bye-bye Bristol City Council. Going to miss it. Hello new challenges!'"

"Yes, I remember that post," Fiona said. "You're right. Sounds as if she's got something fun lined up to fill her time, doesn't it?"

Ever the cynic, Partial Sue said, "New challenges doesn't sound like fun to me. Sounds like more work. That's what you say when you go to a new job, well, in corporate language, to pretend how committed you are."

Fiona had to agree it did seem an odd choice of words. "Yes, it does sound a bit formal. Most people would say, I'm looking forward to putting my feet up or having more time to . . . and then whatever their hobby is."

"Did Sylvia have any hobbies?" Partial Sue asked. "Anything on her social media?"

Daisy shook her head. "No, it's all doggie stuff. I suppose Charlie was her hobby, her passion. Entering him into shows."

"But she'd stopped doing that," Fiona pointed out. "Remember what Dylan Fraser said, she'd had enough of it by then because it was a lot of work."

That last phrase halted their trail of logic, brought it to a place where it couldn't go any further, stumping all of them. Sylvia had no hobbies, and if she wasn't entering dog shows anymore, just what was her new challenge? There were no hints on her social media, so perhaps she'd preferred to keep it a secret.

A contemplative silence descended over the table. Three minds wondering quietly, apart from inside Fiona's head where those annoying, empty underground trains rattled through her brain refusing to join up.

Strangely, they'd read that post before about Sylvia looking forward to new challenges and had skimmed over it, regarding it as a throwaway comment, not meriting any further consideration. Just something people said. But it seemed to hint at a more serious future, or were they reading too much into it, and that was just how Sylvia was? A serious person.

"Are you okay Fiona?" Daisy asked.

"You look like you're chewing a wasp," Partial Sue added.

"That would be more preferable," Fiona replied. A thought had lodged itself deep inside her brain, pestering her but refusing to budge. The mental equivalent of a hangnail, both irritable and painful. "I'm having one of those moments where there's something out of reach that I can't quite grasp."

Partial Sue had her own thought on the matter. "According to both Dylan Fraser and Greg Trelane, Sylvia could be a diva. Liked things just so. Maybe the same went for retirement, and she had it all worked out. Knew what she had planned. Saw it as an opportunity to do something else, rather than a chance to take it easy. Obviously, we don't know what that was — could've been hang-gliding or decoupage for all we know. So maybe she was like us. Being busy was in her nature. She couldn't help herself and had to be involved in something."

Finally, something dislodged in Fiona's brain. "Thanks, Sue. You've just made me remember something that Dylan mentioned."

"What's that?"

"Well, it was only a little aside he made, insignificant, really. We didn't pick up on it at the time, but in the context of this conversation, it might give us something. Not a lead exactly but it could give us the means to finding one."

"A lead to a lead." Partial Sue smiled. "I'll take that as a win. Now, tell us, what did he say?"

CHAPTER 57

Daisy leaned forward, eager to hear a new crumb of a clue. "What was it? What did Dylan say?"

Fiona cleared her throat. "Well, when we spoke to him, he was adamant about Sylvia not entering the dog show, which we now know is true, thanks to Freya. But then he mentioned that she might have been at the show to help out. I didn't think anything of it at the time, probably because we knew that wasn't true either. Sylvia wasn't helping out, she was getting mobbed by people wanting to take selfies with Charlie."

"So how's that relevant?" asked Partial Sue cynically.

"Well, maybe Sylvia *was* planning to help out at the dog show at some point in the future. However, she went there first, to see what it was like."

"To get the lie of the lamb," Daisy added.

"Land," Fiona corrected. "It's the lie of the land. But, yes, exactly."

"So she goes along as a punter," Partial Sue said. "Gets a feel for it, to see if it's something she'd like to get involved in. Make a difference and all that."

"Yes," Fiona agreed. "And I'm sure she could with all her show experience."

"Mm . . ." Partial Sue wrinkled her nose. "Don't get me wrong. It's a great theory, but how do we verify it?"

"I think we should call Dylan Fraser," Daisy suggested. "See if he can shed more light on what he said."

Partial Sue kept pumping the pessimism brakes. "Or if it was just a throwaway comment."

Fiona pulled out her phone. She found the number for his dog salon in the Seven Dials. He answered it after the second ring.

"Hello, this is FUR, Dylan speaking. How can I help you?"

"Hello Dylan. My name is Fiona. I don't know if you remember me, but I came in with my two friends . . ."

Dylan didn't need any more introduction. His tone became laced with melancholy. "Oh, yes, I remember. You were investigating Sylvia's murder. How is it going? Has anyone been caught yet?"

Fiona didn't want to admit that they were no closer to finding the killer than when they last spoke to him. "Well, we have a few leads but one thing we have confirmed is that you were right about Sylvia's entry form being faked."

"I knew it!" Dylan exclaimed. "I knew she wouldn't have entered that competition without my help. Do you know who faked it?"

"No, not yet." Fiona didn't want to get bogged down in explanations about hackers for hire, not when she had a more pressing question that needed answering. "You also said that Sylvia might have been at the dog show to help out. What made you say that? Did she mention anything to you?"

"Oh, no I hadn't spoken to her for months. I'll be honest. It was an assumption but a well-founded one."

"How so?"

"Well, it's a path many competitors take after their show days are over, especially if you're the owner of an ex-Crufts winner. You may not see them in the arena anymore but that doesn't stop them getting involved behind the scenes."

"So, do you think Sylvia was there to get a feel for the place before making a decision?"

"Probably. Sylvia always did her research. I think most people would want to check out a place before committing. Wouldn't you?"

"Yes," Fiona replied. "I think I would. But let's just assume all is well and she's planning on helping out at the Christchurch Dog Show. What would she do there?"

"Knowing Sylvia's eye for detail, I'd say maybe a dog show judge."

The three ladies exchanged horrified looks. Malorie had held that coveted title unchallenged for as long as anyone could remember. She was a permanent fixture, an immovable object. Possibly because no one was foolhardy enough to challenge her. Except someone like Sylvia Steadman. The owner of an ex-Crufts winner would have been an unstoppable force that could've easily toppled Malorie from her lofty position — had she not met an unfortunate death.

"Is everything okay?" Dylan Fraser's disembodied voice brought them out of their silent stupor.

"Yes, sorry," Fiona replied. "Are you completely sure about that?"

"Well, not a hundred percent. But it would have suited her personality being a judge. Sylvia was meticulous."

"Okay, thank you, Dylan. You've given us a lot to think about."

"It's really no problem. I'm glad to help in any way I can. Please don't hesitate to call me if you need anything whatsoever."

Fiona thanked him again and hung up. "What if the new challenge Sylvia posted was to throw her hat in the ring as judge of the Christchurch Dog Club, and Malorie got wind of it."

Partial Sue's eyes lit up. "Can you imagine her reaction — over her dead body, or Sylvia's in this case."

Daisy became the voice of reason. "But Malorie was judging the categories the whole time. Had been all morning.

She was nowhere near Sylvia when she died. How did she inject her?"

"She gets Pippa Stroll to do it." Partial Sue's eyes blazed with possibility. "Pippa injects Sylvia in the crowd, then does her coffee-spilling routine to buy herself an alibi."

"But Pippa would have been spotted near Sylvia, I'm sure of it."

Daisy's words were lost in the furore of Partial Sue's enthusiasm, as she embellished the theory further. "Think about it. Malorie and Pippa both had something to lose. Malorie her job as judge, and Pippa the Best in Show title. Sylvia would have taken both from them, so they team up to take out Sylvia. The enemy of my enemy is my friend."

"But Sylvia hadn't entered the dog show," Daisy pointed out. "She wouldn't have been a threat to Pippa."

"Yes, but Pippa didn't know that," Partial Sue replied. "What if Malorie lied to her. Said that Sylvia was competing and faked her entry form. She shows it to her, and suddenly Pippa's worried. Convinced she'll lose if Barbie's up against an ex-Crufts winner. Then Malorie manipulates her into injecting Sylvia, so they both get what they want."

"But Malorie's the judge," Daisy said. "Surely Pippa would've just asked her to let Barbie win."

"Perhaps Malorie makes up some excuse. Tells her she has her credibility to think about. If she gives Best in Show to Barbie, snubbing an ex-Crufts winner, people will get suspicious. Not that this scenario would have ever happened because Sylvia's entry was all a fabrication." Partial Sue slapped her thigh, dramatically, pleased with how the theory was shaping up. "It all fits. I really think this is how it went down."

Daisy still needed more convincing. "But murdering someone over a local dog show still seems far-fetched to me."

"To us, it is," Partial Sue replied. "But don't dismiss how petty and jealous some people can be. It's a matter of personal pride, and pride's a powerful motivator."

Daisy didn't think so. "Yes, I get that but to go as far as actually killing someone just to get a trophy on your mantlepiece or to keep a job, an unpaid one, that gives nothing in return."

"Don't forget the twenty per cent club discount on pet supplies," Partial Sue joked.

Daisy ignored her comment. "I think murder is a big ask, er, if you ask me."

Fiona was beginning to come around to Daisy's point of view. "I have to admit, there needs to be more at stake for Pippa to go to such extreme lengths."

"Two hundred pounds prize money," Partial Sue offered.

"Would Pippa really kill a rival dog owner for two hundred pounds?" Fiona replied.

Partial Sue shrank a little. "No, I suppose not."

"There has to be a bigger incentive here," Fiona said. "Malorie would've had to sweeten the deal somehow to get Pippa to murder Sylvia. It's a massive risk she'd be taking."

A contemplative silence settled over the shop. Minds deep in thought.

After several minutes, Partial Sue straightened up and spoke more soberly, as something occurred to her. "Hey, hasn't Pippa just come into a lot of money."

"How do you know that?" asked Fiona.

"She told us, remember? When we first questioned her at her salon. She boasted about how she was opening a chain of dog grooming salons. Said she had investment. Where'd she get the money from?"

"The bank?" Daisy ventured.

Partial Sue shook her head. "A bank might lend her the money to turn her current salon into a dog groomer's, but she's opening a chain of four. That's going to take a lot of money. Bank's not going to risk investing in four dog grooming salons until they see how the first one does. Unless . . ."

"She's got a secret investor," Fiona suggested.

"Exactly," Partial Sue replied. "Malorie puts up the money for Pippa's new business venture in return for her services with a syringe. Did you ever read *All The President's Men*? That's where the catchphrase 'Follow the money' comes from. We follow the money, we find out who's behind this. If it came from Malorie's pocket, then we'll know our theory's correct."

Daisy had a problem with the practicalities of this. "But how do we follow the money, especially if Malorie's been hiding her transactions using that hacker?"

Fiona thought for a moment. She felt an inevitable but slightly uncomfortable smile forming on her lips, as she picked up her phone again. "I think we need to get Freya back in here. To do something that might not be strictly legal."

CHAPTER 58

It had been raining. The pavements were wet and gritty underfoot, prompting Partial Sue to insist on driving, just in case there was another downpour and they got soaked. Fiona was adamant that they walked to the community centre, because putting one foot in front of the other had a calming effect on her nerves. Right now, she desperately needed to settle down the tinnitus whining in her ears and the butterflies headbutting her stomach lining. Walking would help, plus, Simon Le Bon needed to do his 'wants'.

The source of her anxiety currently resided within the community centre's salmon-pink brick walls — the Christchurch Dog Club committee — or, more specifically, the thought of confronting them. Its four outspoken members had gathered at Fiona's request and had little idea of what to expect, other than what she had described as presenting them with a minor breakthrough. In reality, it was a breakthrough of the major variety, but Fiona wasn't being falsely modest. She was downplaying it on purpose to give the committee just enough to tempt them into attending an impromptu meeting, but not so much that the killer would be tipped off and make a run for it. That would happen afterwards, Fiona hoped.

She had thought about going to the police with what they'd learned, but unfortunately both pieces of proof that had led them to this point had originated from a not altogether kosher place, acquired through hacking. They didn't want to drop Freya's name into it and would protect their source at all costs. Her evidence would be inadmissible, which ruled out the police, so they would have to skirt carefully around what they had learned, resorting to poking, prodding and flicking the killer, until it became too uncomfortable for them, and they broke cover. Not necessarily holding up their hands confessing, but protesting so much that it became clear that they had something to hide. That was the plan anyway. It could all go pear-shaped one way or another.

Partial Sue had also been thinking about the Amazonian tech guru, but for a completely different reason. "You know, we should have brought Freya. Handy having a kickboxing warrior if things go awry with this lot."

"I don't think that would be a good idea," Daisy said, as they stopped outside the community centre's ugly, tarnished metal doors. "I thought we were trying to keep her name out of this."

"We are, but we could do with back up."

"We have Simon Le Bon," Daisy suggested.

Fiona looked down at her diminutive fluff ball, who stared back with his pretty brown eyes while wagging his tail, neither of which would be much use if things turned nasty. She now regretted bringing him and wished she'd left him at home. "You're right. We need some back up, and I know just who." Fiona began thumbing her phone.

Before Partial Sue could enquire as to exactly who Fiona had in mind, Delia Hawkins, vice chairperson, shoved open one of the centre's creaking doors. "Are you coming in anytime soon? I've got to be in Lymington in an hour." She disappeared with a huff, back inside.

"What is it with her and Lymington?" asked Partial Sue.

"It's nice with all the boats and little cafés," Daisy said. "I haven't been there for ages. We should go."

Fiona had to cut this short. They needed to stay focused on the investigation, not jollies out to Hampshire yachting towns. "Everyone ready?"

Daisy and Partial Sue nodded.

Inside the main hall, the assembled members of the dog club committee sat on a line of plastic chairs, their dogs neatly by their sides, except for Malorie, of course. Bethroned in the midst of them, she perched on her superior high-backed, leather office chair, her three Alsatians sprawled at her feet, pointing in different directions like the lions at the base of Nelson's Column.

Sheepishly, the ladies stood in front of them, as if they were the ones on trial, rather than the other way around.

Malorie got straight to the point, avoiding any superfluous pleasantries. "Well, what have you got for us?"

Fiona went to speak, but the centre's disinfectant-saturated air cloyed at her throat and her words came out croaky and unsure of themselves. "Er, uh-hum, we have some information — about the case."

"We already know that," Delia Hawkins said. "That's why we're here."

"Yes, what's this great revelation?" David Harper plucked his Pomeranian from off the floor who grunted, not assenting to being hoisted up and plonked on her master's lap, as if she were the pet of a Bond villain.

Fiona jumped straight in. "We believe Sylvia Steadman did not enter the dog show."

"But we've seen her entry form," Malorie said.

"We spoke to her dog groomer Dylan Fraser," Partial Sue explained. "He grooms Charlie for all his shows without exception. He's adamant Sylvia wouldn't have entered the show without his expertise."

"In that case, why did Sylvia upload an entry form, then?" Kenneth Prendiville asked.

"We don't believe she did," Partial Sue remarked. "We believe someone faked it."

The committee members threw each other puzzled looks, then turned their gaze back on the ladies.

"Why would anyone fake her entry form?" Malorie asked.

Fiona took a step forward. "Because the killer needed to make it look like Sylvia was in the competition, so it would appear as if a rival dog owner did it."

David Harper laughed dramatically. "But our show is just a bit of fun. Nothing serious. It doesn't count for anything. Are you seriously suggesting she was killed over a regional dog show?"

"No, not all," Fiona reassured him. "We believe the killer wanted us to think that, to create the illusion, distract from the real reason for killing her."

"And what reason was that?" David Harper asked.

"Money," Fiona replied.

"Money?" David Harper guffawed so hard that his head flew back, and he was in danger of ricking his neck. "Top prize is two hundred pounds. Hardly a king's ransom."

"No, but there is money to be made from the club," Partial Sue said.

David Harper checked around the base of his chair, pretending to search for a stash of invisible cash. "And where is this money, pray tell, because I haven't seen it and I'm the treasurer."

"We're a non-profit organisation," Delia Hawkins pointed out. "There's a clue in the name."

"Exactly," Malorie agreed. "I really don't think you've thought this through."

Fiona took a deep, calming breath. "What I mean is, this club has something of great value. It's been staring us in the face this whole time, until recently when Sue joked about it. But it's seriously valuable. We believe it's the motive behind the murder."

All eyes turned on Partial Sue for an explanation. "Your twenty percent club discount. Members love it. It's a great incentive for them to join. Probably why you've got so many of them. However, pet suppliers love it even more. If they're on your approved list, they're quids in. Guaranteed income and customers through the door. Your onsite vet Julie Sheers told us she'd never been so busy."

Kenneth Prendiville furrowed his whole face. "I still don't understand what this has got to do with someone killing Sylvia Steadman."

"We're coming to that." Fiona settled into her deductive diatribe, even allowed herself to pace up and down a little. "Dylan Fraser mentioned something else very telling. Now this might sound a little uncomfortable, as we're all dog lovers here, but he said if the killer was indeed a rival competitor, it would be far more likely that Charlie would be the target, not Sylvia. After all, it's Charlie who's competing and, let's face it, horrible though it is, poisoning a dog is far easier than a human being, and far less tricky or risky. However, the killer wanted Sylvia dead. Not her dog."

"So what reason would they have to kill Sylvia?" Malorie asked.

"She was a threat to their business," Fiona replied. "Well, indirectly."

"Who's business?"

Right on time, the doors to the community centre scuffed and squeaked as Pippa Stroll made an entrance, clip-clopping across the floor on her high heels, Barbie ensconced under one arm.

"Hers," said Fiona.

CHAPTER 59

"Well? Where's the cameraman? The interviewer?" Pippa demanded. "And what are they all doing here?" She pointed at the committee, not caring in the least that they could hear every single one of her blunted words.

"Sorry," Fiona apologised. "I needed an excuse to get you here."

"What? So I'm not being interviewed by the *Southbourne Monitor*?"

Fiona shook her head.

"Right, that's it. I'm going. Complete waste of my time."

She was about to turn on her spindly heels when Malorie halted her. "Pippa, you need to hear this. It concerns you." Malorie caught her up with the ladies' evidence so far. Pippa put Barbie down on the floor while she listened, her face growing redder with every syllable, her nail extensions digging into her palms.

When Malorie had finished, Pippa turned and glared at Fiona, Daisy and Partial Sue. "Are you accusing me of killing Sylvia Steadman? How dare you. I was nowhere near Sylvia when she died. You know that and so do the police." Kenneth fetched her a plastic chair, but Pippa refused to sit.

"You're correct," Fiona replied. "You were nowhere near Sylvia at the time. You have a cast-iron alibi."

"Damned right I do," Pippa snapped.

"You had to have one, though," Partial Sue explained. "Being favourite to win Best in Show, you'd be number one suspect in the whole jealous-rival charade. That was the only flaw in the murder plan, you needed to be above suspicion."

"What murder plan?" Pippa asked. "I'm not part of any murder plan."

Daisy pretended to hold up an invisible cup. "Your latte was part of it. You left the marquee when you knew Sylvia was gasping her last, bought coffee, then bumped into me on purpose so I'd spill coffee all down you. Bingo! You've got an alibi."

Pippa scowled at Daisy. "Absolute rubbish! That was your own stupid fault."

"Hold on! Hold on!" David Harper's outburst made his dog jump. "What's any of this got to do with Pippa's business? I don't get it. Pippa's a hairdresser. Don't tell me Sylvia Steadman was planning on opening a rival hair salon, and Pippa killed her, because that sounds ludicrous, and how did she kill her if she was nowhere near her?"

"Exactly," Pippa sneered.

Fiona turned to her. "Isn't your business about to change direction? You're launching a chain of four dog grooming salons."

"That's right," Pippa replied. "What of it?"

"Nothing," Fiona replied. "They'll probably do okay, seeing as it's impossible to get an appointment around here."

Pippa snorted. "They'll do better than fine. I'm the best groomer around. Just look at Barbie's coat."

"Yes, I'm sure you are," Fiona replied. "However, to really guarantee their success you'd still need to get on the club's approved list of suppliers."

"I suppose." Pippa shrugged.

Partial Sue gestured to the assembled committee. "Only way to do that is have one of you lot vouch for her, nominate her business. As Pippa's just demonstrated, she's not everyone's cup of tea or coffee. Sorry, Pippa, but you can be downright obnoxious." Before Pippa had a chance to protest, Partial Sue continued, "And the club's already got plenty of dog groomers on its list, so who'd bother vouching for her? No one, unless one of you has an interest in seeing her venture succeed."

"A dog in the fight." Daisy looked pleased with her topical word play.

Fiona was hoping for a reaction from the committee at this point. They'd planned it that way, but no one looked the slightest bit uncomfortable. No outbursts, no squirming, no shifting in seats, no sideways glances at the door, hoping to make a swift exit. Fiona would have to press on, applying pressure until the culprit revealed themselves like a blackhead being squeezed. "We know you have an AGM coming up where club members vote on who they want on the committee."

"Hold on. Are you saying one of us killed Sylvia Steadman in cahoots with Pippa?" Finally, a reaction from Malorie, albeit a delayed one. Perhaps the shock of the accusation had needed time to sink in.

"We are," Fiona replied.

An audible wave of outrage swept the room. The collective and indignant voices of the Christchurch Dog Club committee speaking over each other, combined with Pippa Stroll's shrill whining, all ignited by Fiona's two incendiary words.

Malorie silenced everyone with her domineering tone. "I find it highly offensive that you would think any member of this committee would do such a thing. You better be sure of your facts, that's all I'm saying."

"Oh, don't worry, we are." Fiona waited a second or two until their ruffled feathers had settled down. "For instance, we know Sylvia had come down here to retire, but she's not the type to put her feet up and listen to Radio Four all day."

"Not that there's anything wrong with that," Daisy chipped in.

"How do you know she's not the type to put her feet up?" Malorie demanded.

"Dylan Fraser mentioned it," Partial Sue answered.

"Him again," Kenneth Prendiville grumbled, as did the Doberman at his feet. "Are all your deductions based on the musings of Sylvia's dog groomer?"

This stumped Fiona for a second. Apart from Freya's hacked evidence, they were, sort of. "Er, well, yes."

Partial Sue waded in. "He knew her better than anyone else."

"That could all be hearsay," Pippa added. "He said, she said."

Daisy stopped this argument in its tracks. "Sylvia mentions it in her social media posts." She whipped out her phone, found the post in question. "May I approach the bench with evidence?"

Before anyone had a chance to point out that they weren't in court, Malorie, probably not averse to Daisy's deferential formality, said, "You may proceed."

Daisy trotted over and showed her phone screen to Malorie, then each of them one by one. "See, it says, 'Bye-bye Bristol City Council. Going to miss it. Hello new challenges.'" When they'd all had a good look, she rejoined Fiona and Partial Sue.

Fiona continued. "We believe she was planning on getting involved in something after she retired, hence why she said new challenges. We believe it was this dog club."

"But new challenges could be mean anything," Kenneth scoffed. "Maybe she wanted to take up golf or pottery, I don't know."

"But think about who Sylvia was," Fiona replied. "She won Crufts. Has tons of experience when it comes to dog shows. Dylan Fraser told us many competitors get involved behind the scenes after their show days are over. Now think about the timing. Sylvia turns up at your dog show where we know she's not competing."

Kenneth Prendiville opened his mouth to protest.

Fiona gently raised her hand to put him on pause. "Just bear with me for a second. Let's just assume she wasn't there to compete but was there to see what the show was like, get a feel for it, help her decide if it's right for her. And if it is, with her experience she'd certainly be over-qualified for making tea and coffee and selling hot dogs. No, her involvement would be bigger than that. Much bigger. It'd be a waste of Sylvia's talents otherwise. Maybe she's thinking of a more senior role. Maybe even one of your jobs. AGM's coming up soon, just in time so she can put herself forward as a contender for a committee position. What about Malorie's role as dog show judge? Sylvia's got all the experience and expertise anyone could need for that job."

"What? Nonsense!" Malorie snapped. "I'd have heard about it. She would have contacted us. Made enquiries about putting her name forward. Kenneth, you handle communications. Did Sylvia ever contact you, asking about being on this committee?"

Kenneth Prendiville shook his head. "I haven't heard a dicky bird."

"Did anyone else speak to her?" Malorie asked.

They all shook their heads.

"Radio silence on the Sylvia Steadman front, I'm afraid." Malorie folded her arms as if that were an end to the matter.

Fiona didn't speak. Did her best to appear shocked at this revelation, as did Daisy and Partial Sue. The three of them cast their eyes down, humbled and humiliated. Fiona glanced coyly at her audience. "You know, you're right. Sylvia would have made some enquiries first. That's a good point. Darn it. Kind of ruins our theory. Sorry, we may have to go away and rethink this."

The committee shook their collective heads and grumbled under their breath, 'amateurs' and 'what a waste of time', except for Malorie who said, "How dare they think it was one of us?" loudly enough for the ladies to hear clearly. Pippa Stroll went one better by firing a few expletives in their direction.

Delia Hawkins was first on her feet. "Okay, if there's nothing more to report. I'm off to Lymington." The others joined her, gathering up their excited dogs and readying themselves to leave.

"There's just one other thing." Fiona halted their exodus. "I need you to help me understand something."

"Does it need all of us?" Delia asked.

"Please, if it's not too much trouble. It will only take a minute or two."

CHAPTER 60

Reluctantly, everyone took a seat, grunting and complaining, including Pippa Stroll, her petite features twisted into a mask of pure bitterness. The dogs weren't happy about this either. They whined and stared up longingly at their owners, not understanding why the promise of going outside had been curtailed.

"Well, what is it you need help with?" Delia Hawkins perched on the edge of her seat, poised to get away at the soonest opportunity.

"What is it you actually do in Lymington?" Fiona asked.

Delia couldn't hide her guilt. "That's none of your business. It's personal. Can we get on with this?"

"Fair enough." Fiona didn't really care about what she got up to in Lymington. She was delaying and hoping to crank up the discomfort and frustration in the room. Her prodding, poking and flicking strategy about to reach its peak. "Can I ask what it is you do at the club?"

"Me?" Delia appeared confused and a tad embarrassed at being singled out again. "My role, you mean?"

Fiona nodded.

"Well, as vice chairperson I deputise for Malorie when she's not around and take some of the workload off her plate."

Fiona turned her gaze on Malorie. "And what does a chairperson do?"

Rather than answer, Malorie fired back another question. "Fiona, is there a point to this?"

"There is."

"Very well. I'm in charge. I make the decisions. What else would I be doing?" Malorie answered as if this were the most obvious thing in the world. "And I'm the dog show judge — my decision is final."

"And you, David?" Fiona asked.

David sighed. "Really? You need to know what a treasurer does?"

"Humour me."

"I manage the money coming in and the money going out. The budget, the accounts and the bills. Happy?"

"Yes." Fiona smiled. "That gives us a clearer picture of things. Okay, thank you, ladies and gentlemen. We have no further questions."

Pippa and the assembled committee members wasted no time in shuffling to their feet, until Kenneth Prendiville interrupted. "Er, don't you want to know what I do?"

"No, it's okay," Fiona said dismissively. "Malorie mentioned it earlier. You handle all the communications."

Kenneth Prendiville scoffed, offended at this reductive description of his job. "Oh, it's so much more than that. I'm in charge of the club's daily operation, coordinating and organising diaries, making sure everything runs smoothly."

"Oh," Fiona exclaimed. "That a bit of a coincidence."

"What's a coincidence?" The indignancy rapidly faded from Kenneth's face.

"Well, it's very similar to the role of chief administrator," Fiona replied.

"It's exactly the same, I'd say," Partial Sue clarified. "Except a chief administrator would do it for a much bigger organisation, like, oh, I don't know, Bristol City Council."

"Oh, yes," Fiona agreed, as if she didn't know. "Hey, wasn't Sylvia Steadman their chief administrator before she retired to come down here?"

"That's right," Daisy agreed. "That post I showed you was her leaving do."

"You know," Fiona said, "I've just had a crazy thought. Imagine if she did want a position on your committee, she'd be perfect for the role of club secretary. It would fit her like a glove."

Finally, it happened. The shift in the seat, the uncomfortable squirm. Just a small one and it came from Kenneth Prendiville's behind. Pippa on the other hand, remained poker-faced.

"Where are you going with this?" asked Malorie.

Fiona cleared her throat. "At first, we believed Sylvia was after your role, Malorie. But that's only because Dylan Fraser mentioned that Sylvia might want to try her hand at being a judge. But on second thoughts, it's unlikely she'd go straight for the top job. She'd want a role more suited to her abilities to start off with, and that would be Kenneth's. It's essentially the same job but on a much smaller scale. With all her experience as a chief administrator and as an ex-Crufts winner, I'm sure you'd agree, she'd get voted in by club members at the next AGM. It would be a landslide. Kenneth would be off the committee, and he'd lose his influence, especially when it came to picking pet suppliers to go on the approved list. One in particular. A hairdresser turned dog groomer."

"Oh, do shut up, Fiona," Pippa snapped. "You don't know what you're talking about."

"That's rubbish!" Spittle flew out of Kenneth's mouth and his Doberman raised its hackles.

"Is it, Kenneth?" Fiona replied calmly. "You do your annual Zen routine to get voted back in, don't you. Curry favour with club members. But this year, you outdid yourself. Sending out Christmas cards and delaying show categories for people who don't even like you. You must have really wanted to get back on the committee."

"That's true," Delia added. "Karma Ken's been out in force this year."

Ready to burst, Kenneth shot her the foulest of looks. He then turned his fury on Fiona. "Of course I wanted to get voted back in, who doesn't?"

"No, I think it was more than that," Fiona replied. "You were desperate to be on the committee this year, so that you could endorse Pippa's new business, to make sure it got on the approved list."

"And just why the hell would he do that?" Pippa demanded.

Fiona mused on this question. "Mmm . . . Maybe he invested money in it."

Pippa flicked her hair back dismissively. "What rubbish."

Fiona ignored her and turned back to Kenneth. "But then Sylvia comes along and wants your job. She'd wipe the floor with you in the upcoming vote. You'd be off the committee, scuppering your chances of ever endorsing Pippa's business, losing all the money you'd invested. It leaves you no choice. You had to take Sylvia out of the running. You killed her. Faked her entry form to make it look like she'd entered the show and a rival competitor had done it. All so you could protect your investment."

"Kenneth, Pippa, is this true?" Malorie asked. "Have you invested in a business venture together?"

"Course not," Pippa snorted. "These three old bats are deluded."

Kenneth shook his head and chuckled to himself. "You can't believe any of this, surely? We all agreed just a moment ago that if Sylvia was planning on joining us, she would have communicated her intentions. Made enquiries. She wouldn't just turn up at the show and announce her candidacy out of the blue. Where's the evidence: the letters, the phone calls?"

"That's a good point," Malorie said. "If Sylvia was a chief administrator she'd be organised and efficient. She would have done her groundwork. Contacted us first."

"Oh, absolutely," Fiona agreed. "And as club secretary, Kenneth would've been the first port of call when Sylvia got in touch. He'd be first to know of her intentions, which he kept from the rest of you. Now I don't believe she would have contacted him by phone. She'd want things in writing, but letters are too slow. She'd have emailed Kenneth, back and forth."

Kenneth's smile was smug and patronising. "I'm so glad you mentioned emails. That makes sense. She'd want a record of our exchanges, if they actually happened. So where are these emails? There are none in the club's inbox or spam folder. You can have a look on my laptop if you like. Be my guest, and I'd hazard a guess that there are none on Sylvia's computer either. I'm no detective but I imagine the police would check all that."

Fiona nodded. "Yes, you're right. But an email trail between two people can be deleted, if you know the right people. You can hire a hacker off the internet for the right price. Hardly leaves a trace, well, certainly not one the police would find after a cursory look. A hacker can also upload a fake entry form to make it look like it came from Sylvia's computer. Isn't that right, Kenneth?"

"I have no idea what you're talking about." Kenneth appeared to be calm, but his Doberman betrayed him. His ears flicked back and he licked his lips, telltale signs the dog was nervous, picking up on his master's fear.

Time to crank up the prodding, probing and flicking until he broke. "I guess the million-dollar question is who injected Sylvia? You or Pippa? I'm pretty sure it wasn't Pippa. You had to protect your investment, keep her out of the way."

"This is ridiculous." Kenneth fidgeted in his seat, his legs restless.

"Did you come up with the coffee-spilling pantomime, Pippa?" Daisy asked.

"Oh, by the way, we spoke to the man who sold you your coffee," Fiona said. "He told us you poured half of it away and topped it up with cold water. You'd only do that if you knew you were about to spill scalding hot coffee down yourself. But what I can't figure out is why be at the show at all? Why not stay at home, then you'd be completely above suspicion?"

"Personal pride," Partial Sue proposed. "Last year's winner and this year's favourite, I bet you just had to be there, swanning around, showing off. But, I suppose if you hadn't turned up at a show you'd been boasting about winning all year, it'd look suspicious."

For once Pippa had no words. She sat dumbfounded, overwhelmed by the evidence mounting up.

Daisy had her phone out again. She addressed Kenneth, "I must say it was handy having a beautician as a business partner if you're planning on giving someone a lethal injection. Says here on Pippa's website that she does dermal fillers and can make them completely painless."

"Did she coach you before the show?" Fiona asked. "Got you to practice on oranges or something, so when it came to the real thing, you could inject Sylvia without her even noticing, or anyone noticing. Probably helped that everyone's attention and their cameras were pointing down at Charlie at the time. What poison did you use, by the way? We never found that out."

Kenneth stamped his feet as he stood up, clutching his dog's lead. "That's it! I'm not listening to any more of these baseless accusations." Obediently, his Doberman rose with him, as keen as his master to leave this uncomfortable place.

"Stop where you are, Kenneth!" Malorie ordered, as if God himself had commanded it.

Kenneth froze.

Malorie stood and faced him. Her three Alsatians did likewise. "I have my own question that can clear up this mess once and for all. Did you invest in Pippa's new grooming business?"

The club secretary shuffled awkwardly on his feet. Pippa went to speak but Malorie shushed her.

"It's a simple enough question, Kenneth. Yes or no."

Kenneth hesitated for a beat, then made a break for it, tugging his Doberman along with him.

"Kenneth, you coward!" Pippa, now on her feet, shouted after him. "Get back here!"

Malorie gave chase with her three giant Alsatians.

Fiona just had time to scoop up Simon Le Bon into the safety of her arms before Kenneth barrelled past her, nearly losing his footing, not helped by his Doberman, now straining on its lead to reach the door. This gave Malorie time to dart around the other side of the ladies, clutching the leads of her three Alsatians. With her livid red hair, she resembled Boudica controlling a team of powerful chariot horses. Although Fiona doubted the legendary queen ever sported a shampoo and set when going into battle. Maybe things would have been different if she had.

Malorie headed him off and blocked his path to the exit. Kenneth and his Doberman skidded to a halt as they were confronted by Malorie's superior force. Her Alsatians bared their teeth, their hackles raised. In response, the Doberman gave a weak, half-hearted growl.

"Fiona, call the police," Malorie instructed. Fiona immediately dialled 999. "Kenneth, don't try anything. You're no match for me and my three bitches."

Fiona was sure she was referring to her Alsatians and not the ladies of the Charity Shop Detective Agency.

Kenneth sighed, his shoulders slumping, his head bowing in defeat. His dog mirrored his owner, flattening itself against the floor in submission. Sensing the conflict had ended, Malorie's Alsatians stood down, relaxing their coiled muscles and panting happily, their tongues lolling.

"Good girls," Malorie praised them, rubbing their heads one by one, and handing them each a treat from her pocket.

In this brief moment of distraction, Kenneth seized his opportunity. Dropping the end of the lead, he abandoned his Doberman and made a solo sprint for the doors. Just when escape seemed certain, another dog owner came through them in the opposite direction, blocking his way.

"Backup's here," Fiona said.

The intimidating sight of Adrian and Red Bull stood firm in the doorway, causing Kenneth to grind to a standstill.

"You ain't going nowhere, mate," Adrian snarled.

Kenneth immediately retreated, closely pursued by Adrian, eyes blazing with fury. The pair of them forced the terrified club secretary back inside, until he had nowhere to go, trapping him into a corner. Kenneth's Doberman loyally ran to his side, not bothered in the slightest that his owner had abandoned him moments earlier.

Fiona feared a fight might break out between the two dogs, but Red Bull defused the situation, slightly ruining Adrian's hard-man act by rolling onto his back, exposing his tummy, clearly wanting to play.

Sirens whined in the distance. It was as if someone had turned Kenneth's complexion down with a dimmer switch. His skin turned as pale as milk, accepting his fate as all hope faded.

Pippa, on the other hand, continued to protest her innocence, while edging backwards, Barbie in both arms. "He's nothing to do with me. Sure, I had investment in my new business, but it didn't come from Kenneth, I swear."

Fiona knew it had, thanks to Freya's financial digging. "Oh, well, you'll be fine then."

Hope flashed across Pippa's face. "Really?"

Four uniformed police officers burst into the community centre followed by DI Fincher and DS Thomas.

"Oh, sure," Fiona reassured her. "Once you've squared away your accounts with these two detectives, you'll be right as rain."

Pippa swallowed hard and glanced over her shoulder, hoping for a way out the back.

"The only place back there is the kitchen," Daisy informed her. "Unless you want to make coffee."

"No," said Partial Sue. "She'll only spill it over herself again."

CHAPTER 61

Sitting in a theatre had never been so stressful. Normally, Fiona adored catching a show. Theatre was by far her favourite medium of entertainment, apart from books, of course. She loved the anticipation before the curtain went up. Everyone chatting excitedly and taking their seats under soaring ornate ceilings — dazzling Art Deco in the case of the Regent Centre with its elegant, fluted walls and gold-leaf trim. Always a treat and always magical, nothing compared to seeing talented people performing live in front of you. Fiona had booked good seats too, which were perfectly comfortable. But despite all this, she was antsy, and kept fidgeting and squirming.

"What's the matter with you?" Partial Sue asked. "Has someone put itching powder down your back?"

"I'm nervous, that's all."

Daisy caught the tail end of the conversation after returning from the loos. "Why are you nervous?" Daisy asked.

"For the Wicker Man. I'm worried he's not going to be funny, and it will be our fault."

"How is it our fault?"

Fiona swallowed hard. "Well, we should have been more honest with him. I'd hate to see him bomb in front of an audience. Wouldn't wish that on anyone."

"We were honest with him," Partial Sue replied. "He changed his whole act because of us."

"And the last stuff he did wasn't too bad," Daisy added.

Fiona had to admit his material had improved, but they were his friends, they desperately wanted him to be good. How would it go down in front of an audience that didn't know him from Adam and owed him nothing. "What if they get nasty, start heckling him?"

"Fiona, this is Christchurch," Partial Sue replied. "People don't heckle in Christchurch. They write stern letters and give you ticked-off looks."

"Would you like some of this, Fiona?" Daisy revealed a small tub of sticky toffee ice cream.

Partial Sue frowned. "Where did you get that? I thought they only sold them in the interval?"

"No, you can buy them any time. They have them at the counter." Trust Daisy to spot a clandestine supply of ice cream in a regional theatre.

"I am partial to a mini tub of ice cream. Do I have to give a special wink or mention your name?"

"No, I don't think so." She flipped off the lid and dug into the soft dessert with the little plastic spoon provided. She groaned as it touched her tongue. "It's good stuff. Maybe it will calm you down, Fiona."

She declined. "No, thank you. I can't eat at a time like this."

"I'll try some," Partial Sue said. Daisy loaded up the spoon and handed it to her. "Wow that's amazing. I might have to get myself some. How much is it?"

"Two pounds fifty."

Hardly a princely sum but it stopped Partial Sue in her tracks. "No, you're alright. I'll wait until I get home."

Fiona watched the theatre filling up, adding to her nerves. The more the audience grew, the more people there were to witness the Wicker Man's possible humiliation. Partial Sue gave her knee a reassuring squeeze. "He'll be fine. We should send him a text to say good luck, break a leg and all that."

"We already did that." Daisy gasped, as she rolled a big, freezing chunk of ice cream around her mouth.

"Maybe we should send another one."

Speaking of texts, Fiona got a ping.

"Who's that?" Daisy asked.

Fiona examined her phone. "It's a picture from Julie Sheers. It's her and Charlie." She showed it to Daisy and Partial Sue who aahed at the vet squishing her face against her newly adopted dog. It seemed wholly appropriate that the person who'd been with Sylvia in her dying moments, and had tried to save her life, should become Charlie's new owner. And very happy they looked too.

On the other hand, Kenneth and Pippa were on remand, awaiting trial. Both had been charged with the joint murder of Sylvia Steadman. Although, it was more likely that Pippa would be convicted of conspiracy to murder, seeing that it had been Kenneth who'd jabbed the syringe into Sylvia's arm, ably assisted by Pippa who'd been coaching him for weeks. He had seized the chance to slip away from the main arena briefly while everyone had been distracted by the biscuit-throwing debacle. Sylvia had lost her life but at least the pair responsible had been caught. Unfortunately, their two dogs weren't so lucky and were still waiting to be rehomed, in the capable care of Kerry Pritchard, the dog fosterer.

The lights began to dim. An announcer instructed everyone to take their seats that, as far as Fiona could tell from glancing around, were all sold out. She got butterflies and goosebumps all at the same time. The auditorium darkened almost completely, except for the lime-green emergency exit signs. Harsh spotlights lit up the stage, the curtain raised to reveal a lone microphone stand in the middle.

The Wicker Man walked on, entering from the left. He wore a bright-yellow, almost Day-Glo, chunky knit jumper, making him look as if an over-ripe ear of corn were about to perform. The audience clapped half-heartedly, unsure of the etiquette. Were they supposed to clap him now or later? As she joined in applauding, Fiona's heart sank. Not because of how he was dressed (he'd certainly be remembered) but because he had been given the worst slot. Notoriously hard, the opening act had to do the heavy lifting, warming up a cold audience that weren't quite ready to be entertained yet.

He stood in front of the microphone and greeted the audience with an enthusiastic, "Hello, Christchurch!"

The ladies responded, calling out hello back. They were the only ones who did, apart from a few half-hearted murmurs here and there.

"My name is Trevor, but everyone calls me the Wicker Man." At least he'd dropped his Dickensian spiel and hadn't bothered to bring a wicker stool on stage with him. He pressed on regardless. "I don't mind telling you. I was nervous before the show. I had a horrible night's sleep. I kept dreaming FedEx was trying to kill me — it was a logistical nightmare."

Unexpected giggles bubbled up from the back of Fiona's throat, and a light titter drifted through the audience at his clever one-liner. It set the tone nicely for the rest of his act.

"Now, I wasn't supposed to be first on tonight. No, I was scheduled to come on after a record attempt for the world's longest conga, but I told the organisers, there's no way I can follow that."

Patchy laughter but definitely increasing in volume as he began winning more people over.

"You know, my nickname hasn't always been the Wicker Man. Back in the seventies, when I was a big Elton John fan, I worked in a salad bar where they used to call me the rocket man." The laughter increased and there were a few guffaws around the theatre. He continued, clearly encouraged. "Sadly, I got fired from that job so I applied for a position modelling camouflage, but I was unsuccessful — they said they couldn't see me in that role." He waited a beat. This time the laughter swept across the whole theatre. Striding across the stage, gaining in confidence, he stared out across the sea of smirking faces, eager for his next hit of humour. "However, I did manage to get hired at the Rizla factory, but I got the sack from that too because I refused to do things their way. I told them that's not how I roll." Big belly laughs this time. He waited until it subsided before continuing. "Disheartened by work, I went travelling around China. Met a beautiful Chinese girl who was a member of the Communist party, but I had to end it — there were just too many red flags in that relationship." The laughs reached to the rafters. "When I returned home, inspired by my trip to the East, I started a business making origami, but unfortunately it quickly folded."

After that, the one-liners came thick and fast, and most importantly, they were all funny. By the time his set had finished, he had them all wanting more and left the stage to a clatter of applause.

After the show ended, they met him in the bar, clutching an award in one hand and whisky in the other. They each took turns to hug and congratulate their friend.

"Trevor, that was amazing. You were wonderful," Fiona gushed, happy for him but burying her guilt deep down that she'd ever doubted him.

"Third place," he grinned. "Not a bad innings and I got a hundred quid for my trouble." He'd lost out to a magician who'd made himself disappear and then reappear up in the balcony, bewildering and bewitching the entire audience. All except Partial Sue, who swore blind that he had a twin, and had seen them both in Carpetright. But first place had gone to a young girl, barely in her teens who also appeared to do magic, except on a skateboard, flipping it with the grace of a ballerina in ways that would confound Sir Isaac Newton.

"You did bloody brilliant." Partial Sue slapped him playfully on the arm.

"It was hilarious. Just as funny as anything on the telly," Daisy said with a smile.

"Well done, Trevor. Can I buy you a drink?" Fiona asked.

"Normally I'd bite your arm off, but people keep buying them for me." He pointed to a line of whiskies cued up on the bar behind him, ready to be downed.

"So is that the end of the Wicker Man furniture salesman, and the start of Wicker Man the comedian?" Daisy asked.

"Not just yet. I'll keep doing this as a sideline. But it looks promising. A few people have given me their business cards and asked if I could do small gigs for them."

"That's wonderful."

A phone pinged, interrupting the conversation. They all did that thing, checking their phones to see who it belonged to, including a few people around them. Turned out it was Daisy's. She examined the message. They couldn't help but notice her sunny expression dropping with every word she read, until it became sad and downcast. Tears appeared in the corner of each eye.

"Daisy what's the matter? What's wrong?" Fiona asked.

She looked up and they were relieved to see they were not tears of sadness, but ones of joy. "It's from Bella, my daughter. You know I haven't spoken to her in years and we fell out after she married this horrible bloke. Well, she's left him."

Fiona had never seen so much joy in one person's face. Daisy almost toppled over she was so overwhelmed with happiness. "She's coming home! My Bella is coming home!"

THE END

ACKNOWLEDGEMENTS

This book started off as a very different animal (excuse the pun). I'd originally had an idea about dognapping. A dark tale of a gang who prowled the parks of Southbourne and Christchurch, swiping people's unsuspecting pooches. The idea began to take shape, morphing as they sometimes do, snowballing almost of their own volition, complete with set pieces, chases and whiplash twists and turns. The ladies were primed and ready. They'd track down these heinous criminals and bring them to justice, which would, of course, involve all the dogs being safely returned to their rightful owners.

However, there was one thing I hadn't considered, until my publisher, Steph Carey, pointed it out. Cosy crime readers might find this concept a bit traumatic. Though I'd made sure that no animals would come to any harm, a story about owners being separated from their beloved pets wouldn't be an 'easy read', which people have come to expect from The Charity Shop Detective Agency. Steph was absolutely right. But it came as a shock to me that I'd overlooked this, especially as I'm a dog lover and owner myself. I couldn't bear the idea of being parted from my little terrier cross Jess, even though she thinks she's the boss of me. But sometimes you can be so enamored with your own idea that the obvious blindsides you. Lucky for me, I have Steph's amazing judgment, and her very helpful suggestions. She proposed the idea of a dog show instead, and here we are. A massive thank you, Steph. Simply cannot do this without you.

In fact, I couldn't do any of this without the brilliant team at Joffe Books. They're an extremely talented and hard-working bunch of people, not to mention jolly nice as well. Big thanks must go to my editor, the fabulous Anna Harrison whose excellent suggestions have improved this book no end, and to all my amazing beta readers who include Suze Clarke-Morris, Kath Middleton and Paul Lautman, and my lovely proofreader Becky Wyde. I must also thank Lorella Belli from LBLA who's been securing my translation and audio rights. It's an amazing privilege to hear someone bring your book to life, and no one does it better than Zara Ramm. She manages to nail the voice of every new character I throw at her.

There isn't much police procedure in my books. But what little there is has to be correct, believable and totally up to date. To make sure it's all of these things, I call on my good friend, fellow author and full-time police detective Sammy H.K. Smith. Not only does she check my work, modifying it here and there, she also suggests ways around those little issues I may have unwittingly created for myself. Many, many thanks, Sam. Speaking of procedure of a doggier kind, I am indebted to Laura from the Kennel Club who answered all my questions about dog show rules and etiquette.

The biggest shout out must go to each and every person who reads my books. You don't know how much of a buzz it gives me. Knowing that there are people out there enjoying what I do inspires me to keep writing and finding more fiendish cases for Fiona, Sue and Daisy to solve.

Lastly, to the most important people in my life — my family. To Sha, my wife, for all her support and encouragement, even when I'm having a meltdown, and my awesome children Billie and Dan, who constantly amaze and impress me. Big love to my Mum, who brought me up the right way on a diet of Pam Ayres and Victoria Wood, and my sister Jane, who's one of those gifted people who can write from the heart (get those memoirs finished, Jane). And finally, not forgetting Jess the dog whose eccentric canine antics probably inspired me to write something doggie-related.

THE JOFFE BOOKS STORY

We began in 2014 when Jasper agreed to publish his mum's much-rejected romance novel and it became a bestseller.

Since then we've grown into the largest independent publisher in the UK. We're extremely proud to publish some of the very best writers in the world, including Joy Ellis, Faith Martin, Caro Ramsay, Helen Forrester, Simon Brett and Robert Goddard. Everyone at Joffe Books loves reading and we never forget that it all begins with the magic of an author telling a story.

We are proud to publish talented first-time authors, as well as established writers whose books we love introducing to a new generation of readers.

We won Trade Publisher of the Year at the Independent Publishing Awards in 2023. We have been shortlisted for Independent Publisher of the Year at the British Book Awards for the last four years, and were shortlisted for the Diversity and Inclusivity Award at the 2022 Independent Publishing Awards. In 2023 we were shortlisted for Publisher of the Year at the RNA Industry Awards.

We built this company with your help, and we love to hear from you, so please email us about absolutely anything bookish at feedback@joffebooks.com

If you want to receive free books every Friday and hear about all our new releases, join our mailing list: www.joffebooks.com/contact

And when you tell your friends about us, just remember: it's pronounced Joffe as in coffee or toffee!

ALSO BY PETER BOLAND

THE CHARITY SHOP DETECTIVE AGENCY MYSTERIES

Book 1: THE CHARITY SHOP DETECTIVE AGENCY
Book 2: THE BEACH HUT MURDERS
Book 3: DEATH AT THE DOG SHOW

Printed in Dunstable, United Kingdom

65493205R00201